Falling Through Shooting Stars

Nancy Ann Healy

ISBN 10: 0692726632
ISBN 13: 978-0692726631

A Note from the Author

When I first released *Falling Through Shooting Stars*, I was surprised at the amount of feedback I received regarding the story. Many people have struggled with Julia and Katie's story—most notably with Julia. I have spent many hours pondering what it is that troubles people's hearts so deeply about Julia's story. In the end, the conclusion I have reached is simply that Julia's story is painfully human.

Falling Through Shooting Stars was born from a personal journal passage that I had written. It is the most personal story that I have ever penned. As I was reading my journal one day, I began to wonder how I could explore the experience of falling in and out of love through characters. I began writing a journal as Julia, immersing myself in her life, and experiencing her conflicting and competing emotions. Julia's journey is one of questioning, longing, letting go, and learning to love through it all. It's an adventure in living and self-discovery.

Falling Through Shooting Stars is much more than a romantic story. It's a love story of a different kind. It is an exploration in learning to love without expectation. It is as much about accepting the changing nature of life as it is about two people finding each other. In life, we can sometimes lose sight of ourselves in the quest to live within the roles we play for everyone else—spouse, lover, parent, child, boss, employee, friend. Once in a while, just when we think our life is settled, someone comes along that shakes our reality to its foundation. That person challenges us to recall the person that lies beneath the surface, and propels us to seek to become the person we have always hoped to be.

Life is a series of constant changes, and change is the only guarantee any of us have in life. The best that we can hope for is that we find those people who will stand beside us as we grow and evolve as human beings despite all of our faults, quirks, and fears. And, if we are fortunate, one day we find the person who sees all of our parts and loves us not in spite of them, but for all that we are—even in our wonderful, glorious messiness. Love and life can take you by surprise. They are messy and dizzying, and infinitely worth it. But for all its incredible adventures, there is no experience in life quite like falling in love. As Julia says:

"Suddenly, stillness becomes motion and light crashes through darkness, spiraling toward an unknown destination. Is that what falling in love is supposed to be? How did I miss that? It's like *Falling Through Shooting Stars*."

Chapter One

Julia's Journal

I still remember the first time I saw her—Katherine Maureen Brennan. Of course, I had the advantage. I could silently observe at a distance and I did. I remember thinking how fascinating she seemed. There was no denying that she was attractive, and her intellect never seemed a point of debate or denial. She was well-spoken and appeared personable, but you know, you always see what you wish to see at a distance. I hadn't given it much thought, to tell you the truth, the notion that our paths might ever have a reason to collide. I mean, I was just like the millions of other silent observers. She was a personality more than a person. I would see her every morning, like so many others, sipping her coffee at the long desk, smiling as she imparted news mixed with witty conversation. When I think about it now, it seems odd. She was part of my daily routine, and I was a faceless, nameless shadow in the distance. Just like my life, Katherine Brennan was a pleasant albeit predictable inevitability in my day.

Life is funny, though. You move through it sometimes without even paying attention. It just becomes habit—living. You get up, you drink your coffee, switch on the television while you try to stretch the sleep away. You collide in the hallway with growing children and fight for a few minutes of privacy in the shower, hoping that it will provide the final jolt you need to start a new day. Another sip of a cooled cup of terrible coffee and you kiss your wife goodbye. You learn to take it for granted, that it will always be this way. And, that seems perfectly acceptable. After all, it's what you are accustomed to. It's what you committed to. It's what you see when you look backward and what you anticipate down the line. And, isn't that exactly how life is supposed to be? Comfortable. Safe. Secure. Things change, though. Sometimes, just when you think you know exactly what to expect, just when you are sure your life is resolved, and you are agreeable to be resigned to it—it changes. Like the calm before a storm, if the comfortable chaos in my morning routine was the calm, Katherine Brennan was the impending earthquake that would shake my world to its foundation.

NOVEMBER 2014

"Mom, can I grab a ride?"

"Late again, Jacob?" Julia Riley rolled her eyes continuing to sip an ever cooling cup of coffee.

"Come on, Mom…I had…"

"Just get your stuff and do it quickly. I have a meeting at eight-thirty."

"I gotta go," Carrie whispered as she planted a soft kiss on Julia's cheek. "I'm sorry, babe. I'd take him…"

"Just go," Julia chuckled.

"I am sorry," Carrie smiled.

Julia shook her head as two smaller heads followed her wife out the door with the typical, "Bye, Mom."

"Jacob! Let's go."

"Sorry," Jake muttered as he threw his backpack over his shoulder and followed his mother out the door.

Jacob Riley was the first of three children. He was the unexpected first of three and he, unfortunately for him, some days was very evidently his mother's son. Jake struggled to stay organized, burned the midnight oil frequently and spent far more time socializing than he did studying. There were moments now that Julia thought she might seriously throttle him. At seventeen, he exhausted her, but he claimed a piece of Julia's heart that somehow went beyond just parentage. She hadn't given much thought to children when she had found out that Jacob was on the way. Julia had only been married a short time to her college sweetheart, Michael. She had been in her first year teaching Political Science as an adjunct professor at a small university in Massachusetts. Michael had been in his first year of residency at the local hospital. Neither was prepared for the way Jake would change their lives. They had plans. Jake was not in that equation. Seventeen years later, one thing that both Michael and Julia still had in common was how grateful both were for that surprise.

"I have practice after school," Jake offered.

"I'm not sure if I will be able to pick you up, Jake. You might want to call Care."

"Mom?"

"Yeah?"

"Would it be cool if I went to Dad's tomorrow for the weekend?"

"Jake, you can go to your dad's whenever you want, you know that. Did you ask your father?" Jacob nodded. "Not that I mind, but why are you so eager to go to Dad's?" Julia noticed his shrug and the slight flush in his cheeks. "I see. Dad is having a get-together?" she guessed. He shrugged again. "Maybe one that Allison Grant might show up to?" Jake was never good at hiding his feelings, at least not from his mother. His face was always a roadmap to the truth. "She's cute, Jake," Julia smiled.

"Mom!"

"Well, she is," Julia laughed. "A little old for you, though, isn't she?"

"She's nineteen," he said.

"Um-hm, older women already," she goaded him. "Maybe you do take after Care."

Jake laughed. "Care is only three years younger than you, Mom."

"I know. I am just pointing out that you seem to like older women," Julia offered, keeping her eyes squarely on the road.

"And you like younger ones," he teased.

"Nah, Jake...I like 'em all."

"Mom, really?" he sighed as his mother pulled in front of the school. "I'll see you," he called back.

"Jake, do me a favor and *try* to get to your classes on time today?" He shook his head in teenage disgust. "Older women like men who are dependable," Julia called to him.

"Yeah, yeah," he called back with a roll of his eyes. "She's not *that* old, Mom."

Julia laughed as her son disappeared through the school's front door with several friends catching him along the way. It was hard to believe at times that the small towheaded boy she had chased around the backyard was only months away from graduating high school. Time seemed to move more quickly every year.

Julia was thankful for the relationship that she and her ex-husband Michael had been able to maintain. For some people, that was not possible. For Michael and Julia, it never even needed discussion. They had been together since Julia's sophomore year of college, and Michael knew her as well as anyone could. They had simply changed as they grew up. After eight years together, both knew it was time to walk away. Julia knew a part of her would always love him, just as he would always love her. Sometimes, simple moments like watching Jake run into the school reminded her of that fact.

Michael wasn't just a good father; he was a good friend. He had encouraged Julia forward in her career, and he had remained supportive of his ex-wife's decisions both personally and professionally. In fact, he had played a significant role in helping Julia secure her current position at the Fledger Foundation. As much as Julia had loved teaching, being able to work for better education and equality had become ever more appealing to her. It was a different business, but still, it felt founded on the concept of education itself, and that was meaningful to Julia. Now, she just had to utilize her expertise to help with funding projects.

Julia enjoyed meeting people, seeing projects come to fruition, and watching as movement became evident on the new front lines of civil rights. Even if it was a minuscule role, Julia found satisfaction in feeling a part of that change. It seemed another way to effect the future. Listening to her son talk about girls and watching her wife head off with their daughters each morning, it seemed to Julia that the future should be bright. She let out a breath as she pulled into her parking space and made the short trek across the slippery, snow-covered pavement to the door. Julia loved her office. She'd grown to consider its occupants a part of her family. It was a relatively small group, only twenty, not too small that they struggled to make strides, but small enough that there was still an intimate atmosphere.

"Julia!" a voice beckoned from across the common space.

"Everett," Julia shook her head. "What has you so enthusiastic at eight in the morning?"

"Oh, come on Jules…Aren't you curious what Roberts called this meeting for?"

Everett had been with the foundation for just over a year. He was a tall, lanky twenty-three-year-old who started as an intern straight after graduating from Boston College, and Julia sometimes found him to be enthusiastic to the point of annoying. She nudged past him through the door of her office and shook her head.

"Curious? About a meeting that Dan called?" Julia hung up her coat and rolled out her chair. "Not really, Everett. Dan likes meetings. It gives him an excuse to eat the donuts Barbara has forbidden."

"Nah," he plopped in the chair that sat in front of Julia's desk. "Something is up. Something with this new project."

Julia smiled. The foundation had received a grant request for a diversity center in downtown Boston. It was an ambitious project, one that would seek to bring together the diverse community at large through both entertaining and educational programs. The project sought to produce social change and equality by encouraging inter-action between the older generation of Bostonians and its youth. It would tackle race, sexuality, religion, and ethnic barriers by facilitating open dialogue through art. Even with the basic commitment The Fledger Foundation had made, there remained a great deal of funding that would be required. Dan, who was the founder and board president of the foundation and Julia, shared a particular passion for the project. Dan had been somewhat tight-lipped the last week about his latest meetings, and Julia was curious how he intended to help launch the center. It was the type of project they both could get behind with excitement. The kind of project if you can get it off the ground, it could change lives.

"Well, we'll see what Mr. Roberts has to say," Julia offered. "I need to check my email, Everett. Any messages I didn't see yesterday?"

He shook his head, and Julia raised her eyebrow to signal it was time for him to be on his way. Twenty minutes to get situated before a meeting with Dan Roberts was not very long, and Julia found herself mildly cursing Jake for the fact that she was half an hour later than she had intended to be. Knowing her friend Dan, the rest of the day would likely be taking a different course than she had originally planned.

≈ ≈ ≈

"Katie! Jesus H! Where have you been?"

Katie Brennan gave a full-throated laugh. "Where have I been?" she asked as she lifted her coffee cup to her lips.

"Yeah...You know you have an appearance at noon."

Katie laughed a bit harder. "George, have I ever missed an appearance, ever?"

"Well...."

"George, relax. Good Lord, it's only across the building for heaven's sake."

Katherine Brennan was a force of nature, and everyone at JLN understood that. She was easily the most popular news personality that the still-fledgling network employed. She'd started as a field reporter for a major network, but her stunning looks and her ease in front of the camera quickly commanded the notice of more than one network executive. In an era where news and entertainment seemed destined to clash, a personality like Katherine Brennan was a rarity. She was educated, intelligent, well versed on issues and all at once breathtakingly beautiful.

"Katie, you know how Curtis is. He gets ruffled over everything."

Katie smiled and collapsed into the small love seat in her office. It was a typical day. She had awoken at three-thirty, showered, peeked into her children's rooms, thrown on a pair of jeans and a sweatshirt, and headed out the door to make her way to the studio. There was never traffic on her way into the city, and she was grateful for that fact. She always planned carefully to ensure she had a hot cup of Starbucks in her hand before she hit the make-up chair. It was only eleven-thirty, and Katie was exhausted. The morning show had gone off without a hitch, but as usual, she had other engagements she needed to fulfill. One would be as a guest on Curtis Brinker's noon time show covering all the latest news, at least, that's what the network claimed. Katie let out a chuckle thinking about what seemed to constitute news these days.

"Care to share what's so amusing?" George asked.

"News, George. News is amusing."

"Katie, you look tired," George observed.

"Imagine that. I've been up for eight hours already, and I will be up for another ten at least. Stephanie has a concert tonight, and Bill is away. I'm telling you; I need a vacation."

"Well, the holidays are just around the bend," George offered.

"Umm...I know. But, I just committed some time in December."

"I thought you were taking some time off?" George responded in surprise.

"Yeah, well...I am—technically. We're heading to Boston for the holidays." Katie looked across at the clock and rose to her feet. "Guess we should head over."

"Don't sound so excited, Katie," George goaded his boss. Katie smiled at her assistant. "So, are you going to tell me or what?" he asked.

"Tell you what?"

"What we committed to?" George clarified his question.

"*We* did not commit to anything, George. You get a complete vacation from me over the holidays. Just a couple of appearances to help fundraise for a friend's project," she explained.

George nodded. "I can…"

"Take the vacation, George. God knows you need it," Katie laughed. "You look like shit."

"Thanks. You sure it's not you wanting the vacation from me?"

"Me? Never. I love being herded like cattle. And, there is no one I'd rather have prod me than you."

"Well good. Let's get moooving along then," he pushed Katie lightly.

Katie rolled her eyes. "Don't push it, Georgie."

≈ ≈ ≈

"So? What is this all about? I mean besides the donut in your mouth?" Julia asked Dan.

"You know, Jules, you really should have considered a job in comedy," Dan Roberts replied.

"Nah, you just make it easy. What gives?" Julia asked.

"Alright. You know we have a long way to go to fund this Brighton Center. We have to be creative on this one. Technically that is not our job. Our job is to fund the foundation so we can fund the project."

"Yes, Captain Obvious. Thank you for that," Julia laughed. "You clearly have something up your sleeve. What is it?"

"Katie Brennan."

"Katie Brennan is up your sleeve?" Julia poked.

"*The* Katie Brennan from *Coffee with Katie*?" Everett chimed.

"That would be the one," Dan responded.

"Okay?" Julia asked.

"Jules, you could pretend to be excited," Dan told his friend.

"I have no idea what I am getting excited about. What does Katie Brennan have to do with the center?"

"Seems Ms. Brennan and John Fortin, have a long-standing friendship," Dan explained

John Fortin was a well-known local lawyer and one of the founding interests in the center. Julia considered him a friend and had worked with him on several other initiatives. His involvement was one of the reasons she believed the center might actually be a viable project. Fortin was Harvard educated, well-connected, popular in both business and political circles, and he was openly gay. He had worked as an advocate for inner city school funding and in spite of his modesty, it was common knowledge that Fortin often took cases for young black and Hispanic men on a pro bono basis. He was the real deal, the kind of person that Julia had only come across a few times over the years.

"So, Katie Brennan wants to help her friend," Julia began.

"Yes, she's agreed to keynote a fundraising dinner the weekend before Christmas, and she's committed to a day of personal appearances for the foundation," Dan offered.

"Why not just fundraise for the center?" Julia asked skeptically.

"Actually, Jules, she saw you on PBS talking about the projects we have funded the last three years. Seems she found more than one project interesting. When John and I spoke with her on the phone, she was quite curious about the direction you have taken us in as the executive director."

"Huh," Julia said a bit surprised. "Well, Dan, that's great."

"I'm glad you feel that way, Jules."

"Why wouldn't I?" Julia asked. Dan was grimacing, and she sighed. "You want me to plan this fundraiser. Dan, Mandy can handle that."

"Jules," Dan looked at Mandy and smiled, and then he looked back to Julia. "We have six weeks to pull this off—six weeks. You have the connections...And you..."

"Fine," Julia answered. "Mandy, my office in one hour," she shook her head. "She'd better not be one of those needy celebrities, Dan. Who's handling her?" Julia saw Dan smirk. "Well?" she urged.

"No one, Ms. Cynical. Her parents live in Danvers. She'll be here for the holidays. Your contact is Ms. Brennan," Dan told her.

"Fabulous," Julia rolled her eyes. "Send me the...."

"Call John, Jules. He'll explain it all."

❧ ❧ ❧

"You look beat," Carrie said as Julia walked through the door.

"Yeah. What a day."

By the time Julia had removed her coat and made her way to the kitchen table, Carrie was already heating up a plate and pouring her a glass of wine. That was one of the things Julia loved the most about her wife. Carrie took great satisfaction in doing the little things for people that she knew mattered the most to them. People always assumed that Julia called her wife Care as a pet name for Carrie. That was only partly true. Carrie Stevens was one of the most compassionate and caring people Julia had ever met, and the pet name "Care" seemed a perfect fit.

Julia had met Carrie not long after she and Michael had separated. Carrie was exhibiting her photography in the college library. Julia had just finished meeting with one of her students and had the good fortune to trip over a stray backpack and land squarely in Carrie's arms. Looking up from the less than flattering position Julia found herself in, her embarrassment was met by a pair of warm, golden brown eyes. The comforting smile that Carrie offered seemed to all at once banish Julia's blush of embarrassment and replace it with a rush of fascination. A few cups of coffee later, and Julia had found herself suggesting that they meet again for dinner. Julia still wasn't certain that she had any idea where they were ultimately headed, but she surely knew that she wanted to see Carrie Stevens again.

Fourteen years and two daughters later, Julia and Carrie had fallen into a comfortable existence. The years hadn't changed Carrie much at all. She was still curvaceous in the most inviting way, and her eyes still glistened whenever Julia looked at her. They had created a good life—a balanced life. It was the kind of life most people dreamed about. Carrie had opened a successful photography studio in the city, and Julia had found a career that seemed to both fulfill her intellectually and simultaneously provided a substantially better salary than her teaching positions had. Their children were at the center of their lives and Julia and Carrie shared every responsibility, save the fact that Julia had been given the privilege of bearing each of their children.

"Hey, Mom," a voice greeted Julia from the doorway.

"Hey, Megs. How was your day?" Julia asked.

Meghan was their first daughter. She was nearly twelve and already almost Julia's height. Carrie's brother, Ted, had been their donor and Julia was thrilled that Meghan seemed to take after the Steven's side of the family. Both daughters had Carrie's eyes, but Meghan resembled Carrie a great deal in both her physical stature and demeanor. Just as Julia sometimes pitied Jake for taking after her so much, she envied the reflection she saw of her wife in Meghan.

"*Long*," Meghan drew out the word.

"Really? Why *long*?" Julia asked with a smile as Carrie put a plate in front of her.

"We got stuck waiting for Jake," Meghan griped.

"After practice?" Julia asked, looking at Carrie for confirmation.

"Yeah, Ma had to go find him," Meghan complained.

Julia looked at Carrie, who just shrugged. "Should I drink this wine now?" Julia asked.

"He was just off with his friends. Lost track of time," Carrie said.

"Yeah, he does that a lot lately," Julia groaned. "I'll talk to him," she said, watching Meghan grab a can of soda from the refrigerator.

"It's not a big deal, babe," Carrie said. "What about you? You're home late."

"Big benefit to plan for December 20th."

"What kind of benefit?" Carrie asked.

"Eh, you know, dinner, some dignitaries and a keynote speaker," Julia explained as she sipped her wine.

"Another author or another politician?" Carrie asked.

It was typical for the foundation to have well-known authors and politicians speak at fundraisers. The events generally timed to a new book release or the kickoff of either an election season or some piece of important legislation. Seldom was it solicited merely by an interest in the foundation itself which Carrie knew annoyed Julia.

"Nope." Julia looked at her wife and daughter's expressions in amusement and smiled. "Katie Brennan."

"*Coffee with Katie*, Katie Brennan?" Carrie asked.

"Yep. That would be the one."

"Are you serious?" Carrie beamed.

"What? Do you have a crush on the morning host?" Julia laughed.

"Maybe a little," Carrie winked.

"Oh geez, save me Megs," Julia called to her daughter.

"Save you from what?" Jake asked from the doorway.

"Ma has a crush on Katie Brennan," Meghan laughed.

"Who?" Jake asked.

"Never mind, Jacob," Julia answered and turned to her wife. "You like those redheads, don't you? Older ones," she winked.

"*You*," Carrie tugged Julia's hair lightly, "are not really a red-head."

"What are you saying?" Julia scowled playfully.

"Nice try, Jules. You are about as much a redhead as I will ever be a blonde."

"Auburn is red," Julia declared.

"Yeah and brown is blonde. You are a blonde missy. The only reason your hair is that color is to hide all that gray," Carrie said.

"Hey! What's your excuse?" Julia shot back.

"I like being blonde. I have nothing to hide," Carrie laughed.

"Yeah, well, now I know why you wanted me to use that color…Pining away over the news lady," Julia surmised.

Jake rolled his eyes and Meghan laughed.

"Why are you all laughing?" another voice asked.

"Your mother wants us to believe she is really a redhead," Carrie winked.

Jordan entered the room and studied Julia closely. She put her arm around her mother's shoulder. "She has red hair," Jordan defended Julia.

Jordan was a delight. She had just turned eight and was still a bit unsure of many of the jokes that seemed to permeate the Riley household. While she had Carrie's eyes and skin, she was very much like Julia as a youngster. Everything was an adventure, and she thrived on being around people. Jordan would try just about anything once and had given Julia and Carrie most of their lessons in Heart Attack 101. She attempted to fly like Superman when she was three and jumped off the top stair resulting in a broken elbow. Jordan was never content to simply sled down the hill in the backyard. At four, she was emulating everything her brother did including attempting to sled over tree stumps. She was fearless, resilient, and opinionated, a stark contrast to her quiet and sweet older sister.

"All right," Carrie said with just enough forcefulness to convey it was time to settle down. "Let your mother eat in peace. She can't help that old ladies have to hide the gray somehow."

Julia rolled her eyes at the fit of laughter that followed and watched her children clear out of the kitchen. "You know, Katie Brennan isn't any younger than me," Julia quipped.

"Or any cuter, babe," Carrie soothed.

"Nice try. It's too late. I already got the news bulletin."

"Aww…Babe, she probably colors her hair too," Carrie consoled Julia.

"Great," Julia replied. "Let's just hope she's not a bit…"

"Jules," Carrie warned.

"Yeah, yeah…"

"Don't be jealous," Carrie grinned.

"I hate dealing with…"

"I've heard she is very nice," Carrie assured her wife.

"You read too many magazines in the checkout lines," Julia laughed.

"Julia, she is very popular. She will be a huge draw."

Julia sighed. "I know," she admitted as she walked to place her plate in the dishwasher. "I'm beat. What do you say we go finish this wine in bed?"

Carrie smiled quietly. "I'll be in shortly," she patted Julia on the butt. "Try not to fall asleep in your clothes."

"Mmm," Julia groaned. "Six weeks, Katie Brennan. Six weeks. Merry Christmas to me," she chuckled.

Chapter Two

DECEMBER 2014

"You can't be serious? Lunch and dinner? Come on, Dan," Julia griped.

"Relax. It will give you a chance to get acquainted with Katie in person before the benefit tonight," Dan said. "You are going to be with her all day tomorrow, so you might as well get comfortable."

Julia hated dealing with public personalities. It was one element of her chosen profession that many considered a perk. For Julia, it was a nuisance. She had stroked the egos of enough politicians, authors, academics, and the occasional actor to last her a lifetime. While most were polite and engaging, the majority of celebrities she encountered were less than interested in the actual work that they were supposedly "passionately" promoting. She groaned her frustration as she made her way into her office with Dan following close behind.

"What's the problem? Was Ms. Brennan less than cordial when you spoke with her or something?" Dan asked.

Julia flopped into her office chair with a chuckle. "No, of course not. I'm certain that Katie Brennan understands the importance of professional P's and Q's. Always be polite and make every statement quotable," Julia smirked.

"God, you are so cynical," Dan laughed. Julia just shrugged. She would not deny the accusation. Her cynicism was built over time and based on experience. "Just behave," Dan winked.

"Scouts honor," Julia pledged as Dan left her office. "Everett!" Julia called loudly.

"Yeah?" the young man scurried into her office.

"Apparently, I have a lunch date with Dan and John Fortin at noon to review tonight's festivities. I need you and Mandy to run over to The Fairmont and check on things," Julia directed. Everett nodded and turned swiftly on his heel. "And, Everett? Black tie means black tie, not purple, blue, green, or polka-dotted," Julia called to him without raising her eyes from the desktop.

"It's called pizzazz," he called back.

"It's called *black* tie, Everett. Black."

৵ ৵ ৵

Katie Brennan smiled at the host who had begun fidgeting slightly with the menu in his hand. She had never gotten used to the nervous reaction her presence sometimes spurred in others. She had become accustomed to that response as the wife of a major league baseball player, but Katie had never anticipated anyone would find her of particular interest. Her husband Bill Brennan had been in the spotlight from the day she had met him. He thrived in the spotlight and adored the attention. Katie had only begun to launch her career when she had met the star baseball pitcher. She had been content to walk in his shadow. It had never been on Katie's bucket list to anchor anything. Investigative journalism was Katie Brennan's passion. There was little cause for that anymore it seemed, and once Katie had made the jump to television her fate had seemed inevitable.

"The rest of your party is already seated," the young man said to her, careful not to make eye contact.

Katie sighed inwardly and looked at his name tag. "Thank you, Robert. Do you have any recommendations?" she asked him quietly. "Give me the advantage before I walk into the lion's den," she whispered conspiratorially.

The young man looked up, his lips curling into a smile. "Well, most people would say that you should try the salmon or the lobster roll."

"Would they? I didn't ask most people," Katie smiled. "What is your favorite?"

He shrugged, a light pink flushing his cheeks. "I'm a burger kind of guy," he said.

The young man's thick Boston accent made Katie smile broader. He gestured to the table in front of them, and Katie watched as the three bodies who were currently seated rose to greet her. She gently took hold of his arm and leaned into his ear. "Thanks for the tip. I'm on your team," she told him.

"Well, Katie!" John Fortin took his friend into a hug. "Glad you could make it."

"Miss a chance to dine with royalty," she poked at her friend. "Never." Katie saw the questing smile on the woman standing across from her and laughed. "John has never let me forget that while I might one day be a princess, he will forever be the queen," she explained. Julia raised an eyebrow and laughed. "You must be Julia," Katie extended her hand.

"That's what they tell me," Julia responded.

Katie's eyes twinkled as she released Julia's hand. It was immediately evident that Julia Riley was neither impressed nor intimidated by Katie's presence. Katie found it refreshing. "Sorry about my delay. I'm not used to this Boston traffic anymore," Katie explained. "So, did you all order?" she asked.

"No, of course not. We waited for you," Dan told her. "I can't tell you how much Julia and I appreciate you taking this time out," he said as a young waiter approached the table.

"Are you ready to order?" the waiter inquired.

"I think we need," Dan began.

Katie picked up her menu and opened it. "No, no, go ahead. Let Her Majesty start," she joked.

"I'll have the salmon," John Fortin winked at the young man.

"The same," Dan said. "It's excellent, by the way," he offered to Katie. Katie closed her menu and nodded.

"Salmon for you as well?" the waiter asked Katie.

"Actually, I'm more of a burger girl. I have it on good authority yours are excellent." Katie looked up at the waiter who nodded his agreement. "Perfect. Leave it slightly mooing if you don't mind," she instructed him with a wink. "What about you?" Katie looked across to Julia.

"Too bad they don't have a salmon burger," Julia joked, soliciting a smirk from Katie. "I'll pass on both counts, though. Just a bowl of clam chowder," she said.

"Not hungry?" Katie asked curiously.

"Not a lunch girl," Julia answered honestly.

Julia sat for the next hour listening to the conversation at the table. She was surprised at the lack of shop talk. John Fortin and Katie Brennan had known each other since grade school. The pair had talked about homeroom teachers, annoying boyfriends, and over protective parents before anyone mentioned the events planned over the next few days. Julia didn't mind. She found the playful banter endearing. In truth, Julia did not understand what they needed to have a lunch meeting for. Katherine Brennan was a professional. She'd made thousands of these types of appearances over the years. There was no need to review logistics.

"So, Julia?" Katie directed her question across the table. "What made a professor decide to go into non-profit work?"

Julia took a sip of her water and smiled. "Not all that different," she said.

"How so?" Katie asked with genuine curiosity.

Dan sipped the coffee in front of him slowly. Julia's lips had rolled up into a recognizable smirk, and he held his breath.

"Well, both deal with education—for one thing," Julia explained. "Trying to make an impact on the world through knowledge," she continued.

Dan let out the breath he'd been holding. Julia was a professional, but she had a habit of speaking her mind. She was always polite in her dialogue, but she had never excelled at pretending to enjoy what she considered "sucking up" to acquire money. To Julia, the foundation's work should be able to stand on its own merits.

"I can see that," Katie replied. "So, do you enjoy this work more than teaching?"

"Honestly?" Julia asked.

"Well," Katie said. "Honesty is always refreshing in my line of work."

Julia could not help but chuckle. "Touché." She tipped her glass before taking a sip. "Some things I do enjoy more than I did in teaching—yes. Some things not as much. Both have their respective advantages and rewards, and both have their drawbacks. Politics is part of everything. That, I have learned, is unavoidable. Managing personalities and bullshit is just part of life," Julia said with a smile.

Dan nearly choked on his coffee. John Fortin snickered as he watched the two women regard each other with equal amusement.

Katie let out a hearty laugh. "You, Ms. Riley, have no idea. Personality and bullshit seem to be the everyday news," she offered. Julia raised her glass and Katie extended her own in a playful "cheer".

"Well, I suppose we should be going," Dan said. Julia followed her friend's lead, getting to her feet quickly. She felt Katie's hand pull her back.

"Can I quote you on that in my speech?" Katie asked in a hushed voice.

Julia looked into a pair of mischievous blue eyes and winked. "Only if I get royalties," she whispered.

Katie watched as Julia followed Dan out of the restaurant. "She is something," Katie shook her head.

"Julia?" John asked. Katie nodded. "Yes, she is," he agreed. "She likes you, Princess," he said.

"That is surprising; I take it?" Katie asked.

"No. You're the real deal. She just has little use for plastic," he told his friend.

Katie nodded. "Then promise you won't tell her about my nose job," she poked.

"Nope. Loyalty to the royalty," he promised with a laugh.

Katie smacked her friend's arm and sighed. Personal appearances were not one of her favorite parts of her chosen career. The Fledger Foundation funded numerous projects that Katie felt strongly about, and she genuinely wanted to support their efforts. Being raised by two teachers, the importance of education had been drilled into her head repeatedly. She had often pondered leaving behind the spotlight to teach herself. Julia's words had struck a chord within Katie. "Politics and bullshit are everywhere. There's today's newsflash," she silently agreed to the statement.

❧ ❧ ❧

Julia walked into the foyer of the large ballroom purposefully. She offered the customary smile and nod as she passed each table, occasionally accepting the proffered hand of a large donor or local dignitary. Carrie was standing a few paces ahead near the bar speaking with John Fortin, and Julia wanted to reach her wife for a moment before her time would be monopolized. She leaned in and kissed Carrie's cheek softly.

"Sorry, we had some issues with the sound on the stage," Julia explained.

Carrie gave her wife an understanding smile. She had grown comfortable with these events and familiar with Julia's frequent disappearances. For most of the attendees, these evenings provided an opportunity to network and to socialize. For Julia, these evenings were fraught with details and debacles.

"No worries," Carrie winked. "Everything all set now, I assume?"

"One can hope," Julia answered.

"So, where is your guest of honor?" Carrie inquired.

"You'll have to forgive my wife," Julia began to explain to John Fortin. "It seems she is a bit taken with your best friend."

Fortin laughed. "Katie has that effect on people," he said. "Last I saw, Mayor Bremer had her cornered near the fountain."

The group turned its attention simultaneously to the right, and Julia immediately captured sight of the affable morning show host as she entertained the mayor's questions. Katie smiled broadly at the mayor's propensity to ask her a question and quickly answer it himself. She suspected he had already knocked back his fair share of whatever was gracing the glass in his hand. He reminded her a bit of an animated character in a Saturday morning cartoon. Katie found herself torn between her amusement at his comical mannerisms and her need to disengage and circulate. Feeling the weight of a distant stare, she shifted her gaze momentarily. She smiled when her eyes met the matching arched brows of her best friend and a clearly amused executive director.

"Perhaps, I should save her," John Fortin said to his companions.

"No," Julia stopped him gently. "Let me. He'll rope you right in, trust me."

"If you say so," John replied as Julia retrieved a glass of white wine from Carrie's hand with a wink and walked away.

"She's right," Carrie said. "Daniel Bremer is almost as entertaining as he is annoying."

"No love affair with Boston's Mayor?" John teased his friend. "Think she can pull it off?"

Carrie looked off into the distance as her wife weaved through several groups effortlessly to reach her intended destination. "He is no match for Julia," she laughed. "And, before you ask, I would bet the farm on that."

Julia was finding it difficult not to stare at Katie as she approached. Katie had a presence that Julia found difficult to describe. It wasn't Katie's physical appearance that made her alluring, although as Julia drew closer, she could not prevent her gaze from sweeping over the tall redhead. Sensing the presence drawing closer, Katie turned. Julia thought for a split second she might have stopped moving. Katie offered her a genuine smile that Julia immediately recognized as a silent thank you. Katie's green dress painted the twinkle of mirth in her eyes a cerulean similar to the ocean, not quite blue with just a hint of underlying green. Tentatively, Julia sidled up beside her new acquaintance. "

Well, I see you have met our illustrious leader, Katie." The mayor beamed at Julia.

"Yes, I have. Your mayor here is a man of many interests," Katie offered. "Although, I suspect he has actually been gunning for my husband's expertise in Boston."

"Can't blame a man for trying," the mayor answered. "We've got some terrific news outlets here. A new closer for next season...."

"Oh, Daniel," Julia bumped the mayor lightly. "Come clean with Ms. Brennan." Katie quirked an eyebrow at the pair. "Dangerous truths," Julia leaned into Katie and whispered.

"Don't you tell her my secrets, Julia Riley," Mayor Bremer mock scolded. "I'll start thinking those rumors that you want my office are true."

Julia's full-throated laugh traveled through Katie in an unexpected way. She watched in rapt fascination as Julia's lips turned into what seemed to be an ever-widening smile.

"Now, Daniel," Julia narrowed her gaze playfully. "Be careful, or I will give Ms. Brennan the full scoop. And, nothing could cause a mutiny in Boston like a..."

"Uncle," the mayor called out with a shake of his head. "You win, this time, Riley."

"Well, I am sorry to break up your campaigning, Daniel, but I need to borrow our guest for a few moments," Julia looked at Katie.

"It was a pleasure to meet you, Mr. Mayor," Katie said genuinely.

"Likewise, Ms. Brennan," he returned her pleasantries.

Julia gently guided Katie away from the mayor.

"So?" Katie whispered under her breath as both women acknowledged the groups they passed by silently.

"Yes?" Julia asked.

"Mutiny?"

"Ah, yes," Julia nodded. She leaned closer to Katie, bumping shoulders lightly. "Closet Yankee fan. No greater threat for a Bostonian Democrat."

Katie burst out laughing. "You are a bit touched, aren't you?"

"As bad as a high school cheerleader after her prom," Julia said earnestly.

"Sure you don't have any political aspirations, Ms. Riley?"

"Why? Think I'd be successful?" Julia asked.

"No greater threat for a political opponent than a horny cheerleader," Katie replied.

Julia stopped their forward progression to regard the woman beside her. "Can I quote you on that?" Julia asked.

"Only if you run."

❧ ❧ ❧

Julia accepted the customary hug from the keynote speaker, ready to vacate the spotlight for Katie. "You're a tough act to follow," Katie whispered in Julia's ear.

Julia chuckled. "Not for you, Ms. Brennan. Trust me on this," she assured, pulling out of the friendly embrace with a wink.

"What did she say?" Carrie asked her wife as Julia returned to the table, and Katie stepped to the podium.

Julia shook her head in amusement. "Nothing."

Their table had enjoyed surprisingly lively and often candid conversation throughout dinner. Julia had expected Katie Brennan to be engaging and intelligent. What surprised her was Katie's wit and candor, which Julia found refreshing. John Fortin seemed more like the class clown in Katie's presence than he did a well-known lawyer and philanthropist. She could see the wheels in her friend Dan's head spinning. The group had fallen into colorful banter that was far from the usual atmosphere during these events. Julia looked up at the stage and smiled as Katie began her remarks. She snickered when she heard Katie turn on a familiar New England accent.

"Aft-ah marrying a Yankee, my moth-ah will be thrilled to he-ah that Ms. Riley got me to taste the local chowd-ah. Might even get to pahk my cah in the yahd this Christmas." The room erupted into laughter and cheers as Katie took a mock bow. "I have not forgotten my roots," she continued. "That's one of the reasons I jumped at the opportunity to help with this project. I've had the opportunity to travel, explore, and meet all kinds of people in our world. Everywhere I have gone, the story is the same. People simply want their best opportunity. They want the best opportunities for their children, and they want to be accepted for who they are. Being raised by two school teachers instilled in me a deep passion for education. I believe that the only way we can bridge these gaps, the gaps that divide us by gender, by race, by our language, our age, religion, or whom we love, the element we require if we hope to erect enduring bridges that foster equality is education. It starts in our homes—in our local communities. Boston will always be my home."

Julia sat transfixed as she listed to Katie's speech. The words were not only powerful, but there was also a sincerity behind them that left Julia nearly breathless. She listened carefully as Katie laid out the project with a command of the stage and the topic that surprised Julia. At times, she found herself losing the words as she studied the subject behind them. The sensation of warm breath in her ear roused her from her silent pondering.

"Great speech. See? I told you," Carrie whispered.

"Yes, you did," Julia conceded and stood to join in the applause as Katie made her way back to the table, passing the microphone to Dan.

"You owe me a chow-dah," Katie whispered to Julia.

"I'm sorry?"

"Well, I am a journalist. Suppose someone fact checks my remarks," Katie responded evenly.

Julia nodded. "You sure? Lots of great burger joints where we are going tomorrow."

"Consider it your contribution to my journalistic integrity."

"Chowder?" Julia chuckled.

"Hey…Far less has sunk a career," Katie answered with a dire tone as she took her seat.

"I'll see what I can conjure," Julia winked.

≈ ≈ ≈

Julia reached the kitchen still sleepy-eyed. The previous evening's festivities had rolled on much later than expected after John Fortin suggested that Julia and Carrie join him and Katie for a casual drink in the bar. One drink had quickly evolved into several as the foursome became lost in conversation.

"How does she do this every morning?" Julia grumbled.

"How does who do what?" Carrie asked from behind her. "You leaving already?"

"Katie and yes," Julia yawned.

"It's not even six," Carrie observed.

"Yes, I know," Julia groaned. "John has a flight at ten. He roped me into picking up Katie for an early breakfast."

"Oh," Carrie began as she came up behind her wife. "So, you are literally having coffee with Katie," she laughed.

"If I don't have coffee soon, it will be nap time with Julia, not coffee with Katie. Long day in front of me," Julia said with a light rub to her forehead and a wince.

"Aw, babe. I think you might have had one too many glasses of wine last night," Carrie observed.

"Mm. Bad influences. All three of you."

Carrie giggled. "I'm not sure how I crept into that equation."

Julia pulled Carrie to her and squinted in contemplation. "You are smitten with a certain news personality and did not want the night to end," she smiled.

"Smitten?" Carrie began to laugh. "Jules, you are starting to sound like my grandma. The only person I am smitten over is you, you lunatic."

"It's the hair," Julia said with a kiss to Carrie's cheek.

Carrie placed Julia's keys in her hand and shook her head. "Yes, babe. That is exactly what it is. Go on. Don't forget the kids are all going to Michael's today to do their Christmas."

"Isn't he on call?" Julia asked, mentally reviewing her ex-husband's schedule.

"Not until tonight."

"How is it you know more about my ex-husband's schedule than I do?" Julia asked lightheartedly.

"I talk to him more. Have to have someone to compare notes with," Carrie quipped.

"Must be a short conversation," Julia returned. "Not sure when I will be back."

"No worries. I have a few things to do at the studio. Then I am going to finish my shopping. I'll see you when I see you." Carried scooted a still yawning Julia out the door. "Have a good day."

"Yeah..."

"Jules..."

"I know...Gotta go. Wouldn't want to be late for coffee with Katie and the queen."

"The what?" Carrie called after her wife. Julia just waved back with a smile. "Oh, Jules. Behave yourself," she mumbled as she retreated back into the house.

ɛᴠ ɛᴠ ɛᴠ

The day was progressing much more smoothly than Julia had anticipated. She had enjoyed breakfast with Katie and John and had found both of them in a similar condition from the previous evening's festivities. In truth, her head was still aching a bit. She looked on from across the room as Katie now conversed with a group of teenagers at one of the local churches. It was one of several stops to groups who would benefit from the Brighton Center's resources. The cameras rolled, and Katie seemed to effortlessly engage the teens in dialogue about their personal experiences. Julia listened as Katie guided the discussion carefully to navigate what could often become murky waters. Katie kept the group on the topic at hand, relating their personal experiences as to why they believed a center such as Brighton would benefit them. Sometimes, just dealing with Jake gave Julia a headache. She suppressed a chuckle as she mused over the hangover Katie was sporting. Almost as if on cue, Katie reached her feet and accepted the handshakes and hugs of her young friends.

"Something funny, Riley?" Katie asked, coming even with Julia.

"No. I was just wondering how you managed an hour with those kids without a bottle of Excedrin."

Katie nodded with a smile. "Practice."

"Have a hangover often?" Julia asked with a wink.

"Only from sleep deprivation," Katie answered. "Let me know when they make a cure for that."

"It's called sleep," Julia replied.

Julia led Katie through the small crowd that had gathered outside the church and stepped back momentarily to allow Katie to sign a few autographs and shake some more hands. Just watching Katie made Julia tired. Katie seemed to have endless energy. Julia began to consider asking if she could borrow some or even purchase it. She started laughing.

"See? Something is funny," Katie said.

"No. I was just wondering what you would charge me for some of that stamina you seem to possess."

"Under the eight pounds of makeup you see before you, lies a bedraggled old woman," Katie answered as she stepped into the car.

Julia hopped into the driver's seat and shook her head. Katie, she had learned in a few short hours, could be almost as self-deprecating as Julia tended to be. She looked over at Katie and shook her head in amusement again. There was no way that Katie had spent that much time or effort on her appearance. She was a natural beauty. That was evident. Julia pursed her lips and considered her new friend seriously.

"What?" Katie asked.

"I'm just wondering who is hiding under there? Maleficent or Ursula? I don't see any tentacles…" A soft slap to her arm made Julia jump.

"Drive, Riley."

Julia turned the key in the ignition as both women softly snickered. She groaned when she felt the buzz of her phone. "Michael?" she answered curiously.

Julia's ex-husband was well aware of her plans for the day. Instantly, she felt a wave of panic. All of her children were with Michael today. It had become an annual event that she was grateful for. Michael Riley had deemed himself, Uncle Michael, immediately. Julia knew that he loved her daughters almost as much as she and Carrie did. They were Jake's sisters, and Michael wanted them to feel part of each other fully. It was unlike him to interrupt their day or Julia's for that matter unless something was wrong.

"Michael? What is it?"

"Jules," he let out a heavy sigh. "I'm sorry. I tried Carrie. She must have her phone off."

"What's going on?" Julia asked. Katie glanced over and instantly saw the tension on Julia's face. "Are the kids okay?" Julia asked nervously. Katie instinctively put her hand on Julia's arm as a show of support.

"The kids are fine. I am on my way in. Bad accident on Interstate Ninety. Seven cars, multiple traumas."

Julia sighed in relief, a relief she felt a bit guilty for. Someone would be getting a dreaded call. That was not lost on her.

Michael continued. "I'm taking them with me. They can hit the cafeteria until one of you gets here. Maybe you can get Carrie…"

"I'll try. Just tell them one of us will be there soon. Does Jake have his phone?" She heard Michael repeat her question and her son's answer.

"He has it. Jules, I am sorry."

Julia smiled at her ex-husband's genuine concern. She was about to scold him for his apology when Katie's phone rang. "Listen, don't worry about it, Michael. Someone needs you more than those three right now. They get that."

Michael Riley sighed and locked the door to his home. He turned as Jake teased his youngest sister and laughed. "I know. I just wish…"

"Go on," Julia told him. She glanced over at Katie and realized that her new friend had gone completely pale. "I have to go," she said into her phone.

"Okay? Everything okay, Jules? You…"

"I don't know. One of us will be there. I gotta go," she said as she hung up the call.

"I understand," Katie's voice said in a hoarse whisper.

"Katie?" Julia called over. Katie put her phone in her lap, closed her eyes, and exhaled a shaky breath. "Katie," Julia reached across and took hold of Katie's hand. "What's wrong?"

Katie shook her head lightly and turned very slowly toward Julia. "It's Bill. Something…. Seven cars…I don't know. They said they were taking him to…"

Julia felt her body begin to tremble. She knew exactly where they would be taking Katie's husband. "It will be okay," Julia assured. "I know where he's headed."

"How do you? Julia…I…"

Julia offered Katie a comforting grin and a squeeze of her hand. "Don't worry about anything, okay? I'll take care of making the needed calls when we get there." Katie nodded dumbly. "Katie," Julia called over. "It really will be okay."

Katie offered Julia a weak smile. Julia started the car forward and mentally slapped herself. It had been the right thing to say. It was the natural thing to say, but Julia found herself oddly wishing she had not offered such an assurance. She'd lived with a trauma surgeon in her life for many years. One thing Julia did know, there were never any guarantees.

Chapter Three

Julia's Journal:

The funny thing about falling in love is that you don't get to decide when, and you don't get to choose who. It's exactly like being born. One minute, you are nice and comfortable and safe—you know everything around you. It is like a beautiful, solitary cocoon. Then, in one instant, there is a rush of air, and everything is bright, your heart is racing, and some stranger's eyes are looking into yours. You aren't exactly sure who they are. You can't be certain of anything, only that you are a part of them, and they are a part of you. Shivers travel along your spine, and all you desire at that moment is to be held close so that you can feel warm again. You struggle to name what you feel. You can't force the stranger to reach for you or pull you close. You just have to trust that somehow they will, because the truth is, falling in love hurts. It is exactly like being born.

The bustle of a hospital emergency department was one that Julia had become familiar with, but never accustomed to. It was an environment in which her former husband thrived. Underneath all of Julia's bravado, lay a sensitive soul. This place conjured an understanding of the fragility of life that unnerved her. Julia found that reality incredibly breathtaking in its simplicity, and at the same time

34

monumentally disquieting in its reality. This place humbled her and unsettled her. She guided Katie to the reception desk and was grateful to see a familiar security guard.

"Ms. Riley!" he greeted. "Doc said the kids are in the café."

"Thanks, DeAndre. Ms. Brennan's husband was brought in, I believe. Do you think you…"

DeAndre moved his gaze to the woman beside Julia. "Oh…Holy…Your husband?" He recognized Katie immediately. He looked down at the computer screen in front of him and accessed the name. "Yeah. He's in Trauma Two." Julia took a deep breath and nodded her understanding. "I'll let the Doc know you are here."

"DeAndre," Julia leaned over the counter. "I don't think Ms. Brennan should be out here in this waiting room."

"No…Yes, right. How about the inner waiting area? Fewer people there," he observed. Julia nodded.

"Thank you," Katie whispered. "Shouldn't you go?" she turned to Julia "You don't have to go with me, Julia."

"The kids will be fine. Come on," Julia replied.

Katie nodded her silent thanks, accepted the visitor badge that DeAndre handed her and allowed Julia to lead her through a set of automatic doors.

"It's bad, isn't it?" Katie looked at Julia.

Julia forced a small smile. It was never a good sign when someone was rolled into the trauma bays. It did not necessarily mean that Bill Brennan's life was in jeopardy, but Julia knew it increased the likelihood that his injuries were serious or critical in nature.

"I don't know," she confessed. "They have an excellent team here. Believe me."

Katie just nodded again when her phone went off. "George? I don't know. I just got here…. No…What are you talking about?" The edge in Katie's voice was growing by the second. "I don't…"

Julia could see that the normally composed woman beside her was beginning to lose both her patience and her bearings. She stepped in and took the phone from Katie's hand.

"Hello?" Julia inquired.

"Who is this?" George demanded.

"This is Julia Riley. Who is this?"

"Ms. Riley?" his voice calmed slightly.

"One and the same. What can I do for you, George was it?"

"I'm sorry. George Curry. I'm Katie's assistant. Is Katie? Is he?"

"We don't know anything yet, Mr. Curry. We just arrived."

"George, please. Look, Ms. Riley…"

"Julia."

"I'm sorry?"

"Just Julia."

"Right. Look. I don't know what she knows, but the press is already all over this story," George said.

Julia looked over at Katie. Katie had collapsed into a chair with her face in her hands.

"I see," Julia kept her voice even.

"No, Julia. He…Bill…He wasn't in the car alone."

Julia's thoughts instinctively traveled to Katie's children, but Katie had told her that her parents had taken the kids for the weekend while she and her husband finished up their pre-holiday commitments. She listened intently as George continued.

"Look, I think she has long suspected. This is just, well…It seems like it will make speculation reality."

Julia needed a moment to process the innuendo in George's statement. Bill Brennan was having an affair. He had just been caught in a tragic and unexpected way.

"I think I understand."

"I just…They will expect some kind of statement," George explained. "The network will want…"

"To hell with what your network wants," Julia responded a bit harshly. Katie looked up to Julia in astonishment.

George laughed softly. "I'll do what I can here, but they will…"

"I get it. Katie has enough on her plate. I'll tell her," Julia said sternly.

"Keep me in the loop?" George asked.

"I'm sure she will, George," Julia said as she disconnected the call with a roll of her eyes.

"Thank you," Katie's voice betrayed the stoicism on her face.

Julia started to respond when she saw a familiar face approaching. "Stephen…."

"Jules, what are you doing here?" Dr. Stephen Aronson inquired.

Julia nodded towards Katie. "Ms. Brennan and I were on the road when Michael called."

The tall doctor nodded his understanding and turned sympathetically to Katie, who had reached her feet. "Mrs. Brennan."

"Katie, please. Bill…. Is he…"

"He has extensive injuries. Why don't we take a walk to my office? I think you'll find it more comfortable there. I can explain what we know," he suggested to the pair before him.

Katie attempted to smile but felt little inclination toward any good humor. Julia watched her carefully, feeling helpless and oddly frustrated by that fact. She'd grown to like Katie in their short time together. This was not a scenario Julia would wish upon anyone. She gently rubbed Katie's back in friendly encouragement as they followed the doctor through the corridors toward his office. He directed them both to have a seat on a small love seat and rolled a chair out to sit before them.

"Listen, your husband suffered some internal injuries, and a bleed in his brain. Those are of the greatest concern right now. Dr. Riley is taking him into surgery. We need to release the pressure on his brain, and we need to look inside to see what is going on." Katie swallowed the lump in her throat and nodded. "He also has a broken femur, a broken wrist, and crushed vertebrae." Katie nodded again.

"Is he…What are his chances?" she asked softly, almost afraid to hear the answer.

Dr. Aronson looked to Julia and took a deep breath before returning his attention to Katie. "I can't say. I'm sorry. We'll know more when Dr. Riley gets into surgery. I will tell you that the next forty-eight to seventy-two hours will be critical."

Katie nodded her understanding. "What about a statement?" Katie asked. "I already know he wasn't alone. I'm sure the press is waiting."

"We won't release anything without your permission, but yes, the inquiries are steady. Typically, we will just confirm his admission and that his injuries are of a serious nature and are being addressed. As far as the other matter," he paused and took Katie's hand. "That would not be within our purview to disclose. Any statements as to his condition after that will be approved by you."

Katie smiled half–heartedly as Julia's phone buzzed.

"Excuse me," Julia said. "It's Carrie," she explained. She stopped and looked at Katie. "I'll be right back, okay?"

Katie thought for a moment to protest, but she appreciated Julia's company. "Actually, I need to call my parents. They'll be a wreck wondering."

"Use my office," Dr. Aronson offered. "Why don't you just consider this your safe haven for now," he said with a smile. "It will keep curious onlookers at bay. I'll let Julia know. She knows everyone so you will be in good hands."

"Thank you, Dr. Aronson. Honestly, she's gone out of her way already," Katie said.

Dr. Aronson winked at Katie. "Jules is all bark," he chuckled. "Inside she's a marshmallow. She's a good friend to have," he said sincerely.

"I can see that," Katie said with a genuine smile.

"Make yourself as comfortable as you can. It will be a while. Can I get you some awful coffee or soda?"

"Coffee would be great—with a shot of whiskey," Katie attempted to lighten the moment.

The doctor chuckled. "Dr. Riley is a fabulous surgeon. Hang in there. I'll bring you two some coffee. If it makes you feel any better, it tastes worse than whiskey."

Katie appreciated his humor and smiled. What on earth was she going to tell her parents? How was she going to explain to her children that their father was seriously hurt, and how could she possibly hope to shield them from the inevitable? Their father was an unfaithful husband. Katie inhaled a breath for courage and dialed. "God help me," she muttered.

❧ ❧ ❧

"Oh my God, Jules. Is he going to be all right?" Carrie asked.

"I don't know. Michael apparently was taking him into surgery. That's what Steve told us right before you called. It's worse, Care. Apparently he had a woman in the car with him."

"Are you telling me he was cheating on Katie?" Carrie gasped slightly. "Did she know?"

Julia sighed. "I don't know. Look, it's going to get hairy here, particularly when this hits the airwaves. I don't think she should…"

"No. You shouldn't leave her alone. I'll come get the kids. Jules, she can stay in the guest room."

Julia smiled. There was never a moment's hesitation from her wife to help someone. "I don't know what she's going to do. How long he'll be in surgery…Who knows?"

"Well, just do whatever you think is best," Carrie replied. "Can I bring you two something before I pick up the kids?"

"Real coffee. I have a feeling we will need it."

"Done. I'm sorry, Jules."

Julia sniggered. "Don't be sorry for me. I'm used to hospitals and doctors."

"I know. I'm just glad you can, at least, keep Katie company."

"Yeah, me too. I'll see you in a bit."

Julia looked at the door to Dr. Aronson's office and closed her eyes for a moment. She felt compelled to support her new friend, but she also did not want to be intrusive. This was a personal crisis for Katie on many levels. Katie barely knew Julia. Julia was completely conscious of her sometimes overbearing nature, and the last thing she wanted to do was add to Katie's stress in any way. She let out a sigh and decided she would let Katie dictate the course of the day from that moment.

"Hey," Julia called out as she entered the office. She watched Katie raise her head from the position it held on the desk.

"Hey, everything okay?" Katie asked.

Julia smiled solemnly. There was nothing but genuine concern in Katie Brennan's voice. "I think I should be asking you how you are doing," she replied. Katie just shrugged. "Things are fine. Carrie is on her way to get the kids."

"You don't have to stay, Julia—honestly."

"Well, I will leave that up to you. Did you get your parents?"

Another, heavier sigh escaped the woman behind the desk. "I did. They'll bring the kids down tomorrow morning. Maybe by then I'll be able to make some decisions."

"Look, I don't want to impose on your..."

Katie's eyes flew open. "Impose? Julia, you've been wonderful. I mean, a good friend," she smiled gently.

Julia nodded. "I'm happy to keep you company, but you just say the word and I'll..."

"I'd love it if you would stay," Katie admitted.

"Well, good—at least, I know that coffee that I asked Care to pick up won't go to waste."

"Julia?" Katie reached for Julia's hand.

"What?"

"Thanks."

∾ ∾ ∾

The afternoon dragged on in the small doctor's office. Waiting was always difficult. Julia knew the waiting game as well as anyone. She had spent long hours in emergency waiting rooms with both her parents over the years. And, she had endured an anxiousness beyond measure when Jake was twelve. He had been riding his bike in an area that she and Carrie had repeatedly told him to avoid. Coaxed by friends, he followed along down the forbidden path. Julia received the worst call of her life that day. Jake was hit by a car and being rushed to the hospital. Julia had thought she had known panic, thought she understood fear. The wait had been short for news of Jake's condition, but it had felt as if years had passed. They were fortunate that day. Jake had a broken arm, a badly sprained knee, and some severe bruising. He had managed the reminder of his mishap in the form of a scar that remained over his left eyebrow, but he had recovered fully.

Julia looked over at Katie, who had her head tilted back against the loveseat and her eyes closed. Lines of tension and worry creased the normally relaxed figure's eyes and forehead. Julia sighed inwardly. The hospital had released their basic statement just a short while earlier. Pitching favorite Bill Brennan was one of the six patients admitted as a result of injuries sustained in a multiple vehicle accident. He had sustained injuries of a critical nature and was currently in surgery. As soon as any more information was available as to the nature of his condition, a statement would be issued. Katie had insisted on watching from the office. Julia could see that the waiting combined with the other questions she was certain were racing through Katie's mind were taking a toll. She was about to attempt some benign conversation when a soft knock at the door was followed by Michael's face peering inside. Katie sat up immediately. Michael looked over at Julia. His expression was clear. He would not be delivering happy news.

"Mrs. Brennan?" he greeted Katie. "I'm Dr. Riley," he introduced himself. Katie nodded. "So, your husband is out of surgery," he said. "He ruptured his spleen. That is one of the reasons the surgery took so long. We managed to relieve the pressure a bit on his brain, but we need to keep him asleep for the time being, give that some time to heal."

"Is he going to be all right?" Katie asked shakily.

"I think that he will pull through, yes. But, whenever we have bleeding we have to be cautious. His condition is still critical. And, there are other injuries that will need to be addressed further."

Katie tilted her head in questioning. "His leg. The break—there are several fractures in his right leg. I have our best orthopedic surgeons looking at it. Given his career, well…There may be someone else that he will want to consult or perhaps would want you to consult on his behalf."

"Are you saying this could end his career?" Katie asked directly.

"I can't say that. It's not my area of expertise. I've seen worse. But, I won't lie to you. He will require major reconstructive surgery on that leg followed by a lengthy rehabilitation. There won't be any pitching in the next six months to a year, if not longer."

Katie let out a heavy sigh and wiped her face with her hands as Julia placed a comforting arm around her shoulder. "Can I see him?"

"Of course. He won't be conscious for hours. As I said, we need him to sleep for a while. I would suggest you consider some rest yourself. Do you have someplace…"

"I had hoped to head to my parents' in Danvers after today's events, but I have my hotel room for one more night. I can stay there."

"I see," he said. "Is there anyone local that…"

"No, my best friend left this morning," Katie offered him an appreciative smile.

"Well, Carrie and I may not have the queen's palace, but you are more than welcome to stay with us, Katie. I will understand if you prefer the hotel, though. We do have three children who tend to make their presence known," Julia offered. Michael chuckled at his ex-wife.

"You have been far too generous already, Julia. I couldn't ask you…"

"You didn't ask. I offered. And anyway, Carrie would have my head if I didn't try and nudge you just a bit," Julia winked.

Michael reached his feet and took hold of Katie's hand lightly. "Listen, I learned a long time ago not to bother arguing with Julia."

Julia laughed. "Don't listen to him, Katie. He's about the only person who will argue with me just for the fun of it," she teased.

Katie managed an earnest chuckle. "Are you sure?"

"Positive. Why don't you let the good doctor here take you to see your husband? I'll give Carrie a call. Take as long as you need, okay?"

"All my things and the car are at the......"

"Katie," Julia said cautiously but with a hint of assertiveness. "Stop. Minor details, okay? Stuff you do not need to be concerned with right now."

"When she's right, she's right," Michael smiled at Katie.

"You aren't used to not getting your way, are you?" Katie asked Julia.

Julia smiled, relieved to hear at least a moniker of the playful Katie from hours before. "No," she answered. Katie couldn't help but giggle as she stepped out of the office. "Michael," Julia grabbed his arm and he turned. "I can see it in your eyes."

Michael's expression darkened slightly as he leaned into Julia. "I wish it was better news, all the way around."

"What aren't you telling her?"

He shook his head. "I can't, Jules."

Julia groaned. She knew Michael like the back of her hand. Whether it was something about Bill Brennan's condition or something else, she couldn't be sure. More now than ever, she was glad to know that Katie would not be alone. Something was troubling her ex-husband. There was no mistaking that. "All right," she whispered back grudgingly. "I'll meet you back here," she told Katie and received a grateful nod.

Julia watched as Michael led Katie through the hallway. The morning show host carried herself with a quiet confidence that Julia admired. She smiled as Katie acknowledged the people she passed who clearly recognized her. "Grace," Julia muttered as she turned away. That was the word she had been searching for to describe Katie Brennan. She had grace.

❧ ❧ ❧

Afternoon quickly rolled into late evening by the time Julia was able to coax Katie from the hospital. She suspected that Katie was dreading leaving the safety of the hospital walls. The news was buzzing more about Bill Brennan's companion than his condition. Katie had already been forced to field inquiries from her husband's agent, the team owner, general manager, and her own network about his condition. She had been asked to explain what she knew about the circumstances leading up to the accident, and a host of other things. She'd never finished her coffee from hours earlier, and Julia could quite plainly see the exhaustion and frustration that dulled Katie's blue eyes. They looked almost gray now. Katie was about to dial another number when Julia reached out and snatched the phone from her hands.

"What?"

"Enough," Julia said with a shake of her head.

Katie threw her head back and covered her face with her hands. "So many people to call."

"They can wait," Julia said. "What are you going to tell them that you haven't already?" she asked. Katie looked across to Julia in stunned disbelief. "What? Let's go. You can't do any more here, Katie. You heard Michael. You heard the nurses. You need some rest, and you need some food. You aren't going to be any good to anyone when we have to admit you too."

Katie quirked an eyebrow and smiled. "You really are bossy, Riley." Julia shrugged. "I don't feel like facing it right now," Katie admitted.

Julia understood. The press was waiting for her exit. Julia had seen the gathering of what she deemed vultures outside when she had stepped out for some air. She could comprehend that people were interested, but she struggled with the boundaries she felt were too often crossed. Katie and Bill Brennan's marriage was no one's business. This was a trying time for her new friend. Why couldn't people understand that? When Julia reentered the building, she had immediately sought out her ex-husband.

"What if I told you that you don't have to?" Julia offered.

"What are you talking about? You have some secret exit for me to use?"

"Something like that, yes," Julia said with a smirk. Katie regarded her friend curiously as Julia retrieved a set of keys from her coat pocket. "Let's just say that being a Riley has its advantages here," she winked. "We'll be taking Michael's car."

"You know, you are sneaky," Katie said. "But, I appreciate it."

"So, come on, Ms. Brennan. Trust me, if anything changes, Michael will make sure you know immediately."

"How many appearances do I owe you?" Katie joked.

"You don't owe me a thing," Julia said seriously. "But, next time let's try to keep hospitals off the tour, okay?"

"Deal," Katie agreed.

Katie trailed behind Julia slightly, admiring her. She had been pondering how she would have coped without Julia there all afternoon. It wasn't often that Katie spent time with another person who seemed to understand when to speak and when there was no need to fill up the silence in a room. Julia seemed to have a unique capacity in that regard. It had made one of the most painful and confusing days of Katie's life tolerable. Julia had taken control more than once during the afternoon. It was as if she could read Katie's thoughts at times. Katie snickered as Julia unlocked the car.

"What?" Julia asked, seeing the first genuine smile she'd seen in hours play across Katie's lips.

"Oh, nothing," Katie said.

"Mm-hm."

"Just thinking I would pity anyone who ever ran against you, if, of course, you ever sought office. Which, of course, you would never do," Katie winked.

Julia climbed into the driver's seat and turned to Katie, poking at her cheek with her tongue in consideration. "You think I would be any good?" she asked.

Katie could not have suppressed an honest laugh if she had tried. "I think you would be a unique addition," she said.

"Unique, huh? Well, that's one I haven't heard before. I may have to quote you on that."

"Yeah…. When you run—feel free."

"Would you vote for me?" Julia asked, enjoying the bit of levity this banter brought to a taxing day.

"In a heartbeat," Katie answered sincerely.

Julia chuckled as she pulled out of the parking garage. Katie's gaze had drifted out the car window. Katie remained contemplative, but it seemed just a few moments with a change of scenery and a change of subject had returned a bit of color to her cheeks. Julia was about to assure her that things would be all right when she noticed that Katie had closed her eyes. She smiled softly, choosing to remain silent. A moment's peace in this day was precious, and Julia had no intention of interrupting it for her friend. "It will all be all right," she silently assured the woman next to her. "Somehow."

Chapter Four

Katie sat on a large leather chair in the corner of Julia and Carrie's living room sipping what Julia had assured her was a "sure
fire concoction to cure stress and put you to sleep." She let her
gaze drift aimlessly into the flames that flickered in the fireplace a
few feet away and wrapped her hands tightly around the warm mug
in her hands. The evening had been filled with phone calls and inquiries, mirroring the long afternoon she desperately wanted to put
behind her. With a heavy sigh, Katie let her eyes fall closed and
soaked in the warmth that surrounded her.

"Penny for your thoughts," Julia called softly. She tossed off
her shoes and promptly stretched her frame along the sofa that sat
opposite Katie.

"I think this might be the first five minutes today I haven't
thought," Katie replied. "What's in this?'

"Oh, no. I can't give away that secret. It's the secret to my
success."

Katie's eyebrow arched suspiciously. "Should I be afraid?"
she asked. Julia shrugged noncommittally. "Your reassurance is appreciated," Katie said before sighing and returning her gaze to the
fire. "I'm sorry if I've caused upheaval for you," she said tacitly.

They had arrived at Julia's to find a note from Carrie that said she had taken the kids to her parents' for the night. Julia watched closely as Katie traced the rim of her mug thoughtfully.

"Katie," Julia called across the room. When Katie managed to look up, Julia immediately noted the tears in her eyes. "Didn't you see the name on the mailbox when we drove in?" Julia asked lightly. Katie's confusion was evident. "Upheaval. That's our name. It was too long for the kids to spell, so I stuck with Riley. Easier."

Katie managed a slight chuckle at Julia's attempt to lift her spirits. "Do you frequently take in wayward souls?"

"Normally just strays. You know—cats, dogs, birds, reptiles. You're the first of the human variety," Julia winked. Katie nodded in amusement. "I don't want you to feel that way," Julia said sincerely.

Katie released an audible sigh and shook her head. "I'm not sure how I am supposed to feel," she confessed.

"I don't think you are supposed to feel any certain way," Julia answered. "There's no rule book to emotions, Katie. You feel what you feel. You can't control that. You can only control what you do about it."

"That's just it. What can I do? It's not as if I am surprised."

"I'm sorry, Katie."

Katie flashed a smile at Julia. "Oh, don't be. I should have known. I guess maybe I just chose to live in my own fairytale. And now.... Well, I don't know. Apparently, everyone else was living in the real world but me."

Julia frowned at the statement. The news was blaring the long-held rumors of Bill Brennan's extramarital activities. She couldn't imagine how Katie must be feeling. She'd found herself pondering how she would react if she were in the same situation.

Julia imagined if it were her in Katie's position, she would feel conflicted—worried about her partner's health, fearing loss, and at the
same time fighting through humiliation, anger, and sadness. It was
more than anyone should have to deal with. Julia watched as Katie
began to mindlessly trace the rim of her mug again. With another
weary sigh, tired blue eyes fell slowly shut. Julia found that watching
her new friend, her emotions were indeed conflicted. She desperately
wanted to comfort and reassure Katie, and she also wanted to pum-
mel both Bill Brennan and the press. The corners of Katie's eyes
were no longer creased by playful laughter but were now etched in
disquieting emotion. She wasn't sure how she knew, but something
told Julia that Katie needed to breakdown. Just as the thought passed
through her mind, Julia noted the tear that was rolling down Katie's
cheek.

"You know, when we met, I thought he was Lancelot. I
mean it—a knight in shining armor. He was shiny," Katie mused
and then let out a caustic chuckle. "Anything that shiny is too good
to be true." Her thoughts trailed off into silence.

"How did you meet?" Julia asked gently. She was curious,
and it seemed that Katie needed to talk.

"John. John used to handle contracts for several agents.
That's how he met Bill." Katie laughed earnestly. "You know, come
to think of it, he probably just wanted Bill in his court." Julia was
momentarily puzzled until Katie continued. "You know; he takes his
role as Her Majesty seriously. He probably saw Lancelot too." Julia
snickered as Katie continued. "I don't know. We were young. It
seemed like a dream for a long time."

"Youthful eyes," Julia inserted.

"Um. Naïve eyes," Katie replied. "We've always been so different," she said. Julia offered Katie a sympathetic smile. "What
about you?" Katie turned the conversation. She was equally curious

about Julia's life. She had been given the opportunity to observe Julia with both Carrie and with Michael. She wondered how everything had come to pass in the life of her charismatic host.

"You mean, how did I go from being married to a dashing, big city surgeon to becoming a suburban lesbian?"

"Well?"

Julia winked. "You really want to hear this story?" she asked. Katie nodded. "All right. Be warned, it isn't the stuff cable movies are made of."

"Not going to be the template for the next installment of *If These Walls Could Talk*, huh?" Katie joked.

"Nope. No *L Word* either—trust me. My lesbian life is more like a slightly dysfunctional version of *Who's the Boss*," Julia assured her. "But, okay. I'll give you the *Reader's Digest* version. "Michael and I met in college. I was barely nineteen. He had just turned twenty-one."

"Ooo…Older men," Katie teased.

"Older, extremely good looking men," Julia corrected her. "With a future in medicine. My mother didn't raise a fool."

"I'm sure she is very proud," Katie said with a smile.

Julia nodded. "I think she was. I hope so."

Realizing the implication, Katie softened their banter. "I'm sorry, Julia."

"No. Don't be. I had terrific parents. They got to see me marry a doctor and then get my proverbial toaster," she laughed. "And, they got to see all of their grandchildren be born. I miss them, but I wouldn't have traded them for anything. I was lucky," she said.

"So, they were supportive?" Katie asked.

Julia laughed heartily. "Eventually. They were none too thrilled when Michael and I separated. I think my mother came close to a stroke when I told her about Carrie, but we survived," she explained. "To be honest, Michael had a lot to do with their acceptance." Julia could see the intrigue in Katie's eyes.

"You two seem to be close," Katie observed.

"He's my best friend," Julia said with a smile. "We are better that way—as friends."

"You're lucky."

"I know," Julia admitted. "I am. Michael and I were always the best of friends. We've always been able to tell each other everything. That never changed, not even when we separated." Katie nodded. "You're wondering why," Julia said as she released a sigh. "I mean, why we divorced. We grew. Jake was unexpected. Kids were not in our immediate plan. Michael, he loves the fast pace of life."

"And you don't?" Katie asked with a grin.

Julia laughed. "No, I do, but I know when to say when. I like balance. Michael likes speed. I think it's part of the reason he is so terrific at what he does. The thing is, he never slows down. He could never just be still. When Jake came, I needed that more. I needed more balance. We were always on fast forward. Know what I mean?"

"I think so," Katie answered.

"We both could feel it. It was as if the earth shifted beneath us, slipping our foundation. He kept moving forward at breakneck speed, and I slowed down. The gap just grew. Rather than have it become a gaping hole, we decided to just obey that flow. It hurt, but it was best for all of us, Jake too," Julia said assuredly. She saw Katie's eyes twinkling slightly, but with an underlying sadness. "And then, I met Carrie," Julia smiled.

"How did he take that?" Katie inquired.

"Michael?" Julia asked. "Oh, he figured it out before I did," she said with a roll of her eyes.

"What do you mean?"

"That I was falling for her," Julia explained. "Sometimes I think he knows me better than I know myself."

"Sounds familiar," Katie responded.

"John, I take it?"

"Yeah. He usually knows what I think before I think it," Katie laughed.

"Have you called him yet?" Julia asked. Katie shook her head. "Ahhh…Avoiding the inevitable," she surmised. "I understand."

"I'm sure you do. Now, come on, how did you meet Carrie?"

"You gunning for the rights to *Tales of a Suburban Lesbian*?" Julia winked.

"Hey, I never turn down the chance to cover an interesting story," Katie quipped.

"We'll see if it qualifies."

"Julia, I don't think any story with you at its center could be less than interesting," Katie said playfully.

"More like nothing less than clumsy," Julia chuckled to a questioning glance from her friend. "Yeah. That life alert button was designed with me in mind. How did I meet Carrie? I fell into her arms—literally."

"You fell into…"

"Yep. I was teaching at the time. I was in the library, finishing up a meeting with a student. Carrie was exhibiting her photography. True to my incredible form I was not paying attention and tripped over a backpack. Carrie caught me on my graceful descent toward the floor." Julia chuckled at the memory.

"Now, there is a story of being swept off your feet that you don't hear every day," Katie offered.

"Exactly! See, I told you, more klutz than interesting."

"Maybe you are an interesting klutz."

Julia laughed. "I'll take it."

"So, Carrie caught you."

"In more ways than one," Julia said. Katie nodded with a smile. "There was something about her," Julia said. Her voice softened, and she smiled. "I think it was the kindness in her eyes."

Katie watched Julia as she continued. Her affectionate smile was genuine, but Katie was certain that she detected a hint of melancholy in Julia's eyes. "You've been together ever since?" Katie asked.

Julia looked up at her friend. "Yeah. It started as a friendship. Coffee moved to dinners. Dinners eventually became day long outings. Finally, we made it to breakfast," Julia explained with a wink.

"She's a sweetheart," Katie complimented.

"That she is," Julia agreed. "I don't think Care has a mean bone in her body. I think I've only ever heard her raise her voice twice in fourteen years. Both times at me," Julia laughed. "And, she is a great mom to all the kids." Katie nodded. Julia saw her attention retreat back toward the fireplace.

"When I met Bill, it was like a whirlwind. Talk about fast track. Everything was exciting. It was like living in a movie," Katie reminisced.

Julia waited patiently for the story to continue. Katie kept her sights focused on the flames as she continued her tale. Julia pondered the idea that the fire created an ideal, if not ironic setting as she listened. There was an intensity in Katie's life that matched the heat emanating from the fireplace. Katie was, in some ways, watching the life she knew as it was claimed by an uncontrollable blaze. Julia sat quietly, attentive to both the words that escaped Katie's lips and the expressions that passed over her features. Occasionally, Katie's lips would curl into a thoughtful smile. The faint smiles lasted only moments before they gradually receded, always accompanied by a barely detectable sigh.

"He thrives on attention," Katie said. "It's not really that surprising that he would be having affairs," she said with a hint of resignation to the truth. "Attention. Anywhere he can get it. I think that's why he pushed for me to take this job."

"Didn't you want to?"

Katie shook her head. "Not really. It's not like I had tons of choices. Investigative journalism has given way to entertainment news," she said as a matter of fact. "And, digging trenches around the world is not the ideal lifestyle for a mom," Katie said.

Julia understood that concept completely. That had been one of the primary reasons she continually refused to consider running for any public office. Even locally, it would mean exposing her family to the press more. It was not something she wanted for her children. She could hear the passion in Katie's voice. Investigative journalism in the international community came at an even higher price—the risk of personal safety.

"But, that is what you would have wanted to do? I mean, if not for your children?" Julia asked.

Katie nodded. "I know…Bill thought it was insane. And, frankly so did most of the network people, even before Stephanie and Ian. An attractive woman trolling through war zones or digging in archives? That made no sense to any of them."

"Mm. I can imagine," Julia said.

"This job seemed to fit our needs," Katie shrugged. Julia wasn't buying the statement, not for a second. She suspected the job fit Bill Brennan's desires far more than it fulfilled Katie's needs. "It's just, even if it is the softest form of news, it's still news. I don't know how to do that now."

"What do you mean?" Julia asked.

"Kind of hard to be a reliable source for news when you are the news," Katie said flatly.

Julia had not considered that inevitability. Katie set down her empty mug on the side table and put her face in her hands.

"Katie," Julia almost whispered the name.

"I don't know. Everything happens for a reason, right? Isn't that what they say?"

"I've always wondered who *they* are," Julia said. "Who is this *they* we keep hearing about?" she tried a bit of levity. Katie's weak grin tugged at her heart much harder than she could have ever imagined. "But, yes. I believe that," Julia offered honestly. "Maybe not that there is a cosmic conspiracy in our lives, but even the most difficult things lead us where we need to go. It just isn't always where we thought we were headed."

Katie looked up and met Julia's gaze. She felt her heart stop for just a second. Sincerity was evident in Julia's eyes, eyes that on the surface often reflected more humor than substance. Julia Riley was clearly adept at deflecting unwanted conversation and uncalled for intrusions. Katie had witnessed the executive director's skill at utilizing humor to gain control in uncomfortable situations repeatedly during their two days together. Katie considered the depth in the blue eyes that held hers and wondered how many people took the time to peel back the layers of Julia Riley's defenses. There was an underlying vulnerability in the woman across from her. If she hadn't felt the fluttering in her chest, she would have chalked her inquiries up to her journalistic curiosity. She almost didn't trust her voice to have enough power to be heard when she finally managed to speak.

"I don't know how I would have made it through today without you," Katie said as a tear cascaded down her cheek.

Seldom was Julia rendered speechless. She could not seem to formulate a response. Words rumbled through her brain, but they were quickly drowned by an emotional undertow. She thought she was offering a smile in return, but she wasn't even certain that her body could obey her commands against the forceful wave that coursed through her. A familiar panic surfaced, but it was instantly extinguished by something far more powerful. In an instant, Katie had surrounded her. Julia was helpless to struggle against the waves that rose and encompassed her. Her only cognitive thought left Julia wondering if Katie was sharing her surreal experience, or if she had simply gone mad.

Katie tried to shift her focus back to the fire, but Julia's eyes held her in place. She had become pinned by an unseeing, all know-ing force. The day, her questions, her fears all evaporated into nothingness. The heat from the fire that raged beside her paled in comparison to the energy that radiated from the woman seated across the room. Katie felt enveloped by Julia's presence, like a baby in its mother's arms. It was as if Julia held her closer than anyone ever had without needing to touch her. Rational thought was ren-dered powerless. Speech was stifled into silence. It should have been unsettling, but Katie found no inclination to resist the embrace. Should it only last this one moment, she was certain it would be one of the few she would cherish forever. If she could prolong it, even for a fraction of a second, she was positive there was little she would not trade to do so.

Julia battled within, torn between a desire to remain in the solace of what had become a distant caress and a desperate need to regain control. "You need some rest," she heard herself say to Katie. Katie nodded and stood, following her host down a small hallway toward the guest room. Julia opened the door. "If you need anything just help yourself," Julia said. "It's all pretty self-explanatory around here," Julia smiled and started to leave when Katie pulled her back.

"Julia," Katie whispered.

Julia stopped and held her breath in the silence that lingered between them. Katie looked into Julia's eyes as her tears finally escaped freely. Julia reached out and wiped the cheek before her. She didn't have any words. Words would have been empty. Instead, she pulled Katie to her, ending the distant embrace they had shared with a more tangible one.

"It'll work out, Katie."

Katie's words were jumbled by her tears. "I wish I could believe that."

"It always does," Julia said as she placed Katie squarely in front of her. "Now, come on," she said as she pulled Katie into the room. "Go take a long bath and climb in bed…. And, rest." Julia winked at Katie and headed back for the door.

"Julia?"

"Yeah?"

"I meant what I said," Katie told her. Julia tipped her head in confusion. "I wouldn't have gotten through today without you."

Julia nodded. "Yes, you would have, but I'm glad I could be there." She smiled at Katie and closed the door.

"Maybe," Katie whispered as the door softly closed. "I wouldn't have wanted to try."

Chapter Five

JANUARY 2015

"Katie, maybe you should take some more time off," George suggested.

"To do what exactly?" Katie snapped back.

"Come on, two weeks is not a long time. You and I both know that you are exhausted."

"Is that your less than politically correct way of telling me I look like shit? Because, *that* I already know."

George groaned and shook his head. He had worked with Katie since she came on board at the network. His job was envied by many. Katie Brennan was not only considered one of the most intelligent people in the business, but she was also widely regarded as among the most affable and easy to work with. Tension rose off the attractive redhead in waves. Her posture was stiff, and her temper was on a short fuse that George had never experienced.

"Katie, seriously."

Katie dropped into her chair with a sigh. "I'm sorry, George. I am. I am tired. I can't keep vigil next to him while he recovers. I have my own recovery to think about. I have to worry about Stephanie and Ian."

"Exactly my point. Take some time and spend it with the kids, Katie."

"You sound like John."

"Well, for once we agree," George replied.

Katie huffed and shook her head. "I need the distraction. I may have decisions I need to make soon. This is what I need to do right now."

"What kind of decisions?" he asked cautiously.

Katie narrowed her gaze and changed the subject. "Anything I should know before I hit the airwaves again tomorrow?" she asked.

George threw his hands up in defeat. "No," he told her as he headed for the door.

"George," Katie called to him. "I appreciate the concern. Honestly," she said. She watched as he nodded and headed out the door. "Deep breaths, Katherine," she mumbled. "One day at a time."

≈ ≈ ≈

Julia sat behind her desk shuffling papers from one side to the other. No matter what she tried, she could not seem to concentrate on anything. She collapsed her head onto her desk and sighed forcefully. The last few weeks had left Julia exhausted physically and emotionally. The holidays tested Julia's patience at times. It had not always been that way. For most of her life, Julia had anticipated the Christmas season with excitement. She had reveled in the exuberance and anticipation of her children. She had loved the coming together of family. It was one of the reasons she had pressed Carrie into buying their home. It would easily accommodate their extended family. The last few years had seen Julia's excitement shift to a sense of weariness. The absence of her parents made the holidays seem incomplete. She hated to admit the truth, even to herself. She scolded herself repeatedly for what she regarded as selfishness.

Every year the Riley home was filled to capacity for several days. It had seemed easier that way. It would serve as the one place to be everyone's destination, whenever it was most convenient for them to arrive. Julia called it the *Riley Door Policy*—come when you can, bring what you will, stay as long as you need. That meant that from Christmas Eve until New Year's Eve there was a constant flow of guests in and out of her home. Christmas Day alone entailed entertaining Carrie's parents and her brother, his wife, and their two children. Michael always joined them unless he was on call. Michael's parents were always invited, as was his sister and whoever her latest beau was. There were aunts and uncles, cousins, and friends who stopped by. Julia would never put an end to it. All three of her children thrived in the atmosphere, and Carrie loved to be surrounded by family. Julia found that in the last few years, she often felt completely alone in the mass of people. It wasn't that she didn't love them. She did. She just felt like a foreigner in some distant land. Her children were focused on the guests they seldom saw. Julia's parents were gone. Carrie was preoccupied with her family. Julia felt like a shadow cast upon the wall, present but nearly invisible. She could hear the constant conversation around her, but it sounded like a different language somehow, one she could understand but not speak. This year there had been another matter pressing in on Julia's thoughts—Katie Brennan.

Katie had stayed in the area through the holidays. Julia and Carrie's had become a home away from home. It served as a refuge from the pressure of hospital visits for Katie and her two children. It was closer to the hospital than Katie's parents' home. Katie's daughter Stephanie was close to Meghan's age, and her son, Ian was a year older than Jordan. That was the argument Julia mounted when Katie had voiced her concern that she and her children might be overstaying their welcome.

"What are you talking about?" Julia asked.

"Julia," Katie sighed. "You have got to be tired, both you and Carrie. How many people have been in and out of here over the last week? This place is like Grand Central Station. We don't..."

"It's the Riley Door Policy," Julia said.

"Excuse me?" Katie asked.

"Riley Door Policy. Look, you think you are imposing or something..."

"You and Carrie are extremely generous...."

"No," Julia said.

"Yes," Katie disagreed.

"No. You think this is a sign of some kind of benevolence. You should know me better than that already," Julia winked at her friend. "Your children provide a diversion for my children. And, the bonus? I have you to deflect any potential conversation with my sister-in-law. Cindy cannot corner me with you here. See? No Santa here. I am the Miser on Main."

"Um-hum. You don't live on Main," Katie pointed out.

"Sounded good."

Katie laughed. "I would hate for you to have to endure Cindy. She is, after all, clearly evil."

"Yes! See...An imp. Shhh...Now, stop arguing and help me out!" Julia said.

The argument had accomplished its mission. Katie had acquiesced. As the days wore on, Julia began to realize that she was dreading her new friend's departure. She had enjoyed having someone to talk to and to joke with. For the first time in a few years, Julia had enjoyed part of the holidays. She found herself admitting that indeed, her desire to have Katie spend time at the house was selfish.

Julia pushed some papers aside on her desk. She couldn't seem to rid herself of the nagging sensation something was amiss with Katie. Katie had headed back to New York two days earlier, and Julia found that she missed their conversations and their banter. It had become part of daily life. When Katie had called on Monday to say she was going back to work, Julia had been silent.

"I need the diversion," Katie explained. Julia remained silent. "Do you think it's a bad idea?"

Julia sighed inwardly. She thought it was premature. "What I think isn't important."

"It is to me," Katie said assuredly.

"Are you sure? I mean, Katie, you just got home. You just got Bill transferred to the rehab. Why not take at least a few days and catch your breath?" Julia suggested.

Julia felt protective of Katie after the week they had shared with all its ups and downs. Evenings at the Riley homestead during the holiday week saw the adults gathered around the fire for conversation and cocktails. Nearly every evening, Julia and Katie had been the last to fall, spending hours talking about everything and nothing as if they had been friends forever. Julia had confessed everything from the horrors of her first time in the back seat of a car with Michael to her secret passion for disco music. Katie had shared tales of her childhood misadventures with John Fortin. She had disclosed the fact that her best friend had what she regarded as an irrational fear since childhood—a fear of Jawas.

"Jawas?" Julia questioned.

"Yeah, Jawas. You know those spooky little hooded creatures in Star Wars," Katie explained.

"You mean Ewoks," Julia said.

"No, I mean Jawas. Ewoks are furry. Jawas are hooded. How old are you, Riley? What the hell? Were you sleeping through the seventies?" Katie scolded her friend.

"No, I wasn't sleeping. I was dancing." Katie tried unsuccessfully to hide her smirk. "What?" Julia asked indignantly. "Alone in my room or my parent's basement. That's the only way I dance. Ask Michael. I didn't even dance at my wedding. Either of them."

"So, you were a private dancer in your preteens, and now you are a dance floor recluse? What caused that? Traumatic Disco Injury?" Katie laughed.

"Yes, as a matter of fact."

"Oh, please," Katie urged Julia to continue.

"Okay, Miss Sci-Fi geek nineteen seventy-seven, since you are so interested. My next door neighbor, Billy Flannigan walked in on me in my parents' basement. I happened to be acting out 'You're The One That I Want' to the 8-track. Okay?"

"Oh, no," Katie giggled.

"Oh, yes. I had a huge crush on him. My mother told him that he should just come down. He started laughing and doing some kind of frightening hip wiggle to mock me. Then he called me Jiggles Julia," Julia pouted.

Katie tried to act concerned. "What did you do?" she asked.

"Punched him in the face," Julia said. "Gave him one hell of a shiner too."

"You didn't!"

"Yes, I did. And, I don't regret it one bit. That jerk," Julia groaned.

"Did you get in trouble?" Katie asked.

"Yeah. Grounded for a week. Worse? Jiggles became my nickname for two years," Julia explained.

"That is awful," Katie comforted Julia for a moment before the laughter she had been fighting to contain erupted.

"It's not funny. It was mean," Julia declared.

"I know," Katie continued to laugh.

"Katie!"

"What?"

"You were mean, weren't you? You were a mean little girl," Julia said with an accusatory finger point.

"I was not mean!" Katie defended herself. *"Only to John,"* she whispered.

"Oh, no. What did you do?" Julia asked.

"Nothing that terrible."

"Katherine Brennan...."

"Oh, all right! It is an irrational fear; you know?" Katie said. Julia implored her with a glance. *"Jawas! It's irrational,"* Katie repeated. *"Anyway, we were camping in the back yard one night. I begged my father for one of those dress up kits, you know...And I sort of...Well, I waited for John to pass out and then I,"* her voice dropped in shame.

"What did you do?" Julia asked again.

"I dressed up as one of those little things and popped in the tent with a flashlight."

"You did not do that to him!" Julia said as she began to laugh. *"That's horrible! He's probably scarred for life!"*

"No, he's not. He just refuses to ever wear anything with a hood. And, he doesn't like them much on anyone else either," Katie confessed.

"Did he punch you?" Julia wondered.

"No. He just peed in his sleeping bag."

Julia pulled her head up from the desk and started to chuckle at the memory. Katie had planned on heading into her office at the studio for a few hours that afternoon, and Julia wondered how her day was progressing.

ॐ ॐ ॐ

Katie was sitting at her desk scrolling through emails when a familiar ping notified her of new mail. She rolled her eyes in anticipation of another dull network memorandum. Paying more attention to the coffee in her hand than the images on her screen, she startled and sprang out of her seat when familiar music began to play.

"What the hell?"

Katie moved closer to the screen for inspection of the email and began shaking her head. She picked up her cell phone without diverting her attention from the image in front of her.

"Julia Riley," the voice answered.

"May the force be with you," Katie greeted Julia.

"Oh, hello, Princess. You must have gotten the message I implanted in that droid," Julia cracked back.

Katie laughed. "Dancing Jawas? Dare I ask where you found that one?" Katie inquired.

"Hey, you're not the only one with experience in research, you know," Julia answered. "I thought maybe you could use a little distraction on your first day back."

Katie sat back in her chair and smiled. "You have no idea how timely that was," she said.

"Tough day?" Julia asked.

"Not really," Katie said with a sigh. "I just can't seem to concentrate on anything—at all."

"I know the feeling," Julia whispered to herself.

"What? Did you say something?" Katie asked.

"Nothing, just waving someone out of my office. Seriously, how are you making out?"

"Aside from everyone trying to convince me I shouldn't be here, you mean?" Katie said with a frustrated groan.

"Ah. I see. They're just concerned about you."

"Mm. Some. The others are worried about ratings. How will the public react to the reappearance of one embarrassed morning show host? That's what they are concerned about," Katie said.

Julia considered how to reply. She had made it a point to try and avoid any news segments or articles about Katie and Bill Brennan. Listening to people talk about her friend's marriage, Katie's personal life in any way, unsettled Julia. Katie put up a believable façade of control. She smiled at the cameras and politely declined any comments, but Julia was certain the constant attention was wearing on her friend.

"It will all pass. Some senator is bound to get caught in a public restroom or something."

Katie laughed. "You are classy, Julia," she joked.

"Hey, I don't make these things happen. I'm just stating the inevitable."

"Well, I hate to wish ill on anyone, but if you know any desperate senators feel free to encourage them," Katie replied.

"I'll check my Rolodex after lunch," Julia promised.

"You do not have a Rolodex, Riley. No one has a Rolodex anymore," Katie said.

"Not much of a researcher," Julia responded in kind.

"What?"

"You were in this office. I most certainly do have a Rolodex. I'm an old-fashioned girl."

Katie snickered. "That must be where you catalog all your 8-track tapes."

"Easy does it, Nancy Drew," Julia cautioned.

"Thanks," Katie said softly.

"You're welcome."

Silence lingered on the line for a moment. "Listen, I have to go. George will be back any minute," Katie explained.

"Me too. I have a meeting in ten minutes. Listen, just try and take it easy, okay?"

"You worried about me, Riley?" Katie joked. Julia didn't respond, and Katie sighed. "Scouts honor," Katie promised.

"Mm-hm."

"What? You doubt me?" Katie asked. "I promise. I might have to look at that email a few more times, though."

"You do that," Julia said. "I'll talk to you."

"Yes, you will. Thanks, Julia."

Julia hung up the call and shook her head. She was pleased that her attempt at adding a bit of levity to Katie's day seemed to have been successful. She had noted the tension in Katie's voice. Julia could easily picture the worried creases at the corners of Katie's blue eyes. "I think it's going to take more than dancing Jawas," she mused.

"What?" Everett asked as he slid into the chair in front of Julia's desk.

"Don't you knock?" she asked pointedly.

"When the door is closed," he batted his eyelashes. "Now, why were you talking about those disgusting little creatures?" he asked.

Julia rolled her eyes. "Never mind, Everett. Don't tell me you are afraid of movie monsters."

"Me? No. I've dated a few, actually."

"Somehow, Everett, that does not surprise me at all," Julia said with a smile.

"So, who was your line blinking for? Anyone interesting?"

"We're late, Everett."

"Aw, come on Julia! Word is Fortin is lining up some more heavy hitters to help out."

Julia pulled Everett from his seat and spun him around. "This is not the red carpet fashion show. Now, let's go," she told him.

"You're no fun," he whined.

"Oh, I'm lots of fun."

"And, anyway," he said with the wave of his hand. "I would be fabulous on the red carpet. Hey! Your friends with Katie now, right? I'll bet she could…."

Julia prodded him forward. "Late, Everett. Late."

♥ ♥ ♥

Katie quietly made her way into her husband's room. She had engaged in a lengthy mental debate while in the car as to whether or not she had the patience to endure this visit. Stephanie and Ian had made it clear that they wanted to see their father. Ultimately, that won out over any of her reservations. It had been a trying week. There were moments that Katie could have sworn years had passed within just an hour. A consistent lack of sleep was adding to an unusually short fuse that ran directly to her patience or lack thereof. The network was urging her to accept an interview with someone—anyone. Katie simply was not comfortable with that scenario. Her agent had implored her to agree and made numerous suggestions as to which personalities would likely grant gentle interviews, "family centered," he called them. Katie groaned as she replayed their conversation. She did not require anyone's insight regarding her colleagues as to who may or may not be willing to spin a positive tale about her family situation. Katie had traveled in these circles long enough to have an understanding of the personalities that often competed with her. The reality was that anyone she sat down with would pose questions that she simply could not answer with any honesty. Pleading the fifth in a celebrity interview would neither be helpful nor would it be believable. She forced a small smile onto her lips as she took a seat next to her husband's bed, and listened to her children bombard him with questions. A long week was ending on a stressful note.

Time passed painfully, slowly, and stressfully. Katie listened to the conversation in the room as best she could and occasionally offered a half-hearted grin to one of her children's questions. She could scarcely do more at the moment against her struggle to keep both eyes open. She flinched at the sound of a slightly raised voice.

"Did you hear me? Katie?" Bill called to his wife.

"What? I missed that," she shook her head slightly.

"Obviously. Where have you been all night?" he asked. "I said that David spoke with Marty at the network. He said you were reluctant to grant any interviews."

"That's true," she replied.

"Well, he felt that my participation might ease your mind. I talked to Dr. Ratcliffe. He seems to think I am up to the task. Marty will set something up with June Neville next week. We can tape it here in one of the offices."

Katie felt her eyebrow begin to twitch. A smile tainted with evident sarcasm played over her lips. "Stephanie," she addressed her daughter.

"Yeah, Mom?"

"Why don't you take your brother down to the vending machines near the family lounge? Get a snack and watch some television. I need to talk to your father for a few minutes."

Stephanie shrugged and said goodbye to her father. She directed her younger brother to follow and accepted a few dollars from her mother before heading out the door as instructed.

"What's wrong?" Bill Brennan asked.

"Why on earth would you agree to an interview with anyone without discussing it with me first? And, why the hell is your agent speaking to Marty?" Katie asked heatedly.

"Well, you can't avoid it forever, Katie. Ignoring the press is making it worse for both of us. This injury might end my pitching days, but we still both have careers to think about," he answered.

"Oh, we have a hell of a lot more than careers to think about," Katie snapped.

"What the hell does that mean?" he asked.

"Careers? How about our marriage?" she shot at him.

"Katherine, you have to know that she meant nothing to me," he said.

Katie rolled her eyes and shook her head. "Well, that just makes it all better, doesn't it, Bill? What does that make you exactly? I should feel better that you are screwing people just because you can?"

"Jesus, Katie. I made a mistake."

"A mistake? As in one?" Katie's voice dripped with a deceptive sweetness.

"Katie…"

"You know, it's bad enough to get a call that your husband has been in an accident. It's stressful enough to sit and wait not knowing if he will survive or how he will recover. Do you have any idea how unbelievably upsetting it is to try and devise something to tell your children? To sit and contemplate what you will tell them if their father doesn't make it? On top of that, you have to wrestle with the discovery that everyone on the planet seems to know your husband is unfaithful except you. So, now you are a wife beset with worry and humiliation. You don't get to apologize. Not here. Not now."

"I know you are angry."

"Angry? I'm disgusted. I cannot believe that you spoke for me after making a complete ass of me in front of the entire world. You are worried about your career? My God, Bill!"

"What's done is done," he said softly.

"Are we talking about the interview now or the fact that you can't keep your dick in your pants?"

Bill Brennan looked up in astonishment. Katie seldom swore. She rarely lost her temper. He'd often heard people comment that Katherine Brennan would have made the perfect political spouse. This was a side of his wife he had never experienced. He shook his head in disbelief.

"You want to back out of the interview? Go ahead," he said.

"I think we both know that cannot happen now," Katie sighed. "Do not speak for me again, Bill. I mean it."

"Katie, we need to talk about this."

"No. We don't. I know everything I need to know. I really don't need any more details," she assured him.

"Are we going to be okay?" he asked sheepishly.

Katie exhaled forcefully and closed her eyes. This conversation confirmed all the reasons that she believed granting any interviews was a mistake. She was angry. He was in denial. They were faced with a great deal more recovery in the future than broken bones. The bones, those would heal eventually. The trust that had been broken, that was a diagnosis that remained undetermined for Katie.

"I don't know," Katie finally answered. "If by okay, you are asking will you and I make it through this—the answer is I don't know."

"I'm sorry, Katie."

Katie nodded. "I know you are," she said. "I'm just not certain if you are sorry for hurting me, or sorry for getting caught," she said honestly. She watched his face grow pale. "I think that's enough for tonight—for both of us. I'll bring the kids by tomorrow afternoon."

Bill watched as Katie made her way to the door. He considered calling her back, but her posture stopped that inclination. He let his head fall back onto the pillow with a soft thump. The pain in his legs made it difficult for him to concentrate on anything. As he watched Katie disappear, he wondered if the surgeons could suggest a remedy for the pain in both their hearts.

∾ ∾ ∾

It was almost midnight when Julia's phone rang. Just as it was most evenings, she was sitting by the fireplace, a glass of wine in one hand and a book in the other. Winding down was a skill that Julia had never mastered. Many nights, she fell asleep with a half-consumed glass of wine on the table beside her, and a book draped over her chest. Jake had come home an hour earlier from a friend's house. Michael was working. Carrie and the girls had retired hours earlier. She couldn't imagine who was calling so late. She looked at the number scrolling across the screen and felt a tug in her chest.

"Katie?" she answered in concern.

"It's late. Sorry," the response came.

Julia immediately detected two things: Katie had been crying, and Katie had been drinking. "What's wrong?" Julia asked.

"I just can't believe it," Katie answered.

"Katie, what happened?" Julia asked with growing concern. The two had not spoken since Katie's first day back to work. A brief email to say hello was the only contact Julia had received. "Katie?"

"It's Bill."

"Is he all right?"

"Oh, yeah. He's fine. Physically, anyway. I mean, he's as fine as anyone can be who has a jigsaw puzzle for a leg, but the real puzzle, Julia? The real puzzle is his brain," Katie said.

Julia tried not to snicker at the slight slur in Katie's voice. It was obvious that her friend was upset, but it seemed clear no one was in any imminent danger. "His brain?"

"Yep. I used to think it was in his head."

"Used to?" Julia asked.

"Well, yeah. Now I think it's in his pants," Katie offered.

Julia suppressed a chuckle. "I see. Care to explain this theory?"

"Well, it's the only one that makes sense! How dare he!"

"I agree. How dare he what?" Julia asked.

"Who does he think he is?" Katie's voice climbed an octave.

"I don't know," Julia said.

"Exactly," Katie said.

Julia finally snickered. "Katie, how much have you had to drink?"

"What makes you think I've been drinking?" Katie asked suspiciously. "I'm not drunk, Julia."

"Of course, not."

"I'm pissed off *and* drunk."

"Well, that explains it then," Julia said. "Are the kids there?"

"Asleep for hours," Katie said.

"So, I think I can gather why you are drunk."

"Yeah!" Katie exclaimed. "Because I am pissed off."

"Yeah. I got that memo. Why are you pissed off?" Julia asked.

"He agreed to an interview, Julia," Katie said, suddenly sounding eerily sober.

"What kind of interview?" Julia wondered.

"Oh, one with June Neville for the two of us. You know, to talk about the accident, our family, and all that great stuff," Katie said, sobering with each word.

Julia winced. "He agreed without telling you? Is that what you are telling me?"

"Bingo."

"Oh, Katie…"

"What the hell, Julia? How am I supposed to answer someone else's questions when I can't even answer my own?"

Julia wasn't certain how to respond. "I'm sorry."

"Lot of that going around tonight," Katie chuckled.

"What are you going to do?" Julia asked.

"Don't have much choice," Katie said. "I just…. God, everything is…"

"It will work out," Julia said softly.

"I'm sorry," Katie said sincerely.

"For what?"

"Bothering you at midnight," Katie said. "It's not like me."

"That's what friends are for," Julia replied.

Katie sat down on her sofa and nodded silently.

"Katie?" Julia called.

"I don't know what I'm going to do, Julia. It's all such a mess."

"Have you talked to John? What does he say?"

Katie huffed. "Talking to my parents or John—they'd have Bill in full traction and me in divorce court tomorrow."

Julia smiled. She would never tell Katie, but she felt that admission to that club would be easy to gain, and one she might enjoy being a part of. Something about Katie brought out a fierce protectiveness in Julia. The only thing that seemed to supersede her need to protect Katie was Julia's honest desire to see Katie happy. She hadn't given it any thought until Katie's call. As she listened to her friend, Julia began to realize that Katie Brennan affected her in unusual ways.

"They love you," Julia reminded her friend. "They just don't want to see you hurt."

"I know. I wish it were all that simple."

"Maybe you should stop trying so hard to figure it all out," Julia suggested. "Take it one day at a time for now. You'll know what to do when the time comes."

"I think you have more confidence in me than I do," Katie admitted.

"I wish I had something more to offer," Julia said.

"I'm just glad you were there…I mean…Then—now. I just needed to talk to someone. I knew you would let me—talk, I mean."

"Anytime at all," Julia replied. "Are you going to be okay?"

"Yeah. I will be. Everything happens for a reason, right?" Katie said with an uncomfortable giggle.

"You already know what I think about that," Julia said. "Hang in there, okay?"

"Yeah, I will."

"Call whenever you want," Julia said, realizing she was hoping that Katie would do just that, and often.

"You should go to bed," Katie observed.

"I'll make you a deal. You hang up and go do that, and I will do the same. Well, I will as soon as I am finished with the chapter I am reading in this book.

"I don't know. Can I trust you?" Katie asked.

"Scouts honor," Julia promised.

"You were a Girl Scout?" Katie asked skeptically.

"A Brownie. It counts."

"Sure it does," Katie laughed. "Deal."

"Good night, Katie."

"Night."

Chapter Six

I turned and the world stopped. I'm not certain if it stopped for a moment or if an eternity passed. Stillness. Complete stillness. Did I know I loved you then? I must have asked myself that question a million times. Did I know? When did I know? Did I know the moment I saw you? The moment our eyes met? Was it when I heard your laughter? Perhaps it was that moment we sat silently looking at one another from across the room. No words. Were there words I should have said? It seems that there are no words, and yet I find myself searching and digging, scraping the bottom of my soul to find some explanation, some way to dismiss or justify this insanity of unexpected emotion. Am I searching for a reason or a way to reach you? I don't know.

I ask myself why? My life is comfortable. Isn't it? My life is what so many crave. I hear that—the enviable family, a relationship to be coveted. In one moment of stillness, you set my world spinning. Ironic. One moment. And now, I am falling helplessly. When I was a little girl, I thought all the stars in the sky were the people who left us. I would imagine them looking down on me. When one of those lights streamed across the sky that meant they would return to the person they were meant to find—someone fell in love. I never imagined what that fall would feel like. Suddenly, stillness becomes

motion and light crashes through darkness, spiraling toward an unknown destination. Is that what falling in love is supposed to be?
How did I miss that? It's like falling through shooting stars.

"Mom!" Meghan yelled through the house.

Julia took another sip of a tepid cup of coffee and attempted
to squint away a mounting headache. January was a long month.
She'd often pondered how strange it was that the beginning of a new
year always seemed to drag on for eons. It was cold. She left the
house bathed in a hazy indigo each morning and seldom returned
home before the sun had disappeared from the sky. Her children, no
matter how much older they were, inevitably became restless in the
winter. Activities lessened during this time for everyone except Julia.
Her job seemed to amp up into high gear every January. New expec-
tations were being set by the board and that meant hours of planning
and projection for Julia. It was one of the few times each year that
she missed teaching.

"What is it Megs?" Julia called out through the house.

Meghan came bounding into Julia's office with a furious
glare. "I have to be at school by five-thirty," she said.

Julia winced at the pounding in her temples. "I thought Jake
was going to drop you off? I told him he could use the car."

"Jake isn't back yet, and neither is Ma. I can't be late, Mom.
It's tryouts. I don't want to lose my chance and if..."

"I got it, Meghan. I got it," Julia replied evenly.

Meghan had been encouraged to audition for the spring musical at school. The family had been treated to several weeks of
Meghan singing *Anything Goes* at the top of her lungs. For the first
few days, Julia had found it amusing and endearing. Over the course
of the last few nights, it had threatened to launch her headache into

a full-blown migraine. She had a mountain of work facing her, limited time, and it seemed there was a conspiracy afoot to keep her from making any progress.

"Where's Jordan?" Julia asked.

"In her room, I think," Meghan said.

"Fine. Get your sister and your jackets, and meet me in the kitchen in five minutes," Julia instructed. "When do you need to be picked up?

"Should be done by eight-thirty," Meghan called back as she scurried through the house.

"Fabulous," Julia muttered. "I hope your brother is home by then."

❧ ❧ ❧

John Fortin looked into the passenger seat of the car at his best friend. "Are you ready for this?"

"Define ready," Katie replied.

"Katie, if you don't feel comfortable giving this interview, don't," he told her.

"I wish it were that simple," she said sadly.

"It is that simple. You are the one making it difficult. Why do you do that to yourself?"

"Bill is right about one thing; we can't keep avoiding it. I just wish it wasn't live," she said. "No control at all."

John looked at Katie with pleading eyes. "Just don't do it, Kate. You don't owe anyone a thing."

Katie smiled as reassuringly as she could. "You never call me that unless you are worried," she observed.

"Call you what?" he asked.

"Kate."

"I am worried," he admitted.

"I'm just glad you are here," Katie said.

"You ready to head inside?" he asked.

"No," she chuckled. "I'm not sure whether I feel like I am about to walk down the aisle or be placed in front of the firing squad."

John opened her door and scrunched his face in displeasure. "Same difference, if you ask me," he told her.

Katie winked. "One of these days, Your Majesty, you will fall against your will."

"I'd sooner face the firing squad," he grinned evilly.

"Yes, well…. Sometimes it doesn't feel all that different," Katie said softly.

"Katie…"

Katie shrugged. "Or maybe, the firing squad is just the inevitability at the end of the aisle. After all, that hood keeps you from seeing the truth."

John looked at his friend sympathetically and then scowled. "Listen Princess Jaded, first of all, it's a veil, not a hood. Hoods are evil. No one should ever wear anything with a hood. We have covered this. Secondly, green and black are not your best colors. They are mine. Trust me on this one." He watched as Katie attempted to square her shoulders in confidence. "Don't let that asshole do this to you," he whispered.

"You mean the one I walked down the aisle for?" she asked. "See, there is a reason we wear veils."

"Yeah, well…Aisles are not one way, Princess. You can always walk back in the other direction."

"Yes, that's true, but it is a much lonelier walk," Katie replied.

John held the door open to the large building for his friend to walk through. "Rehab," he silently thought. "I'm not sure they have a regimen to heal this."

❧ ❧ ❧

Julia sat down in front of the television in the family room with a glass of wine. Tension riddled her muscles. Katie had called briefly earlier in the day, and Julia instantly detected the anxiety in her friend's voice. Julia had tried to be supportive, even attempted to lighten Katie's mood, but her attempts at humor were met with nothing more than a forced chuckle. She hoped that this interview would prove a step toward some closure for Katie. She feared it might turn out to be the catalyst to opening a larger wound than the one her friend was already struggling to heal from.

"Have you talked to her at all?" Carrie asked as she sat down beside her wife.

"Only for a few minutes this morning," Julia replied.

"You look worried," Carrie observed.

Julia shrugged in an attempt to appear less concerned than she felt. "She was stressed about it."

"Why did she agree to it?" Carrie asked.

"She didn't. Bill did."

"Couldn't she back out?" Carrie wondered.

"I'm sure she could have. I think part of her just wants it over with," Julia said as the show began.

"You are referring to the interview, aren't you?" Carrie asked.

Julia offered her wife a faint, unconvincing smile. She was referring to the interview, but the more she talked to Katie, the more it became evident to her that Katie was profoundly unhappy with her husband. Julia was certain that a good deal of the disgust and despair she heard in Katie's voice was the product of recent revelations. She had begun to suspect that there were deeper roots to Katie's discontent. She let out a small sigh as the piece they were waiting for was introduced.

"I'm sure it will be fine," Carrie said. "She's a professional. They all are." Julia nodded.

Tonight, I am joined by two of America's favorite personalities. Two people who have seen enormous success. Two people who have faced tragedy. This is their story.

Julia took a sip of her wine and shook her head slightly as the camera panned to Katie and Bill Brennan. Katie appeared calm and relaxed, but Julia could see the stiffness in her posture. She wondered how many people would pick up on the subtle cues that Katherine Brennan was not comfortable.

꙳ ꙳ ꙳

Katie fought the urge to wring her hands in her lap. She mentally reminded herself of all the lessons she had learned over the years in her profession: *sit on your jacket, square your shoulders, look ahead.* Repeating the obvious seemed the only chance she had of remaining calm and in control. She thought for a moment at the irony of this situation or at least, her handling of it. Here Katie sat. She was about to answer some of the most personal questions she had ever been posed, and she was reviewing a clinical checklist of mundane tasks in an effort to appear unemotional. That was not what the audience was hoping for, and she knew it. A few tears would please them. A forlorn expression or a loving gaze offered to the man beside her would evoke the intended response from viewers—sympathy. That would make for great television. "Not today," she muttered.

"What is it?" her husband leaned into her ear and asked.

"Nothing," she replied with a wry grin. "How are you doing?" she sought to redirect the conversation.

Katie remained angry about many things. Bill was still recovering. She could see a fine sheen of perspiration on his forehead that was produced by pain. It was not the pain that Katie was suffering. Bill's was physical. Regardless of any anger, she did not revel in his discomfort.

"I'm fine," he assured her. "Thanks for worrying, though."

Katie nodded. "I'm sorry you are in pain," she said sincerely.

"I'll survive," he said.

"We're going in two minutes," June said as she took her seat. "I promise to make this as painless as I can," she told the couple seated before her.

"We appreciate that," Bill offered with a smile worthy of a politician.

Katie just nodded mutely. She knew June Neville well and regarded the woman as a professional who possessed admirable ethics. June Neville was not a sensationalist by any means. Katie also understood this profession. It was June's job to uncover something, some nugget of emotional intrigue that would peak the audiences' interest and incite conversation or even debate. Human interest stories were meant to pull at heart strings. Katie was not in the mood for anymore tugging in that department.

"All right. Here we go," a voice called out. "In five, four, three, two, one...."

❧ ❧ ❧

Julia's eyes were fixed intently on the television screen. She heard the door open in the distance and Meghan enter the house singing. Carrie saw the twitch of her wife's temple and rose to her feet to quiet their children. She put her hand on Julia's shoulder.

"I'll go see how the audition went," Carrie said. Julia nodded her thanks.

Carrie stopped in the doorway to regard her wife. She'd noticed the growing affection between her wife and the attractive morning host that had quickly become a friend. In some ways, she welcomed it. As personable as Julia was, many of her relationships centered on her work. Carrie often wished that her wife would find some outlets and friendships that were decidedly personal in nature. Katie seemed to fill that void for Julia. There was a hint of something else in Julia's eyes that made Carrie sigh inwardly. She wondered if her wife had even noticed it—attraction. She watched the woman she loved for another moment, pondering that question before heading off to complete her task.

$$\approx \approx \approx$$

"It can't be easy for you, Katie," June Neville observed.

"You mean, the accident or the affair?" Katie returned.

"You learned about the affair after the accident as I understand it," June replied.

Katie nodded. "That's true, yes."

"That must have been d...."

"Devastating?" Katie broke in. She surprised herself with her terse reply. "Yes, it was."

Bill Brennan shifted nervously and then spoke. "It was completely unfair to Katie, and to my family—to everyone," he said.

June shifted her focus to him. Katie listened silently as her husband continued.

"But, Katie has been extraordinary. I don't know how she handles everything. This, our two children, me…And, I'm just so grateful that she is standing beside me through all of this." Katie felt her stomach twisting into knots as Bill's hand took hers. "I am lucky," he said. The camera panned to Katie, and Katie forced an awkward smile.

Julia watched in utter disbelief. As the camera zoomed in closer, Julia noted the deepening crease in the corner of Katie's eyes. She'd seen that before. Katie was smiling, but the sparkle that customarily lit her blue eyes had been replaced with a fiery flicker. She'd seen that too. Julia rested her face on her hand with a quiet groan.

"Sounds like they are trying to work things out," Carrie said.

Julia rubbed her eyes as she heard June close the interview.

"So, there is a future for Mr. and Mrs. Brennan?" June posed the final question. Julia looked back up at the screen. Katie barely concealed the grimace that Julia could see taking shape.

"Of course," Bill Brennan answered. He placed a kiss on Katie's cheek. Julia let out a nervous chuckle when she saw Katie flash a grin laced with far more teeth than sincerity.

"Well, it seems adversity does indeed strengthen us sometimes," June said. "Thank you both for taking the time and sharing your story. I know everyone wishes the best for your recovery, and for your family." Julia sat shaking her head.

"What?" Carrie asked.

"I have a feeling the immediate future is not going to be very rehabilitating for Mr. Brennan," Julia said.

"Why is that?" Carrie inquired. "They seemed…"

"Are you kidding?" Julia finally turned to her wife. "Did you see her face?"

"You know her better than I do," Carrie said quietly.

"Well, I know her enough to know she is less than thrilled with everything. And, she does not like to be spoken for. That much I do know," Julia said with an affectionate chuckle.

"I'm going to head to bed," Carrie said. "You coming?"

Julia kissed her wife on the cheek. "In a bit," she said. She watched Carrie as her wife nodded and began to leave. "Hey," Julia called. "How'd the budding star make out?"

Carrie smiled. "She seems to think she did well. Guess she'll know next week. You might be living with the next Patti Lupone, you know," Carrie laughed.

"Oh, God, Care," Julia rolled her eyes.

"Night, Jules. I love you," Carrie said more softly than usual.

"Love you too, Care," Julia called as she retrieved her glass of wine and the book that was lying on the table.

"Don't stay up all night, okay?" Carrie said.

Julia turned and winked. "You worry too much," she said. "I'll try not to wake you."

"You can," Carrie said. "It's Friday."

Julia snickered. "Noted."

෩ ෩ ෩

"John, would you excuse us?" Katie requested some privacy. John Fortin looked at his best friend sheepishly. "And, close the door, please," Katie instructed him as he left.

"Katie? What's wrong?" Bill Brennan asked his wife.

Katie kept her back to the man behind her, who was jostling himself gingerly in the bed. It had taken every ounce of self-restraint she possessed not to lose her temper violently at his proclamations during their interview. She could feel the prickly heat of her simmering fury scratching from within. Slowly, she turned to face her husband.

"What's wrong?" she repeated his question.

"Yeah, I thought that went well," he said. "You didn't?"

A caustic bout of laughter escaped from Katie. It took her a moment to calm her nerves enough to answer his question. "I guess it did—for you."

"What are you talking about?"

"Perhaps that head injury affected your short-term memory more than the doctors told me," she said.

"Katie…"

"I thought that we had an understanding," she continued. "At least, I thought that you understood me."

"What did I do?" he asked.

"Speaking for me? Speaking for us?"

"When did I do that?" he asked. "I just answered truthfully."

"And, what exactly do you think the truth is, Bill?" Katie asked. "You led her to believe that you and I were on the mend."

"Aren't we?" he asked. Katie stared at him vacantly. "What are you saying? Are you saying don't want to work things out? Is that it? I said I was sorry."

"Yes, you did. I'm sure you are. Sometimes sorry just doesn't cover it, Bill. I can't even trust you to respect my wishes, much less my feelings," she said.

"I told you she meant nothing to me."

"And, I told you that almost makes it worse. You think this is just about an affair? A string of affairs?" Katie's voice increased gradually. "It's about respect, William. Respect. Your lack of respect for me, for my feelings, for what I want in my life."

"What are you talking about? I have always respected you! When have I ever been disrespectful?" he shouted.

"Do I need to get you a dictionary? Do you not understand what the word respect means?" Katie asked. "You think making decisions for us without asking for my opinion or consent is respecting me? Really? How exactly is sleeping with other people showing me any respect? You respect me, just not our marriage, is that it?"

"I don't know what you want from me," he said with an exhausted sigh.

Katie released a heavy sigh of her own and shook her head. "And that, Bill is precisely the problem. You don't."

"So, tell me, Katie! Talk to me!"

"If I have to tell you how to show respect, I'm not sure we have much left to talk about. I have two children already to teach those lessons to. You are supposed to be my partner, not my child," she said sadly.

"So, what are you telling me?" he asked.

Katie hung her head and pushed back her tears. "I don't know, Bill. I'm not sure I have much left to say, and that says everything." She reached the handle of the door and pushed it open.

"Katie, please..."

"I'll drop the kids by for a visit tomorrow," she promised.

"What about you?" he asked.

Katie shook her head. "I don't know," she said as she walked through the door. "I really don't know," she whispered.

❧ ❧ ❧

The evening had been quiet. John Fortin watched his best friend as she stretched out on the sofa and closed her eyes. He'd never seen her look beaten in his entire life. That was the only word he could think of to describe what he saw. Katie looked defeated—completely.

"Princess, you need to eat something."

Katie opened her eyes and let out a huff. "I know. I just don't feel like it."

"Well, you won't feel any better starving."

"My stomach feels twisted," Katie explained.

"I know," he said compassionately. "Let me go figure something out. Will you, at least, try if I do?" he asked. Katie smiled. John took that as her agreement. "You can always come home," he said as he left the room.

Katie closed her eyes again and sighed. "Home?" she asked herself. "I don't even know where that is anymore."

❧ ❧ ❧

Julia tried to focus on the words in front of her. She was struggling to pay attention to the story on the page. Every few sentences, Katie seemed to invade her thoughts. The distraction was weighing on more than her mind; it was pressing on her heart. As crazy as it sounded, even in her private thoughts, Julia could swear she could sense Katie's misery. She'd picked up her phone several times to call but then placed it back beside her. She knew John was with Katie. He was Katie's best friend. Katie didn't need anyone else to cause her stress. That's what Julia told herself. With a groan, she flopped the book in her hand onto the table and grabbed her phone again. Before her mind could mount another protest, she made the call.

❧ ❧ ❧

Katie tried unsuccessfully to relax. Her mind was reeling. Her thoughts were a jumble of colliding and competing emotional responses that she could not seem to put in any order. She had just closed her eyes when she heard her phone buzz. She prayed it was not her husband. Without opening her eyes, she pressed the button. "Hello?" she answered nervously.

"Hi," Julia's voice responded. "Sorry, if I am interrupting you."

Katie unconsciously smiled as a sense of relief washed over her. "The only thing you interrupted was my headache."

"I'm sorry."

"For interrupting a headache? I should be thanking you," Katie said. "Did you watch it?" she asked.

"I did," Julia said quietly.

"Brilliant, wasn't it?" Katie offered her sarcastic assessment.

Julia wasn't certain how to respond. She could feel Katie's pain through the phone. It wasn't just anger that tainted Katie's words; it was grief.

"Are you all right?" Julia asked worriedly.

Katie held the phone away from her and looked at it in amazement. Julia had become her confidante through unexpected upheaval. She realized as she placed the phone back to her ear, that she wished Julia was with her now. It was the first clear thought Katie had managed in hours. The reality startled her.

"I'm okay. Well, not really," Katie confessed.

Julia had already surmised the truth. "Is John still there?"

"Yeah, he's spending the weekend. Thank God," Katie said.

"Well, you could always torment him with hoodies," Julia suggested. "Might be worth at least a few laughs."

John walked into the room and heard Katie giggling and stopped in his tracks.

"Share my torture, huh? That's your solution, Riley?" Katie asked.

"Not a solution, just a diversion," Julia admitted.

"Evil. You have an evil streak underneath all that bravado," Katie joked.

"No. Devious maybe. I'll go with devious, but only if it serves a higher purpose," Julia told her friend.

"And, what's the higher purpose in tormenting the queen?" Katie inquired. She was enjoying the playful conversation. It was exactly what she needed, right when she needed it most.

Julia heard the lilt in Katie's voice that had been absent when she had first answered the phone. She could picture her friend's eyes beginning to twinkle in amusement.

"Tell me this, are you smiling right now? And, be honest," Julia said.

"You think you made me smile?" Katie asked. "A bit confident, aren't we?"

"Are you?" Julia asked.

"Yes, Riley, you caught me."

"Well, there's the higher purpose. Devious to the bone, that's me," Julia declared.

"I'm glad you called," Katie said, closing her eyes as the full weight of the statement hit her.

"I wasn't sure if I should. I just wanted to check on you. I know you have…"

"And again, you save my sanity. This is becoming a habit of yours," Katie said.

"That's what friends do," Julia replied honestly.

"Maybe one day I will be able to return the favor," Katie said.

"Who says you haven't already?" Julia asked.

Katie sighed. "Is everything okay there? I'm a terrible friend, aren't I? I didn't even ask how you are."

Julia sipped her wine and shook her head. The sudden concern in Katie's voice amused and touched her. "I'm fine. We are all fine, except that we are living with a short version of Patti Lupone, or, at least, someone who thinks she is the short version of Patti Lupone."

"There's a shorter version?" Katie quipped.

Julia laughed. "Yes, her name is Meghan Riley."

Katie immediately understood. Julia had sent her a one-line email earlier in the week saying that *Anything Goes* was about to become *Everything Goes* if she did not get a reprieve from the song soon.

"That's right. I forgot all about that! Her audition was tonight. How did it go?"

"Apparently, well. Which means I might be headed for a padded cell soon," Julia said gravely.

"Part of parental penance," Katie offered her assessment.

"I guess so," Julia agreed. "Listen, I know John is there. I just wanted to…"

"Make sure I wasn't drunk again?" Katie joked.

"Nah, I wouldn't blame you if you drank all of Manhattan."

Katie's genuine laugh brought a smile to Julia's lips. "I haven't even had a drop, but that is tempting," she said. "I might just be able to do it too."

"I have all the faith in the world in you," Julia said. "I know I keep saying it, but it will get better."

"I know," Katie said. "I know it. I just find it hard to believe."

"I'll let you go. Tell Her Majesty to take good care of you."

"I will do that. Say hi to Carrie for me," Katie replied.

"I will. Good night, Katie."

"Good night, Riley. Thanks for, well, you know, being so devious."

Julia chuckled. "You are welcome. Talk to you soon."

"Yes, you will."

Chapter Seven

"**E**verett!" Julia called out sternly. "What the hell is this?" she asked him when he entered her office.

"What?" he asked.

"This," Julia held up a copy of her schedule. "Do I look like an octopus or something?"

Everett was about to answer that the purple flush to Julia's cheeks could be mistaken for a certain Disney villain that did, in fact, possess tentacles, but he thought better of it. "What's wrong with your schedule?" he asked a bit sheepishly.

Julia threw the schedule onto the table in front of her and glared at the young man. She was feeling completely exhausted and utterly overwhelmed. There were not enough hours in the day anymore. It was that simple. Everett had taken it upon himself to schedule meetings for Julia as early as eight in the morning, which meant leaving home to arrive at the office an hour earlier than normal. He had booked appointments for her almost every afternoon after four o'clock, some as late as five-thirty. Her schedule ensured that most evenings she would be lucky to make it home by the time her youngest daughter was headed for bed. When she finally did manage to arrive home, her mornings would necessitate a late night of preparation for the following day. She was feeling stretched beyond limits that she found acceptable, and it was adding to her profound state of irritability.

"Let me ask you something, Everett. Do you like having a life? I mean one that happens outside of this building?"

Everett grinned and nodded. "You know I always have somewhere to be," he replied.

"Yes, well, I suggest that you look closely at your social calendar for the next two weeks," she said dryly.

"Why? Are we doing something exciting? Big event?" he asked.

Julia was certain she was going to explode. She balled her hands into a fist and stared at the young man across from her harshly. She had just opened her mouth to speak when the phone beeped. Everett, seeing the executive director's rising fury, flashed a cheesy grin and scurried to her desk to answer it.

"Julia Riley's office. How can I help you?" he answered sweetly.

Julia stood a few paces away, simmering. She had called him into her office with the intention of filleting him and eating him for lunch, and she was looking forward to it.

"Oh no, she's right here. No, I'm sure she's available. Hold one moment," he said. Julia put her hand up to protest when Everett interrupted her. "It's Ms. Brennan," he said.

Julia nodded and made her way to the desk. She picked up the receiver as Everett attempted to scurry off. She picked up the line and pointed the receiver toward him. "We're not finished," she told him.

Everett had his back to her and offered a slight wave. He knew that if Julia could see his expression she would be furious. Katie Brennan had just unknowingly saved his day, maybe his life.

It had not escaped his notice that there was one thing lately that could shift Julia Riley's foul mood on a dime. That happened to be a call from a particular television personality.

"Did we start something I am unaware of?" Katie asked.

"What?" Julia responded in confusion.

"You just said that we weren't finished."

Julia shook her head. She felt the tension that had plagued her morning beginning to ease. "No," she laughed. "Everett. I swear I am ready to throttle that kid."

"What did he do this time, show up to another black tie dinner in plaid?" Katie teased Julia.

Katie was aware that Julia was extremely focused professionally. Julia expected a great deal from her staff. Everett often tested Julia's patience. Katie also had surmised Julia's honest affection for the young man. She suspected that was one of the reasons the young intern was able to push her friend's buttons so often. It was almost like having an annoying little brother, which Katie understood from personal experience. Katie could picture Julia tapping her pen on the desk repeatedly. She had witnessed that habit a few times during her short stay at the Riley residence. When Julia was irritated or deep in thought, she tapped. If Julia had a spoon, she would use it to bang out rhythms on her mug or plate. If Julia had a pen, she would click it endlessly or tap it on the table. And, on more than a few occasions, Katie would fight to hide her smirk as Julia drummed the steering wheel of the car or even her knee with her fingers.

"He just doesn't think. Well, either that or he thinks I am a robot," Julia explained. "It's fine. I just won't be doing any pleasure reading for the next few weeks—or any pleasure anything for that matter," Julia huffed.

"If you are busy…"

"I'm never too busy for you," Julia answered without any thought. Realizing how the statement might be received, she continued. "I need a forced break every now and again," she said.

Katie listened to the slight hint of panic in Julia's voice and wondered if her friend was all right. "Maybe you need to slow down a little," Katie suggested.

Julia started drumming her pen on the desk. "I'll try and have Everett pencil that time in," she said.

"Stop drumming," Katie said.

"What?"

"I can hear it. You're stressed out," Katie observed.

"Think you have me figured out, huh?" Julia asked.

"Not really, but I think you might want to invest in an actual drum set before you put a hole in that desk."

Julia laughed. Lately, she found herself considering investing in a punching bag or some martial arts classes just so she could kick something—anything. The problem was she had no idea how she would fit that into her schedule. She sighed.

"Consider your suggestion noted. You didn't call to encourage my burgeoning musical talent. What's up?" Julia asked. Katie paused for a moment. It was evident that Julia was feeling pressured. "Hello?" Julia called over the line. "Not enough coffee for Katie this morning?" she joked. "What's going on?"

"I'm going to be in the area this weekend for a family thing. Just, well...I thought maybe you could have Everett pencil me in for a cappuccino sometime Saturday. If you have time we could make it dinner—my treat."

"Saturday, huh?"

"Julia, don't worry if you can't. I understand. It's totally last minute."

"No, I can. It's just I have Meghan and Jordan on Saturday. Care has a photo shoot out of town," Julia explained.

"Well, I was going to leave the kids with my parents, but why don't we all just have dinner?" Katie suggested. "Tell Carrie to join us."

"I'm sure she would love to, but she won't be back until Sunday afternoon. So, I am afraid you will have to settle for three of the four Riley women," Julia said.

"That is quite disappointing," Katie chuckled. "Honestly, I would love to see Carrie too."

"I know. I'm sure she'll be bummed. How about dinner at our place? The kids can entertain themselves, and we can catch up. I can look forward to an adult conversation that does not revolve around raising money. It doesn't, does it?" Julia tried to ask seriously. She heard Katie's soft laughter and smiled. "Plus, I get a reprieve from the theater for a few hours," Julia said.

"Oh yes, the budding Broadway star," Katie said.

"Indeed. Just come over whenever. I'll figure something out."

"Julia, I said it was my treat. You and Carrie put up with us for almost an entire week. It's the least I can do," Katie offered sincerely.

"Fine. You spring for pizza and soda. I have the adult beverages covered. Deal?"

Katie shook her head. Julia was impossible. "You drive a hard bargain, Riley," she answered. Julia gloated. "Deal," Katie agreed. "Around four o'clock good for you?"

"Perfect," Julia said. "I'll see you then."

"Hey, try not to end up on *Deadly Women* or anything like that between now and then, okay?" Katie snickered.

"Scouts honor. No killing annoying interns," Julia promised. Katie laughed. "See you Saturday," Julia said.

"Yes, you will."

❧ ❧ ❧

"I don't understand," Bill Brennan told his wife. "You were just in Massachusetts. What do you need to go back there this weekend for?"

Katie attempted to keep her voice even and unemotional. There were a number of reasons that she felt she needed to get away from New York for a few days. Her husband's persistence in wanting to discuss their marriage was at the top of that list. Katie needed space to work through her emotions. Her brother's visit home gave her the perfect excuse. She hadn't seen him in over a year. Apparently, he had a new love interest. Katie had to admit that she was curious. The trip would allow her to satisfy that curiosity, give her some space from the man a few feet away, and as a bonus she would have the opportunity to see her two closest friends. She missed John, and she missed Julia. They played extremely different roles in Katie's life. At the moment, Katie needed both some perspective and some levity.

"Bill, Tommy will be home. I haven't seen him since last October," she said.

"Why can't he come here?"

Katie's patience was being pushed to its limits. "Why should he have to come here?" she asked pointedly. "It's only a three-and-a-half-hour drive for me. He's only in the area for three days. Why should he have to make that trip?"

"Well, he knows the situation," Bill offered.

"What *situation* is that?" Katie asked.

"Our situation," he replied.

Katie took a deep breath and exhaled it slowly. "The entire western hemisphere knows our situation. Are we talking about this," she waved her hand around the room. "Or are we discussing the situation of our marriage?" she inquired.

"Both," he answered.

"I see," Katie said.

"Katie, I need you here. I need you right now."

Katie pursed her lips and nodded. "I'm confident that you will manage from Friday to Monday without me. You've done it for much longer periods for many years."

"What about the kids?" he asked. "I won't see them either."

Katie sighed. "Neil will bring them by Friday morning before he brings them to the studio."

"Why is Neil…"

"Because, Bill, I have a show to tape before I leave later that morning. Neil is going to stay over. That way I don't have to get the kids up at the same ungodly hour as I do."

"So, now Neil is staying over?" he asked with a hint of accusation in his voice.

Neil Jeffries was a longtime friend of both Katie and Bill Brennan's. He had been a sportscaster at the local network Katie worked for after graduating college. Neil's aspirations, however, were always to write books. For the last seven years, he had been making a significant name for himself writing biographies of some of the sports world's greatest legends. Katie trusted Neil completely. He was one of the few people in New York that she considered a close friend. He was between projects and more than happy to help Katie in any way that he could. The tone of her husband's voice took Katie off guard for a moment. When it dawned on her that he might be insinuating she was having an affair with Neil, she started to laugh.

"Is something amusing?" Bill Brennan asked.

Katie kept laughing. "It is true what they say about mirrors, isn't it?" she shook her head. Bill looked at her severely. "You think I am having an affair with Neil?" she asked him.

"Well, what would you think?" he asked.

"I should think that would be quite obvious. All the rumors about your escapades and I put my faith in you every single time," Katie said in disgust. "I ask one of our oldest friends to help me out, and your immediate conclusion is that I am having an affair," she said sadly. "Well, I am not having an affair. In fact, sex is the farthest thing from my mind these days."

Bill looked at his wife closely. "I'm sorry, Katie. That will pass. Once I am out of here and we can...."

"I don't know when that will pass as you put it," Katie said. "But, if what you are worried about is my sleeping with someone else, you can put your mind at ease. If I had such an inclination, I would either walk away from it, or I would walk away from you first," she said assuredly. "I have to go."

"Aren't you going to come say goodbye?" he asked.

Katie looked at him in disbelief and sadness. "I'll see you next week," she said.

❦ ❦ ❦

"Katie?" Julia looked at her friend.

"Huh?"

"Where'd you go there?" Julia asked with a wink.

The pair had enjoyed a late afternoon of pizza and laughter with their children. Meghan and Stephanie had finally decided to head off to Meghan's room for some "girl talk." Jordan and Ian had claimed the television in the family room for an evening of movies and popcorn. Finally, Katie and Julia had a chance to breathe. Julia had lit a fire and poured them each a glass of wine. They had been midstream in a conversation about the Brighton Center when Julia noticed that Katie had mentally checked out.

"I'm sorry, Julia," Katie said with a sigh of exasperation.

"Nothing to be sorry for," Julia said. "You want to talk about it?"

Katie thought for a moment and then nodded. She took a large sip of her wine and looked back at her friend. "You do have more of this?" she asked. "This may take a while."

"I do. I have no place to be until Monday morning, and as you well know, I have plenty of extra rooms. So, get comfortable," Julia instructed Katie. "And, let's hear it."

"I don't know where to start," Katie confessed.

Julia offered her friend an encouraging smile. "Just start wherever," Julia said. "If I get lost I will ask for directions. I promise," she winked.

Katie giggled. "You're crazy, Riley."

"Probably a safe bet," Julia agreed.

"I don't know. I just can't be anywhere near him. I just...I don't even know if I am angry anymore. I just feel sad—sad and disgusted."

"I'm going to go out on a limb here and guess that we are talking about Bill," Julia said.

"Who else? Do you know that he actually insinuated I was having an affair with one of our best friends?" Katie barked. "Can you even believe that?"

Julia wasn't at all certain how to respond. "Maybe he was just..."

"Oh no," Katie cut Julia off. "One of our closest friends, in fact, one of my only close friends in New York. We've known Neil as long as we've known each other. Neil offered to stay over Thursday in the guest room, so I didn't have to bring the kids to the studio with me when I left. He even offered to take them to see Bill beforehand. And, do you think that my husband might just say, thank you? No. He immediately suspects that Neil is staying over to get it on with me. Unbelievable."

"I'm sorry, Katie."

Katie let out a heavy sigh and rested her head against the back of the chair she was sitting in. "Yeah, I guess it's hard to see anyone else when you are so consumed with your own reflection. I don't know anymore, Julia. That's why I had to get away. I can't even look at him. I don't want to end up hating him, and I'm afraid at the rate we are going, I might."

Julia smiled. "I don't think you are capable of hating anyone," she said honestly. Katie glanced over at Julia doubtfully. "You're hurt, and you're angry. It's going to take time to work through that." Julia watched as Katie dropped her face into her hands. "Katie…"

"It's not just the affairs, Julia," Katie said in almost a whisper. "The truth is I don't know if I am more furious with him or with myself," she continued. "I knew. Of course, I did. I just chose not to believe it. For years, he would come home from a road trip and I would dedicate myself to pleasing him. I tried to be perfect. I tried to be more than he could ever want. I was determined to convince him that I was enough," she said. "Maybe I was trying to convince myself. I don't know. I've never been good at failure."

Julia watched Katie's inner turmoil begin to surface. She couldn't fathom how any person would need more than Katie. Her heart was breaking for the woman across the room. Katie was intelligent, had a wicked sense of humor and a quick wit. And, Katie

Brennan was breathtakingly beautiful. It wasn't only Katie's appearance that made her alluring. Katie possessed charisma, an energy that immediately filled a room when she entered it. Julia struggled to remain silent. She desperately wanted to intervene and somehow make Katie understand that she was desirable on every level. Bill Brennan was a first-class idiot by Julia's standards.

"Eventually, that changed. I just didn't want to bother anymore. I know I'm not perfect. Believe me. I'm not. I think I was happier when he was away. Maybe it really is my fault," Katie said softly.

Julia was not standing for that statement. "Bullshit," she said. Katie looked up in surprise. "He must be the dumbest man on earth," Julia offered her assessment. "Has he been tested for that?" Julia asked. Katie's eyes narrowed in confusion. "The stupidity gene. Has he been tested?" Julia asked.

Katie snickered. "I wasn't aware they had one."

"They do. He'd fail. Anyone who would cheat on a woman like you is either certifiably insane or intellectually challenged. Either way, it isn't you," she said.

"Can I quote you on that?" Katie asked. She loved the way Julia could brighten her spirits in a heartbeat.

"Yes," Julia answered. "Listen, I'm kidding, well, sort of. I am not trying to make light of how you feel."

"I know that," Katie assured her. "I need to figure out what to do. I don't want to just exist in a marriage because it's what everyone expects."

"Who is everyone?" Julia asked. Katie sighed again. "Katie, whatever you decide to do, someone will judge you. That's the way people are. You know that. If you stay and try and work it out, some people will say you are weak and submissive—that you need a man to complete you. And, if you can't do that, some people will think you weren't willing to do the work. So, in the end, the only thing you can do is what feels right to you."

Katie looked at Julia and smiled. "You tired of saving my sanity yet?" she asked.

Julia smiled. She had never tried to analyze how Katie made her feel. She hadn't attempted to explain the feeling until now. Being in Katie's presence felt a great deal like coming in from the cold and being wrapped in a warm blanket.

"I don't think I've saved you from anything," Julia said. "But I'd die trying." The words came naturally, without hesitation or conscious thought and startled them both.

Katie stared at Julia blankly. The sincerity of Julia's statement was unmistakable. The swell of emotion that rose within Katie took her breath away for a moment. Katie had always relied on her ability to discern and describe her feelings and experiences. She categorized her life in many ways, just as she had filed her stories and ordered her interviews. It was logical and sensible. She sorted her senses in an effort to comprehend what they meant. That skill had served her well in nearly every facet of her life. Julia managed to spin Katie's world upside down with just a simple sentiment. Emotion had, in an instant, suffocated thought and reason. A faint whisper in the back of her mind was calling to Katie to get up and run, but she seemed to have been rendered both speechless and paralyzed.

Panic. Julia began to panic. "Where the hell did that come from?" she screamed silently. She wanted to clarify what she was saying. She needed to give her words the proper perspective. Julia's thoughts swirled about violently. Reason would drift by, the brief hint of a concrete explanation making an appearance before being sucked under by a forceful whirlpool of unexpected feeling. The friendship between Julia and Katie had developed instantly. Their friendship had become a central part of Julia's life overnight. Julia couldn't define what she saw flickering in Katie's blue eyes from across the room. Perhaps it was the reflection of the fire that danced across them that had trapped Julia's gaze. Julia could not pull her gaze away and it was beginning to unsettle her nerves.

Katie felt an involuntary grin take shape. Amid the myriad of competing thoughts and emotions, only one thought had become completely clear; Julia cared about her, and that mattered more to Katie than anything in recent memory. She finally managed to formulate a response.

"No dying, Riley," Katie winked. "Not allowed."

Julia wasn't convinced that she was still breathing. The thought that she might have already died and been transported to some strange realm passed through her mind. At the moment, it seemed a real possibility. She smiled at Katie with an uncharacteristically embarrassed nod. Julia looked at her glass, which at some point had been drained of its contents in search of a distraction.

"I'm running on empty," she noted. "How about you?" Katie lifted her wine glass and finished the last sip, before handing it to Julia. "I'll be right back," Julia promised. She had never been so grateful for a justifiable escape in her life.

"What the hell just happened?" Julia scolded herself when she reached the kitchen. "Get a grip, Riley," she chastised herself. "She's your best friend for Christ's sake." The verbal assessment took Julia aback for a moment. She stared at the empty wine glasses and shook her head. She looked forward to Katie's calls, to her emails, and most of all to her company. Katie had unexpectedly become the part of the day that Julia looked forward to the most. She chuckled and finished the task at hand. "Well, maybe you should just tell her that," she reasoned.

Katie watched Julia's hasty exit and could not help but be amused. Her gaze retreated into the fire again and she sighed in contentment. She felt a sense of peace in Julia's presence that seemed too often to allude her in life. Julia had an uncanny ability to understand what Katie needed at any given moment. It was not necessary for Katie to detail events or emotions for Julia. Julia seemed to understand Katie, to be able to anticipate the shifts in her mood and the underlying thoughts and feelings that drove them. Katie wondered how common it was to find someone that complimented you so naturally. John was the only other person Katie could claim to feel that level of comfort with, and somehow that was drastically different. She wasn't positive how to describe the difference. She heard Julia's footsteps approaching and made a note to revisit that puzzle later.

Julia handed Katie her glass and resumed her seat. "I don't like seeing you so torn up," she explained. "I have a lot of friends, Katie. I am lucky in that way, I guess. It's been a long time since I had anyone I felt this comfortable talking to. Michael is terrific. He is my closest friend in many ways, and Carrie, well…But I…."

"I think I understand," Katie said. "I feel the same way."

Julia nodded. "I know I say it all the time, but it really will be all right. Things have a way of working out."

Katie looked at Julia and remained silent for a few moments, studying the subtle signs of both truthfulness and skepticism that competed for dominance in her friend's expression. "You really believe that?" Katie asked.

Julia chuckled. "Not always," she admitted. "But, I know it."

"I know what you mean," Katie muttered.

Chapter Eight

Julia's Journal:

It's interesting how we spend most of our lives hearing about falling in love—anticipating that. I think most people long for that—the way your heart begins to skip a beat every few seconds just at the mention of someone's name. There is an exhilaration when you fall in love that is unmatched by anything else in the human experience. Unexpectedly, without explanation, someone passes through your thoughts, and you stop all movement, all reasoning, just to imagine them a few moments longer, willing them not to leave you. Everything and anything will remind you of that person—a song, a sunset, the sound of laughter or the feel of a cool breeze. It's as if your soul begins to cry out across time and space, calling out through imaginary distance to another that has taken up residence within. Maybe the secret to life is learning to fall in love each day.

No one tells you that you can fall out of love. Sometimes you don't notice the falling out. It's a great deal like watching the leaves fall to the ground in autumn. When you first look, everything is beautiful, a myriad of vibrant colors. Slowly, one at a time leaves fall from their branches. I wonder how long it takes the branches to notice. Do they feel the weight as it falls away, or does realization only come when they are laid completely bare? Maybe that is the only way to describe falling out of love. Remnants of what once was a part of you remain, leaving you forever changed. You have been sheltered and fed, just like the branch of a tree. Then, one day you find that the vibrant colors, the shelter, the shade, the flourishing of what has nourished your soul has slowly withered to a shadow of itself. You are left exposed and open—naked to the world. No one tells you about falling out of love.

MARCH 2015

Katie walked slowly down the hallway, silently rehearsing what she would say to her husband when she visited. She had avoided any time alone with him for days, making sure that their children were in tow each time she visited. Katie's brief trip back to Boston had brought a great many things into focus for her. Her family had made it clear that they would support any decision she made regarding her marriage. It was evident that her parents and her brother thought she would be happier apart from Bill Brennan. John had been less reserved in his assessment. He blatantly made Katie aware of his analysis. He had long regarded her relationship as toxic and confessed that he had struggled to remain silent for years. He told Katie that she was a shadow of herself in Bill's presence for a long time. She withheld her humor more when her husband was around. John could feel the tension between Katie and Bill Brennan for years, and he had wondered when Katie would finally admit it to herself. And then, there was Julia.

Julia. Julia had consumed Katie's thoughts for the last few days. She and Julia had stayed up talking well into the early morning hours on her most recent visit. Long periods of silence would stretch between conversations. Strangely, Katie did not feel uncomfortable in the quietness. She welcomed it. It was during those stretches of stillness that she felt the closest to Julia. Katie did not seek to disguise her emotions with Julia, and she could not seem to suppress them. When they had finally decided to retire for the evening, Katie had felt a void take shape that she could not understand. In the morning, when they parted company, she had lingered in Julia's doorway, feeling that there was something she should say, but having no idea what that should be. Julia had hugged her goodbye with another encouraging promise that everything would work out. Katie had closed her eyes as Julia whispered in her ear. "I'll always be here if you need me." Katie had replayed the moment a million times.

Katie stopped just outside the door to her husband's room. She tugged on her blazer and took a deep breath.

"Hey," Bill greeted her. "I'm glad you decided to come by alone." Katie closed the door with a solemn smile. "Everything okay?" he asked.

Katie pulled a chair next to the bed where he was seated. She sucked in a deep breath for courage. "I think we both know that everything is not okay," she said calmly. "We need to talk."

"Okay?" he asked hesitantly. Katie sensed that Bill was not going to make this painless. She took his hand and looked at it. Images of their past invaded her thoughts. She had thought she would feel a sense of relief in this decision. Right now, all she felt was grief.

"Katie? Are you okay?"

"No," she whispered. She looked up at him and tilted her head with a crooked smile. "You know, I still remember the day I met you," she began. He smiled and caressed her hand, feeling suddenly hopeful. Katie sighed. "I remember when I told you that I was pregnant with Stephanie, the look on your face," she recalled as her eyes began to moisten. "I don't know when we lost that," she confessed. His smile instantly disappeared. "We did. We lost it a long time ago."

"We can find it again," he said.

"No. We can't," she told him. "I can't."

"What are you saying?" he asked fearfully.

Katie squeezed his hand. "I'm not going to make you go through all of this alone, Bill." She watched as relief washed over his face. "I'll stick by you publicly until you are out of here, at least, until you decide what you want to do."

"What I want to do about what?"

"With your career," she said.

The prognosis for Bill Brennan's pitching career was grim at best. It seemed clear that his days donning a uniform and strolling to the mound had come to an end. Katie mourned that loss for him. In many ways, she knew that would be the most profound loss for her husband. Losing their marriage would pale by comparison. The ball field was Bill Brennan's home, his best friend. Katie and Bill had become virtual strangers. He was constantly traveling and the scarce moments that they did manage to share had been fraught with tension for years. The distance that kept them apart physically had crept into their intimate relationship. It was an ethereal separation that was just as tangible, and monumentally more painful. Katie looked at her husband empathetically.

"I can't do this anymore," she said.

"So, what? That's it? What about counseling? What about...."

"Bill," she said softly. "Don't do this. This is hard enough."

"Hard enough for who?"

Katie shook her head. "I don't want to fight. I just want my life back."

"Your life? What about our life?" he shot back at her.

She took a deep breath and released his hand. "My life has been your life for almost our entire marriage," she said. "It hasn't been our life for a very long time. You've gone your way, and I have been on my own with the kids."

"You knew what it meant to be married to a ball player when you signed up," he said.

"No. You make our marriage sound like it is a contract you negotiate with your agent. I didn't *sign up* to marry a ball player. I made the decision to marry you—the man I loved. That's what I signed up for. I didn't expect this. I didn't want this to happen," she said truthfully.

"Obviously, you did," he said. "What is it? Is there someone else?"

Katie shook her head. "Yes, there is." She watched his face flush in anger. She continued before he could speak. "Me. That someone else is me," she said.

"Katie, wait…"

Katie kissed her husband on the forehead. "I'm tired of waiting, Bill. I've waited a long time for things to change. The only person who can change them is me," she said.

Bill Brennan closed his eyes in resignation of the truth. There was no malice in his wife's tone or her declarations. He had shared his life with Katherine Brennan long enough to realize that she was serious. She hadn't come to discuss their relationship. She had come to inform him of her decision.

"I'm sorry, Katie," he said. "I wish…"

"I know," she said with a somber smile. "Me too."

ॐ ॐ ॐ

Julia laughed as Jordan chased Meghan out of the kitchen towards their bedrooms. "Where do they get that energy?" she mused aloud.

Carrie smiled and wrapped her arms around Julia's waist. "I think that must come from the Gallagher gene. I don't recall any evidence of that on the Stevens side," she laughed.

"Oh, Lord, sometimes I think I forget that I was ever a Gallagher at all," Julia said.

"Well, your father certainly never forgot," Carrie said with a wink.

"No, he did not," Julia agreed.

Julia's father had teased her endlessly about not keeping her maiden name. She was his only child, after all, he repeatedly reminded her. It was always playful, but Julia suspected there was a hint of truth in his joking. Her parents had always wanted more children. She suspected he had always envisioned a son to carry on the family name. Marrying a doctor, and an Irish one made the reality more palatable for James Gallagher. Julia snickered as she recalled her father.

"Thank God I took an Irish name when I married Michael. Can you imagine?" she shook her head.

"No," Carrie answered with a chuckle. She smiled at her wife and moved closer to Julia, stopping to kiss her tenderly.

"What was that for?" Julia asked curiously. Carrie smirked. "Oh," Julia breathed knowingly. "Too many romance novels for you lately, huh Stevens? Or too much Hallmark Channel?"

"Maybe I just miss you," Carrie said honestly.

Julia nodded her understanding. Her schedule had been daunting over the last month, to say the least. She had barely found time to nap most days. Frequently, she fell asleep on the couch sometime in the middle of the night. She had been home late nearly every night and out the door with a quick wave in the morning. Julia sighed and kissed Carrie's forehead.

"Why don't you head up? I'll pour us some wine and be there in a few minutes," Julia promised.

"Jules, if you have work to do…"

Julia shook her head. Hopefulness and disappointment mingled in her wife's expression. "No. Work can wait," she assured Carrie.

Carrie's appreciation was evident in her smile and the kiss that she placed on Julia's cheek as she headed off. Julia watched her wife leave and turned to retrieve some glasses and a bottle of wine. As she started to open the bottle, her thoughts drifted to a similar scene a week ago. "I hope she's okay," Julia thought. She hadn't spoken with Katie in several days, and she wondered how things were panning out for her friend back in New York.

℞ ℞ ℞

Katie plopped in front of the fire with a glass of wine. She was thankful that her children had both fallen asleep quickly. Her conversation with her husband was replaying like a broken record in her mind. The decision to end their marriage had not come easily for her. Katie was relieved that she had found the courage to voice it finally, but facing Bill had been more painful than she could have imagined. She felt inadequate again, unable to devise a way to mend their broken relationship. She'd waltzed through numerous ideas and strategies over the last month, but none had held any promise. It was like trying to fill an empty cup that had no bottom left. No matter what she poured into it, it would pass right through, accomplishing nothing but adding to her sense of frustration and failure.

Katie sipped the wine in her hand slowly as memories of the last fifteen years danced through her thoughts. She felt the occasional tear slip over her cheek. How had she reached this point in her life? She had loved Bill Brennan once. She recalled their first date. She replayed the memory of their wedding repeatedly as if she were watching it on television. She closed her eyes and remembered watching him hold their children, seeing him jump in celebration on the pitching mound, all the moments she cherished. Katie sighed as she mentally relived her marriage—the happy moments, the sense of possibility that had become a distant echo. She shook her head wondering how they had lost each other. Now, she would mourn the ending of what she had once dreamed would last an eternity.

The fire crackled. The faint sound of music seemed to paint Katie's memories in unique colors. She closed her eyes and let the warmth of the fire caress her skin. A small smile took shape as her thoughts drifted elsewhere—Julia. Katie breathed in the momentary sensation of Julia surrounding her, the feeling of safety and completion that seemed to encompass her in Julia's presence. She could swear she could hear Julia's laughter. It was a sound that warmed her more than the heat of any fire ever could. "I'll always be here if you need me," she heard Julia's voice softly promise. Katie felt an overwhelming emotional burst clench her heart. Startled, her eyes flew open before closing again with a realization that stole the air from her lungs. Katie's tears escaped freely.

"Julia," she whispered.

❧ ❧ ❧

Julia felt Carrie's breath against her neck whispering endearments. She closed her eyes and quieted her thoughts. She had made love to Carrie slowly. She had focused all of her energy on that task. Something was clawing at the back of her mind, and she needed to quiet it. She had been successful at silencing thought and translating it into a physical sensation until now. Now, Carrie's hands traveled the expanse of Julia's form, and Julia felt a sudden wave of panic. She desperately wanted to lose herself in Carrie's touch. She screamed at her mind to be quiet, as she listened to Carrie's soft declarations.

"I love you," Carrie told her, and Julia closed her eyes.

Carrie's lips traveled slowly over Julia's thigh and Julia sighed.

"Please," Julia heard herself encourage her wife.

It was delicious. Julia craved release. She looked down at Carrie, grabbed the sheets and gave over to the sensations that were coursing through her body, feeling the rising tide as it steadily built momentum. She struggled to steady her breathing as the waves began to crash over her. The emotions that were fighting their way to the surface were irresistible. Julia closed her eyes in surrender. Katie. The thought, the vision that appeared in her mind as her body lost all control caused her eyes to fly open in alarm. Katie.

⁓ ⁓ ⁓

Katie put her face in her hands and cried. Julia. She attempted to order her thoughts, to will them back to Bill—to her children. There were so many things Katie needed to consider. How would they tell their children that the life they had always known, that their family was about to change forever? What would she do? Should she stay in New York? What about Bill? Where would his career take him and how would that impact her future? Katie shook her head. No matter how many questions she posed, Julia continued to creep into her thoughts. She desperately wanted to pick up the phone and call. She wanted to hear Julia. She wanted to see Julia. Katie rubbed her face and scolded herself. She needed focus. She needed to concentrate on her family. Julia was a constant distraction.

"I miss you," she admitted through her tears, knowing that there was only one solution now. Katie felt her heart break in two. "I'm sorry, Julia," she cried softly.

෬ ෬ ෬

Julia waited until she was certain that Carrie had fallen into a restful sleep. She looked down at her wife and closed her eyes with a ragged breath. Carrie was the gentlest soul she had ever known. She kissed her wife's head and reveled in the softness, feeling the first silent tears begin to slip from her eyes. Julia made her way into the bathroom and turned on the shower. She needed to be alone. She needed something to comfort her. She needed to somehow wash away the sadness that had embedded itself in her heart. It was a familiar grief, one that came when confusion was suddenly silenced by clarity.

Julia stepped under the flow of the hot water and allowed it to wash over her. She could feel her body shivering despite the heat of she had hoped would serve as a soothing caress. Carrie's face flashed in her mind, the tenderness and understanding in Carrie's eyes, the complete trust. She remembered the moment that she had fallen into Carrie's arms. Carrie had held Julia through laughter, loss, tears, and the promise of new life. They had shared everything. She recalled their first kiss. When she wondered, had they grown apart? And then, without warning, a pair of blue eyes that twinkled with amusement and sincerity appeared before her. Katie. Julia missed Katie unlike she had ever missed a person in her life.

A violent collision of sadness and hopefulness, love, and fear forced Julia to the shower floor. The water cascaded over her while emotions coursed through her in forceful waves. She wrapped her arms around her knees as the myriad of feelings and thoughts plaguing her finally escaped in desperate sobs.

"Oh, God," Julia cried.

Her body quaked in disbelief. How could this happen? She loved Carrie. She had a life with Carrie that she treasured. Katie. God, she missed Katie. The tears seemed endless. She wondered if anything could wash away the fear and the sadness that besieged her soul. Katie. The answer came in an instant.

"Oh, Carrie," Julia cried. "I'm so sorry."

Chapter Nine

May 2015

"It's a fabulous opportunity," Katie said to Bill.

"I know it is. It means you are going to be saddled with the kids more than ever, Katie," he reminded her.

"Bill, I have never felt saddled, as you put it. You have a chance here to keep doing something you love, teaching it in a way. So, take it. Go and coach," she told him.

"What about you?" he asked.

Katie smiled and touched her husband's cheek. "I don't know. We both know my life is not there. We both know it's time."

"To make an announcement, you mean?" he guessed. Katie nodded. With a deep sigh, Bill Brennan nodded his agreement. "You know that I still love you, don't you?" he asked.

Katie smiled again. She did know that he loved her. She loved him, but it was different now. Bill had been home for four full weeks. He was stronger and more mobile. They had shared quite a few enjoyable evenings with their children before retiring to separate rooms. Acknowledging the fact that they had been leading separate lives had inadvertently brought them closer together. It was a drastically different relationship now. There were no more lies or suspicions, no more hiding or half-truths to keep them apart. They could speak honestly, and that had made time together far more meaningful than it had been in years. It did not change the inevitable. Katie was certain Bill understood that. She kissed him on the cheek affectionately.

"I know you love me," she said. "I love you too, but not the way I once did," she said assuredly. "This job is right for you. The kids need stability, Bill. I need that."

"You hate New York," he reminded her. "You only came here because of me," he said, feeling a sense of guilt over that reality.

"Well, everything happens for a reason," Katie told him.

"So, you are going to stay here? Stay in New York?" he asked.

"For now. The kids are in school. It's best for now," she said.

"Do you want me to call and…"

"I'll have Marty put something together," Katie offered. "We can prepare the statement and have David release it. I'll make sure that Marty lines up a couple of interviews for us together."

Bill Brennan looked at his wife and nodded sadly. "Katie," he said. "I…Well, a lot of people would not be so generous."

Katie shook her head. "Our problems are not all your fault, Bill. We were both in this marriage."

"Only one of us…"

"It's in the past. At least, it is in our past. We have two children to think about. I'm not going to sour them on this family or you. There is no reason to do that."

"You could come to California," he suggested sheepishly.

"No. I'm not sure where my life is headed, but I am sure it is not there. You go and be the best pitching coach the major league has ever seen," she encouraged him. "We'll cheer you on from here. And, even if I am in New York," she began, "Now, I can cheer for my Red Sox guilt free. I'll redeem myself with my dad, if nothing else."

"I wish I could find a way to redeem myself with them."

"With my parents?" she asked. Bill nodded again. "Just be the best dad you can be," Katie told him. "That's all that matters now."

"Katie?"

"Yeah."

"For whatever it is worth, whoever manages to catch you— that's one lucky guy," he said earnestly.

Katie tried to smile. The statement, however, unsettled her. "I'm not sure that's in the cards for me," she told him. Katie gave her husband a peck on the cheek. "Good night," she said as she left the room.

Bill Brennan watched her walk away slowly. "Sure it is, Katie. He's out there somewhere. Trust me."

ॐ ॐ ॐ

Julia sat at her desk reviewing the coming day's agenda. It had been a difficult period for her. She had been pulling away from her family more with each passing day, finding excuses to stay late at the office, scheduling late meetings, and deliberately arriving home after everyone had retired. After a month of growing tension, Carrie had finally confronted her. That had been a month ago today. The memory of that conversation had been consuming Julia's thoughts all morning.

"What is going on with you?" Carrie asked.

"What do you mean?" Julia responded as she walked around the table to retrieve a glass.

"Julia!"

"What?" Julia jumped at Carrie's uncustomary yell.

Carrie let out a strong sigh. *"Would you please just sit down? We cannot go on like this."*

Julia was determined to avoid any meaningful conversation. She had convinced herself that whatever feelings she had for Katie, they were nothing more than a passing infatuation. It wasn't that uncommon she told herself. If she just kept her distance from everyone and gave it some time, it would all pass into oblivion. Things would go back to normal. The problem was, Julia no longer knew what normal was. Everything was amiss in her life all of sudden.

"What are you talking about?" Julia asked Carrie calmly as she took a seat at the kitchen table.

"Julia, it's bad enough that you are avoiding me..."

"I'm not avoiding you," Julia said. Carrie just raised her eyebrow. "It's just been crazy. You know how it gets some..."

"Stop," Carrie said firmly. "Just stop. You and I have been together for almost fifteen years. I know you as well as anyone. You have always had too much work. You have always made time for all of us. Even when things might have gotten a bit distant between us, you were here for the kids. Now, what is going on with you?" Carrie asked pointedly.

Julia could feel her body beginning to tremble. "I don't know," she said softly. Carrie looked up at the ceiling and then closed her eyes. "Care..."

"Is it someone else?" Carrie asked.

"What?" Julia gasped.

"Is it? Is there someone else you want to be with, Julia?"

"Care," Julia looked at her wife. "Are you happy?"

"With you?"

"With us," Julia clarified.

"Honestly? I don't know right now, Jules. I feel like you pull away a little more every day," Carrie said sadly.

Julia nodded. "I'm just overwhelmed."

Carrie shook her head. "I think we both know there is more to it than that. What do you want, Jules?"

"What do you want?" Julia asked.

"I want my marriage back. I want my wife in my bed. I want to be a family," Carrie told her. "Fifteen years, Julia—I feel you slipping away by the minute."

Julia made her way to her wife and held her. "I'll try harder. I don't ever want to hurt you."

"I know that," Carrie admitted. "I just wonder what happened. This isn't what I want for our life," Carrie said. Julia nodded. "Is that what you want? To work on it, on us?" Carrie asked.

"I want to try," Julia said honestly. "I really do."

True to her word, Julia had tried. She and Carrie had made a concerted effort to be home together with their children more regularly. They had enjoyed some wonderful evenings and weekend afternoons playing games, watching movies, and just sitting at the dinner table. One thing remained a challenge—intimacy. Julia loved spending time with Carrie and the kids. Carrie still made her laugh, and it always tugged at her heartstrings to watch her wife with their children. Still, something was missing in their marriage, and Julia could not put her finger on it. She'd pondered it for hours, night after night once Carrie had fallen asleep. Julia would watch Carrie in the faint light and wonder what she was doing wrong. There had to be something she could do to reconnect with her wife.

Julia still viewed Carrie as beautiful. She still looked forward to sharing her day with her wife, but there was an element that just was lacking. It was like trying to bake a cake with flour and water, but without any eggs. It just would not come together. After a lengthy conversation, she had made an agreement with Carrie to focus on their relationship closely for the next month. Julia had prayed, had hoped, and had invested everything she could think of to make inroads—to shift the tide. Today, Julia's heart was heavy. She had seen the dismay in Carrie's eyes the night before as they retired. There was no possible way to deny the distance between them. Julia rubbed her eyes, feeling the onset of a migraine.

"Hey, boss lady," Everett called as she skipped into Julia's office. Julia did not move. "Did you see the paper yet?" he asked. Julia looked up at her young intern and scowled. "Aww, come on Julia!" he said as he threw a copy of the morning paper on her desk. "Look in the entertainment section."

"Why would I do that, Everett? Did Boy George make a sudden comeback and no one told me?"

"Who?" he asked.

Julia shook her head and picked up the paper. She reluctantly followed his instructions and froze.

"Big news for your news lady friend, huh?" Everett winked.

Julia's migraine was gaining momentum by the second. "Everett, the ending of a person's marriage and family is not something to get all Bob Fosse about," she drawled with irritation. "It's someone's life, not a bad movie musical."

Everett looked at Julia and sighed. "I figured you knew already."

Julia looked back at the young man before her and nodded. "I have to get ready for my nine o'clock meeting," she said with a motion towards the door.

Everett followed her cue and stopped abruptly. "Julia? I'm sorry. Katie seems like a nice person. I didn't..."

Julia sighed. "I know.... And, she is a nice person," she said. He nodded and closed the door to give his boss her privacy.

Julia picked up the paper and groaned. She hadn't spoken to Katie in nearly six weeks. After leaving several messages, and a handful of emails without receiving a response, Julia determined that

Katie was either dealing with a difficult situation at home or had re-evaluated the meaning of their friendship. Either way, Julia had promised herself she would not make any more overtures.

"Oh, shit," she said with a sigh before picking up her phone. "You are a complete idiot, Riley," she scolded herself as she pressed the number.

∾ ∾ ∾

"How are you doing, honestly?" George asked Katie as she entered her office.

"I'm fine, George," she assured him. "This is something Bill and I have known for a while. We just decided not to make it public until we were ready."

George looked at Katie skeptically. "No offense, Katie, but you look exhausted."

"This isn't exactly my idea of fun," she told him. "It sucks if you really want to know the truth."

"I know. I just want to help if I can," George said.

"I appreciate that," she winked.

"Oh geez! I almost forgot. Your phone went off during the broadcast," he said as he handed it to her. Katie smiled and took the phone, and immediately went pale. "Katie?" George called to his boss. "What's wrong?"

Katie forced an uncomfortable smile. "Nothing. Nothing, just tired, I think. I have a few things to wrap up here and then I am going to try and head home a bit early." George understood Katie's soft direction to leave. He nodded his understanding and left his boss to her tasks.

Katie stared at the phone for several minutes. The last week had taken its toll on her emotionally. She and Bill had explained to their children that they had decided to divorce. She hadn't been certain what she should expect. To her pleasant surprise, both of her children seemed to take the news in stride. When she approached her daughter later to have a chat, Stephanie had ended up comforting her.

"It's okay, Mom, really."

"You know that your father and I both love you, and I don't want you to think I am taking you away from him at all," Katie assured her daughter.

"Mom," Stephanie said with a slight roll of her eyes. "Dad is never here. We mostly see him at the holidays anyway. It's not like it will be all that different."

Katie smiled and nodded. She knew that it would be different, but Stephanie and Ian had grown accustomed to long separations from their father. That made the news more bearable for them. Their main concern had been where they would live. For the time being, Katie promised they would remain in the home they knew. She was also deliberate in preparing them. She explained that while she would not uproot them during a school year, she would not promise them forever in New York. Her tears began to fall as she offered her daughter another apology.

"It's okay, Mom," Stephanie said again. "Don't be so sad. I promise you will still get to yell at me to pick up my room," she goaded her mother.

"Wise guy," Katie had bantered back. "I love you, Steph."

"I know, Mom. I love you too."

Katie was grateful for her children. They were her pride and joy, the most important people in her life. While she was relieved that they were both coping, she remained cautious. The press had yet to get their hands on the story, and both Stephanie and Ian were old enough to feel the fallout when that happened. She looked back at the phone and closed her eyes. Part of her wanted to delete the voicemail, but something much stronger compelled her to listen.

"*Hey. It's me, but I guess you already figured that out,*" Julia's voice said.

Katie ran her tongue over her bottom lip and chuckled lightly at Julia's greeting. She missed Julia's voice. It always calmed her.

"*Listen, I think I can pretty much figure out that you don't want to talk to me. I mean, unless you were abducted by aliens or something and that charming woman I see on the television is some kind of pod person.*"

Katie swallowed hard. Julia's attempt at humor did little to disguise the underlying hurt in her voice.

"*Anyway, look…. Obviously, I saw the paper. Not that I am surprised, really. I am sorry. I guess I just wanted you to know that I hope you are okay. Everything happens for a reason, remember?*"

"I do remember," Katie said as she felt tears begin to well in her eyes.

"*Well, I just wanted you to know…. I'm always here if you need me, even if you never call. I wanted you to know…Well, I have to go make sure Everett hasn't set anything on fire with that thing he is pretending is a suit.*"

Katie smiled, even as her tears continued to fall.

"*Take care of yourself, okay? I'll see you.*"

Katie traced the phone with her finger. "I hope so," she whispered. Her face fell into her hands as sobs of reality and pain racked her body. "I'm sorry," she whispered, not sure whose forgiveness she need more, her own or Julia's.

❧ ❧ ❧

Carrie sat on the edge of the large bed, in the home she had shared with Julia for nearly eleven years. Her cheeks were tear stained as Julia knelt before her. "Are you sure this is what you want?" Carrie asked.

Julia held Carrie's hands tenderly. "No," she confessed. She wiped a tear from her wife's cheek. "It's what I need. I think we both do, Care," Julia said honestly.

"You don't love me," Carrie replied.

"I do love you," Julia promised. "I do. I just feel…Care, can't you feel it? We just…The passion we had. That feeling of…"

"Jesus, Julia," Carrie interrupted her wife. "Of course, I know. What did you expect? That we would be like love-struck teenagers forever? We have three kids, bills, careers, and a million other things to balance!"

Julia stood and paced the floor. "I know that."

"You know that? What am I doing wrong?" Carrie asked.

Julia spun around in alarm. "What?"

"What am I doing wrong?" Carrie repeated.

Julia could hear the mixture of raw sadness and anger in Carrie's voice. "You haven't done anything wrong. Why would you say that?"

"It must be me," Carrie said. "You want to end our marriage, Julia. What the hell am I supposed to think? You can't seriously expect a relationship to stay the same as…."

"I don't," Julia said as she made her way back to Carrie. "I expected us to grow. I just hoped it would be closer together and not farther apart," she said softly.

Carrie wanted to argue, but she was quickly losing the energy to fight. "I'll go and stay in the studio loft," Carrie said as her tears broke forth again.

"No," Julia said as she took Carrie into her arms. "I will."

"That doesn't make sense," Carrie said. "I work there anyway. You love this house. That's why we…"

"I loved this house because I wanted it for us—all of us," Julia said. "I made this decision. I'm not going to change anything more for you or the kids than I already am," she explained. She felt Carrie pull back and watched as her wife attempted to compose herself. "I know you are angry," Julia said. "I don't blame you."

"I am. I am angry," Carrie admitted. "I'm hurt and confused. I am terrified."

"I know," Julia said. "Me too."

"Then don't go," Carrie pleaded.

"You don't know how badly I want to stay. How much I will miss…"

"I know you'll miss the kids…"

Julia stopped Carrie midstream. "I will miss you, Care. I will."

Carrie nodded and sighed. Julia grabbed the bag she had packed and kissed Carrie's cheek. "I'll be here tomorrow so we can talk to the kids."

Carried nodded again. "Jules?"

"Yeah?" Julia stopped and answered.

"I hope you find what you are looking for," Carrie said.

"Oh, Care. I hope we all do," Julia said.

Julia turned back and placed a light kiss on Carrie's lips. "No matter what happens, I will always be here for you. Don't you ever doubt that," she promised.

Carrie could not answer. She watched as the woman she had shared the last fifteen years of her life with walked out of their bedroom door. She sat perfectly still until she heard Julia's car pull out of the driveway and promptly collapsed onto the bed. Carrie pulled a pillow to her and hugged it as if it were her lifeline. "Jules," she cried.

She looked up and glanced around the room then closed her eyes tightly. There were reminders everywhere of a life she somehow understood had just been forever changed. Pictures of Jake, Meghan, and Jordan surrounded her, pictures of her standing wrapped in Julia's embrace. She likened the grief to mourning a death. With a deep breath, she retrieved the photo that sat beside the bed. Julia was laughing as Carrie kissed her on the cheek. Jake had taken it three years ago on a skiing trip. Carrie clung to it with her pillow and grieved. It was a death. Julia would never have walked out the door if she believed they could repair their marriage. Carrie felt a cold shiver pass through her before succumbing to the emotional exhaustion of the evening.

"Jules," she whispered again. "I'll miss you."

≈ ≈ ≈

Julia sat at the kitchen table, nervously fiddling with the glass in front of her. She had arrived early in the afternoon. She had cried. Carrie had cried. They needed to decide how to break the news of their separation to their children. There was no happy way, no way to sugar coat the news or to make it more palatable for anyone. Julia immediately noticed the weariness in Carrie's eyes and she hated herself for causing it. Carrie was much calmer than she had been the previous evening. It seemed her anger had dissipated and given way to profound sadness. Julia would almost have preferred the anger. Carrie looked broken and that tore at Julia's soul.

Carrie reached over and stilled Julia's hand. Julia closed her eyes momentarily at the tenderness of her wife's touch. Carrie was devastated, yet she was comforting Julia. Julia pushed back her tears as she watched Carrie turn to address their three children.

"Listen, this is something that we both agreed to. Believe me, we both love you. Your mom and I...Well, we did not come to this decision easily, but it's where we are and we are all going to have to figure out how to get through it—together," Carrie said.

"Together? That's a joke. So, what? That's just it?" Jake yelled.

"Jake," Carrie cautioned him gently.

"No. What? You two just can't handle it. So, what? You just leave, Mom? That's your solution? It's that easy to just leave us?" he bellowed.

"Jake," Julia tried to keep her voice calm. "I'm not leaving you. I'm just going to stay at the studio for a while until Care and I can work through some things," she said.

"Until you can work through things or until you decide who is going to live where?" he asked pointedly. "What about us?" he demanded. "What are Meghan and Jordan and me supposed to do, huh?"

Julia sighed. Carrie intervened. "Jake, your mother will do still do all the things she always has, so will I. She just won't be here at the house every day."

"I'll still pick you up...We'll still," Julia began.

"You know what? Don't bother. You want to leave us all so badly? Go ahead. Obviously, you have more important things to do," he said viciously. "It's your decision to leave."

"Jake, your mother and I," Carrie made another effort to intervene.

"Why are you defending her, Care? Don't. I heard you two. I heard you crying when she left last night."

"Jake," Julia said gently.

"Save it. I don't need this, and I don't need you," he told Julia as he turned to leave with Meghan chasing after him.

"Jacob!" Carrie yelled to him. "Don't talk to your mother that way. Get back here! Meghan!'

"Let them go," Julia said sadly. "They have every right to hate me right now."

Carrie shook her head. "No, they don't. They have a right to be hurt. They don't have a right to talk to you that way," she said. "And, I am going to make sure they both understand that," Carrie said with a light squeeze to Julia's shoulder before leaving the room.

"Mom?" Jordan whispered to Julia. Julia looked at her youngest daughter as tears fell down both their cheeks. "Don't you love Ma anymore?" she asked.

Julia embraced Jordan and kissed her head. "Of course, I love your mother," she said. "Sometimes people just need to be apart. It doesn't mean they don't love each other."

"But you don't want to be married?" Jordan asked. "I thought if you loved somebody you wanted to be with them?"

Julia rested her head on Jordan's and closed her eyes. The innocent statement held far more truth than Jordan could have realized. Julia didn't know how she could explain to her daughter that being a part of someone's life didn't always mean living with them. Being part of a family, loving another person, meant letting them go every bit as much as it meant holding on. She could scarcely comprehend that reality as an adult.

"Oh, Jordan," Julia sighed. "Sometimes you have to love someone enough to let them go."

"You mean like how Jake is going away to college?" Jordan asked innocently.

Julia chuckled. Maybe Jordan could understand things better than the rest of them. She hadn't thought about it, but there were definite similarities. "A bit. People grow, like your brother. It's time for him to discover who he is without us there all the time. It's part of growing up," she said.

"But, you and Ma are already grown up," Jordan observed.

Julia chuckled lightly. "Well, I don't know about that. We are older. I think we are always growing up in our own ways."

"Mom?"

"Yeah?"

"Does Ma still love you?" Jordan asked.

"Yes, Jordan. Ma still loves me. And we both love you," she assured her daughter.

Jordan pulled back and smiled at her mother. "I love you too. Will you still pick me up on Fridays?"

"Yes. And, I will still be there whenever you need me and so will Ma. That will never change," Julia said.

Jordan wiggled her way closer to Julia and hugged her. "Okay, but I get to sleep on the futon when I come over," she said. "Meghan can't have it every time."

Julia giggled. "Deal."

Chapter Ten

Carrie hung up the phone with Julia and let out a heavy sigh. They had been living apart for a month. It had been nothing short of a roller coaster ride. Jake and Meghan were furious with Julia. Julia had insisted that they be allowed to work through their feelings in their own time. Carrie had obeyed that wish reluctantly. In four weeks, Jake had yet to stay in the room with his mother for more than five minutes. Meghan had only visited the loft apartment once. And, while Julia had made light of the visit, Carrie could see the evident pain in her wife's eyes. There had been no animosity in the separation between Carrie and Julia, but there had been more than enough disappointment and sadness to replace the space animosity could have filled. The situation with their two eldest children, however, was different, both continued to be hostile toward Julia.

A month of independence from Julia had begun to give Carrie perspective on their relationship. She still missed Julia, but as time continued to pass, she began to realize that their marriage had become complacent and comfortable. It was pleasant. She loved Julia. That was not a question. There had been a rift between them romantically for a long time. Intimacy at some point had become defined by quiet time in front of the television or on the front porch

135

without the presence of their children. Looking back over a number of years, intimacy had seldom entailed long embraces, physical affection or making love.

Carrie hadn't realized in the day to day chaos of family life how much she had missed that. She had accepted the nature of her relationship with Julia. Part of her wanted it back. The longer they lived apart, the more Carrie began to realize that she craved something more. She had stepped back from pursuing many of her career interests to support Julia's endeavors, and she had been happy to do so. Jake, Meghan, and Jordan meant everything to Carrie. She would do it all again without a moment's hesitation. She was beginning to realize that at the end of those chaotic days, she wanted a partner that held her, that slept beside her, and that needed her as something more than a second parent and friend. It sounded cold to her ears, but Carrie could not help but label her marriage to Julia as a business partnership. It was one founded on shared interests and ideals, and one in which affection and love existed, but it lacked passion and connection. That was something Carrie not only wanted, but it was also something that she needed. She took a sip from her coffee cup and prepared herself for the arrival of her wife. It was time for Carrie to present Julia with her needs and decisions. She hoped that Julia would agree and understand.

ớ ớ ớ

"Julia?" Michael gently nudged his ex-wife. "You didn't come here for my coffee. What's wrong?'

"Everything," Julia chuckled. "Carrie wants me to come over for dinner while the kids are at her parents' house."

"And that is a bad thing?" Michael asked. "I thought you two were getting along."

"We are," Julia said. "Sometimes I see her, how much she has struggled to handle all of this—the kids. God, Jake hasn't said a full sentence to me since I left. The only good thing to come out of any of this so far is the time I've gotten with Jordan one on one."

"Jordan is a lot like you, Jules," Michael chuckled. "And, Jake? Jake is seventeen. Half of him thinks he's invincible, and the other half is pissed off at the world. You can't let him keep treating you like this."

"You sound like Carrie."

"Well, she's right. So, what is it? Are you regretting the fact that you left?" he asked.

"Sometimes. There are times that I think it would be easier just to go back. Maybe somehow we would all hurt less," she admitted.

"But, there's more, isn't there? Is that really what you want, to go back to Carrie? What about you, Jules? There is something else, isn't there?" he raised a brow at Julia.

"Yes. I guess there is," she confessed.

Julia had tried to place Katie in the past for months. Nothing had worked. No matter what she did, no matter how much time passed, Katie inevitably was a part of her daily thoughts.

"So? How about you just say it? It's just us here now. Truth."

Julia looked at Michael and rested her head against the back of the couch. She closed her eyes, willing the breath to return to her body. She had never been able to keep secrets from him. A heavy sigh escaped her lips, and she shook her head.

"I don't know," Julia said with a sigh.

It was difficult to form words around the tightness in her throat. The pressure in her chest seemed to spread throughout her body. Emotion danced with reason and then spun reason away on its heels. Julia's truth was straining against any rational thought. It no longer remained content in the prison she had carefully constructed for it. She inhaled a breath for courage and resigned herself let it go.

"It's like I woke up, and there it was—not even a discovery. Like the universe banged on my door, screaming, 'Where have you been? Wake up! Look. She's right there.' And, there she was," Julia said.

Michael regarded his ex-wife intently. Julia had always relied on her principles to guide her. He sensed now that her principles and beliefs about many things were fighting an epic battle with her heart. He wasn't certain if he should push, but something in him felt inclined to do so.

"Katie," he guessed. Julia looked up with an astonished gaze. "I have known you a long time," he winked. "Are you in love with her?" he asked softly.

Julia shook her head. "Love? She's my friend. At least, I thought she was. Jesus, she doesn't even want to talk to me. If I think about it, I hardly know her, Michael."

"What do you need to know?" he asked.

"Michael! Jesus! This is insane. I've lost my mind," Julia snapped.

"I'm not so sure it's your mind you've lost," he answered. Julia looked at him and gave an uncomfortable chuckle. "Well?" he asked. "Jules, why can't you just admit what you feel?"

"Let me count the reasons."

"Do any of the reasons change the reality?" he returned. He watched as her face fell in silent defeat. "You are trying to reason with love? If that's the case, then you have lost your mind."

"Is that a clinical diagnosis, doctor?" Julia feebly attempted humor.

"I'm a trauma surgeon, not a psychiatrist."

"Pretty much the same thing in my case," she said.

Michael moved to sit beside her and smiled when Julia's head collapsed onto his shoulder. "Tell me," he encouraged her.

"I'm not sure I know how," Julia confessed. "It doesn't make sense. All I know is, it feels like there is a hole in me that I can't fill. I never noticed it was even there until…."

"Until Katie," Michael gently finished her thought. "And now?"

"And now? I don't know. Part of me is almost grateful. Isn't that bizarre?"

"Bizarre?" he inquired.

"Yeah, bizarre. My whole life is upside down. And, Katie?" Julia laughed. "We're barely friends if I stop and think about it. But, that night after the accident, we were sitting there in front of the fire, she looked at me as if she expected me to say something. I wasn't sure I was conscious, or breathing for that matter. I have never," Julia stopped abruptly to compose herself. "I thought I knew what it felt like."

"What?" Michael asked her.

"Love. I'm not sure anymore," she admitted as a tear washed over her cheek.

"It will be all right," he assured her.

"I don't know, Michael. I can't imagine having never felt that now. I swear my entire life passed in those few minutes in front of that fire. And, it makes me so angry sometimes."

"Angry?" Michael asked curiously.

"Yes, angry. I don't want to ever lose that moment, even if it's just a memory, and I know I will never have it again."

Michael sighed and nodded. "I wouldn't be so sure about that," he said. He could feel Julia's light shaking and pulled her closer into his embrace. "Maybe you should stop trying to put it all in those boxes you like so much, Jules. Let it be for now." He took a moment before continuing. "What about Carrie?" he asked.

"I love her."

"I know," he said. "But, Jules, you are in love with someone else."

Julia held her breath and tugged at her lip. "Maybe sometimes that just doesn't matter," she observed.

"When you convince yourself of that, you let me know," he said with a kiss to her head. "I can't tell you what to do. Don't you think you owe it to Katie to…"

"We haven't spoken in months," she said sadly. "It's like she just vanished. I don't know. Too much is happening all at once. Maybe I just need to let it be what is was, and accept what it's not."

"Maybe you should stop being so stubborn and just call her."

"I wish it were all that simple," Julia said to coin Katie's favorite phrase.

"Few things in life that are worthwhile are simple," he reminded her.

"Yeah, I know. Carrie may forgive me. I'm not sure the kids ever will," she said sorrowfully.

"You know better than that," he told her. "Sounds like you already have your answer, Jules."

Julia closed her eyes. "Why doesn't that make me feel any better?"

Michael pulled his ex-wife closer. "Because you love them all, and you don't want to hurt any of them."

"Mm." Julia sighed. "You give me too much credit, Michael. I'm not that selfless. I don't want to lose any of them," she admitted.

"I know," he said. "You don't give yourself enough credit either. You're many things, Jules. It isn't selfish to want to be with the people you love."

"Yes, it is," she said.

"Then we are all destined to be convicted of that crime," Michael told her. "Give it time, Julia. It might not all turn out the way you'd like, but that doesn't mean they can't all be a part of your life."

"I guess we will see."

≈◡ ≈◡ ≈◡

Julia sat on the sofa with a glass of wine. She could see the hint of apprehension in Carrie's eyes. They had enjoyed a casual conversation over dinner, but she was certain there was something more on her wife's mind. "What's up?" she finally asked.

Carrie took a deep breath and chuckled. "No fooling you, huh?"

"Fraid not," Julia winked.

"Okay. Here goes," Carrie said. "I want you to move home," she said in one breath.

Julia was stunned. "Care..."

"Let me finish," Carrie held up her hand. "I want you to move home and I will move into the loft over the studio."

"What?" Julia asked in confusion. "Carrie...No. I am not..."

"Julia! Please, let me get this out. Please," Carrie pleaded. Julia nodded with a ragged breath. "Look, there are a few reasons. I've been thinking about this for a while. I have a chance to shoot a piece for a major magazine on the women's music scene," Carrie said.

"That's fabulous, Care," Julia said.

"Yeah. It is. But, Julia, it will mean I am away for three weeks documenting a national festival tour with The Pedestals," Carrie explained.

"That's why you want me to move home?" Julia asked. "You don't have to move to the loft, Care. I will stay here until…"

Carrie smiled. "No. I want to start taking more of these assignments. I'll need to be in the studio more when I do. You know it's something I always said I wanted to pursue when the kids were older," she said. Julia smiled. "And, Julia, you have got to confront this issue with Jake and Meghan," Carrie said flatly. She saw Julia begin to mount an argument and stopped it. "Don't. I have respected your feelings, but this has gone far enough. You are their mother. They need to respect you. They need to respect us and move past this. I know you hate confrontation, but it has gone far enough. It's killing you, and inside it is killing them. I can't stand by any longer and pretend it is all right. It's not. No matter what, I love you. I won't watch you allow yourself to be beaten up so you can somehow appease your guilt," Carrie said. Julia closed her eyes and groaned. "No more guilt. It isn't helping anyone. Jake graduates in two weeks. We are going to celebrate that, and you are going to be a part of it the way that you should be. You two are not spending his last two months home at odds. I won't stand for it. It's time to put this family back together," Carrie said. "That may look different now, but we are still a family."

Julia sighed and nodded. "Are you sure this is what you want?" she asked. Carrie nodded. "Okay," Julia said as she set her glass down. "There is something I need to talk to you about too."

Carrie held her breath and braced herself. "Go on," she said calmly.

"I'm leaving the foundation," Julia told her.

"What?" Carrie asked. It was not the direction that she anticipated their conversation was about to take.

"You know that I get offers all of the time to consult privately," Julia explained. "I think it's time I struck out on my own. I've been thinking about it for a while."

"When did you decide this?" Carrie asked curiously.

"Just now."

"What?" Carrie shook her head in disbelief. "Jules…"

"It makes sense. I want you to go and do what you have always wanted. You and I both know that will mean more travel. If I'm on my own professionally, I will have more flexibility. Plus, the money is good. I have the contacts," Julia said.

"I don't want you to make this decision because of me," Carrie said honestly. "We can make it work."

"Carrie, no matter what has happened, there is never going to be a decision I make…. I will always consider you, your feelings, how it will impact our children and our family. That hasn't changed because we aren't living together, and it never will. It's the right time for me. This just helps me make that final leap and do it," Julia said honestly.

Carrie smiled. "Jules, when I get back…We," she faltered and closed her eyes.

"I know," Julia said quietly. "We have realities to settle. I know. I'll start the ball rolling while you are away."

Carrie shook her head. "Some days I still can't believe this has all happened."

Julia understood. "I know. You know that I love you?"

"I know that," Carrie said with a solemn smile. "You just aren't in love with me."

Julia did not respond. "What about the kids?" Julia asked. "Do you want to tell them together?"

"About which things?" Carrie let out a nervous giggle.

"Point taken," Julia said.

"I will tell them about my decision when they get home tomorrow. When I get back, I think we should tell them about the divorce together," Carrie sighed.

Julia covered her face to still her emotions. "This sucks."

"Sure does," Carrie agreed.

"I'm proud of you," Julia said through some tears.

"Of me? What for?"

Julia smiled. "Oh, I think you know. You are a terrific mom, Care. There have been so many days I've wanted to just stay in bed. You've put everyone else first, even me," Julia said in awe. Carrie smirked. "What?" Julia asked.

"There were a few nights I wanted to throw your books in that fireplace," Carrie admitted. Julia had no doubt that was the truth, but she could see the twinkle in Carrie's eyes. "There are more nights that I just miss you," Carrie said honestly.

"Me too," Julia said.

"I know."

"When do you want me here?" Julia changed the subject.

"I leave on July 2nd."

"Going to play groupie. Sounds like an adventure," Julia joked.

"I think my groupie days are over, but it certainly will be a change from the pace I am used to," Carrie laughed.

"Care, if you want me here when you talk to the kids…"

"No," Carrie said. "I'll call you tomorrow after I talk to them. Why don't we plan on a family dinner Sunday?"

"Are you cooking?" Julia asked lightheartedly.

"No. You still know how to turn on the grill, don't you?" Carrie poked.

"Understood," Julia laughed.

"Good."

≈ ≈ ≈

"So, what's with the family meeting?" Jake asked Carrie.

"Just jump right to the point, Jake," Carrie chuckled.

"Well?" he asked.

"Before we start this, I want your word, Jacob, and you too, Meghan, that you will sit here and listen to what I have to say," Carrie told her children.

"If this is about her," Jake began.

"Jacob Riley! I have had enough of this from you," Carrie said sternly. She had never been the disciplinarian in the family and Jake wiggled slightly in his chair at her tone of voice. Carrie sighed. "I mean it. You two have gone quite far enough with the way you are treating your mother," she said with disgust.

"She's the one who left," Jacob mumbled.

"Yes. She is," Carrie agreed. All three children looked up in shock. "She did not leave any of you."

"No, she left you," Meghan said sadly.

Carrie sighed again. "No, Megs. She didn't. She stepped away. I know that hurts, but as much as that hurts all of you, you need to understand how difficult it has been for her."

"I heard you," Jake said softly.

"I know you did, Jacob. You heard your mother leave, and you heard me crying. I am sorry that you overheard any of that. You were not meant to."

"How can you just act like it's okay?" Jake began to raise his voice.

"Jake," Carrie softened her tone. "Listen to me. I love your mother. I will always love your mother."

"She doesn't love us that much," Meghan muttered.

"Yes, she does!" Jordan snapped. "You two are so mean," she said as she began to cry.

"Enough!" Carrie put her foot down. "Jordan, come here," she directed her daughter into her lap.

"Your word," she looked at Meghan and Jacob. They both nodded.

"Good," Carrie said as she wiped away Jordan's tears. "Your mother is moving home."

"You mean you…" Meghan popped up in her chair.

"No. I asked her to come back to the house so that I can move into the loft for a while," Carrie said.

"So, now you are leaving us?" Jake snapped.

"No one is leaving anyone," Carrie said with a warning tone. "And, no one is leaving this table until everyone understands that." She watched as Jake and Meghan looked at the table and avoided her gaze. "I have an opportunity to take an assignment with a major magazine. Your mother supports that fully. I'll be away for three weeks in July."

"And then you will come back here?" Jordan asked innocently.

"No. Your mom is going to stay in the house. I will be at the studio more than I have been. It makes sense for us. And," she reached across the table and grabbed Jake and Meghan's arms. "It makes sense for you. You need some time with your mom," she told them.

"I don't…" Jake began to argue.

"Stop it," Carrie told him. She sensed that there was more to Jacob's actions than just anger, and she had an inkling what it might be. "Meghan, would you and Jordan give me a few minutes with your brother, please?" Meghan nodded and led Jordan from the room. Jake continued to shift uncomfortably in his chair. "Okay, Jake, let's have it," Carrie said.

"I don't know what you are talking about," he mumbled.

"We can play twenty questions, but that will take a lot longer," Carrie said with a poke to his arm. She could see her son wrestling with something.

"It doesn't matter," he told her.

Carrie could see the tears in his eyes. At seventeen, crying was completely uncool. Crying in front of your parents was a catastrophe from which one would surely never recover. "Jake," Carrie urged him.

"What about me?" he asked her. His eyes finally lifted to meet Carrie's, and there was no more holding back his fear. "You leave now and that's it for me. I'm not like Meghan and Jordan."

It was the answer that Carrie had suspected had been driving Jacob's behavior. Meghan was impressionable and following along, not understanding what was plaguing her brother's mind. Carrie moved her chair next to Jacob and looked at him lovingly.

"You think because your mom had you before I met her, that you mean less to me than your sisters do?" she asked him. Jacob stared blankly at her as he struggled to keep hold of his tears. "You were just about to turn three when I met your mother," Carrie said. "Do you know that you were part of our first real date?" He shrugged. "Jacob, I didn't give birth to either of your sisters. Do you think that I love them less?"

"No, but they are Uncle Ted's..."

"I see. You think because biologically they are my nieces that makes them more my children than it does you?" she asked him.

"Maybe," he said.

Carrie smiled and shook her head. "You know, one of the main reasons your mom and I wanted to have more children was you." He looked at her doubtfully. "It's true. We wanted you to have siblings, and honestly, I always wished that I could have been there when you were born. I missed a part of your life."

"I don't remember that," Jake said sincerely.

"I know," Carrie winked. "For a long time, I worried about what you would think as you got older. Your mom and dad have a great friendship. You already had two parents who loved you. I was just Care," she told him.

"Just because I don't call you Ma, like Meg and Jordan, doesn't mean you aren't my mom," Jacob said honestly.

"Mm-hm. I know that and just because we don't share the same DNA doesn't mean you aren't my son," she countered. Jacob began to falter, and Carrie pulled him to her. "Jake, no matter what could ever happen and no matter how old you get, both your mother and I will see you as the little boy we used to take to the playground."

Jacob's tears finally defied his will, and he collapsed against Carrie. "Why did this have to happen?" he asked her.

Carrie's tears mingled with her son's as she comforted him. "Oh, sweetie," she said with a kiss to his head as if he were still a toddler. "Things just change sometimes. I know it's different, but we're still a family."

"It sucks."

"Yes, it does," Carrie agreed with a chuckle.

"Do you still love her?" Jake asked hesitantly.

Carrie sighed. "I will always love her," she replied honestly. "It's just not the same as it was, Jake. I wish it were."

Jake pulled back from the embrace and wiped his tears with the back of his hand. "She probably hates me right now," he said.

Carrie laughed. "I think you know that is not true. She's hurt, Jake. You have always been the light of your mother's life. This hasn't been easy for her either."

"Aren't you pissed at her?" he asked.

"I was," Carrie admitted. "But, the truth is that she saw things I wasn't willing to see." Carrie could see the confusion in her son's eyes. "One day you will understand what I mean. Right now, you have some fences to mend," she told him.

He nodded. "What am I supposed to say?" he asked.

"Well, neither you nor your mother has ever been known to be short on words," she joked. "But, what you both lack in brevity, you make up for in pigheadedness," she chuckled. She watched as a smirk crossed his face. "So, when she gets here tomorrow," Carrie said as Jake looked at her apprehensively. "Yes, Jake, your mother will be here tomorrow for a family dinner. Perhaps, you should just start with hello."

He nodded. "Care?"

"Hum?"

"Would it be okay...I mean, sometimes...If I called you Mom? Now that it won't be so confusing," he hurriedly explained. Carrie was stunned. "Well, would it?"

"Of course," she said. "I love you, Jake.

"I love you too.... Mom," he answered, feeling suddenly lighter than he had in months.

❧ ❧ ❧

Julia was flipping burgers, sipping on a beer when the sound of the back door startled her. She was surprised when she looked up to see Jake approaching sheepishly.

"Hey," he greeted his mother.

"Hi, Jake," Julia replied.

"What are you doing?" he asked, not knowing how to start a conversation.

Julia smiled inwardly. She couldn't imagine what Carrie had said to their son, but she couldn't wait to ask. This was the most talkative he had been in a month. Julia pointed to the grill.

"Care relegated me to burger duty," she explained.

"Can I help?" he asked.

Julia eyed him curiously. "Not unless you want to stand here and watch meat cook," she winked. He shrugged and started to turn away. "But, I wouldn't mind the company," she called after him. He shrugged again with a smile that portrayed all of his insecurity and sat down on one of the deck chairs. "So, are you excited about graduation?" she asked him.

"I guess," he said.

Julia closed the grill and took a seat next to him. "You guess?" Julia quizzed him. Another shrug was the only response she received. "Jake? Look, if there is something you need to say to me, you can say it."

He looked up at his mother and sighed. "I'm pissed that you left."

"I know," Julia said.

"Now, you are coming back and Care has to leave."

Julia rubbed her forehead in frustration. "I know, Jake. I'm sorry. I really am."

"What am I supposed to do when I come home from school?" he asked his mother.

"What do you mean?" Julia asked.

"I mean, where is home, Mom? Kids go home from college, right? Where is that going to be? Here? At Dad's? With Care? How am I supposed to choose between three parents? It's bad enough choosing between two," he explained.

Julia felt her temples begin to throb. She had pondered a wide array of issues that she felt sure her children were concerned about. Somehow, this had completely escaped her consideration. She rubbed her eyebrow in thought and shook her head.

"Shit," Julia groaned.

"What?" Jake asked. "Did you just swear?" he tried not to laugh at his mother. Julia could outswear a sailor in the right circumstance, but she seldom let them slip in front of her children.

"Yeah, I did," Julia chuckled as she realized her slip. "Is that what you think? That you have to choose between the three of us?"

"Don't I?" he countered.

"No," Julia responded emphatically. "Absolutely not. You can stay anywhere you want, Jake. We will all make a point to spend time with you unless you don't want that," she finished.

"No matter what I do, someone's feelings are going to be hurt," he observed.

Julia nodded and took a sip from her beer. "That's probably true," she said. Jake looked at his mother in surprise. "What? You want me to tell you that because we are all grown up, we don't have feelings?" she asked him. "You'll be eighteen in a month, Jake. You can handle some truth," she said.

He looked at Julia and braced himself. Something told Jake that his mother was about to give him a dose of honesty that he had not expected. "What do you mean?" he asked.

"You are right," Julia said. "All of us will hope that you want to stay where we are. That's a fact, and when you choose to stay with Care or your dad, I'll be disappointed."

"Yeah. See what I mean?" he mumbled.

"I do see what you mean," Julia said. "That's one of the shitty things in life sometimes, Jake," she said with a raise of her beer. Jake watched his mother carefully as she continued her uncharacteristic candor. "What I mean is that you can't always have everything just the way you'd like. Sometimes you have to make choices, and sometimes no matter how much you hate it, your choices are going to hurt someone you care about."

"You're talking about leaving Care," he said with a grimace.

"No. Although, that is certainly a good example," Julia admitted. "Jacob, all you can do in life is your best—try and be honest. Tell the people you care for that you do care for them—that's about it. Sometimes there are no good choices or bad choices but just choices to make."

"How can you say that?" he asked her. "If you are going to hurt someone, how can that be a good thing?"

"It isn't. Look, you are exactly right. No matter who you choose to stay with, two of us will miss you. That's a fact. We'll miss you because we love you, though, not because you did something to hurt us. We know that you love us. Hurt is a selfish emotion, Jacob."

"You think I am selfish?" he asked. "You think Care is selfish for being hurt?" he asked his mother in disbelief.

"I think we are all selfish. We all want to be happy. We all want to be loved, and none of us wants to feel pain. It's like when someone dies. Our grief is not for them as much as it is for what we will miss. It's not a bad thing, Jacob. It's just part of being human," she said with a smile.

Jake remained silent for a few moments. He watched his mother return to the grill to check their dinner. She was sipping her beer and humming quietly. He smiled at the familiar feelings it prompted.

"Mom?" Julia turned to the sound of her son's voice. "Do you think you will ever love anyone again?"

Julia studied her son carefully. She let the question roll around in her mind for a few moments and then smiled. "Are you asking me if I think that I could love someone other than Care, or if I think I will ever be with someone other than Care?" she asked.

"What's the difference?"

"There's a big difference," she said. "The answer is, I don't know," she told him.

"What if she does?" he asked. "Won't that bother you at all?"

Julia sighed. "Probably," she chuckled. "But, that is exactly what I mean. Selfishly, yes—it probably will hurt when she finds someone new," Julia confessed. Jake nodded. "But, I hope she does," Julia said sincerely.

"Why?"

"Because, Jake…Loving someone isn't about keeping them. It's about letting them go."

"That doesn't make sense," he said.

"No? Sure it does. You know, your little sister helped me to understand that more than I ever had," Julia said proudly. Her conversation with Jordan the night they had explained that Julia would be leaving had opened her eyes. "It's like watching you go off to college six hundred miles away," she explained. "I wish you would stay right here," Julia admitted. "I love you enough to let you fly farther away."

"Not the same," Jake said.

"Isn't it?" she asked him. Julia turned off the grill and sat down beside her son again.

"Mom, the burgers…"

"They'll wait," Julia said. "Loving someone means holding on when they need you to and setting them free when the time comes. You can only hope that when they land, it will be close to you again. If you really love them, you will love them no matter how far they fly or where they nest. And, sometimes that is painful, but it is always worth it, Jake. Always."

Jake felt his mother place a kiss on his cheek and smiled.

"I know the last couple of months have been hard," Julia told her son. "I know how much my leaving hurt you," she admitted. "I love you. Care loves you. Your dad loves you. I hope you know that," she said honestly.

Jake nodded. "Where do you think you will land?" he asked his mother.

Julia smiled. "I don't know, Jake," she laughed. "I really don't know."

Chapter Eleven

JULY 2015

"Steph! Come on!" Katie called up the stairs. She was already running later than she wanted. This would be the first trip for Stephanie and Ian to their father's new home in San Diego. The last thing Katie needed on top of the anxiousness that had settled in her stomach was to miss their flight. "Steph!"

"I'm almost done!" Stephanie yelled back.

"Sweet Lord," Katie muttered to herself. "She's twelve. What the hell is going to happen when she hits sixteen?"

"What did you say, Mom?" Ian asked as he slipped on his jacket.

"Nothing. Just wondering what on earth your sister is doing. Steph!"

"Probably looking in the mirror. Again," Ian rolled his eyes.

Katie snickered as Stephanie finally made her way down the stairs. "Geez, Mom. I thought you were gonna have a heart attack there," Stephanie said with a pat on her mother's shoulder.

"Very funny," Katie replied. "All your hairs in the proper place now?" she poked at her daughter while Ian taunted Stephanie in the background.

"Ha-ha," Stephanie said. "Knock it off you little troll," Stephanie pinched her brother's arm.

"Oww!"

Katie forced a smile. "Are you two through now?" she asked her children. They both giggled. "Excellent. Then, can we please leave?"

Katie watched Stephanie and Ian race to the waiting car and exhaled forcefully. The trip to the west coast had timed perfectly for Katie. She had been slated to interview Rachel Shears, a rising star on television, and it happened to coincide with her soon to be ex-husband's request for a visit. She suspected there was more on his mind than just seeing their children. Katie had asked him if there was anything she should be concerned about. He had attempted to placate her fears, but his efforts had a tone that she immediately recognized. There was something Bill Brennan was not telling her. That made Katie incredibly uneasy. She had some news of her own that she needed to deliver, although she expected hers would pale by comparison to whatever Bill had in store for her. She stopped just shy of the car and inhaled a deep breath. "Here we go."

≈ ≈ ≈

"You all set?" Julia asked Carrie.

"I hope so," Carrie replied. She looked at Julia and frowned. "What's wrong?" Carrie asked.

Julia shook her head. "Nothing. Honestly. I guess it will be a little weird," she said.

Carrie sniggered. While they had not lived together for a couple of months, Julia and Carrie still spoke almost daily. It was one of the realities that came with juggling three children's busy schedules and their own. The truth was, Carrie was going to miss seeing Julia as well.

"We've never been apart more than a few days," Carrie said. "At least, we've always seen each other at some point."

Julia sighed. She knew that she was going to miss Carrie, and she understood that this was a necessary evolution in their new lives. Julia was immensely proud of Carrie. Carrie was a talented photographer and Julia looked forward to seeing what the future held for her wife—her wife. She wondered when she would stop referring to Carrie that way mentally. Soon, Carrie would be her ex-wife. That reality was not lost on Julia. They had filed the papers the day after Jake's graduation. There was a finality to it that Julia had tried to avoid pondering.

She and Carrie had decided not to wait to tell their three children about the divorce. There was no reason to procrastinate. Jake and Meghan were coming around slowly. Keeping it from them for even a few weeks might have appeared a deception. After Jake's graduation, Julia and Carrie made several important decisions. The first had been to tell their children that their separation was permanent and would be legal. The second had been to initiate a new ritual, a weekly family dinner. The last had been to make a pact that no matter what changes occurred in their lives, they would make an effort to continue family gatherings. It had helped to begin to heal some of their wounds. Now, Carrie would be gone for three full weeks. Shortly after her return, they would take Jake to college in Virginia. Everything was changing rapidly.

Carrie had hedged on following through with her assignment earlier in the week, saying she didn't feel comfortable leaving. With Jake leaving in a few weeks, Carrie had confessed to Julia that she was having second thoughts. Julia had listened quietly before telling Carrie that this was her time and she needed to take it. When

Carrie broke down, Julia had rocked her gently until she finally regained her composure.

"*You have to go,*" *Julia said.*

"*No. I don't think I should. He'll only be here a few more weeks,*" *Carrie cried.*

"*Care, he'll be back. Jake understands. He's excited for you. You need to go do this.*"

Carrie trembled in Julia's embrace. "*I feel like there are too many goodbyes. I'm tired of goodbyes. I don't want to miss...*"

"*I understand, but think of all the people you will meet,*" *Julia offered.*

"*They are strangers,*" *Carrie said.*

"*Only because you haven't met them yet,*" *Julia winked.* "*Now, come on. You need to pack so you can go off on the road and be a groupie.*"

"Jules? Hey, are you sure everything is okay? I lost you there for a minute," Carrie said.

"I'm fine. Maybe a little jealous of your impending adventures."

"I think you have watched *Almost Famous* a few too many times," Carrie laughed.

"Funny."

"Sometimes I am," Carrie quipped.

Julia walked Carrie to the car and threw Carrie's bags inside. "Be safe," she said.

Carrie narrowed her gaze playfully at Julia. "I'll try not to sleep with too many guitarists," she joked.

Julia nodded. "Mm-hm. Enjoy it, Care."

"The guitarists?" Carrie laughed.

"Already on your way to breaking some hearts, huh?" Julia asked lightly.

Carrie shook her head. "Think I'm more into the healing," she said seriously.

Julia nodded. "I'll talk to you," she said with a kiss to Carrie's cheek. "You know," she pulled back and looked at Carrie. "If you did meet a sexy guitarist, I'd be happy for you."

Carrie smiled. "I know," she said with a touch of melancholy. "With my luck, it'll be a frumpy grandmother."

Julia laughed as Carrie started to pull away. "Wait! Hey! What do you mean with your luck? I'm not frumpy! And, I don't have any grandchildren!" Julia shouted after the car. Carrie just waved out the window. "Well, I don't. Wait…. Jake!"

∾ ∾ ∾

Katie sat on the patio at her husband's new home while he retrieved them each a beer. She was feeling unsettled. Bill was nervous, and Katie wanted to know why.

"Here you go," he said.

"Thanks," Katie replied.

"So? What do you think?" he asked. "The kids seem to like it."

"It has a pool," Katie remarked with a grin. "You may never see them inside again."

"One of the bonuses to moving here. The pool, I mean," he clarified.

Katie nodded. She shifted a bit in her chair and looked at Bill intently. Katie held his gaze firmly, silently imploring him to give her his news.

He sighed. "You want to know what prompted this visit," he said. Katie just lifted an eyebrow. "There's a few reasons, Katie. It's not like the kids wouldn't have been here in a few weeks to visit.

I'm not officially coaching until next March. You know that. Right now, I am still going through my physical therapy, mainly doing administrative things. I have some interviews later this month. This was an ideal week."

"Uh-huh."

"And besides, you mentioned you had some news yourself," he said.

"Somehow, I have a feeling my news is not going to be very thrilling once we get to yours," Katie said.

"I guess we'll see. So, what is it? Neil finally manage to sweep you off your feet?" he asked.

"God, Bill. What is it with you and Neil? I thought we moved past all this when you came home," Katie rolled her eyes.

"Well?" he urged his wife.

"No. Neil has not, and will never sweep me off my feet, as you put it," Katie replied evenly.

"So, what's your news?" he asked.

"My contract is up in October at the network."

"And..."

"And, I am asking that they move the taping of the show to Boston, along with some changes in format and in control over the content," she said.

"What if they refuse? Katie, you know the networks like to keep their..."

"If they refuse, I will leave," she interrupted him.

"Leave? And do what?" Bill asked.

Katie took a sip of her beer and shrugged. "I don't know—teach, maybe."

"As in school?" Bill asked. Katie shot him a disgusted glare. "I mean, why not look into local broadcasting or what about..."

"Bill, either they agree or they don't. Until I know that, I can't make any career decisions. I have plenty of possibilities. Either way, I'm moving home," she said.

"So, home is Boston?" he asked.

"Home is where the people I love the most are," Katie answered honestly.

Bill Brennan nodded his understanding. "Your parents and John must be thrilled."

"They don't know yet. No one does. I have some things I need to put in order, like the house. Unless you want it. If not, I want to put it on the market when I get back."

"I've been thinking that I should look into something small, a condo maybe, something closer to the kids. You know, so I can see them there more often," he answered. "But, no, I don't want the house." Katie nodded. "What else?" he asked.

"Obviously, I need to find a new house. I want to do that before the kids start back to school in September," Katie said.

"You haven't told them?"

"No. Our divorce isn't even final until next month. Believe it or not, I still think significant things concerning our children should be discussed between us before they are told to them. I would hope you agree," Katie said.

Bill sighed. "I do agree. That's part of what I wanted to talk you about." Katie waited curiously for her husband to continue. "I've been doing a lot of thinking since the accident."

"About?" Katie asked.

"About where we went wrong. I never intended that, Katie, everything that happened. I made a lot of mistakes. I don't want to make the same ones again," he said.

"I'm not sure I follow you," Katie admitted.

Bill took a deep breath and released it slowly. "Yvette and I, well, we've been talking about things."

"Yvette? Yvette Summers? As in the Yvette that was in your car the day of the accident? That Yvette?" Katie asked as unemotionally as she could manage.

"Yes," he said. "That Yvette. Katie, we…Yvette and I…"

"Are you trying to tell me you are seeing her again?" Katie asked.

"It's more than that," he said.

"I see."

"She's…. Katie, she's pregnant."

Katie began to laugh uncontrollably. She was so disgusted and so completely taken off guard that laughter was the only response she could manage.

"I can't say I expected that reaction," Bill said. "You find this funny?"

Katie composed herself and shook her head. "No, I don't. I find it pathetic."

"Pathetic?" he asked harshly.

"You want to tell me that the woman you were sleeping with when we were married…At least, the last one…. The one you told me meant nothing to you, is pregnant with your child, and we aren't even divorced yet," she said. Bill started to respond and Katie talked over him. "Oh, and you think that telling me while our children are several yards away in your pool is a good idea. What did you expect?" she asked.

"Look, if you had wanted to work on our marriage, I would never have started seeing her again," he said.

Katie laughed again. "I'm sure," she said. "Okay…So, Yvette is pregnant. What now?" Katie asked Bill.

"We're going to get married," he said in one breath.

Katie arched her eyebrow. "Should I expect an invitation before or after our divorce is final?" she asked.

"Give me a little credit," he replied.

"Oh, I give you lots of credit, Bill. Believe me."

"Why are you so upset? You are the…"

"I'm not upset that you are seeing someone. I am concerned that our children are at impressionable ages, about to go through a move, are just dealing with our split, and you want to announce a new marriage. That's a lot to ask of a twelve and nine-year-old, don't you think?" she asked him pointedly.

"I understand that. I didn't plan this, Katie. It just happened. I want to do the right thing here. Don't you want them to have that example?"

Katie sighed. "Look, you don't need my permission, and you don't need my absolution. But, please do me a favor."

"What?" he asked.

"Don't drop Yvette on them until the divorce is final," Katie said.

"That's not an easy request. She lives here," he said.

Katie stared at her husband in disbelief. "Jesus Christ!" Katie had to take a deep breath to calm herself. "She lives here? You want me to leave Stephanie and Ian here with the two of you—together? They know, Bill. They've seen the news. You know what Stephanie has gone through with the teasing at school. Why would you subject her to this?"

"To what? What am I supposed to do?"

"I don't know. Have Yvette stay with a friend. You haven't seen the kids for over a month. They need to be secure with you before you ask them to accept anyone else, pregnant or not. God, especially Yvette Summers. Yes, you will have to tell them. At least, let them think this trip was all about them. I think you can hold your news until the divorce is final. Babies take a while," she reminded him.

Bill Brennan sighed. "I'm sorry. I wasn't thinking about that," he said sincerely.

"No, I know," Katie replied. "I know you aren't trying to be hurtful, Bill. It is hurtful."

"I'm not trying to hurt you…"

"Not to me," Katie said. "To the kids."

"Would you tell me?" he asked Katie.

"Tell you what?"

"If you were involved with someone else?" he asked.

"If it was serious enough, of course."

"So, nothing serious?" he continued.

"I'm not seeing Neil, Bill. I'm not seeing anyone," she said. "If and when I do decide to have a relationship, I can promise you it will only be if I find someone I know values our relationship and my children as much as I do."

"Is that a judgment on Yvette or me?" he asked.

"Neither. It's a fact about me. You asked me a question. I gave you an honest answer."

"I'll figure something out for this week. She won't like it, but…"

"If she loves you and she values you, if she honestly wants a life with you, she will respect your decision. She'll understand the fact that your children have been through a great deal this year, and that you need to put them first right now," Katie said. "She'll be there when you are ready."

Bill nodded. "You might be right, but not many people are like that, Katie. They aren't patient enough for that."

Katie chuckled. "No, maybe there aren't that many, or maybe there are just a few who love you enough to wait for you.

Most of us just don't have the patience to wait long enough to find them."

❧ ❧ ❧

THREE WEEKS LATER

"So?" Julia asked Carrie.

Carrie had regaled the family with some entertaining stories about life on the road with a popular club band. She had shared a few of her favorite pictures. Julia sensed there was something Carrie was holding back. She was both curious and beginning to become concerned. The few conversations that they had shared while Carrie was away indicated that the assignment was going well. It was clear to Julia that Carrie was struggling with something. She was having difficulty determining whether that something was a potentially positive thing or if something had occurred that had upset Carrie in some way.

"What?" Carrie asked.

Meghan and Jordan had grown bored of their mothers' company and the decidedly adult conversation. They had retired to the family room to entertain themselves with a movie. Jake had excused himself with a kiss to Carrie's cheek to go spend some time with his friends. That had left Carrie and Julia alone for the first time in over three weeks.

"Care?" Julia said with a slight chuckle. "You don't think that three weeks apart means I have forgotten everything about you, do you?" Julia asked. "Something is on your mind. It sounds like you had a great time. From what you shared, it looks like it will be a fabulous piece," Julia observed. Carrie nodded apprehensively. "What happened? Did you break some guitarist's heart after all?" Julia asked lightly. She watched Carrie closely as Carrie toyed with the napkin in front of her, refusing to meet Julia's eyes. Julia tugged at her bottom lip gently as she processed the reaction. "She must be something pretty special," Julia said honestly.

Carrie looked up with watery eyes. "Nothing happened, Jules."

Julia smiled in earnest. "And, it would be all right if it had, Care."

"Would it, really?" Carrie asked.

"Yes," Julia said as she took hold of Carrie's hand.

"I don't know if that makes me feel more relieved or sad," Carrie admitted.

Julia nodded. "I didn't say it doesn't hurt," she admitted with a wink. "Because, it does hurt a little to know that someone has captured your attention enough that you are afraid to tell me." Carrie looked at Julia apologetically. Julia smiled. "But, if someone has, and I think someone has, then I am happy for you, Care."

"I don't even know what it means, Jules," Carrie said. "We're just friends."

"But part of you thinks that it could be more," Julia guessed. Carrie nodded. "Why is that upsetting you?" Julia asked.

"Why? Jules…. God, my life has been with you for almost fifteen years. Our family means everything to me. You know that," Carrie said. Julia waited for her to continue. "I'm not ready to…. We're not even divorced…"

"We're separated," Julia said.

"I'm not ready," Carrie said softly. "I'm not ready to be dating anyone."

Julia sat quietly for a moment. She studied Carrie and then chuckled. "Love's a bitch," she said.

"I'm not in love, Julia," Carrie snapped defensively.

"Okay. Lust is a bitch."

"Julia!"

"What?"

Carrie started to snicker slightly. "Stop. This is so…"

"What? Strange? You mean talking to your soon to be ex-wife about your new girlfriend," Julia goaded.

"I don't have a girlfriend. A friend. Just a friend," Carrie said.

"A friend, that maybe, just maybe you think could be your soon to be girlfriend?" Julia asked with a smile.

"How can you be so calm?" Carrie snapped again.

"Care, you think because I am teasing you that I don't feel anything? God, come on. I'm not in love with the idea of seeing you with anyone else, and I didn't expect you to find someone so soon…"

"Jules…"

"Will you just be quiet for one minute?" Julia scolded Carrie lightly. "Look, I was kidding when you left about finding a sexy guitarist, but I meant it when I said that I would support you when that happened, and I will."

Carrie sighed heavily. "We're just friends." Julia nodded. "But, I think she would like it to be more than that."

"And you wouldn't?" Julia asked gently.

"I don't know. I'm so confused," Carrie said as her tears began to surface again.

"Why?" Julia asked.

"Because I feel like I am betraying you," Carrie said.

Julia scooted her chair closer to Carrie. "Don't do this to yourself, please, Care."

"It's too soon."

"If you honestly feel it is too soon, then tell her that," Julia said. "But, don't walk away from something that might be good for you because of me," she said honestly. "I love you. You know that. I accepted what leaving meant. We both did."

"Then why does it hurt so much?" Carrie asked. "How can I feel so excited and so devastated at the same time?"

Julia wiped away Carrie's tears and smiled. "Because things have changed. Because it is proof of the finality of us," she said compassionately. "Because it means risking your heart again. That means not knowing the outcome."

Carrie looked at Julia knowingly. "Speaking from experience?" she asked.

Julia offered her wife an uncomfortable smile. "I just want you to be happy," she said sincerely.

"I know," Carrie said. "But, Jules, I just met her."

"Did that matter when you met me?" Julia asked.

"It's different," Carrie replied.

"How so?"

"Because I did meet you, Julia. We had a life together for a long time, one that still means a great deal to me. And, while I know that you have moved past that…Well, I don't know that I am ready to let it be the past yet."

Julia allowed her tears to fall. "You really think that? That I am past us? Carrie…Listen to me. You will always be a part of my life. No one will change that, and something new can't diminish our time together. Nothing could ever do that."

"You think I should see her," Carrie surmised.

"I think that you should do whatever it is your heart is telling you to do."

"What if I don't know what it is telling me?" Carrie asked.

Julia smiled. "You do know. You're just too busy trying to convince yourself otherwise," she said with a wink.

"I still love you," Carrie whispered.

"I know," Julia said. "And, I love you. But, we both know that love changed a while ago. So, tell me about her. What's her name? It is a her? This.... Wait...Let me guess, a guitarist?"'

Carrie shook her head in genuine amusement. She could detect the underlying hint of sadness in Julia's voice, but she was touched by Julia's determination to be supportive and encourage her.

"Yes, it is a her. Bess, and no. Drummer," Carrie answered her wife's playful questions.

Julia nodded. "Bess, huh? All right, tell me about the drummer named Bess."

Chapter Twelve

Julia's Journal

It's a funny thing the way people talk about time. I never paid much attention until recently. Time seems to explain everything in life for people. They blame it for what they cannot recapture. They look to it to justify choices and changes. Time is an explanation, a scapegoat, and a dreamscape it seems. I never thought about time itself. Did you ever notice that when you are struggling in life, people always begin to talk in terms of time? Give it time. It takes time. Time passes quickly, don't take it for granted—as if time were responsible for our lives. What is time—really? We count it in the ticks of a clock, the turns of a calendar, and the number of candles on a cake. Those are milestones. They are the things that we check off on our list while we fail to pay attention to what is happening around and within us.

When I was very small, my Nana and I would look at the stars together. I had all kinds of ideas about what they were. I thought they might be the people who had passed before me keeping watch, maybe memories or even dreams. I suppose I never totally let go of those whimsical ideas. Nana always said that when a star fell, that meant that someone fell in love. A shooting star was a soul suddenly finding its way to another. It signaled a return. I looked out at the stars tonight. As one fell, I found myself pondering that its descent happened thousands, perhaps millions of years ago. It was only reaching me now. It had taken all those ticks of a clock, all those turns of a calendar before I saw it, yet it was there the whole time. And, there is that word again—time. Perhaps time does not even exist. It's just space that we fill up with milestones while we are waiting for that collision.

AUGUST 2015

"I'm glad that you had time to fit me in," John Fortin said.

"I am curious," Julia admitted. "I am used to your impromptu calls for lunch or one of your soirées, but a proposition? I can't say I expected that from you."

"Well, you are single now, are you not?" he winked.

"In more ways than one, it would seem," Julia replied.

John nodded. "I was referring to your impending departure from the foundation this month," he said gently.

"I know."

"How are you doing with all of this?" he asked.

"Being single as in striking out on my own professionally, or being single as in dealing with the fact that my ex-wife has a younger, extremely attractive new girlfriend?" Julia asked.

"Both," he answered sincerely.

John, Julia, and Carrie had been friendly for years. They had grown much closer once John had begun partnering with the Fledger Foundation. He admired both women. John had watched both as they struggled through their separation in different ways. He understood it remained difficult and painful for Julia. She looked tired, more tired than he could ever recall seeing her. He'd pressed her to get together for a visit before she and Carrie left to take Jake to college.

John had been to dinner with Carrie and Bess over the weekend. He'd taken the opportunity to bounce an idea that he had off of Carrie. He was planning on suggesting to Julia that she accept an interim position in development at The Brighton Center. Carrie had used that as an opening to confess that she was a bit concerned about Julia. John hoped this meeting might accomplish both some of his professional goals, and with any luck, give him some personal insight to the sometimes evasive Julia Riley.

Julia looked at John and took a deep breath. She could see concern and curiosity mingling in his expression. "Carrie's worried about me, huh?" she guessed.

John shrugged. "Not just Carrie," he said.

"I'm okay," she winked. "Let's do the easy part. I'm excited about starting the agency," she told him. "It's just a lot of work, a lot of getting my ducks in a row. The flexibility is important right now. I didn't have that with the foundation, but...Well, there are financial realities I have to consider."

"If it helps ease your mind, I looked at your contract. There is no clause to prevent you from working with entities the foundation supported," he told her. Julia released a sigh of relief. "On that subject," he began. Julia looked at him suspiciously. "What would you say to coming on board at Brighton as the Interim Director of Development? Maybe help Dana with some marketing strategies as well."

"John, I'm leaving Fledger for the flexibility. I need to be home more right now for the girls. Things are happening for Carrie quickly. I don't want her to feel she has to make compromises in her career—not now. It's her turn."

"I know. This position would be part-time. You can still consult on the side. One year. We'll provide an office; you set the schedule. I need you, Julia. One year, and then we can talk. If all goes as we hope and expect, well, maybe you'll decide to join us in some capacity permanently. If not, you go with my blessing and full support." He handed her an envelope. "The proposal is in there. You look it over this weekend. Talk to Carrie. Let me know." Julia nodded. "One question—what prompted the name change? Gallagher? Julia, everyone knows you as Riley. I don't care, but don't you think it will hurt, I mean…Well, you won't be as recognizable to your contacts, at least, not immediately."

Julia had wondered when the questions would come about her decision to use her maiden name professionally. She had debated the pros and cons. In the end, the decision came down to identity— Julia's need to reclaim, or perhaps redefine hers.

"I considered that," she said. "I'd like to think my credibility is predicated on more than being called Riley."

"It is, so why the change?" he asked cautiously.

"Maybe I just need to feel like I am my own person right now. Not just somebody's wife or mother," she explained. "Just me. I need to find me again."

John nodded. "I know it's been hard for you. I know that you…"

"I really am okay," Julia assured her friend. "I'm learning more about me…It's just…Well, I just miss her," she practically whispered.

John looked at his friend and took a deep breath. "Which her?" he asked. Julia looked up in shock. "Oh, come on, Julia," he said.

Julia shook her head. "Both of them," she said flatly.

"I thought so," he replied.

John watched as Julia made a feeble attempt to smile, and decided to steer the conversation away from all things Katie, at least, for the moment.

"What do you think of Bess?" he asked.

"Carrie's happy. The kids like her. She's been nothing but friendly toward me. What's not to like?"

"And, that makes you want to hate her, I'll bet."

Julia laughed. "Pretty much."

"Sorry, Julia," he smirked.

"You shouldn't be. Carrie's an amazing woman. Anyone would be an idiot to let her go."

John raised his brow. "Second thoughts?"

Julia shook her head and smiled. "No. I'm happy for her. Bess is great. They seem to fit. Just feel like feeling sorry for me," she admitted.

"That's what I thought," he winked. He watched as Julia's smile slowly faded, and her expression became distant. "She misses you, you know?"

Julia looked up and nodded. "Fifteen years is a long time."

"Not Carrie," he interrupted her. Julia froze. "She misses you. She makes a point not to ask about you, but she also makes a point to listen extra closely to any conversation your name is likely to come up in."

"Is she okay?" Julia asked tacitly.

John thought for a moment about his response. Katie had invited him to come stay in New York for the weekend and spend some time. He sensed there were things she wanted to tell him. Next week, the news would break about Bill Brennan's impending fatherhood and marriage. John scowled as the image of his best friend's ex-husband passed through his mind.

"John?" Julia asked with growing concern. "Is Katie all right?"

"Yeah. I probably shouldn't tell you this," he groaned. "But, for some reason, I feel like I should."

Julia felt her heart drop rapidly in her chest. She was certain that John Fortin was about to drop the bombshell that Katie was involved with someone new.

"That son-of-a-bitch is getting remarried, and he got that wench pregnant already! Can you believe that? I hate that guy."

Julia's head was spinning. It had taken her a moment to process John's revelations. "Bill? Bill got someone pregnant?"

"Yeah, that beat to hell, far less witty version of a young Blanche Deveraux that was in his car. I can just imagine what caused *that* accident," he muttered.

"Wait a minute. Are you telling me that Yvette Summers is pregnant with Bill Brennan's baby?"

"Are you listening to me?" John said exasperatedly. "Catch up! Cliff Notes version, ready?" Julia nodded. "Okay. Katie went there last month with the kids. He had some news. His news? He was living with an already knocked up Yvette, and they were getting married. End story."

"Jesus Christ," Julia grumbled.

"Pretty sure he was not in on this one," John quipped.

Julia tried not to chuckle. "How'd she take it?" John laughed. "Never mind, I think I can guess."

"Yeah, I know you can," he said. "Why don't you just call her, Julia?"

Julia shook her head and sighed. "I tried," she said softly.

"What?" he asked.

"I tried. More than once. I just can't anymore," Julia said.

"I'm sorry, Julia. She's…Well, Katie's been distant from everyone the last few months, even me. When she's home, she's with the kids. Just…To be honest, I was surprised when she invited me for a visit this coming weekend."

Julia nodded. "I really do hope she's okay," she said honestly.

John could hear the dejected tone in Julia's voice. He took a deep breath and released it in a huff. "Me too," he said. "What about you, Julia? Are you honestly all right?" he asked softly.

Julia smiled. John could be flamboyant and dramatic one minute, and the next completely transform into a soft-spoken, thoughtful friend. She appreciated his genuine concern.

"I am okay. I swear," Julia promised. "And, I appreciate both the offer and the concern. Honestly."

"I know," he said. "Do me one favor?"

"I promise; I will make a decision about the offer quickly."

"No," he said. "I get it. I do. Just, think about calling her," he said hopefully.

Julia closed her eyes. "Maybe in time."

❧ ❧ ❧

"So, what's up, my princess?" John Fortin asked his best friend.

Katie smiled and took another sip from her wine without answering. She loved to torture John. It wasn't malicious. He just lacked patience, always had, and she delighted in getting a reaction from him.

"I thought you'd be all Scarlett O'Hara on me, what with the impending doom," he said dramatically.

"Good thing you never wanted to be a casting director," Katie drawled. "The only thing Ms. O'Hara and I have in common is our first name," she kicked him lightly. "You can be such a drama queen sometimes."

"Hello? Titles matter," he kicked her back. "So, my dear, do dramatics," he grinned. "Now give it up! The suspense is killing me!"

Katie laughed. "Fine." She reached over to the table beside her and handed him a large envelope.

"What's this?" he asked.

"Open it," she instructed him.

John opened the envelope and slid out its contents, studying them curiously. "I don't get it."

"No? You're a lawyer. Look at the evidence."

"What are you.....Holy shit!" he shot up from his seat exuberantly. "Is this what I think it is?" Katie nodded. "You're moving home?"

Katie tipped her head in acknowledgment. John jumped up and down a few times as if they were still children and then stopped abruptly. Katie watched as concern slowly etched itself across his brow.

"Wait, what about the show? Kate, if you come home…"

"You worry too much," she winked. "I'll be taping the show from the Boston affiliate's studio."

"You're serious," he said in disbelief. Katie nodded. "How did you…"

"Wasn't as difficult as you might think. The show's market share has increased every year. It's never quite made it to the number one slot, but I think we might just change that," she said.

There was excitement in Katie's voice and that interested John. "You think moving the show will make a difference?" he wondered aloud.

"I do. It will be even less cookie cutter, and with a bit more balance in fluff versus news."

"Oh my God, who did you bribe? You got more control over the content? I've been telling you to push for that for years. How did you get them to agree?"

"That was easy. My contract was up October 31st. I had refused three renewal proposals. I made one of my own. There are the typical clauses, but I'm not concerned."

John beamed. "I'm so proud of you," he told her. "And so happy for me!" Katie chuckled. "What about this week? I mean, they know—the network—about Bill and the tart, and that whole wedding thing."

"Yeah, they know. The truth is, I would have moved home no matter what. The kids need the change and the stability. It has been a shitty year for Stephanie since the accident. You know how kids are at twelve and thirteen. This news did not help. When we told them two weeks ago about Yvette, what was coming, well…Steph doesn't even want to see him. She certainly does not want to be in this house anymore."

"I'm sorry, Katie. I'd like to kick his," John stopped himself. "He is a narcissistic ass sometimes, but he does love those kids."

"I know," Katie agreed. "But, he doesn't think about them when he makes decisions. He doesn't think period sometimes. He needs to start doing that if he is going to earn back Stephanie's trust. Ian, he follows his sister's lead. Me? New York is not for me. It never has been. We all deserve to heal. That can't happen here, not for me and not for the kids."

John surveyed his best friend's mannerisms in detail. He could tell that Katie's thoughts had traveled elsewhere in an instant. He wondered where those thoughts might have landed. He softened his tone deliberately.

"Why come back to Boston? You could go closer to Bill." Katie shook her head. "Don't get me wrong; you know how I feel. I just…I know how important family is to you," he said compassionately. "What about school? When? You're sure?"

Katie looked at John with a shy smile. "I close on the house at the end of the week. Mom is going to stay there on the weekdays until the show moves so that the kids can start school. The last show tapes in New York on the eighteenth with John Myers filling in. I will be in Boston permanently a few days before that to ensure we are ready to go. I need to be where the people that I love are. That's in Boston," she said.

John understood. "There are a lot of people who love you there too," he told her.

She winked and rose to retrieve their bottle of wine. "I hope so," she whispered to herself.

John didn't have to hear his best friend's private musings to know what she was thinking. He sighed inwardly. He'd puzzled over Katie's friendship with Julia at first, even feeling a slight pang of jealousy. It wasn't until he heard Katie on the phone with Julia after the Brennan's infamous interview with June Neville that John realized Katie's feelings for Julia had deepened. He still wasn't sure if Katie realized just how deep those feelings ran. He'd never seen anyone affect his friend the way Julia Riley could. Part of him wanted to jump up and scream at her to wake up. John knew that would be a mistake for them both. This was something Katie and Julia had to face in their own time. He grinned as the new developments took shape in his head.

"Won't be able to keep avoiding her now," he said as he imagined potential scenarios. "A gentle nudge might just be in order," he chuckled.

"Something funny? Katie asked as she returned with the wine.

"Nope," he said. "Just can't wait to have you home," he raised his glass in a toast.

❧ ❧ ❧

TWO WEEKS LATER

"So, how was the trip down South?" John asked his friends.

Michael rolled his eyes. "Dramatic," he looked at Carrie and Julia.

"No, it wasn't," Julia smacked him. "It was great. Jake's excited. Nervous, but excited."

Michael was making faces at John, and Julia smacked him again. "You need to stop. Don't you think we missed your sniffles, Dr. Riley. Allergies were acting up again, huh?" she teased her ex-husband. Michael dismissed her with another roll of his eyes.

"He is excited," Carrie said. "But, it was hard, you know? Just seems so strange to have him so far away," she said, casting a sympathetic gaze at Julia. "Jake in college. How did that happen? God, time flies."

"I think Jordan is already missing him, and it's only been a couple of weeks," Julia laughed.

"Well, he'll be home before you know it," John said with a smile.

John had arrived with two bottles of champagne. Carrie and Julia had exchanged smirks at what they called his Tigger Dance when he bounced onto Julia's deck. They had both assumed that his celebratory mood centered on Julia's acceptance of the position at The Brighton Center. As the afternoon wore on, Carrie began to wonder if there was something else driving their friend's unusual enthusiasm for life. No matter what the topic, John's reaction was all sunshine and daisies. Julia had cornered Carrie in the kitchen briefly and asked if she thought John was high. Carrie laughed and shrugged, offering her conclusion that he must have gotten laid finally. For the last hour, Julia had tried to banish that image from her mind.

"I remember when I left for college. I was terrified when my parents left," John said with a slight shudder. He quickly recovered and offered his friends an enthusiastic smile. "Then, about forty-eight hours later I realized I was free. I loved college."

"You seem awfully chipper," Michael observed.

"Yeah, you do," Carrie agreed. "What gives, Your Highness?"

John Fortin shrugged with a smile and took a sip from his beer. "Can't I just be in a good mood? What's not to be happy about?" he asked. Michael, Carrie, and Julia all looked at him in disbelief. "Okay! I give. I'm just happy that my selfish wishing has finally been granted."

"What did you do put your teeth under your pillow and pray to the Tooth Fairy?" Julia laughed.

"Laugh it up, Ms. Gallagher, is it now? You are the only lesbian I know who rents a truck from U-Haul to move *out*, not in. Then changes her name in her forties."

"We're not talking about me," she reminded him curtly, avoiding Carrie's eyes.

"Oh, please...She's fine. Aren't you, Carrie? She's got that cute little musician courting her now."

Carrie smacked John. "Enough. We're not talking about us, nosy...What gives?" Carrie asked.

"You two are worse than a den of..."

"John!" Carrie and Julia scolded him in unison.

"Oh, be that way... I was just..."

"If you don't fess up, I am going to send you a troop of dancing Jawas," Julia warned.

John's eyes flew wide open. "She told you that? When did she tell you that? It's a damn good thing she's moving home then! She's lost control of herself!" he declared. Julia froze and stared blankly at John.

"What the hell are you two talking about?" Carrie asked in confusion.

"The princess airing my dirty childhood laundry! I thought she hated tabloid television!" John rolled his eyes. Seeing the confusion play over Carrie's face, he continued. "Hello! Katie! I'm talking about she who is supposed to be my best friend."

"Katie's moving to Boston?" Carrie asked.

"Yep. Can you believe it? She got them to agree to tape her show here," John explained.

Julia felt her stomach lurch violently. "Excuse me," she said quietly and headed for the kitchen.

Carrie closed her eyes for a moment and sighed.

"What?" John asked. "What did I say?"

Carrie offered John a small smile and turned to Michael.

"I'll go," Michael began.

"No," Carrie stopped him. "I think this time it should be me." Michael nodded his understanding.

"I missed something, didn't I?" John asked.

"No. You just weren't thinking during your colorful tangent," Michael said with the raise of his brow.

John closed his eyes and groaned. "Oh shit," he mumbled. He looked at Michael apologetically. "All the talk about the center and Jake. I just...I can't believe I just blurted that, of all things out."

"Well, there was no easy way to tell her," Michael said.

"I know, but I also know..."

"We all know," Michael said with a smile. "It's just getting her to do something about it. She's hurting, John. She hides it pretty well, but…"

"I know. She's not the only one," John said with a sigh. "Stubborn," he muttered.

"More like scared," Michael corrected his friend.

Carrie reached the doorway to the kitchen and leaned against the wall. "You okay?" she asked Julia.

"Yeah, of course," Julia tried to answer lightly. Her hands firmly gripped the counter in front of her in a futile attempt to steady her emotions.

"Jules," Carrie called to her ex-wife. Julia remained still, willing her breath to return. "Julia!" Carrie called for her attention.

"What?" Julia asked without changing position.

Carrie made her way to Julia and pulled her to the kitchen table. "Sit," she ordered.

"Care, I am fine."

"How long have we known each other?" Carrie asked.

"What are you…"

"Just answer the question, Julia," Carrie directed.

"Fifteen years," Julia answered.

"Yes. I've seen you sick. I held your hand when you gave birth—twice…"

"Carrie…"

"No. You sit there, and you listen to me," Carrie said firmly. "We have shared just about everything two people can in life. Wouldn't you agree?" Carrie asked. Julia nodded. "So, why is it you think you can hide the truth from me? Look at me," she implored Julia. Julia slowly and steadily met her ex-wife's gaze. "You were right about a lot of things, Jules—a lot of things. We had lost ourselves. Not just you, both of us. God knows I still love you. I always will."

"Care…"

Carrie waved a warning finger. "And, I know you will always love me. But, Julia, you can't keep running from Katie."

"I'm not running from anything!"

"You don't think I know, that we all know? Christ, Jules, the mention of her name and you turn pale. Maybe there is a reason Katie is coming back home."

"I'm sure there is," Julia mumbled before looking back at Carrie. "There was never anything between Katie Brennan and me, Carrie."

Carrie smiled. "I love you, Jules. I know that nothing happened between you, not like that. But, be honest, at least, with yourself. Maybe nothing will never come to pass between you, not the way you would like, but she means something to you."

"It doesn't matter," Julia said so softly Carrie barely made out the words.

"Yes. It does."

"No. It doesn't," Julia said. "I was just caught off guard."

Carrie sighed heavily. "Julia, just think about it. You two were friends at the very least. Just give her a chance." Julia looked at Carrie warily. "For your own sake," Carrie said.

"Do you realize how bizarre this conversation is?" Julia asked.

Carrie chuckled. "More bizarre than you telling me to date Bess a month ago? A few months ago, I could barely look at Katie Brennan on television," she admitted. Julia's face fell. "Julia, you don't have to say anything. You were right about a lot of things.

Things change. But, Julia, something made you realize that we had grown apart. Something made you feel the need to change things in our life. And, I think if you are honest, we both know who that was."

"I…"

Carrie smiled. "You have always said that people come into our lives for a reason. Maybe that was Katie's reason for coming into our lives, just to help us see. Then again, maybe there is more to it than that," she said with a gentle grasp of Julia's hand. "You think back to what you told me when I came back from my trip. Turn it around. You can try and fool yourself all you want, Jules, but don't fool yourself out of a chance, at least, at a friendship that obviously means so much to you." Carrie rose from her seat and kissed Julia on the cheek.

Julia grabbed Carrie's hand and stopped her from leaving. "That's one lucky musician," she said. Carrie smiled. "I'm happy for you, you know?"

"I do know," Carrie answered. "That's one of the reasons I fell in love with you all those years ago. I want you to be happy too, Jules. You put on a good show, but underneath it is the softest soul I know. You don't fool as many people as you think."

Julia chuckled. "I'll take that under advisement," she said. Carrie winked at her.

Julia watched Carrie leave and threw her head back with a sigh. She'd always expected that she and Katie would eventually cross paths again. It seemed inevitable. They had too many friends and interests in common to avoid that forever. Her emotions were engaged in an epic battle now. Was she glad that the inevitable would come to pass sooner rather than later? Would she have preferred to prolong their distance as long as possible? She collapsed her head onto her hands in exhaustion.

"Give her a chance?" Julia sighed. "I'm sure she hasn't even given it a second thought," she said with the shake of her head, not realizing John was standing in the doorway.

John had made his way to the kitchen intending to apologize. He looked at Julia sympathetically in the distance. His heart ached for his friends. "Two of a kind," he mumbled before slipping away again silently.

Chapter Thirteen

The afternoon breeze felt refreshing on Julia's face as she strolled through Boston Commons. She loved autumn in New England. The tops of the trees were tipped with color, a burst of red, orange, and yellow painting the tallest branches. She had never been able to determine why, but something about the fall always invigorated her. It was strange when she took the time to examine it. Great beauty always seemed to precede great loss. She savored a deep breath of the crisp air and pondered how that reality reflected her life. Great beauty had preceded great loss. She sat down on a bench in the park and allowed the scenery and sound to wash over her. It seemed that this year, more than ever, autumn was a metaphor for her life.

Leaving the foundation had thus far proved a healthy and prosperous decision. It wasn't a financial boon, but she was grateful for the change. The freedom in her schedule, the diversity in her tasks, and the ability to spend more time with Meghan and Jordan were helping Julia to achieve a sense of both peace and accomplishment. Still, there was something missing. Julia inhaled another deep breath and looked skyward as the clouds drifted by. She was lonely. She cherished time with her children, enjoyed her work more than she had in years, and had found more time to socialize recently. To

Julia's surprise, she had even cultivated an enjoyable friendship with Bess. That had given Julia a new perspective on her relationship with Michael.

People had always marveled at Michael's ability to remain so close to Julia after their divorce. Often, people had asked Julia if it surprised her that her ex-husband and Carrie had become such close friends. Why shouldn't they, she always wondered? Now, people asked how she could be so accepting of Bess. Julia chuckled at the thought. Sometimes it felt a bit strange to be with Carrie and Bess, but that seemed to subside a little more with each passing day. Carrie was in love. Julia was grateful to see the sparkle in Carrie's eyes return with a renewed clarity and brilliance. Perhaps, that was the purpose behind all of the loss.

Julia watched as a single leaf fell from a tree a few inches away. Its descent was so graceful. Gently it floated toward the ground. Julia mused that it appeared a lonely journey. Great beauty precedes great loss. Katie. She shut her eyes in silent contemplation. She had tried to forget about Katie. She had attempted to rationalize the emotions that she felt. It all seemed hopeless to her now. Katie had burst into Julia's life like the vibrant colors that paint the trees every autumn. And then, just like the leaves, she disappeared. Julia looked at the singular orange leaf that now rested on the ground.

"How lonely," she thought. Why did the most wondrous parts of life always seem to fade away so quickly? Julia bent over and picked up the leaf, turning it over and over again in her hands. Perhaps, there was no answer. She sighed. "So beautiful," she said. "And, so alone."

❧ ❧ ❧

"Jules, you don't have to take the girls. We can get someone to stay with them," Carrie said. "Bess even said she'd…"

"Would you stop?" Julia chuckled. "Did it ever occur to you that I might just want to be with the girls this weekend?"

"Yes. It also occurred to me that you might be hoping to avoid Katie," Carrie said pointedly.

"I told you before; I'm not avoiding anything. I promised the kids I would take them to Salem this weekend. Meghan's doing that report. I've been looking forward to it," Julia explained.

Carrie studied her ex-wife's demeanor closely. "You could just take them for the day. You don't need to stay all weekend. It's not like you are going to be driving for hours," she said.

Julia took the opportunity to collapse onto the sofa. "I know what you think, and I understand you mean well, but I need this weekend with the kids. *I* need it. It's been slow going with Meghan, getting her to want to spend time with me. I promised."

"I know," Carrie said. "Eventually, you are going to have to face Katie."

"And, eventually, I will. This isn't about Katie. It's about the kids and me. We've had these plans for weeks. If I decide to change that now for one of John's affairs…."

Carrie stalled Julia's explanation with her hand. "I hear you. I know. I just feel guilty sometimes, I guess."

"For what?" Julia asked in utter confusion. Carrie shrugged. "What on earth would you feel guilty for?"

"I just…You've been so terrific to Bess, and I…."

"I like Bess," Julia said sincerely.

"I know," Carrie grinned. "But, I hate seeing you…"

"Alone?" Julia guessed. Carrie nodded. "Listen, Yente, relax. Stop worrying about my love life, or lack thereof. It's weird."

"I'm not trying to be your matchmaker," Carrie said. "You could use more friends that you aren't always talking business with."

"You worry too much," Julia said. "Stop worrying and stop feeling guilty. Things are going well for me." Carrie looked at Julia doubtfully, and Julia started laughing. "Jesus, you have been hanging around John too much. The dramatics must be contagious."

"It's not dramatic to worry about the people you love. You do it constantly," Carrie said.

"We're not talking about me anymore."

"Only because you won't have the conversation," Carrie poked.

"Were you always this persistent?" Julia asked.

"No," Carrie replied. "That's a recent development."

Julia sighed heavily. "Sometimes, Care, it is lonely," she admitted. She watched Carrie's face fall. "But, that's mostly when the girls aren't here. It's quiet."

"Missing the noise? Never thought I'd hear that," Carrie said with a pat to Julia's knee.

"I like the quiet sometimes. It's just there's no one here. I've never lived that way, Care."

"I know. We can talk about changing some of the girls…"

"No. Stop worrying. It gives me time with me. I'm learning that sometimes I like my own company."

"And?" Carrie asked.

"And, sometimes I am a real pain in the ass," Julia laughed.

"There is hope for you," Carrie winked. "Message received. I can't help but worry about you," she said.

"Old habits die hard, huh?" Julia asked lightly.

"Maybe some habits aren't meant to be broken," Carrie replied.

Julia smiled in earnest. It amazed her some days how far she and Carrie had traveled. Carrie hadn't changed, but she had blossomed. "You know, Jordan wants a drum set," Julia said with a raised brow.

"Oh boy," Carrie laughed. "Sorry about that, Jules. Bess has been giving her lessons."

Julia laughed. "No, no. I was just thinking if she takes to it, I should enjoy my moments of silence. It might get a little louder than I am used to here soon."

"I don't normally gamble, but I'd lay odds on that one," Carrie smirked.

"Thanks for the support," Julia said.

"Anytime," Carrie winked.

❧ ❧ ❧

"Is she here?" Carrie asked John Fortin.

"Oh, she's here somewhere," he winked. "You know, when she is around, people sometimes tend to swarm."

"Ah, the price of celebrity," Bess laughed. "Like bees to honey."

"More like buzzards if you ask me," John rolled his eyes.

Carrie patted his arm. "Jealous?"

"Of the attention? No. Of always losing my best friend in the crowd, maybe," he admitted. "I'll tell you the truth. It's always been that way, even when we were in school."

Carrie looked across the room and caught sight of Katie out of the corner of her eye. John's admission did not surprise her. Katie Brennan was personable, intelligent, and as much as Carrie hated to admit it some days, Katie was stunning. She looked back to her friend.

"She looks great," Carrie said softly.

Bess looked at her feet for a moment and then at Carrie. "You okay?" she asked her girlfriend.

Carrie smiled broadly. "Yes, I am. Oh, now don't you two look at me like that. Believe it or not, I am hoping those two will settle whatever happened between them."

"I know," Bess said. "But, I also know that Katie Brennan was not your favorite person for a while."

"My issue. People can't help what they feel," Carrie said to her girlfriend.

"No, they can't," Bess agreed with a longing gaze at Carrie.

"I have got to stop hanging out with lesbians," John said. "You are like your own damn Hallmark Channel."

"Yeah, yeah," Carrie laughed. "Why don't you go see if you can rescue your friend from the buzzards," Carrie suggested. John looked over to the corner where Katie remained surrounded by several attractive men.

"Careful," Bess cautioned. "They might swarm you," she whispered.

"One can hope," John said with a cheesy grin. "Besides, she can't have all the fun. Paybacks are still do for The Jawa Betrayal."

"The what?" Bess asked.

"Don't ask. It's safer," Carrie told her.

"Okay, I'm going in," John announced.

༄ ༄ ༄

John sidled up to Katie and whispered in her ear. "Hoping to run into someone?" he asked. Katie twitched a bit at the question and offered her best friend a sideways grin. "She's not here," he said flatly. Katie's eyes widened. "It's her weekend with the kids. You might collide with Carrie, though," he said.

As if on cue, Katie captured a glimpse of Carrie standing beside an attractive younger woman with long black hair. "Who's with Carrie?"

"That?" John asked.

Katie stared off at the scene a few yards away as the attractive woman draped an arm around Carrie's shoulder.

"That would be Bess," John told her.

Katie turned to John, stunned. "What do you mean it's *her* weekend with the kids?" she asked.

John shrugged. "Guess you weren't on that memo list," he said dryly. He loved Katie, but she could frustrate him like no one else. "Katie, Julia left Carrie in May. Carrie's been dating Bess for almost two months." Katie searched John's eyes for any hint of a joke. "I'm not kidding," he told her.

"Why didn't you say anything?" she asked him a bit harshly.

"I may be the queen, but I am not a gossip. It wasn't my place. It was Julia's."

"You know perfectly well that Julia and I haven't spoken in...."

"I do know—about six months. I most certainly do know. Still, not my place," he said.

Katie sighed and shook her head. "I can't believe it."

"Really?" He looked at her skeptically. "Why does that surprise you so much?"

"She must have been...."

"It's been hard for them both," John said. "Believe it or not, I think it was worse for Julia, even if she is the one who ended it."

"I do believe it," Katie muttered.

"Maybe you should call her," John slipped in his suggestion.

"I'm not sure that would be so well received," Katie said sadly.

"Oh? So, what then? Just come to my parties and hope that she can't avoid you?" he asked. "What exactly happened with you two?"

"Nothing," Katie answered. "We just…. I don't know, life got crazy. We just sort of moved apart."

"More like turned tail and ran."

"What?" Katie looked at her best friend harshly. "Jesus, John, you make it sound like I am in love with her or something."

John raised his eyebrow and shook his head. "Well, in my experience if the shoe fits, Princess, you should go ahead and wear it." Katie's mouth flew open in astonishment. "You know, maybe that knight in shining armor you've been dreaming about all these years just happens to be more like a lady in waiting. Thing is, you'll never know if you're too chicken shit to show up to the ball," he told her.

"I…."

"Save it. You two were made for each other. Stubborn, opinionated…And, stubborn," he said. "Don't look now, but the former Mrs. Riley is on her way over. Make sure you get home before midnight, Cinderella," he whispered in her ear. He placed a kiss on her cheek as Carrie reached them.

Carrie nodded to John before addressing Katie. "Katie," she said with a smile. "How are you?"

"I'm doing well. How are you?" Katie asked sincerely.

"Good," Carrie answered honestly. "It's been an interesting year," she offered with a wink.

"John told me. I'm sorry to hear about…"

"Well, I was sorry too," Carrie admitted. "We all were, but we got through it," she said. Katie nodded, and Carrie followed her stare as she glanced over toward Bess. "Yeah, things have changed a bit," Carrie chuckled.

Katie gave a small smile. "How is...I mean how are," she fumbled her words.

"You can say her name, you know," Carrie said. "Julia's doing all right." Katie nodded again. "Look, I have no idea what happened between you two," Carrie began. Katie swallowed hard, and Carrie saw the attractive redhead's cheeks flush. She made a mental note of the reflexive response to her statement and raised her brow slightly. "It's none of my business," Carrie continued. "Well, except that I love Julia." Katie listened closely, wondering where Carrie intended to head with the conversation. "I do know that she's missed you," Carrie offered truthfully. Katie's face fell. "She won't admit that, mind you. She is Julia after all," Carrie said affectionately. Katie snickered. "I'll tell you what I told her when John not so gently announced you were moving home." Katie looked at Carrie curiously. "I told her that she would be foolish to pass up the chance for a friendship that obviously means so much to her. Based on the expression on your face, I'd say you could use the same advice," Carrie said.

"I wouldn't really blame her if she didn't want to talk to me," Katie admitted.

Carrie nodded and clasped Katie's hand. "You'll never know if you don't try," she said. "I'd better go find that drummer of mine. Somebody will be trying to steal my date."

"Carrie? I.... Thanks."

Carrie winked. "Don't thank me yet. Trust me; she wants to talk to you, Katie. Like I said, she is Julia. Don't expect too much out of the gate."

Katie watched as Carrie made her way across the room and let out the breath she had been holding. John was right. She had hoped to run into Julia. It would have been an excuse to break the ice, or, at least, to step out onto it. Could Carrie be right? Could Julia actually miss her? Want to talk to her? Katie let out a sigh and put her questions aside. She'd mastered that endeavor these last few months where Julia Riley was concerned. One more day wouldn't hurt.

᪣ ᪣ ᪣

Julia's morning had been more hurried than usual. She had a full plate for the day. One that included three interviews, a meeting with the President of the Chamber of Commerce, and lunch with a group of civic leaders. The Brighton Center seemed to be gaining attention daily. John credited Julia's expertise with the instant rise in corporate donations and inquiries benefiting the project. It seemed that no matter what name Julia used, her decision to come on board with the center had increased its viability and prestige overnight. In a few weeks, Julia had found that her twenty-five hour per week schedule was no longer adequate to meet the growing demands of her position. John had insisted that she not stretch herself. The center had planned to break ground in March, which meant that creating a framework for attractive sponsorship opportunities was imperative. The new donors wanted to be certain that their support would be front and center. That left Julia scurrying to adjust numerous details. If she was not going to increase the number of hours she invested at the center's temporary office, she needed to hire more staff as soon as possible.

"Great," Julia groaned as her gas tank chimed empty. The entire day had been a comedy of errors. The only thing she had managed to accomplish without incident and on time was getting Meghan and Jordan on the bus for school. Fifteen minutes into her drive to work her cell phone had rung. Bess was out of town for several days with her band, and Carrie's SUV had decided to die in the driveway. Fifteen minutes forward had quickly turned into fifty minutes backward. By the time Julia had managed to jump-start the SUV, fight her way back through traffic, and reach the office, she was already twenty minutes late for an interview with her first intern candidate. She had thought that her bad luck was behind her when the candidate proved both qualified and good-natured. That turned out to be a fleeting hope.

Luck, it seemed was not on Julia's side. Half an hour before her lunch meeting, Everett had appeared in her doorway. At first, Julia was ready to dismiss him. Then she saw the streaks that painted his cheeks. And so, Julia sat as a captive audience for her former intern's story. It wasn't a broken heart or a lost job that had brought him to his mentor's door. Everett's mother had fallen ill. He had to resign from the foundation and head back to Indiana indefinitely. He was devastated. Julia's heart broke for him. He had tested her patience often, but she had immense affection for the young man. He was intuitive, bright, and personable. She called and informed the host for the luncheon she was due to attend that she would likely be tardy. It seemed that this day was made to test her resilience.

"Who the hell did I piss off?" she muttered as she climbed out of her car. "Let's just hope you make it to the gas station through traffic," she patted the vehicle with a chuckle. "Seriously, I need coffee and a quiet afternoon. God willing… Please," she continued her dialogue with the car. "I'm talking to a car. Jesus, I have lost it. What else could possibly happen?"

🙞 🙞 🙞

Katie walked down the corridor holding a carrier with two coffees, wondering if the trembling she felt in her hands was evident to the rest of the world. After a few more martinis at John's party for liquid courage, she had gotten up the nerve to ask her best friend some more pointed questions about Julia. With a great deal of persistence that bordered on badgering, he confessed that Julia had left the foundation to open a consulting agency. She had accepted a one-year, interim position with the Brighton Center to help devise a funding and marketing strategy for the center's first two years.

Katie had spent the majority of the week back in New York tying up loose ends before officially moving her show to Boston. It had provided her with a distraction for a few days. Returning to Boston on Wednesday, she had tossed and turned throughout the night, finally deciding it would be more productive to get up and pace the floor until she could leave. As soon as the clock read seven, she headed out the door to her office. She had an agenda today, and no one was going to stand in the way of it. No one that was, except perhaps the focus of that agenda, the person whose office she now sought on her trek down this corridor. Katie scanned the names on the doors inside the small building that served as the interim home of the diversity center. She battled a growing feeling of nervous frustration as she approached the end of the hallway.

"Looking for someone?" a voice asked over her shoulder. Katie spun on her heels and came face to face with the focus of her days' agenda. "He stepped out for a bit," Julia said, assuming that Katie was looking for her best friend. Katie nodded. She heard Julia, but the words became lost in the low hum of the voice that she had sorely missed. "Hello?" Julia waved a hand in front of Katie's face.

Katie was positive she was about to pass out from a lack of oxygen. She barely trusted her legs to support her weight, much less her brain to string together any articulate speech. She had practiced, reviewed, tossed out, revised, and rehearsed again what she would say when she saw Julia. Now, it all failed her. Julia saw the color drain from Katie's cheeks and grabbed hold of her arm to steady her.

"Katie?" Julia called to her friend.

"I didn't come to see John," Katie said softly, nodding to the tray in her hand. "Double cappuccino?"

Julia watched as hopefulness mixed with apprehension in Katie's eyes. Time had changed very little. The worried creases that pulled at the corners of Katie's eyes simultaneously tugged at Julia's heart. Julia could pretend, and she would try, that seeing Katie was the most normal thing imaginable. In some ways, it was. Just seeing Katie standing in the hallway had instantly filled the hollowness that had haunted Julia for months. She desperately wanted to reach out and touch the cheek just inches away. Instead, she allowed a smile to take shape and nodded to the nameplate on the door Katie had just passed.

Katie read the name and looked to Julia in confusion. "J.R. Gallagher?" she asked.

"That would be me," Julia explained. "Unless there is some-one else on staff who is in desperate need of what you have there," Julia pointed to the tray in Katie's hands. Julia gestured for Katie to follow her inside the office.

"You changed your name?" Katie asked.

"Long story," Julia said as Katie walked past her. Katie tipped her head slightly to signify her unspoken question. "Longer story," Julia said.

"I'd love to hear it sometime." The words escaped before Katie could hold them back.

Julia just smiled. She was determined not to give away how happy she was to see Katie, happy but terrified. The only thing that allowed Julia to remain in control of her emotions was the tinge of terror evident in Katie's eyes. It was an anxiety that Julia felt equally. She found herself silently asking, "How did we get here?"

Katie handed Julia her cappuccino and sighed. She'd rehearsed it. She might as well say it now. "Look, I know I have no right to ask you for anything," Katie began. Julia slowly sat in her chair and listened as expressionless as she could manage. "The truth is, I wouldn't blame you if you never wanted to talk to me again. I really would like to hear that story," Katie added. She took a deep breath and closed her eyes before looking directly at Julia. "I know you might not believe this, but I miss you." Julia's heart stopped at the unexpected admission and then hammered so powerfully she wondered if Katie could hear it. Katie smiled, retrieved a card from her bag, and handed it to Julia. "Just...I have no right to ask, but...Well, you decide. My address is on the back. The number's the same, but that's there too. Bill is flying in for a few days with the kids this weekend. I'll be home all day Saturday if you wanted to talk or have another one of those," she pointed to the cup in Julia's hand that Julia was fingering nervously. "Or maybe something stronger," Katie lifted her eyebrow.

Julia nodded. "I have some commitments in the morning," she heard herself say.

"It doesn't matter when," Katie said. "I just—I wish we could start over," she confessed. Julia nodded her understanding. "Well, I'll leave you to it," Katie said. She turned and made her way to the door.

"Katie?" Julia called out. Katie turned to face Julia with a deep breath that she deliberately held.

"I'll see you Saturday," Julia said simply. Katie released her breath and gave a solemn smile to her friend. She made her way through the door, shutting it softly. She felt her head collapse against it, her hands tracing the steel, wishing she could reach back through somehow.

≈ ≈ ≈

Julia made her way to the porch of Bess's house and had just lifted her hand to knock when the door opened in front of her. Carrie's eyes met hers, and Julia's tears were given instant permission to make their escape. She looked at Carrie helplessly, and Carrie pulled her into an embrace.

"You saw her," Carrie guessed. She felt Julia nod on her shoulder. "Was it that bad?" Carrie asked.

"No," Julia chuckled through a sob. "And, yes."

Carrie tried not to laugh. "How hard on her were you?" she asked. Julia's laughter mixed with her tears. "Made her sweat it a bit, huh?" Carrie asked knowingly. Julia nodded again. "Come on," Carrie grabbed Julia's hand. "Bess is grilling. Beer and burgers?" she asked.

"Do you know how much I love you?" Julia asked as Carrie wiped the tears from her ex-wife's cheeks.

"In fact, I do," Carrie winked. "Even if it is only for my beer now." Julia laughed. "And, I love you too," Carrie said honestly. "Now, come on. I have a feeling I might need that beer as much as you do for this visit."

Julia followed Carrie through the house and shook her head in pleasant disbelief. Somehow they had managed to maintain the friendship that was always at the heart of their marriage. Carrie was happy, and Julia was surprised that she felt no jealousy in Bess's company. Bess had treated Julia as a friend, never an adversary, and Bess loved all of the children. Julia's thoughts drifted to Katie as she watched Bess kiss Carrie on the cheek. She drew a pattern in the condensation on the beer in her hands.

Carrie could no longer hide the satisfied smirk on her face. "All right, Jules…. Now, you pay the piper. Out with it…. *All.*"

Chapter Fourteen

Katie paced back and forth in the living room, readjusting picture frames, moving pillows, anything to keep her hands busy. She hadn't spoken to Julia since their brief visit earlier in the week. She had only received a short voicemail from Julia to say that she would arrive sometime after two o'clock. It was nearing two-thirty, and Katie's mind was racing. Deep down, she felt confident that Julia would not stand her up. A tiny voice nagged at the back of her mind, warning her not to become too hopeful about any promised appearance or what any appearance might mean. She sat down on the sofa and put her face in her hands.

"Please, just let her show." Katie sucked in a ragged breath when she heard a car pull in front of the house and she lifted her head slowly. She closed her eyes and willed her feet to carry her to the front door.

᷾᷾ ᷾᷾ ᷾᷾

Julia reached the front door with two grocery bags in her hands. Before she could set them down to ring the bell, the door opened.

"You came."

"I said I would," Julia answered smartly.

"With…What is all that?" Katie asked.

"Well, if you let me in maybe you will find out," Julia quipped. Katie nodded with a smile, feeling the first sense of their natural connection return. She looked at Julia to ask her question. "Kitchen," Julia answered instinctively. Julia followed Katie through the house into the kitchen and set the bags on the large island at the center of the room.

"I don't usually ask my guests to do my grocery shopping," Katie joked.

Julia stopped her endeavor and pushed a bag aside to focus her attention on Katie, who was standing on the opposite side of the kitchen island. Julia let out a small sigh and sat on the stool in front of her, directing Katie to do the same. Katie felt her heart drop instantly. Julia decided to get to the point. "You said that you wished we could start over."

"Yes, I do," Katie replied.

Julia took a deep breath and nodded. "I don't," she said.

Katie closed her eyes and bit her bottom lip to quell her tears. She jumped when she felt Julia's hand on hers and looked up. Julia shook her head and closed her eyes before continuing.

"Starting over would mean trying to forget how we met, trying to put aside all of that time," Julia said with another shake of her head. "I don't want to forget any of it, or pretend all that time isn't part of who we are. It's too important to me," Julia said honestly. Katie tried to say something but could not formulate a response. "So, maybe we should just start fresh," Julia suggested. Katie smiled and looked at the bags with a curious smirk. "It's killing you, isn't it?" Julia asked. Katie shrugged. "Mm-hm." Julia pulled out several items and placed them in front of Katie. "As I recall, I agreed to help keep your integrity intact," Julia explained. Katie remained perplexed, and Julia rolled her eyes. "The day we met, you made a now famous speech in which you claimed to have sampled some chowder," Julia reminded her.

Katie chuckled. "We were on our way to lunch when…"

"All hell broke loose," Julia finished Katie's sentence. "So, if we are going to do this, whatever this is," Julia began and received a quirked eyebrow from Katie. "I figure we need everyone's integrity intact. Seems like this is as good of a place to start as any," Julia explained. Katie just shook her head softly and smiled. Julia looked over her head and grabbed a pot. "Best chowder you will ever have. I promise," Julia said.

Katie marveled at the way Julia moved about, and at the ease of the conversation that ensued. She had just finished handing Julia a ladle and had turned to retrieve a bottle of wine when she heard Julia start humming. "God, I missed you," Katie whispered softly, intending it only for her ears.

"Good to know," Julia said. Katie froze. "And, just so there's no question, I missed you too," Julia finally admitted without lifting her focus from the pot in front of her.

ﻬ ﻬ ﻬ

Afternoon turned quickly into evening and found Julia and Katie in the living room sipping wine from a second bottle. They had enjoyed playful banter and light conversation about their children's lives, the house, and work. All of it was interesting, and all of it mattered. Both women knew that the time had come for a more emotional conversation, one that neither could avoid any longer. Katie took a deep breath. Julia was running her fingers over the rim of the wine glass in her hand.

"Julia," Katie said. "What happened? With you and Carrie, I mean," she asked gently.

Julia took a sip from her glass and returned to tracing patterns on its edges. "I don't know. Truthfully?" she asked. Katie nodded her encouragement. "We just fell out of love, I think. I mean, I love her. She loves me, but it just wasn't," Julia closed her eyes and stopped. She was not ready to divulge the complete truth to Katie, not even close. And, the truth was that Julia had realized that what she felt for Carrie was drastically different from the emotions just the thought of Katie could evoke. There had never been a moment that Julia had considered Katie the cause of her marriage's ultimate breakdown. Julia's feelings for Katie, however, were the catalyst for her to admit what she lacked in her life. Julia had tried to deny that reality to herself for a long time. Ironically, it was Carrie who forced Julia to face the truth about the role her feelings for Katie played in changing the course of their marriage and their lives. It turned out that the missing pieces Julia felt in the marriage she and Carrie shared were mutual. Comfort had, at some point, shifted to complacency. Passion had faded into placating personalities. Both Julia and Carrie had grown content, but neither could have claimed to be fulfilled.

Katie watched as a myriad of emotions played across Julia's face, each one flickering and fading in an instant. "Julia?"

"We lost ourselves," Julia shrugged. "I don't know, Katie. I spent my whole life intent on being the best I could be for everyone else—the best daughter, the best wife, the best mother. And, I loved being...I love *being* all of those things. I just forgot who was beneath it all," Julia said.

"Hence the name change?" Katie guessed.

"I became a Riley when I was twenty-three. When Carrie and I decided to have Meghan, well, we just thought it would make it easier for all of the kids, make them feel part of the same family if they shared the same name. She never took my name. I never took hers, for professional reasons mainly. It just worked," Julia explained. She glanced up to Katie nervously. "It probably sounds ridiculous. I just needed some place to start. I needed some place to find myself again, so when I left the foundation, I decided to give the agency my maiden name. It was a start. Crazy?"

"No," Katie said. "I'm just sorry I wasn't there for you through all of it."

Julia shook her head. She had been thinking a great deal about the distance that had crept between them, or rather, the distance Katie had placed between them. It had been difficult for Julia to understand why Katie had pulled away from their friendship so abruptly and so completely, and it had hurt her deeply. As she sat talking with Carrie and Bess after Katie's appearance that week, she realized that the distance had been necessary for them both. They might have had very different reasons for needing space, but it did not alter the truth. That space had allowed both Katie and Julia to settle the lives they were leading separately, and the relationships that deserved their full attention. Everything had a purpose, even when it meant suffering through pain.

"I know you are sorry. To be honest, it was awful for a while. At first, Carrie was furious. Then she was just so—broken. I almost went back more than once. Jake and Meghan would barely speak to me for the first month. I stayed at the studio downtown until we could figure things out," Julia told Katie.

"What happened?"

"Time. Time happened. I'm just thankful it didn't take any longer. We realized, both of us, we'd been living apart in the same house for the better part of three years. It shifted things. We started to be able to talk again. Actually, we started to communicate more than we had in all that time. Carrie wanted to focus on some new projects and be closer to the studio. It's her turn," Julia said. "She compromised a great deal to be available for the kids' needs and accommodate my schedule." Julia shrugged. "I always have people approaching me to consult. So, we made the decision that I would move back to the house and strike out on my own. I control my schedule more. The money is good, and I can be there for the kids. Carrie can pursue those projects," Julia said. "The hardest part was when I moved back into the house."

Katie looked at Julia for an explanation. Julia sighed and closed her eyes before finding the strength to speak at least a part of her truth. Her voice fell in reflective quietness. "I missed Carrie. She had always been there, every day, every event," Julia explained.

Katie understood. She had experienced something similar to her great surprise when Bill had first moved out.

"And," Julia barely managed to keep her voice at an audible decibel. "I missed you," she confessed. She looked up into Katie's misty eyes. "I just couldn't understand why," Julia said. "Why didn't you just talk to me? We talked about everything."

"Not everything," Katie said with a deep breath. "Oh, Julia. I was a mess. I mean a bigger mess than I had ever been. I didn't know where to turn. I was angry and afraid. I needed to find me too, I guess," she said.

Katie had been debating how much she should admit to Julia. The most important thing in the world to her was Julia's presence in her life. She would do anything to preserve that now. She had spent the week agonizing over John's words. It wasn't that Katie hadn't recognized that she felt something powerful for Julia. It had been precisely because of those feelings that Katie had needed to step away. Julia had the ability to consume Katie's thoughts, and Katie had feared that in the midst of so much change, that would cloud her judgment. The moment she had turned and had seen Julia in the hallway earlier in the week, Katie's denials had ended and any hope of avoidance had been brought to a screeching halt. Katie didn't just love Julia. John was right. She was in love with Julia.

Julia watched as Katie struggled inwardly, wondering what was troubling her so deeply. "Katie," Julia called to her.

"I missed you," Katie said.

"I believe you," Julia said compassionately. A tear rolled down Katie's cheek and Julia crossed the short distance that separated them. She knelt in front of Katie and wiped it away.

"No, Julia, you don't understand. I just...I couldn't need you. I couldn't need anyone and I did," Katie admitted. She was finding it increasingly difficult to speak through the bursts of emotion that kept rising without warning within her. Katie looked at Julia and lost herself. A sensation she had closed her eyes to recall many nights enveloped her—Julia. Julia was barely touching her, but Katie felt surrounded by her. "I still do—need you," Katie finally said.

Julia needed a moment to process the words. She gently took Katie's hand to coax her to open her eyes. When Katie's eyes found Julia's, Julia smiled. "Everything has a purpose, Katie. It will be okay."

Katie smiled. She felt Julia's arms finally surround her and laid her head on Julia's shoulder. Julia closed her eyes and reveled in the feeling of Katie close. "I know it will," Katie whispered.

વ્યું વ્યું વ્યું

"So?" John asked Katie.

"So what?" Katie replied dryly.

"Come on now, Princess. What happened with my favorite fundraiser?"

Katie gave her best friend an odd look. "You trolling for Girl Scout Cookies again?" she asked as seriously as she could manage. John groaned. Katie couldn't hold back any longer and erupted into laughter. "Well, you're in luck, she was a Brownie."

"Are you drunk?" he asked her. "I'm talking about Julia!"

Katie laughed harder. It took her a few minutes to catch her breath. "So was I," she said. John threw his hands up in the air. "Oh, never mind," Katie rolled her eyes. "What about her?" she asked her friend. John glared at her. "What?"

"Did you talk to her yesterday or not?" he asked pointedly.

"Maybe."

"Katie!"

"You don't have to yell," Katie chuckled.

"Well, given your annoyingly happy mood, I assume it went well?" he raised both his eyebrows.

"What is it with you?" she asked.

"Maybe I would just like to see you happy," he answered sincerely. Katie narrowed her gaze playfully. John rolled his eyes again and sighed. "You missed her, admit that much," he implored her.

Katie smiled. "I did."

"And?"

"Julia is the best friend I have ever had, other than you, of course," she told him.

"Look, you don't have to tell me anything, but…"

"We talked. And, we talked. And, we talked some more," Katie said. "We had a lot to talk about," she said quietly.

He nodded. "Katie?" he urged his friend gently. Katie's mood had seemed to shift in an instant.

"We still have a lot to talk about. We have some fences to mend. I have some fences to mend," Katie said with a sigh before allowing her eyes to meet her best friend. "I hurt her."

John pursed his lips. "Did she say that?"

"She didn't have to," Katie answered honestly. "I know I did. I knew it when I stepped away. She left me a message when we announced the divorce. Did she say anything? No, of course not. She didn't say that last night either. She doesn't need to say it, John. I already know."

The sadness in Katie's voice pained John. He watched as Katie closed her eyes. "Why did you, step away, I mean?" Katie shook her head. "Kate?"

"Because I love her," Katie answered truthfully. John had not expected Katie's candor. He stared at her for a moment. Katie looked at her best friend with a lopsided, uncomfortable grin. "You look surprised. Aren't you the one who told me if the shoe fit, I should wear it?" she asked him.

"I did. I just didn't think that you…."

"You didn't think that I knew what I felt? I didn't. I knew I needed her in my life. I couldn't need anyone, not Bill, not my parents, not you," Katie took a deep breath and paused. "And, most of all, not Julia. You were right. I didn't know what that meant, at least, I hadn't admitted it," she said.

"And now?" he asked cautiously.

"And now? I love her, John. More than anything, I want my friend back in my life. And, John?" she called for his undivided attention. "If that is all it ever is, that will be all right."

John nodded. "When did you figure it out?" he asked.

Katie wasn't certain how to answer her friend's inquiry. She had been mulling over that question all week. When did she know? She offered John a genuine smile. "I'm not sure I can answer that, and I'm not sure it matters," she said. "I just know that I am glad to have her back in my life."

"Well, for whatever it is worth, I think she loves you too," he said. Katie just smiled. "What are you going to do now?" he asked.

"Take it one day at a time. Rebuild my life and see where it leads."

"What if…."

Katie shook her head with a smile. "Someone once told me that everything happens for a reason. I just have to believe all of this will lead me where I am supposed to go."

"Where do you think that might be?" he asked.

"I don't know," she answered honestly. "I do know I need to be here to find that out."

∾ ∾ ∾

"What's wrong?" Julia asked Carrie.

Carrie smiled and ignored the question. "How did it go with Katie?"

"Change the subject much?" Julia asked.

"Only when I need to," Carrie answered. "You are right. I do have something to talk to you about, but it isn't dire."

"But my dinner with Katie is—dire, I mean?" Julia snorted. Carrie rolled her eyes. "Okay, fine. We had a long talk."

"How do you feel about that?" Carrie asked.

Julia smiled. "I'm relieved to know that I didn't do anything to have made her walk away from our friendship."

"Is that what you thought?" Carrie asked.

Julia shrugged. "I didn't really know what to think at the time. So much was happening, I guess part of me wished I had Katie to talk to," she explained. Carrie gave an uncomfortable nod. "But, now…. I don't know, Care. I think we both needed time."

"Jules," Carrie began cautiously. "Does she know? How you feel about her?"

Julia bristled slightly. "I'm not sure I know." Carrie's expression remained unchanged. Julia understood that was a sign of her ex-wife's skepticism. "Why are you looking at me like that?"

Carrie let go of a heavy sigh and moved to sit beside Julia. "Look, if you really don't know, and I mean deep down, if you really aren't sure how you feel, that is one thing. If you are avoiding that for my sake, you need to stop."

Julia took a moment to center her thoughts. She looked at Carrie with an expression that mirrored so many emotions, Carrie almost began to cry. "I love her," Julia said without removing her gaze from her ex-wife. "I do. I love her, Care. I just don't know what that means for either of us."

Carrie patted Julia's cheek. "I know, Jules. For whatever it is worth, I think you just need time—both of you," Carrie tried to support Julia.

Julia nodded. Discussing her emotions was not Julia's favorite pastime. She was still reeling from her evening with Katie. She had woken up that morning with a pounding headache caused by the jumble of uncontrollable thoughts and emotions Katie's return had produced. Julia had looked at the phone on and off all day, forbidding herself to give into temptation and call Katie.

Carrie understood Julia as well as, if not better, than anyone. She should. They had celebrated life and endured the pain of loss together. Carrie would always claim a part of Julia's heart, and that made these conversations even more unsettling for Julia. Carrie seemed happy now, but Julia could not help but feel a twinge of guilt. She loved that Carrie was so determined to be supportive in their new relationship dynamic. Right now, it was too much for her. Julia needed time to process all of it.

"As fascinating as this conversation is," Julia said sarcastically. "That was not the purpose of your visit."

"No, more like the bonus round," Carrie chuckled.

"What's going on?" Julia asked. Carrie's sudden intake of breath signaled Julia this was going to be a stressful conversation. "Care? What's wrong?"

"I wouldn't say anything is wrong, Jules. I got a call last night," Carrie said with a sad smile.

"From?"

"From Jake."

∾ ∾ ∾

Katie had been both surprised and delighted when she heard Julia's voice on the phone. She did not require more time with Julia to know that making the call had not been easy for her friend. Julia was a master at maintaining an air of confidence and control. It had been a simple call to thank Katie for dinner that weekend. Katie had immediately pointed out that Julia had cooked their dinner. Katie could read the tension in Julia's voice over the phone and casually suggested that they meet for lunch. Now, they sat at a small table in the corner of a local fish market. Julia was making patterns in the condensation on her water glass.

Katie watched her closely and smiled. "Julia?" she called over knowingly. "What's going on in that head?" Julia looked up and frowned. "Hey," Katie began to grow both concerned and frightened. "If you need to take a step back…"

"It's Jake," Julia said.

Katie was puzzled. "Is he okay?" she asked.

"I don't know, Katie. Apparently, he called Carrie the other night and broke down crying," Julia explained.

Katie pursed her lips to keep her smile from edging forward. The first few months of college were an adjustment for everyone. She was sure that Julia understood that. Jake was Julia's first. He was, in many ways, the apple of her eye. Katie had seen that immediately. She suspected that Julia was worried, and feeling a bit slighted at the knowledge that Jake had called Carrie and not his mother. "Julia," Katie said gently. "I'm sure he's just getting used to everything."

"I know. That's what Care said."

"Have you called him?" Katie asked. Julia shook her head. "Why not?"

"I promised Care that I would wait a few days. If I call now, he'll suspect she told me how upset he was," Julia explained.

Katie smiled at her friend. "He probably was too embarrassed to call you," she suggested.

Julia nodded. "Maybe. I told you, he was angry at me for a long time. I don't know if he will ever forgive me," she said sadly.

"Maybe it's you who needs to forgive yourself," Katie said cautiously. Julia's head popped up. "Just listen. You can't keep beating yourself up, Julia. Don't look at me like that. I know you, and that is exactly what you are doing. Did you stop to think that maybe he felt awkward because he had treated you badly for so long?" Katie asked.

"He had every right," Julia said.

"Somehow, I doubt that he would agree with that now," Katie suggested. Julia looked at Katie doubtfully. "He was hurt and angry, Julia. That wasn't because he doesn't love you. It was because he does love you, both you and Carrie. He lashed out. That's normal. You told me things had been better between you two lately."

"I thought so," Julia said. "So, why wouldn't he talk to me? We used to talk about everything."

Katie reached across and put her hand over Julia's. "Because he is eighteen, because he is embarrassed, and because he doesn't want to disappoint you. Because…Julia, he hurt you, and he is old enough to know that."

"That doesn't matter," Julia said. "I understand."

"I know you do. That doesn't mean he knows you do. What did Carrie say?" Katie asked.

"Pretty much the same thing you just did," Julia told her.

"Give yourself a break, Riley," Katie said. Julia shook her head and groaned. "You do deserve it. Wait a couple of days and give him a call."

"Easier said than done," Julia sighed.

"I know. Honestly, I can't even imagine how strange it must be to have him so far away."

"I miss him," Julia admitted. Katie squeezed Julia's hand in reassurance. "It sucks."

Katie laughed. "He'll be home for Thanksgiving, won't he?"

"Yeah, but that's almost two months away. And, I'm not even sure who he is going to stay with that weekend," Julia explained.

Katie hadn't thought about that. Just because Jake came home, that didn't mean the home he would arrive at would be Julia's. "He'll be close, no matter what. You will have time with him," Katie reminded Julia.

"You're pretty good at this, you know?" Julia said with a smirk.

"What's that?"

"Putting me in line," Julia chuckled.

Katie smiled. "I enjoy a challenge," she quipped.

"I choose to take that as a compliment," Julia replied.

"You should," Katie said honestly. "Now, eat. Her Majesty will have my head if I make you late."

"Nah, he doesn't have the stomach for anything that bloody," Julia said. "Maybe the rack, no guillotine."

Katie laughed. "You're crazy, Riley."

Julia winked. Just being in Katie's presence lightened her spirits. "I'm glad you're here," Julia said softly.

"Me too."

Chapter Fifteen

Julia's Journal

Puzzles. I was watching Ian and Jordan working on a puzzle together tonight, one of those giant puzzles that have five thousand and some odd pieces. I think Katie is a bit sadistic sometimes. She likes to throw down a challenge, even to the kids. I thought I was bad. Ian was getting frustrated. I thought that I should intervene, but as usual, my daughter beat me to the punch. Jordan took hold of Ian's shoulders and explained that it was important to do the frame first. "Then you can see the outline of the picture," she told him. Jordan might just be the wisest person I know. I'm not sure where she gets that from. Heaven knows I seem to learn something from her every day.

It occurred to me that if my life were a puzzle, I had spent the first thirty-something years constructing its frame. Once I had reached the middle, I seemed to get lost. It was as if I couldn't find that one piece that would bring it all together. I kept studying the frame. I could see the outline. The colors in the middle were taking shape, but I still could not make out the whole picture. I sat listening to Jordan as she instructed Ian. He always listens to her. They are like yin and yang, those two. Jordan and Meghan seemed almost as happy as I was to hear that Katie was in Boston. I'd forgotten, or maybe I had just been so wrapped up in my own feelings that I didn't think about the fact that our children are so close in age. They had become friends as well. Our distance meant that their friendships had suffered. Our kids seemed determined to make up for lost time. Funny how puzzles come together. That one piece you are looking for is right there, and yet you somehow don't see it. The instant that you find it and click it into its place, the picture comes into focus.

OCTOBER 2015

"Where have you been all night?" Katie asked Julia.

"What do you mean?" Julia asked. Katie just chuckled. "I'm sorry," Julia said knowingly.

"No need to apologize. You just seem distracted," Katie observed.

Julia had been distracted on and off for weeks. The pair had settled into a comfortable routine over the course of the last month. It had not escaped Julia's notice that Katie invited her for dinner whenever the girls were at Carrie's. Julia welcomed the company and enjoyed the time that they shared together. Most nights, it filled the void for Julia that not seeing her children every day had created. Julia's relationship with Katie's children was growing naturally, and that meant the world to her, but at times, it made Julia miss her children all the more. Katie often observed Julia silently, pondering the thoughts that were churning in Julia's brain, and knowing the emotions that tugged at her friend's heart.

Julia remained concerned about Jake. She had confided in Katie that she thought he might be border-lining on depression. Being homesick was a common malady for college freshman, but Julia said that Jake sounded worried, almost insecure. He had always been a confident person. Julia had tried to get to the root of what was bothering her son, but phone calls and emails made that difficult.

She could not read his expressions and body language at such a distance, and she could not shake the feeling that he was holding back with her. Julia's fatigue was evident to Katie. Katie guessed that Julia's mind was racing over possible scenarios with Jake nightly. Katie could listen, but she felt Julia was in need of more than just a sympathetic ear. Katie reached for an envelope and placed it in front of Julia.

"What is this?" Julia asked. Katie shrugged as a mischievous grin crept across her lips. Julia opened it. "A plane ticket to Richmond?"

"Well, yes," Katie confirmed the obvious. "Followed by a car drive to Charlottesville." Julia's eyes grew wide. "Before you say anything," Katie stalled any commentary from her friend. "I've been asked to give a lecture on the changing role of women in media. It's part of a forum on media and its effects on public policy." Katie took a dramatic pause. "At UVA. I thought…" Before Katie could finish, she found herself in one of Julia's impromptu hugs. Katie laughed. "I thought it would give you a good excuse to visit Jake," she said as Julia pulled back. "Of course, it means you will be forced to spend a weekend with me."

Julia sat back and looked at Katie in complete wonderment. Julia understood that this was not intended as a romantic overture. Part of Julia wished it was. This trip was part of Katie's carefully constructed plot to provide Julia with an excuse to visit Jake, an excuse that would prevent her from looking like a mother hen.

Julia smirked suspiciously. "You were invited, huh?"

"Well, yes, I was," Katie said.

"Um-hum."

"What?" Katie feigned innocence.

"Perfect timing," Julia said.

Julia was aware that Katie's favorite uncle was a professor at The University of Virginia. Julia shook her head affectionately. It seemed to her that every moment provided another reason for her to love the woman across from her. This was one of the moments she wished she could express that freely to Katie.

"So? What do you say? You up for a long weekend?" Katie asked.

"Don't lectures usually take up a day's schedule?" Julia inquired knowingly.

"Yes, they do, wise guy," Katie responded. "But, I am speaking to several classes on Friday as well, and I was invited to participate in a panel discussion on Saturday that will be a public event. That includes dinner with some of the university's administration and the other panelists. I thought, well, I thought perhaps I could coax you and Jake into accompanying me."

Julia suddenly found it difficult to breathe. Jake had been full of questions for Katie when she had stayed at Julia's the previous winter. He had always maintained that he would follow his father's footsteps into medicine, but Julia suspected her son's passions could be found elsewhere. It seemed that Katie might have caught on to that fact as well.

"I don't know what to say," Julia admitted.

"How about, I'll be ready when you pick me up," Katie suggested.

"What about the kids?" Julia asked.

"Funny you should mention that. Seems they have been conspiring behind our backs," Katie laughed. Julia was truly curious now. "Oh yes, Meghan apparently convinced Carrie that she and Bess should take them all to Salem for the Halloween festival. It's imperative for her further research. That's what Carrie told me."

"She finished that report a month ago," Julia snickered.

"Yes, I heard."

"When did you talk to Care?" Julia wondered.

"When she called to ask me if I would object to Ian and Steph spending a weekend away with the girls," Katie explained.

"When was that?" Julia asked.

"Wednesday."

"And, let me guess, you took that opportunity to suggest that next weekend might be a good time for that particular adventure," Julia laughed. Katie shrugged. "Does my ex-wife know your master plan?"

"Yes, she does, Riley. In fact, my aunt and uncle's condo happens to be available that weekend, so she and Bess have a place right in the heart of it all to stay with the kids for free."

"Perfect timing," Julia said. "Funny how that all happened."

"Isn't it, though?" Katie replied sweetly. "So, are you in, Riley?"

"I'll be ready when you pick me up."

❧ ❧ ❧

ONE WEEK LATER

Katie squeezed Julia's hand under the table and whispered in her ear. "Relax," she said softly. She sensed Julia's tension. Julia was a master of conversation. While Julia had engaged in the dinner discussion, she had been content to listen far more than speak. Katie knew the topic that commanded Julia's thoughts—Jake.

Jake had an event the he had to attend on campus Friday evening and had to decline an invitation to have a late dinner with his mother and Katie. He had seemed genuinely interested in attending the panel discussion on Saturday. Katie had made a concerted effort during the panel discussion to glance out at Julia and Jake whenever possible. Julia's thoughts were preoccupied with Jake. Jake, Katie had noticed, was listening intently to the discussion on stage. Katie recognized the twinkle in his eye. It mirrored the playfulness in his mother's when Julia was excited about something.

"He seems to be enjoying himself," Katie observed.

Julia returned Katie's gentle squeeze silently. Jake was engaged in a conversation with another student at the table about her studies. He was questioning her about her thoughts on the panel discussion that afternoon. Julia had to admit that Jake did seem to be relaxed. She knew Jake like the back of her hand. Julia could tell that there was still something troubling him. She couldn't imagine what could be so grave that Jake felt he couldn't confide in her.

"I just wish he would talk to me," Julia whispered back to Katie during a break in the conversation. Katie squeezed Julia's hand again.

As dinner came to a close, the conversation moved to the large foyer of the university president's house. Katie's uncle managed to corner Julia. He was curious about Julia's take on the next election cycle. Julia had groaned inwardly at the table when Katie had shared how many people were constantly courting Julia to run for public office. Julia had smiled appreciatively but had taken the opportunity to kick Katie lightly under the table. Katie's response was a million-dollar smile worthy of every camera that had ever been aimed in her direction. If Julia had taken the time to analyze it, she would have recognized the pride and affection in Katie's eyes as she spoke about Julia. Now, Julia watched as Katie expertly navigated her way to the small veranda where the bar had been placed.

"Sneaky," Julia chuckled.

Katie leaned on the stone rail and savored the crisp night air. The indigo sky was dotted with millions of white lights. A single cloud seemed to float across the moon, and Katie admired its freedom from her vantage point.

"Hi," Jake called from behind her.

"Hey, Jake," Katie turned to greet the young man.

"I wanted to say thanks," he told her.

Katie smiled. "You don't need to thank me, Jake. I hate traveling alone. You bailed me out on this one," she told him. Jake nodded uncomfortably. Katie studied him and pursed her lips. "So, how do you like UVA?" she asked.

"I like it," was his simple response. Katie's eyes narrowed as Jake shifted his weight nervously, suspecting there was something he wanted to ask her. "How did you know?" he asked quietly.

"Know what?" Katie inquired.

"Did you always want to be a journalist?" Jake asked.

Katie inhaled a deep breath. She guessed that her suspicions were about to be confirmed. Katie directed Jake to sit beside her on a bench that sat a few feet away from the hubbub of guests. "No," she answered his question. "For a while, I wanted to be a race-car driver," she chuckled.

Jake looked at her and snickered. "A race-car driver?" he questioned. He liked Katie. She was fascinating, articulate, and easy to talk to—more so than any of his parents at times.

"Yeah. What, you don't think girls like racing? Ever heard of Danica Patrick?" Katie quipped. Jake laughed as Katie continued. "I don't know if I knew I wanted to be a journalist," Katie said honestly. "I just knew that I wanted to discover things. I wanted to uncover truths and write about them," she said. Jake nodded. "Both of my parents were teachers," Katie explained. "My mother taught English, and my father taught History. They are both passionate people," she said affectionately. "I guess they planted that seed.

Maybe it just runs in our genes; I don't know. I thought about teaching, but finding those great stories, for me? There is nothing quite like that," she said whimsically. She looked at Jake and noticed the pensive crease in his young forehead. "Jake?" she gently nudged him. "You seemed engaged in the discussion at the table," she noted.

Jake brightened slightly. "Monica is brilliant."

"That would be the young woman you were speaking with at dinner," Katie surmised. "Seemed as though you two were already acquainted."

"Oh yeah," he said with a smile. Katie bit her lip to keep from grinning too widely. "She's the president of the Women's Policy Group on campus, and she's involved in student government. She's always speaking somewhere. She'll be president one day; I'll bet," he chuckled. "To tell you the truth she reminds me a bit of my mom."

Katie felt her heart flutter slightly. It wouldn't take a genius to recognize Jake's crush. Katie could see the similarities between the object of Jake's affection and Julia. As far as Katie was concerned, anyone like Julia would be easy to fall in love with. Her smile edged forward as he continued.

"Monica wants me to get more involved. They need more men involved," he explained.

Katie nodded. "That's true, Jake. Men still hold the majority of power and the authority in business and government. It's a fact— for women to achieve a stronger presence, they require the support of their male counterparts. They require their advocacy as well."

"I know," Jake said enthusiastically. "There's too much suppression still," he said passionately. Katie quirked an amused brow at him. "Imagine if Congress looked like our society?" he said to her. "Policy would change almost immediately."

"Sounds like you have a real passion there, Jake," Katie observed. He shrugged. "Is that a bad thing?" she asked.

"No. I guess not," he said. "But…"

"But?"

"Well, I'm studying Biology," he pointed out.

Katie smiled. "Is that what you want to study?" she urged him gently. She watched his eyes close in defeat. "Jake?"

"No," he whispered. Katie nodded. "I mean, I love it. I really do, but what good is all the medicine in the world if people can't get treatment?" he asked seriously.

Katie put her hand on his knee. "Jake, what is it that you want to do?"

"It doesn't matter," he said.

"Of course, it matters," Katie told him. "This is between you and me, okay?"

"I don't know. I guess I'd like to study policy; you know? Government. People who understand the healthcare system need to change it," he said. "I've seen my dad so many times stressing over patients who are leaving the hospital, and he knows they won't get the right care afterward. Insurance, you know? No insurance. Not enough insurance. So many are moms. And, what about that?" he asked. "What about moms? My parents were lucky. We live where we never had to worry. What about Meghan and Jordan?" he continued his diatribe. "Do you know how many kids only have one parent legally because where they live, their other parent can't adopt them? It's stupid."

Katie thought her heart might burst open. Jake was just like Julia. She imagined that Julia was just as idealistic at eighteen. "So?" Katie said. "I am guessing that Biology is not really the major you want to pursue." She watched as he shook his head. "Sounds like you have an answer, Jake."

"Yeah, but how can I tell them?" he asked.

"You mean your parents?" Katie guessed.

"I already disappointed them once," he said sadly.

Katie smiled at him empathetically. "I don't think you could disappoint your parents if you tried, Jake." He looked up at her skeptically. She could see his eyes imploring her to convince him. "Wanting to change the world is certainly never going to disappoint them," Katie assured him. "Why don't you just tell them?"

"They expect me to be a doctor," he said.

Katie patted his knee. "Well, maybe that's because they think that's what *you* want to do," she said. "I do know one thing," she told him.

"What?" he asked.

"Your mom loves you," she said.

"I know."

"And, you are a great deal like her," she chuckled.

"I know," he said with a smile.

"Tell her, Jake. Give her a chance. I think she just might surprise you," Katie said. She got up from her seat and saw Julia approaching. She leaned back into Jake's ear. "Talk to her," Katie encouraged him. When Katie stood back up, she came face to face with Julia's curious gaze. "Quite the young man you have," she complimented Jake to Julia sincerely. "I'll leave you two to talk," she told Julia.

Julia held Katie's gaze for a moment. She recognized the silent promise Katie was trying to convey without words. "Everything will work out."

∾ ∾ ∾

"So," Julia began as she took a seat next to her son. "Did you enjoy today?" she asked him.

"Yeah," he answered honestly. "Katie is awesome."

Julia felt her cheeks flush slightly. "Yeah, she's pretty okay, isn't she?" she remarked. "So, what were you two doing over here so conspiratorially? Should I be sleeping with one eye open?" Julia joked. Jake shrugged. "Jacob?" Julia sighed heavily. "What's bothering you?" she finally asked him pointedly.

"Mom?" he looked at his mother.

Julia immediately recognized the fear in his eyes. "Jake? What is it? Do you not like it here? Talk to me."

"No. It's not that, it's just," he stumbled and then took a deep breath. "Katie says I should just tell you the truth."

Julia smiled. "Katie usually gives pretty good advice in my experience."

"I want to change my major," he said in one rapid breath. Julia was puzzled for a moment. Jake's nervousness grew. "Never mind," he said softly,

"Wait, Jake," Julia directed her son to look at her and she smiled brightly. "It's just not what I expected you to say," she explained.

"What? Did you think I was on drugs or something?" Jake chimed.

"No," Julia said. "I wasn't sure what was on your mind. Why didn't you just tell me? Or, tell Care or your dad if you couldn't tell me?"

"I don't know. You always wanted me to be a doctor. All of you," he said. "I didn't want to let you down," he admitted sadly. "I already did that once."

Julia took a deep breath and shook her head. "Jacob," she said with a sigh. "You didn't disappoint any of us. And, we never wanted you to be anything but happy. You always loved following your dad around from the time you could crawl. You always wanted to go with him to his office. You were full of questions, and always curious about how things worked. We just tried to follow your lead," she said. Jake nodded. "What is it that you want to study?"

"I'm not sure," he said. "Policy, political science. I want to try to change things. Like you," he told her.

Julia could not prevent the tear that escaped her eye from rolling down her cheek. "I have no doubt that you will do exactly that," she said proudly.

"Dad will be disappointed," Jake said.

"No, Jake, he won't," Julia said assuredly. "Neither will Care. It doesn't matter to us what you study or what you do for a living. If you had wanted to be a mechanic or a surgeon, it wouldn't have mattered to us. If you want to go be a teacher or a lawyer, it's your life—yours. Just be the best you can be at whatever you choose," she said. Julia chuckled softly.

"What?" Jake asked.

"Oh nothing, sometimes you start down one path and you end up someplace entirely different than you imagined," she observed.

"Mom?"

"Hum?"

"Do you think you might? Ever run for office, I mean?" he asked almost hopefully.

"I don't know," Julia answered truthfully. "One thing I have learned is to never say never."

A comfortable silence settled between them until Jake broke it. "I'm glad you came," he said. Julia looked at her son and smiled. "She really is pretty awesome," Jake said with a grin. Julia jumped slightly at the innuendo in her son's voice. Jake laughed. "I'm not that stupid, Mom."

Julia shook her head. "Oh yeah? Who is this Monica you were talking to?" Jake blushed. "I'm not that stupid either, Jacob," Julia said with a wink. "Does she know?" Julia teased her son.

"Does Katie?" he returned in kind. Julia sighed. Jake nodded and put his arm around his mother. "Don't worry, Mom. Your secret is safe with me," he assured her. "But, just so you know, that would be cool with me."

Julia nodded and a brief expression of sadness crossed her face. "I'm not sure that's what is meant for Katie and me," she said honestly. Jake smiled sympathetically. He wondered how his mother could be so intuitive where other people were concerned, and so blind to her own life. Julia shifted gears. "Now, about this Monica.

Chapter Sixteen

NOVEMBER 2015

It wasn't often that Julia had an occasion to visit Katie at the television studio. Their schedules typically made it more conducive for the pair to meet someplace downtown during the weekdays or for Katie to swing by the Brighton Center's offices. Julia secretly enjoyed the rare opportunities that allowed her to visit Katie at work. It gave her a chance to witness a side of Katie that few people saw. Most people saw Katie in front of the camera. Behind the scenes, Katie was a force of nature to be reckoned with. She was professional and good-humored, but Katie was also demanding and focused. Julia had popped in once unannounced and managed a covert glimpse at Katie in action as she addressed several of her staff. Katie's focus was never the camera when she was off-screen. It was always content, and she was determined that her staff understood that.

Julia acknowledged several familiar faces as she made her way to Katie's office. She caught sight of Katie behind the glass. Katie's back was turned, but it was easy for Julia to determine Katie's mood by the way Katie stood with her hand casually tossing her hair. Katie was frustrated. Julia paused and Katie turned to see Julia in the hallway. Julia flashed a sheepish grin and held up a carrier with two coffees. Katie's expression relaxed into a smile, and Julia continued her trek forward, curious as to the conversation Katie was engaged in on her phone.

Katie accepted her coffee from Julia with a frustrated grin. "No, I heard you," Katie said into the phone. "Do I understand? By that, I assume you mean am I capable of comprehending what you just told me," she said pointedly. Julia took a seat and sipped her coffee quietly. "Oh, I comprehend it perfectly. I just would appreciate it if, for once, you might consider my feelings in something."

"Bill?" Julia mouthed her question to Katie. Katie nodded her affirmation.

"Well, it doesn't really work for me—no. Since you were supposed to have the kids for Thanksgiving, I made my schedule accordingly," Katie said pointedly.

Julia cringed at the tone of Katie's voice.

"No, Bill, I can't. My parents are going to Florida to see Aunt Dani for the weekend." Katie's aggravation was visibly growing by the second. "Well, of course, I will figure it out. I always do. Just so we are clear, I am accommodating you this year. Next year, the kids are with me for Christmas," Katie said flatly.

Julia tried to tune out the conversation unfolding inches away. It was impossible. Katie wasn't only frustrated; she was angry. Katie seldom got angry.

"No, Bill, I don't think that we will be discussing it. Those are my terms, and they are not negotiable. Um-hum. Sure. I'll talk to you then. Yes, you too," Katie finished her conversation in a sickly sweet voice. "Unbelievable."

Julia remained silent as Katie collapsed into her chair.

"Hi," Katie said softly.

"Hi," Julia replied. "Sorry, if I interrupted."

Katie smiled. "Typical conversation, and for the record, you are always a welcome interruption," Katie told Julia.

"Would I be correct in guessing that Bill wants the kids for Christmas instead of Thanksgiving?" Julia asked.

"You would be. He was supposed to spend the long weekend with the kids at his parents' house. I guess Yvette made other plans for them," Katie said with a sarcastic smile.

"Oh, boy," Julia whispered.

"Oh, boy is right. What the hell am I supposed to do now? Mom and Dad will be in Florida. I have a show to tape on Thanksgiving and on Friday."

Julia considered the statement for a moment. "Have the kids stay with me," she offered. Katie looked across her desk with genuine surprise. "What? It's not like any of the kids will object," Julia pointed out.

"True," Katie laughed.

Julia and Katie's children had grown attached to each other. It had become a frequent occurrence that Julia and Katie ended up spending time together solely because their children demanded it. Katie looked at Julia seriously. As much as she wanted to accept Julia's offer, she was reluctant to. Jake was planning on staying with Julia for that weekend. That was because Carrie and Bess were taking all three of the Riley children skiing over Christmas vacation, and leaving on Christmas day. Bess was taking Carrie to visit with her family in New Hampshire over Thanksgiving. Katie did not want to intrude on Julia's time with her children.

"Julia, this is your family time."

"And?" Julia asked.

"You know what I mean," Katie said.

"Katie, you are part of that family, you know," Julia said assuredly.

Katie felt the truth in Julia's words wash over her. "Are you sure?"

"Yeah, I am," Julia said. "Besides, it gives me more minions to put to work."

"I have to be at the studio at five in the morning, you know?"

"Yes, I do know," Julia replied.

"Yes, and I gave Marion the weekend off. So, I don't have anyone to watch them."

"Were you not listening to me?" Julia asked with a chuckle. Katie sighed. "Bring them over Wednesday night. No big deal, Katie. It's not like they haven't spent a weekend before."

"Yes, but not one that entails you trying to prepare a meal for…How many people is it now?" Katie asked.

"Well, with you and the kids that would make nine," Julia said.

"Nine?" Katie asked.

"Yeah, nine. Michael, us, the kids, and Everett," Julia said.

"Everett is back in Boston?" Katie asked.

"Not yet. He arrives a few days before Thanksgiving. It's his first holiday without his mother. I thought he could use a place to go," Julia explained.

"Of course, you did," Katie said. "You really are a softy, Riley," Katie observed. Julia rolled her eyes. "And, I really don't want to impose."

"You couldn't impose if you lived there," Julia said without thinking.

Katie's heart skipped a beat. Julia wasn't conscious of her words. She was so consumed in convincing Katie that she should spend the holidays with the Riley clan that she was not stopping to censor herself.

"And, anyway, on Friday we have the Tree Trip Tradition. The kids will have a blast," Julia said.

"The Tree Trip Tradition?" Katie asked.

"Yeah."

"Dare I ask?" Katie giggled.

"Well, Friday morning, the kids haul all the ornaments down from the attic and test all the lights. And then, in the afternoon we all pack in the car and go cut down our tree. Well, Jake will do that," Julia explained. "We stop and pick up some pizza on the way home, and Friday night we eat pizza, decorate the tree, and watch Christmas movies. Tree Trip Tradition," Julia explained.

One of the things that Katie loved about Julia was the child-like quality Julia possessed when it came to her family. Julia was, Katie had determined, the most compassionate person she had ever known. Julia loved to do things for other people. It was no surprise to Katie that Julia hesitated to enter the political world and opted for the non-profit sector. "God, I love her," Katie thought silently. It was a realization that ran through her heart often.

"You really should consider running for office," Katie said.

"Why is that?" Julia asked.

"You know how to make a compelling case," Katie replied.

"Oh yeah? So, did I convince you, Ms. Brennan?"

"I'd vote for you," Katie supplied.

"So, turkey for nine?" Julia asked hopefully.

"You are crazy, Riley," Katie chuckled. "Turkey for nine. I'll even bake."

"Ha! I knew there was a Betty Crocker Cookbook somewhere in that house!" Julia declared.

"Crazy, Riley," Katie laughed.

"About you," Julia thought, suddenly looking forward to the holiday more than she could remember.

❧ ❧ ❧

THANKSGIVING

"Are you sure you don't mind me taking him away? I would have taken him today, but things just got away from me this week. I can't believe I misplaced J.T.'s contact information. I almost blew the interview," Katie said.

Julia laughed as she watched Jake throw his backpack into Katie's car. "That's why you need a Rolodex," Julia chided.

"No one has a Rolodex, Riley. No one except you," Katie returned.

"Umm…But, I never lose my contacts. Computers get fried, the internet goes down, I'm still in the know," Julia gloated.

"Yes, I'm sure you have an 8-track player somewhere in this house too. Just in case your iTunes somehow disappear into the clouds," Katie quipped.

"Katie, things get saved in the cloud. They don't disappear there. And, sadly, my 8-track player was lost to one of my mother's many yard sales somewhere around nineteen-eighty-three."

"That must have been devastating," Katie laughed. She turned to see Jake sliding into her car. "Julia, are you sure you don't mind Jake spending the night at my house? It's just that it's an early morning."

"Are you kidding? Look at him. Michael said the only thing he talked about all afternoon was spending tomorrow at the studio with you. Well, that and Monica," Julia chuckled.

Katie had offered to let Jake accompany her to the studio for Friday's taping of her show. Julia had enjoyed watching excitement light his eyes when she said that she thought it was a perfect idea.

"I'm just happy to see him so excited about something. Are you sure he won't be in your way?"

Katie glanced over to her car, and Jake waved. She had grown fond of Julia's eldest. He was a great deal like his mother with a youthful exuberance that warmed Katie's heart. "I'm positive."

"You know, he might keep you up all night if you let him," Julia said. "I haven't seen him this excited since that Christmas we gave him the skis he had been begging for. He was nine."

"Well, he'll be talking to himself after ten. I am beat," Katie said.

"You could've just crashed here," Julia said. Katie smiled. "Well, make sure you pack to stay here tomorrow. And, bring some extra stuff for Ian and Steph."

"What?" Katie chuckled. "Is this tree tradition of yours a pajama party?"

"Tree Trip Tradition," Julia corrected. "And, yes."

"Uh-huh."

"Just do it," Julia said flatly.

Katie couldn't have denied Julia if she had wanted to. Julia had been prattling on about the next day's festivities all afternoon. Katie couldn't imagine how Julia was not exhausted after entertaining all day. She wondered if Julia has secretly been popping caffeine pills.

"Did you spike the cranberry sauce or something?" Katie looked over Julia's shoulder toward the living room where four kids were laughing. It seemed everyone had an abundance of energy except her.

"No, that's tomorrow, and it's not cranberry sauce, it's eggnog. Secret to surviving Rudolph."

"Pizza and spiked eggnog? That is your secret to surviving Christmas cartoons?" Katie asked. Julia nodded. Katie leaned in and kissed Julia on the cheek. "You are one of a kind," she said.

Julia smiled. "I'll see you tomorrow."

"Yes, you will."

"Pack a bag!" Julia called after Katie.

Katie waved to Julia as she got into the car. "Your mother is nuts," she said to Jake.

Jake laughed. "Yeah, sometimes. That's why we love her, though."

"I guess it is," Katie said as she pulled out of the driveway.

෴ ෴ ෴

The sound of Burl Ives' voice seemed to fill every nook of the Riley house. Katie was gaining an understanding of Julia's egg-nog remedy's origins. Julia had her head under the large tree that Jake had cut down. The only visible part of Julia were her feet, which stuck out from underneath a swath of green branches. Jake was following the directions of the four younger kids as to where to position the behemoth. Katie tried not to laugh at the scene unfolding in front of her.

"A little left," Meghan directed as Stephanie whispered in her ear.

"Too far!" Jordan yelled out.

"Stop! There! Right there," a chorus of voices rang out.

"Finally," Katie heard Julia grumble. Katie chuckled.

Julia turned the screws in the stand to secure the tree firmly and scooted herself out from underneath. "I'm getting too old for this," she huffed.

Katie's outstretched hand greeted Julia's escape. "Come on, old lady," Katie joked. "Let's get you some eggnog."

Julia accepted Katie's help up and allowed herself to be pulled toward the kitchen. "Jake! Make sure you use all the lights!"

Julia called back. Katie snickered. "What are you laughing at?" Julia griped playfully.

Katie turned to face Julia and smiled. Pine needles stuck out of Julia's hair at peculiar angles. It was adorable. Katie became enraptured by the sight. She reached out and started gently removing them, taking the time to study Julia's features as she did. She froze when she felt Julia take hold of her hand. They stood perfectly still, Julia's fingers lightly caressing Katie's hand.

"You have tree in your hair," Katie barely whispered. Katie took a deep breath. Her heart had taken her head prisoner at the moment, and she began to lean forward.

"Mom!" Meghan yelled. "Jake is not listening!"

Julia closed her eyes and let out her breath, trying to find a way to recover naturally. Katie was equally shaken and took the opportunity to brush the pine off Julia's shoulder.

"Eggnog?" Katie asked Julia.

"Perfect," Julia answered. "I'm coming!" she called out. "Duty calls," she said with an impish grin.

Katie collapsed her head on the counter in frustration. "Jesus, Katherine. Get it together," she scolded herself. "Eggnog. I hope you have plenty of rum to go with that," she mused.

꙾ ꙾ ꙾

"Night, Mom," Jake said with a kiss to his mother's cheek. Julia smiled when he repeated the same affectionate action with Katie. "Night, Katie. Thanks for taking me today."

"You're welcome," Katie said with a smile.

"Tell those girls to settle down," Julia directed her son.

"They are wired," Katie observed.

"Too much sugar," Julia laughed. "That never changes. I should have thought twice about all that soda."

"Mmm," Katie yawned.

"Tired?" Julia asked.

"Relaxed," Katie responded honestly.

"You up for my After the Kids Pass Out Tradition?"

Katie squinted at Julia. "Do you have a tradition for everything?"

"No, just the important things," Julia replied. "So, go and get your jammies on. Oh, and, bring down that blanket on the end of the bed."

"What?" Katie laughed.

"Did I stutter? Jammies, slippers, blanket—that's part of the tradition."

"Who else knows about this tradition of yours?" Katie asked suspiciously.

"No one. Just you and me," Julia said.

"Uh-huh. And, how long has this tradition of yours been in effect?"

"Unofficially or officially?" Julia asked. Katie folded her arms across her chest and bit back her laughter. "Oh, fine. Unofficially, about six years. Every year after the kids all go to bed I settle in with a big mug of hot chocolate and a splash of Kahlua and watch *Christmas Vacation*. It's a thing. Officially, it's existed since about eight o'clock last night."

Katie grinned. "A new tradition, and I am the only one in the know. Really?"

Julia waved off Katie's theatrics. "Are you going to go get ready or not?"

Katie pretended to consider the request for a second before answering. "Are you making that cocoa?"

"If you go get changed then you will find out," Julia told her. "No jammies mean no cocoa, no movie, no Julia."

"You drive a hard bargain, Riley," Katie huffed. "Okay, you win. But, just so we are clear, I expect to see you making that cocoa in your jammies." Julia painted on a scowl. "No jammies mean no blanket, no Katie."

Julia scrunched her face in disapproval. "Fine."

Katie got up and headed for the stairs. "I'll bet they are Tigger or Smurfs too," she called back to Julia.

"You wish!" Julia scolded her as she followed behind.

"We'll see," Katie laughed.

≈ ≈ ≈

Katie made her way back into the living room with the blanket that Julia had requested. She flopped down onto the couch just as Julia walked in with their cocoa. "Nice jammies," Katie smirked.

"Aren't they?" Julia replied.

Katie shook her head and laughed. "Donkeys?"

"Democratic Donkeys," Julia returned.

"Where's my phone?" Katie asked urgently.

"What do you need your phone for?" Julia wondered.

"I want proof," Katie said. "If you ever run for office, I have the inside scoop as to the level of your party loyalty."

"Cute," Julia winked as she handed Katie her cocoa. "Okay, Ms. Braniac."

"What does that mean?" Katie asked.

"Nice and comfortable in your Yale sweats, are you? Show off," Julia groaned. "You know they turn out more Republicans."

Katie laughed. "You cannot hold the Bushes against Yale, Julia. As I recall, Billy did a stint there as well."

"Yeah, yeah," Julia conceded. She sat down next to Katie and clicked on the television.

Katie sipped her cocoa and looked at the tree in the corner. "It's a beautiful tree," she said. Julia nodded with a broad smile as the movie started.

A short time later, Katie's eyes began to grow heavy. She fought to keep them open, but they seemed to have a mind of their own. Julia pressed a button and reclined the couch.

"I love this couch," Katie moaned in appreciation.

Julia chuckled. "You can go to bed, Katie. It's okay."

"Uh-uh. Just need to rest my eyes," Katie yawned. Julia watched as Katie continued to fight her sleepiness. Slowly, Katie began to drift off, and her head landed on Julia's shoulder. Julia moved slightly and put her arm around Katie. Thinking Katie was asleep, she placed a light kiss on Katie's head.

"Thanks for sharing your tradition with me," Katie said as she finally gave over to her exhaustion.

"No one in the world I would rather start a tradition with," Julia told her sleeping friend as she let her eyes fall shut. "No one."

৵৩ ৵৩ ৵৩

Jake had made his way downstairs for a drink and wandered into the living room. The Christmas tree was still lit, and he was curious who would still be up. He stopped and shook his head at the sight on the couch. Katie was fast asleep on his mother's chest. Julia's head was resting on hers. They looked content. Jake grabbed another blanket from the hallway closet and covered them both up. He stepped back and considered them again. He was sure that he had never seen the expression that graced his mother's face before. He'd seen her cuddled with Carrie countless times over the years. He had covered her up on more than a few occasions when she had fallen asleep on the couch with a book. Right now, Julia looked peaceful. She looked younger, Jake thought. Katie's lips were turned up into a contented smile. He took a few extra moments to study them and found himself wondering how they couldn't see it. They just fit.

"Just tell her, Mom," Jake whispered as he left the room. "She might just surprise you."

≈ ≈ ≈

Katie woke first. She wasn't immediately sure of her surroundings, but she knew instantly whose body she was pressed against. She considered just feigning sleep a bit longer. She was used to being close to Julia. Their relationship had always been demonstrative, but this was different. At some point in the night, their positions had shifted to a decidedly more intimate embrace. Katie closed her eyes again, selfishly wishing that their close proximity had been deliberate. She breathed Julia in, savoring the last moments of Julia's arms around her. Reluctantly, she extricated herself from Julia's grasp. Katie stretched her neck and was surprised to find that she felt more rested than she could remember. She looked back at Julia with a longing she had never experienced. "How can I miss her when she's right here?" she wondered.

"Hey," a voice whispered.

Katie turned to see Jake standing a few feet away. A wave of fear tinged with embarrassment swept over her.

Jake smiled knowingly. "Come on," he said softly.

Katie followed Jake into the kitchen. "Jake, your mom...I mean your mom is..." Jake just kept smiling as Katie faltered. "She's my best friend," Katie said.

"I know that," Jake said. He poured Katie a cup of coffee which she accepted gratefully.

"Why are you already up?" she asked him.

Jake chuckled. "Already? It's ten o'clock," he told her. Katie nearly spit her coffee out. "Don't worry about it," Jake assured her, anticipating where Katie's thoughts had immediately traveled. Had anyone else walked in on her cozy slumber with his mother? "They are all in Meghan's room playing some game. They've been in there for hours," he told her. Katie breathed a sigh of relief. "And, I don't know about Stephanie and Ian, but I don't think you need to worry about Meg and Jordan," he said.

"Jake, nothing is going on between your mom and me," Katie said.

"I know that too," he said, taking a sip from his cup of coffee. Katie looked at him curiously. "Do you want there to be?" he asked Katie.

Katie shook her head. "I do not think this is an appropriate conversation for us to be having," she said.

"Guess that answers that question," Jake laughed.

"Jake…"

"It's cool," Jake assured Katie. "Don't worry about it."

"Don't worry about what?" a bleary-eyed Julia asked as she entered the room. For the second time in a few minutes, Katie nearly expelled the coffee in her mouth violently. She choked slightly. "You okay?" Julia asked Katie. Katie just nodded. "So, who is worried?" Julia asked.

Katie looked into her cup helplessly. Jake rescued her. "Katie. You know, she was worried that no one made breakfast."

"Oh," Julia yawned. "Holy shit! It's after ten."

"Yep," Jake said.

"How long have you been up?" Julia looked at Katie.

"About fifteen minutes."

Julia nodded. Unlike Katie, she vividly remembered pulling Katie into her arms. "Where are the kids?" she asked.

"In Meghan's room," Katie said.

"They haven't eaten?" Julia looked at her son.

Jake was having an increasingly difficult time keeping a straight face. He had never seen his mother or Katie behave so nervously. He was completely aware that his mother was fishing for information. Had anyone seen her holding Katie as they slept? For a moment, he considered allowing her to simmer a bit. Katie looked up at him with a pleading glance. Katie seemed to be able to convince him of almost anything.

"I brought them some Pop-Tarts and juice about an hour ago," he said, putting his mother out of her misery.

Katie mouthed the words "thank you."

Jake couldn't hold back his chuckle. "I'm gonna go say goodbye to them. Dad will be here in half an hour."

Julia turned to Katie. "Morning," she said. Katie just smiled. "You want something to eat?" Katie couldn't answer. She just stared at Julia blankly. "Earth to Katie," Julia called playfully.

"Julia?"

"You okay?" Julia asked gently.

"Yeah, of course. Just, you know, don't you? I mean, that...Well, how much you mean to me," Katie finally managed.

Julia smiled. "I think so."

"I don't know what I would do without you," Katie said quietly.

Julia took Katie's hand. "I'm not going anywhere," she said. Katie nodded. "Katie, I'm not going anywhere. I promise."

"You're my best friend, Julia," Katie whispered. "I don't want to lose you."

"Hey, where is this coming from?" Julia asked. She could see the insecurity in Katie's eyes. Julia mentally reprimanded herself for taking advantage of the previous night's events. She had thought that Katie was close to kissing her in the afternoon. Now, all she saw was apprehension in Katie's eyes, and it broke her heart. Perhaps she had misread the signals. "I don't start traditions unless I intend to keep them," she said. Katie looked up hopefully. "And, you're my best friend too. You're stuck with me for good." Julia winked at her friend before turning to start on breakfast.

"I hope so," Katie mused silently. "I hope so."

Chapter Seventeen

DECEMBER 2015

Two weeks had flown by. Julia had barely seen Katie since Thanksgiving. Katie had been in New York, Miami, and Chicago to tape a string of shows on location. They had spoken daily, but Julia found that the phone was a sorry substitute for Katie's company. The distance had Julia reeling slightly. Thanksgiving had proved to be an emotional roller coaster. In spite of Julia's reassurances, and Katie's professions about not wanting to lose Julia, Julia was feeling anxious. Julia's gut told her that the recent distance was due to schedules and commitments. Still, the separation was reminiscent of the months that she and Katie had spent apart, and that terrified Julia. She had been delighted when Katie had called from Chicago to talk about the upcoming holiday.

"So, what are your plans?" Katie asked.

"Sleep, work, and more sleep," Julia answered. "The kids are leaving with Carrie and Bess at eleven on Christmas morning."

"How are you doing with that?" Katie asked.

"I can't complain. I had them all weekend over Thanksgiving, and they will all be at the house Christmas Eve," Julia said. Katie knew that no matter what Julia said, the idea of being apart from her children over Christmas was painful for her. That was something she understood

completely. Stephanie and Ian's holiday departure had been plaguing her thoughts for weeks. "What about you?" Julia asked Katie.

"Putting the kids on a plane Christmas Eve morning, and heading to my parents' for the holiday. I'll be home Wednesday. Makes me so mad. I arranged to have the week off and didn't need to," Katie griped. "Oh, well."

"I'm sorry, Katie."

"Not your fault. Listen, do you have plans this Saturday?" Katie asked hopefully.

"Nope. Carrie has the kids this weekend," Julia said.

"I know. How about an early Christmas at my house?" Katie suggested.

"An early Christmas? Is this a tradition I should be aware of?"

"No, you are better at those, I confess. And, besides, I'd like to think we might actually see each other on Christmas one of these years," Katie replied. Julia smiled on the other end of the line, feeling a sense of relief wash away her anxiety. "How about it? My parents are taking the kids for their Christmas celebration this weekend. What do you say? I'll even dust off my Betty Crocker Cookbook."

"See? You do have one!" Julia answered excitedly.

"Anyone with a mother who was born before nineteen sixty has a Betty Crocker Cookbook," Katie replied evenly. "So, I will see you Saturday? Four o'clock work for you?"

"Yeah," Julia said quietly.

"Everything okay there, Riley?"

"Yeah. Guess maybe I just miss you a little," Julia admitted hesitantly.

Katie inhaled a deep breath. She had been agonizing over Thanksgiving. Perhaps, Jake was right. Maybe she should come clean with Julia about her feelings. That thought simultaneously produced exhilaration and trepidation for Katie. She had committed every texture, every scent, and every emotion that had flowed through her while Julia *had held her to memory. The thought that she might never feel that connection again was nearly unbearable for her. The last two weeks had been hell for Katie. She missed her children; she missed Julia's children, and she missed Julia.*

"I miss you too," Katie said honestly. "I'll call you when I get in on Friday."

"Katie, if it's too much, we can…"

"It's not too much."

"Okay, I'll talk you soon," Julia said.

"Yes, you will."

❧ ❧ ❧

"Jules?" Carrie said with a smirk. "It's just dinner. It's not like you don't see Katie all of the time."

"I know," Julia said.

"So, why are you pacing the kitchen floor?" Carrie laughed.

"I'm not pacing."

Carrie shook her head and laughed harder. "You are pathetic, Jules. Why don't you just admit it? Just tell Katie how you feel about her."

Julia sat down at the kitchen table and put her face in her hands. "I can't," she mumbled.

Carrie sat across from her ex-wife and reached for her hand. "You know, one of these days you are going to have to forgive yourself," Carrie said flatly. Julia's head popped up. "I know you, Julia. I know how much Katie means to you." Carrie sighed at the consternation on Julia's face. "Okay, you win. For now, anyway."

"Thanks," Julia groaned.

"There is something I wanted to talk to you about," Carrie said.

"Everything okay?"

"Yes…. It's…. Well, Bess asked me to move in," Carrie explained.

Julia's reaction was unflinching. "About time, isn't it?" Carrie shrugged uncomfortably. "Weren't you just trying to convince me to profess my undying love to another woman?" Julia laughed. Carrie lifted an eyebrow at her ex-wife. "And, you think that I will be shaken by this earthquake of yours?" Julia inquired playfully. "Care, you basically live there now," she stated the obvious.

"But, I don't live there now," Carrie said.

"Is there some reason that you would not want to make things more official?" Julia asked. Carrie sighed. "Care?"

"No. I just…. It's not like I expected this all to happen so soon," Carrie replied.

Julia nodded. "You mean falling in love with someone else?"

"Yes, or starting a life with someone else," Carrie answered.

"But, you have already done that," Julia observed. Carrie looked at Julia with unshed tears glistening in her eyes. "Care, if you are worried about me, don't be. I'm happy for you."

"I know you are," Carrie said. "I guess I just thought it would be you."

"What do you mean?" Julia asked.

"I mean, I thought it would be you to move on first."

"I'm not sure I know what to say," Julia responded softly. "Things tend to work out the way they are meant too, Carrie. I really am happy for you."

"Jules? Are you sure you are okay with Bess and I taking the kids away over the holidays? I mean, Jake is only home for a few weeks, and he is your…."

"He is our son," Julia stopped Carrie's diatribe. "And yes, I am sure. I will miss them. I'll miss you," Julia said honestly. "Hell, I will even miss Bess," she chuckled. "This is our life now."

"It's Christmas," Carrie said sadly. "We've always spent Christmas as a family. We promised we would keep our family traditions as much as possible."

"Yes, we did. Our family is different now," Julia pointed out.

"I know," Carrie said tacitly.

"It's bigger," Julia said with a smile. Carrie nodded her appreciation. "Maybe we need some new traditions. And, let's face it, it won't be long before the kids have families of their own."

"Bite your tongue," Carrie scolded Julia.

"You know what I mean."

"Yeah, I do," Carrie admitted. "I just don't ever want you to think that I am…"

"Stop," Julia said flatly. "We'll figure it out as we go. That's what we have always done."

"True enough," Carrie agreed. "I love you, Jules."

Julia kissed her ex-wife on the cheek. "I know. I love you too."

"Promise me you will do something for yourself while we are away?" Carrie implored Julia.

"I promise I will keep myself busy."

Carrie got up from the table and took Julia's face in her hands. "You are stubborn, Julia Riley, but you have a big heart."

"You're biased."

"No, just honest. Just…Give yourself a chance, Jules."

Julia giggled at Carrie's persistence. "You are relentless, Care."

"I like Katie."

"So do I," Julia laughed. Carrie smirked. "Okay, Yente, that's enough. You have boxes to pack. I have presents to wrap."

"What did you get her?" Carrie asked curiously as they headed to the door.

"Nosy, nosy. Something she needs," Julia grinned. "And, something she loves."

Carrie smiled and kissed Julia on the cheek goodbye. "In that case, all you need is a bow on your head," Carrie thought silently.

"Have a good weekend, Jules. Say hello to Katie," Carrie said.

"I will. I'll pick up the kids Monday."

Carrie waved and hopped in her car. "Oh, Julia," she sighed. "I should wrap up a giant anvil and drop it on your head," she snickered as she backed out of the driveway.

❦ ❦ ❦

"You got that dinner from Betty Crocker?" Julia asked with the raise of her brow.

"What? You doubt me, Riley?" Katie said with a gentle whack on Julia's arm.

"I wouldn't dream of it. Pretty fancy for Betty's day," Julia said.

"You would be amazed. She is a woman of the world now. Even has her very own website," Katie offered seriously.

"Uh-huh," Julia smirked.

Julia had enjoyed dinner immensely. It wasn't often that she got to spend an entire evening alone with Katie. They had enjoyed a lively, adult conversation over dinner, a dinner that Julia had noticed Katie had put considerable effort into preparing. Now, they sat in Katie's living room relaxing with a glass of wine. Gentle jazz harmonies echoed in the background. Soft light was cast across the room by the Christmas tree. Julia looked across at Katie as she retrieved two boxes from underneath the tree. Katie was casually dressed in jeans and a dark green sweater that brought out the changing color of her eyes. Julia watched every move that Katie made. Katie was the most magnificent person Julia had ever known. She was elegant and charming, the kind of woman that many would assume was tainted by conceit. Katie was nothing of the sort. She was humble and real. Julia wondered if Katie had any idea how breathtakingly beautiful she was. And, to Julia, Katie represented the most incredible sight in creation. Julia struggled to steady her emotions as Katie made her way back across the room.

"You okay?" Katie asked, noticing the flush in Julia's cheeks. "You're a bit flushed."

"And you're gorgeous," Julia thought silently. Julia smiled at Katie. "Must be the wine."

Katie grinned, seeing a hint of something else in Julia's eyes. "Mm. You want to open your presents?" Katie asked.

"You know, you didn't have to get me anything," Julia said honestly.

"This from the woman who unloaded a sleigh's worth of presents into my house?" Katie laughed. Julia had shown up with several armloads of gifts for Katie's family.

"The kids wanted to shop. You know how it is," Julia shrugged.

Katie pursed her lips in amusement. Sometimes the biggest kid in the Riley household was Julia. It was one of the parts of Julia's personality that Katie loved the most. Katie handed Julia a large box. "You go first."

Julia considered the box before her thoughtfully. "Nothing is going to jump out at me, is it?"

"I don't know," Katie answered. Julia took an additional few minutes to study the wrapped present. Katie looked on, shaking her head at Julia's childlike antics. "Would you just open it?" Katie finally implored her friend.

Julia pretended to be wounded but complied with Katie's direction. She got through the wrapping to reveal a large, plain box. Julia looked at Katie curiously, but Katie just shrugged. Slowly, Julia peeled the tape back and reached inside to retrieve the contents. She closed her eyes and shook her head in amusement when her present was finally revealed. "Are you trying to tell me something?" Julia asked as she held up the 8-track tapes.

"You need to practice," Katie explained. "I figured I would start you out on something familiar, you know, start at your own speed."

Julia licked her lips and tried to withhold her laughter. She pulled out the old 8-track tape player and looked at Katie as seriously as she could manage. "The Bee Gees, Donna Summer, Village People…"

"Don't forget Grease!" Katie chimed.

"I wouldn't dream of it. Is disco making a comeback?" Julia asked.

"Not necessarily, but it's something you have some experience with. One of these days, Riley, someone is going to drag you onto a dance floor—all of these events you attend and whatnot. You need to be prepared. Isn't that the scout's motto?"

"It's the Boy Scout motto," Julia returned. "And, I only dance in the privacy of the shower these days."

"Not anymore. Branch out of the bathroom, Riley. You have a bedroom and a basement. Pick one," Katie told her.

"I'll think about it," Julia said. She grabbed a box next to her and handed it to Katie. "Here you go," she said. Katie shook the box. "Oh, just open it."

"Should I be afraid?" Katie asked.

"Probably," Julia replied. Katie ripped open the wrapping and rolled her eyes. "What?" Julia asked. "*You* need to be prepared, Brennan. Now you have proper backup."

"Always looking out for me, huh?" Katie asked as she held up her Rolodex.

"Or looking out for me," Julia replied. "This way you can never say you lost my number."

Katie smiled at Julia. There was an undercurrent of pain in Julia's playful statement. "I don't need any backup to remember where to find you," Katie said softly. She reached beside her and handed Julia a second gift. "Here."

Julia sensed a shift in Katie's mood and opened the present without comment. "Katie," she spoke the name softly when the contents of the box were revealed.

Katie watched as Julia's fingers traced the glass of the picture frame. "I hated this week," Katie said honestly. "I know, Julia…I know that I hurt you once…"

"Katie…"

"No, listen. You never want to talk about this."

"There's nothing to talk about," Julia said sincerely. "That's the past."

"Yes, maybe it is. I hated not seeing you the last two weeks," Katie said. "It didn't feel right. I know part of you was feeling like I was pulling away again."

"Katie…"

"Julia, please. I just want you to know that I don't ever want there to be a time in my life that you are not a part of. So, maybe that will help remind you."

Julia nodded. She looked down at the picture that Katie had framed. Jake had taken it of the two of them with his phone when they had visited him in October. Julia realized that Katie must have asked Jake to send it to her. She looked back to her friend with an appreciative grin. "I love it," Julia said.

Katie breathed a sigh of relief. The gift was her way of trying to say "I love you" without words. She was certain by the glistening in Julia's eyes that Julia understood Katie's emotional sentiment, but it was also clear that sometimes there was no substitute for words. "I'm glad you like it. I had Jake email it to me."

"Here," Julia said, handing Katie an envelope.

"What's this?" Katie asked. Julia just smiled and waited for Katie to open it. "Julia," Katie whispered.

"I hope you don't have plans," Julia said.

"I can't believe you did this," Katie said.

Katie sat in stunned disbelief at the pair of tickets to the Boston Pops Orchestra for New Year's Eve. Katie was a music aficionado. She listened to classical, jazz, swing, pop, rock, Broadway musicals, and country. Julia was fairly certain that every artist that had ever recorded was represented somewhere in Katie's collection. Between work commitments and raising two children, Katie seldom managed to see a live concert or show. It was one of the few guilty pleasures that Katie confessed to Julia she often missed.

Katie's lingering silence was beginning to unnerve Julia. "It was presumptuous, I know. If you have plans…"

"Plans?" Katie looked up in alarm. "No…I mean, I guess I do now," she corrected herself. Julia smiled in relief.

Katie slid over and kissed Julia on the cheek. "You are the best, Riley, you now that?"

"Yeah, but you can feel free to tell me anytime," Julia quipped. She looked at Katie and kissed her on the forehead, wishing she had the courage to say more. "You're pretty okay yourself, Ms. Brennan."

Katie pulled back, needing to put some space between them before she lost her senses. "You up for a movie?" she asked Julia.

"You going to fall asleep on me?" Julia teased.

"No," Katie promised. She got up and headed for the television. "But I certainly could think of worse ways to spend the evening," she mumbled to herself.

Julia was busy cleaning up their mess. "Did you say something?" Julia asked.

"No, just wondering if you'd rather listen to those 8-tacks," Katie said.

"Cute," Julia replied. "You might be the only one I would dance for," Julia thought. Julia chose humor as her response instead. "This is not my bedroom," she said. "And, I am not alone."

Katie made her way to the couch with about ten witty retorts on the tip of her tongue. She thought better of them all. "Merry Christmas, Riley," she said as Julia took a seat beside her.

"Merry Christmas, Katie."

～ ～ ～

ONE WEEK LATER

Katie walked into Julia's office to find her hovering over the computer. "Hey, there," she greeted the woman behind the desk. The moment that Julia looked up at Katie, Katie's eyes opened wide in concern. She'd never seen dark circles under Julia's eyes like the ones glaring at her now. Julia's skin looked almost a light gray.

"What are you doing here?" Julia asked through a cough.

"I think the question is what are you doing here?" Katie asked.

"What do you mean?" Julia coughed again. "I work here. I thought you were going to be at your parents' house until tomorrow."

"I decided to come home early. Thought maybe with the kids away, you could use some company," Katie said. "You look like you could use an undertaker," Katie raised her eyebrow. Katie noted the wheezing sound that accompanied Julia's chuckle.

"I am always happy to have your company," Julia said honestly. "I just need to finish a couple of things," she said as she rose from her chair. "I need to check the," Julia's thoughts trailed off as she became lightheaded.

Katie found her feet quickly and guided Julia back into her chair. "Julia," she whispered. Katie put her hand on Julia's forehead. "Jesus, you are burning up. How long have you been like this?" she asked with growing concern. Julia just shrugged. "Julia?"

"I'm okay. I'm sure I'm just overtired, and I caught a cold. Let me just finish setting up these appointments for…"

Katie reached over and clicked off Julia's computer. "That's it. The only appointment you have is at the walk-in clinic—right now." The firmness is Katie's voice caused Julia to look up sheepishly. "I mean it, Riley. Now."

Julia started to laugh, but her laugh was immediately silenced by a coughing fit. "Katie…"

Katie had already retrieved Julia's coat and was standing back in front of her. "Don't bother arguing," Katie told her flatly. Julia stood up, wavering again as Katie steadied her. "What the hell are you doing at work?" Katie asked with growing worry. Julia just shook her head. Katie sighed. "Come on. Let's go get you feeling better," Katie suggested. Julia nodded. She was too sick to argue, and she knew it. Katie was looking at her with so much tenderness and worry that Julia would never have refused her anything. "Good," Katie said. "Glad that's settled."

෴ ෴ ෴

Katie hopped back into the car with Julia's prescriptions in hand and looked at Julia, who was shivering despite the blasting heat. She shook her head and reached across to Julia. "Let's get you home, Riley. You need to follow the doctor's advice and rest." Katie watched as Julia labored for a breath. Julia deliberately kept her gaze out the window. "Julia?" Katie called to her.

"I don't want to go home," Julia mumbled.

Katie sighed. "Why not?" she asked gently. Julia continued to stare out the window silently. "Julia?"

"It's too quiet," Julia answered in a whisper.

Katie squeezed Julia's knee. "Okay," she said. Julia turned to Katie with a questioning glance. "Then we'll go get your things and you can come to my house."

"You don't have to take care of me," Julia mumbled.

Katie gave another gentle squeeze to Julia's knee before starting the car with a smile. Julia had no intention of trying to dissuade Katie. Katie's mind was made up, and Julia was secretly relieved, both to have someone with her, and that Katie was that someone.

෴ ෴ ෴

Julia's house had been quiet when Katie and Julia entered. Much quieter than it had been the year before, Katie mused. It was almost impossible for Katie to believe that a full year had passed since she had met Julia. And yet, there were times that Katie felt an entire lifetime had passed within that year. It had been just over a year since Katie had received the call that changed her life forever. It had been Julia that had supported her through those agonizing first days. Katie rested her head against the large leather chair in Julia's living room and closed her eyes. She remembered the first time she had sat in Julia's living room, in the very chair that she now occupied. A smiled painted her lips as she recalled Julia seated across from her. No matter how many emotions and questions had plagued Katie's heart and mind, Julia had always been able to quiet them.

Katie opened her eyes and strained to listen. Julia had insisted that she was fine to go gather some things. Katie was trying not to hover over Julia, but she couldn't help but be concerned. In addition to Julia fighting against what the doctor had determined was a severe case of bronchitis, a double ear infection, and a sinus infection, Katie was certain that something was weighing on Julia's mind. Julia had barely been able to stand on her own power at the clinic. That was enough on its own to worry Katie. There was more driving Julia's unsteadiness than just her physical illness. The moment they had pulled into the driveway, Julia had become withdrawn. The longer that Katie waited for Julia's return, the more concerned she became. After a few more minutes of attempting to convince herself that Julia was an adult and fine, Katie finally gave up. No logical argument seemed capable of quelling her instincts. She reached her feet and headed up the stairs.

A faint sound greeted Katie from Julia's bedroom as she made her way through the hallway, and she picked up her pace. Katie's heart dropped when she reached the door. Julia was lying on the bed, clutching a pillow, sobbing uncontrollably. It was no secret to Katie that Julia did not enjoy appearing vulnerable. Right now, Julia was more vulnerable than Katie had ever seen her, and it only made Katie love her more. With a deep sigh, Katie made her way to the edge of the bed and reached out for her friend.

"Julia," Katie called gently to her friend. "Talk to me." She saw the shake of Julia's head. "Julia…"

Julia turned slightly to face Katie. Her eyes were rimmed a bright red, and Katie winced at the wheezing sound coming from Julia's lungs. Being emotionally upset was adding to Julia's physical distress, and her illness was making Julia all the more susceptible to the emotional tide that had taken hold of her. Katie reached out and traced the outline of Julia's face gently. The only word she was able to discern through Julia's tears was, "quiet." Katie leaned down and pulled Julia to her. She half expected Julia to resist the embrace, but Julia willingly collapsed into Katie's arms, a new flood of emotions availing themselves in her tears.

"Not quite that *Riley Door Policy* you are used to, is it?" Katie guessed. Julia managed a slight chuckle but continued to cry. "I know, sweetheart," Katie said softly as she rocked Julia gently. "I know." Julia continued to cry as Katie held her. "That's why you went to work, isn't it? You're missing them," Katie guessed. Julia nodded against Katie. "Sweetheart, it's okay," Katie tried to soothe her.

Julia looked up at Katie and managed a small smile. "I'm being a baby," she finally said as her tears began to subside.

"Because you miss your family?" Katie asked. "I don't think so."

"No, because I am the one who left them," Julia said.

Katie sighed and instinctively held Julia tighter. Julia carried a great deal of guilt. She was the caretaker, and Katie knew that some part of Julia felt that she had failed in that endeavor. "I'm sure they miss you too. I know how you feel," Katie said.

Julia looked at Katie sympathetically. This Christmas was Katie's first holiday apart from her children and Julia knew that was painful for Katie. "Aww, Katie...I'm such a jerk. I know you miss Steph and Ian."

Katie nodded. "I do," she admitted. "You're not a jerk. You know, I came home early because I missed you." Katie said the words so quietly that Julia barely heard her.

Julia smiled and was about to tell Katie how much she had missed her, but her lungs had other ideas. The coughing spell that hit Julia racked her body and Katie was helpless to do anything but wait for it to subside.

"Okay," Katie said as Julia finally caught her breath. "I know you don't want to stay here, but I think for tonight you need to stay put. We need to get that medicine into you. The last thing you need is another trip outside in the freezing cold."

"Producing that show has made you bossy," Julia laughed through another cough.

"Says the politician," Katie returned. "Let's find you something more comfortable and I'll see about heating you up some soup."

"Katie, you don't have to stay with me," Julia said as she made her way off the bed. Julia noticed the slight flicker of sadness in Katie's eyes.

"Do you want to be alone?" Katie asked.

Julia shook her head. "No," she said definitively.

"Then stop telling me what I don't need to do. Someone needs to keep you in line, Riley. Those kids will be back Sunday night, you know," Katie reminded her.

Julia nodded. She started toward the bathroom and lost her balance. Katie was at her side in an instant.

"It's the ear infection," Julia explained.

Katie cupped Julia's cheek affectionately. "For once, Julia," she said thoughtfully. "Please, let me take care of you."

Julia looked at Katie for a long while without responding. She was at war with herself. The more time they spent together, the more challenging it became for Julia to keep silent about her feelings. "You take care of me all the time," Julia said honestly. "You don't even know it." She placed a kiss on Katie's cheek and made her way to the bathroom.

Katie stood dumbfounded for a moment. She closed her eyes and caught her breath. She'd been tempted to say the words, "I love you." Why was that so hard to say, she wondered? She did. She loved Julia. She'd known it for months. Something still held her back. "I just can't lose you," Katie said. "I just can't."

❧ ❧ ❧

"You okay?" Katie asked Julia.

Katie had managed to coax Julia to eat something and to swallow down her medicine. There were moments when Katie would catch Julia pouting. Katie would have found that infuriating with most people. When it came to Julia, Katie found it endearing. Katie was certain that Julia did not want to seem needy. As sick as she was, Julia was worried about Katie's needs, asking if Katie had eaten enough, was warm enough, wanted a pillow, what did Katie want to do. Katie's answer was to suggest they watch some movies in the family room. It would keep Julia quiet, and provide the right atmosphere where Katie could surreptitiously keep an eye on Julia. Julia needed to sleep. Katie kept watch, noting that Julia's eyes would grow heavy before Julia would slowly pry them open again. Every so often, Katie noticed that Julia would grimace and start rubbing her temples with the heels of her hands. She suspected that Julia's earlier emotional breakdown had conspired with her illness to bring on a headache, one that was making the sleep Julia needed impossible for her to achieve.

"Just a headache," Julia confirmed Katie's suspicion.

Katie grabbed the pillow next to Julia and placed it in her lap. "Come here," she directed Julia. Julia looked at Katie hesitantly. "Come on, Riley. I promise it will be painless. In fact, it might help with the pain in your head."

Julia thought for a second that she should protest. The combination of pain, fatigue, and medicine was making her woozy. Her defenses were down. When Julia's defenses were lowered, she often spoke without thinking. She had come dangerously close to telling Katie how she felt several times already. Julia offered Katie a sheepish grin and placed her head on the pillow.

"I know you are enthralled by this movie," Katie joked. "It will still be here tomorrow. Close your eyes," she said softly as her fingers began a gentle massage of Julia's temples.

Julia did as Katie instructed. She worried for a split second that Katie's touch would produce a passionate response from her. After their close call in the kitchen at Thanksgiving, Julia had been finding it increasingly difficult to suppress her attraction to Katie. At this moment, Katie's tender caress generated something far more profound than desire, something Julia had never experienced with another person. Katie's touch had a healing quality, and not simply for the throbbing in Julia's temples. Julia felt peaceful. She felt her body relax as Katie's voice carried softly to her aching ears.

"Go to sleep," Katie said gently.

Julia instinctively snuggled closer to Katie. She could feel her body willingly begin to submit to the rest she required. Sound became distant. The conscious world fell away from her, and she let herself fall with it. Katie smiled when she felt Julia's head press firmly against her. "I wish you were really here," Julia mumbled.

Katie looked down and realized that Julia had reached a place that existed somewhere between sleep and wakefulness, the place where dreams and reality collided. "I am here," Katie whispered. She played with Julia's hair and kissed her on the head.

Julia had become lost to the waking world. She could feel Katie holding her, but in the foggy world of drug-induced sleep, she found that reality impossible to process. Julia had been falling asleep for weeks wishing that she could hold Katie—wishing that she could somehow will it into reality. She longed to hold Katie again, and she feared that it would never come to pass. If this was a dream, Julia did not want the dream to end. She inhaled deeply. The light scent of Katie's perfume tickled her senses, and the warmth of Katie's hand as it combed lovingly through her hair calmed her.

Julia sighed in contentment. "I love you," Julia said sleepily.

For a moment, Katie held her breath. Julia was asleep. She wanted to believe that the words were meant for her, but she was terrified to believe it was so. Katie had just closed her eyes when Julia mumbled in her sleep again.

"Katie."

Katie leaned over and let her lips linger on Julia's forehead. "I love you, Julia," she spoke the words aloud.

Katie knew Julia was in a different world now. In some ways, she felt guilty for speaking the words at this moment. Julia deserved to hear them, and not when Katie felt it was safe. Katie couldn't help herself—not now. She watched Julia sleep. An expression of contentment painted Julia's face. Julia's features would soften each time

Katie's hand connected with her skin, and Katie was certain that she had never loved a person more. Katie closed her eyes again and reveled in Julia's closeness. She felt a tear slip over her cheek as her feelings and her fears made themselves known. She could not imagine her life without Julia in it.

Katie had no intention of sleeping, not wanting to miss one moment of Julia in her embrace. It felt natural. It felt right, as if this was where she had always belonged. She wondered how she would tell Julia that. Katie was as sure as she could be that Julia loved her, but she sensed a reluctance on Julia's part to move their relationship in a new direction. Katie remained at a loss as to how to build that bridge. It was becoming impossible to avoid. She needed Julia, and she was beginning to realize she needed much more than playful banter and long talks. She needed more than Julia's friendship. Katie wanted to spend her life with Julia—all of it.

"I love you so much," Katie whispered.

Julia moved closer. Katie closed her eyes when Julia's arm wrapped around her waist. "I love you, Katie," Julia said without waking.

Katie sighed. "I know you do, Riley. I know you do."

Chapter Eighteen

Julia's Diary

Life is a funny thing. It goes on around you every moment. Sometimes, you forget that you are a part of it at all. You seldom think about the fact that life is temporary. You take it for granted that tomorrow will come. You see the evolution in your children's faces. You see the subtle shifts when you look in the mirror, but they happen so gradually that you fail to realize what they mean. In life, there is an ending.

Love. Love is different. You fall against your will into a bottomless sea of emotion in love. Sometimes you float. Sometimes you sink. Sometimes you fight to swim against the tide. Love is like an undertow. You can fight it with every ounce of energy you have, it is far more powerful than you, and it inevitably sweeps you under. Once love takes hold, it remains. Love is what remains when life finds its ending. It is the bridge that connects where we have been, where we now reside, and where we ultimately need to travel.

JANUARY 2016

Julia watched Ian as he gave Jordan the tour of his grandparents' house. Julia had been surprised when Katie invited the Riley clan for a day at her parents' home. She had met Katie's parents a few times during Bill's hospital stay the previous year, but she had not seen them since. Katie's parents spent a good deal of time trav-eling since retiring. But, Katie's professional commitments in December and January had prompted her parents to stay home for the winter to help Katie with Stephanie and Ian.

Bob and Ruth McAllister were warm, generous people. It was easy for Julia to see where Katie had acquired both her good-nature and her good looks. Katie's parents had welcomed Julia and her children as if they had been part of the family for years. It made Julia's heart ache slightly for her parents. Jake was sitting beside her, talking with Katie's father about history and government. Bob McAllister seemed to delight in Jake's curiosity and openness to de-bate. Katie had skipped off into the kitchen with her mother. Julia wondered what the McAllister women were discussing.

"Katherine," Ruth McAllister looked across the counter at her daughter. Katie smiled. "Is there something you want to tell me?" she asked. Katie's confusion was evident. "Kate?"

Katie shook her head. "There's nothing to tell," she said.

"You are in love with Julia," Ruth said flatly. Katie smiled sadly. "Does she know?" Ruth asked. Katie shook her head. "Why not?"

"It's not that simple, Mom," Katie said.

"It never is," Ruth chuckled.

"Gee, thanks for the encouragement. You don't seem all that surprised," Katie remarked.

"I'm not. Should I be?"

"No," Katie replied.

"It wouldn't be the first time you fell for an enigmatic woman," Ruth said with a smirk. The remark startled Katie. Her mother laughed. "Maggie Spencer. Ring any bells?"

Katie groaned. Maggie Spencer had been a college friend. Katie had never told her parents about their brief liaison, and she had no desire to discuss it now. "Maggie was a friend, Mom."

"That you had a relationship with," Ruth said without missing a beat.

"What? Why would you say that?" Katie asked. "That was over twenty years ago."

"So? I wasn't born yesterday. I do have two children as you may recall. Contrary to your hopes, the stork did not drop you on my doorstep," Ruth teased. "You are an open book, Katherine. That girl broke your heart, and you leapt right into Bill's arms."

Katie sighed dramatically. It was true. The only person she had ever confided in about Maggie was John. As far as Katie knew, no one else had any knowledge of the nature of their relationship. "Did John tell you?" Katie asked.

"No one needed to tell me anything. It was written all over your face, just like it is now," Ruth said.

"Big difference now," Katie said.

"Yes, Julia is not Maggie," Ruth observed. "She's a grown woman, a woman who is clearly crazy about you."

"Maybe," Katie said. "I wish it were that simple."

"Kate," Ruth said. "What are you worried about? Your career?"

Katie laughed. "Not at all."

"Then what is it? Bill?" her mother asked.

"No. I just don't want to jeopardize what we already have," Katie answered truthfully. Ruth McAllister laughed. "Why is that funny?" Katie inquired.

"You are risking more by not following your heart," Ruth said seriously.

"We are not you and Dad," Katie reminded her mother. Ruth just grinned. "Oh, just say what you want to say," Katie said with a roll of her eyes.

Ruth grew more serious. "Time passes quickly, Kate. Very quickly. Look at the kids. Before you know it you will be having a conversation like this with one of them in your kitchen. Things change, and when things change it is loving someone that will keep you steady, letting them love you."

"I don't want to lose her," Katie admitted.

"I can see that.

"What if she doesn't…"

Ruth took hold of Katie's shoulders. "If you want to have the big rewards, Kate, you have to take the big risks. Eventually, everyone leaves," she said softly with a smile. "That's part of life too. Take the ride while you can, sweetheart." Katie nodded and put her head on her mother's shoulder. "Tell her."

"I don't know how," Katie said.

"Yes, I think you do."

"I'm not sure…"

Ruth hugged her daughter and whispered in her ear. "You'll know when the time is right. You'll feel it. When you do, you tell her. Don't argue with yourself, Kate. That won't get you anywhere except lonely. Just follow your heart."

ॐ ॐ ॐ

TWO WEEKS LATER

Julia was engrossed in her email when Katie stepped into the doorway of her office. "Must be fascinating reading," Katie said.

"Hey," Julia grinned, thankful for the interruption. "What brings you downtown at this hour?"

Katie chuckled. "Why are you still here at this hour?"

"I asked you first," Julia reminded her.

"God, you can be so frustrating sometimes," Katie observed.

"So?" Julia asked. Katie placed an envelope in front of Julia and directed her to open it. "What's this?"

"Let's not play twenty questions, Riley. Just open the damn envelope," Katie ordered.

Julia huffed and did as she was told. She pulled out the contents and looked at Katie quizzically.

"You missed our New Year's Eve date," Katie explained. "While I enjoyed spending the evening with Her Majesty, I would have preferred the original arrangement. So, the next show is February 12th. Unless there is some beautiful woman wooing you for Valentine's Day that weekend, I thought maybe you would like to try again."

Julia stared at Katie for a moment. "You want to spend Valentine's Day together?" she asked. Katie's heart stopped for a minute. Julia laughed. "I would love to go to the symphony with you, but, on one condition," she said.

"My present comes with your conditions?" Katie asked in amusement.

"Yes. I am the one who ruined New Years, and here you are trying to make it up to me."

"You did not ruin a thing," Katie said.

Julia had been sick for a full week. If Katie were to be truthful, while she hated seeing Julia so ill, she had enjoyed taking care of Julia. Katie had all but moved into Julia's house until New Years. The kids were all away, and Katie loved just being with Julia. It didn't matter to her if Julia was sleeping or if they were sitting playing Scrabble. Spending time with Julia was better than any gift someone could wrap. She had been disappointed that Julia was not up to their planned event on New Year's Eve. Katie had wanted to give the tickets away and stay with Julia, but Julia took it upon herself to call John and forced the issue. Katie's proposal for a do-over was as much for Katie as it was for Julia.

"Well, you let me take you to a fabulous dinner beforehand, and we will call it even," Julia said.

Katie contemplated the offer. "That means I don't have to work with Betty that night?"

Julia laughed. "No. Betty can have the night off. So can Ina, Rachel, and the rest of the cookbook brigade."

"You really are an expert negotiator, Riley," Katie said. "Deal."

"Now, seriously, what are you doing down here at night? Where are the kids?" Julia asked.

"Her Majesty is taking them to dinner. It happens—occasionally," Katie explained.

"Does that mean you are free for dinner?" Julia asked.

"That depends."

"On what?" Julia asked.

"On whether or not Betty and the girls will be needed," Katie explained.

"Nope. I was thinking more along the lines of dial out, deliver in."

"Lazy," Katie chided.

"Exhausted," Julia replied.

"Why are you here so late?" Katie asked, bringing the conversation full circle. "I was surprised to see your car when I dropped the kids off to John."

Julia rubbed her eyes in frustration. "We're scheduled to break ground the first week in March. There's so much to coordinate—sponsors, donors, dignitaries, and we are still working on a skeleton crew here. I was on the phone all morning with the city, dealing with permits. Six weeks goes fast. I still have about four emails I need to deal with before I can leave."

"Well, why don't you finish what you need to here? I'll stop at Feng's and pick something up, find one of those terrible science fiction movies you love, and you just come over when you are ready," Katie suggested.

"He really is a total idiot."

"What?" Katie asked.

Julia was so tired that she was thinking out loud. "Bill. I told you a long time ago he should be tested for that gene. Who the hell would let you go?"

Katie managed an uncomfortable grin. She realized that Julia was musing aloud unintentionally. It wasn't the first time. Exhaustion and illness were the two things that always seemed to lower Julia's defenses.

"Well, I don't know about that," Katie said. "I do know there will be Chinese food on my table in about half an hour. See you in a bit?"

Julia nodded. Katie smiled and waved goodbye as she left.

"Well, I do know," Julia continued her assessment of Katie's ex-husband privately. "He'd fail. Thank God the kids got your intelligence," she chuckled. Julia returned her focus to her work. She warned her computer with the wag of a finger. "No more emails. Four and we are done. No more. I do not have the stupidity gene. There is a beautiful woman with Chinese food on her table waiting for me. Four. Not one more," Julia said. "Sweet Jesus, listen to me. You are losing it, Jules." Julia shook her head as she pictured Katie. "Admit it, when it comes to her—you lost it a long time ago."

❧ ❧ ❧

FEBRUARY 2016

It had been a while since Julia's house had been full of people for any type of party. Meghan and Jordan had been spending most of their weekdays at Julia's. Carrie's career had taken off. She had gotten jobs in Paris and San Francisco in the last month. Bess was on the road frequently with her band. The kids had tons of activities. Julia was so preoccupied with the Brighton Center's upcoming groundbreaking ceremony that she had put her consulting to the side temporarily. She was grateful for Katie. Katie had stepped in more than once to pick Meghan up from a rehearsal or to make sure the kids were all fed until Julia could get free. Finally, Julia had begun to catch up. Bess and Carrie were home for the next few weeks. The only person missing for an impromptu get together was Jake. Julia had insisted on a Saturday afternoon indoor barbeque.

Katie had forgotten how these gatherings energized Julia. Julia loved a house full of people. Katie watched Julia fondly. She had been concerned that Julia was running herself ragged over the last two weeks. Julia had taken on a great deal of work outside the scope of her responsibilities at the Brighton Center. So much so, in fact, that Katie was finding it difficult no to blast John about the situation. She didn't, opting to be as supportive as she could for Julia. She had been staying with the kids almost nightly for the last two weeks. Julia apologized and promised to make it up to her at some point. Katie wanted to laugh. It wasn't an imposition. It gave her a reason to spend time with Julia. She chuckled as she watched Julia work the room.

"She loves this," Carrie said, coming up beside Katie.

"Yes, she does," Katie beamed. "She can work a room of politicians or kindergartners with the same ease," she observed.

"That she can," Carrie agreed. "Listen, I wanted to say thanks for helping out so much the last couple of weeks. It was the worst time for me to be away—I know."

"You don't need to thank me," Katie replied truthfully. "There isn't anything I wouldn't do for Julia or for the kids."

Carrie nodded as a smile edged its way onto her lips. "Well, still, you both could use a break," she said. "Bess and I will be home for a few weeks. You let me know if we can do anything."

"Actually," Katie began. "There is one thing." Carrie's eyes opened wider. "I'm taking Julia to the symphony for Valentine's Day," Katie said. She saw the sideways smirk that Carrie was attempting to conceal. "To make up for our New Year's bust," Katie clarified. "I was thinking…"

"Say no more," Carrie stalled Katie with her hand. "We can take the kids that weekend, Ian and Steph too."

"Carrie, it's your first Valentine's Day with Bess. It just would help on Friday if you could…Well, if you could watch the kids until my dad can come to get them," Katie explained.

"It's your first Valentine's Day too," Carrie pointed out.

Katie nodded. "Not really the same thing," she said.

Carrie looked at Katie and shook her head. "Good time to change that, then." Katie's cheeks blushed uncomfortably. "Relax," Carrie said. "She calls me Yente, you know," she chuckled. "She can be pretty thick-headed in case you hadn't noticed," Carrie offered her assessment. Katie smiled. "We'll take the kids, Katie. Spend the weekend with Julia. She is a hopeless romantic underneath it all."

"Carrie, I…"

"It's okay, Katie," Carrie assured her friend. "I just want her to be happy."

"I'm not sure that…"

Carrie just smiled and patted Katie's arm. "I am sure," she told Katie. "And, the symphony on Valentine's Day? Good plan."

Katie sighed as Carrie winked and walked away. She hadn't admitted it to herself until Carrie pointed out that it was her first Valentine's Day with Julia. It was her plan. It was her hope to break through the final wall that stood between them. She closed her eyes in silent resignation. It was time.

"What are you doing over here all alone?" Julia asked.

"I'm not alone," Katie quipped.

"Not now," Julia said.

"I was talking to Carrie," Katie said.

"Oh? Where is my ex-wife?" Julia asked.

"Not sure," Katie replied.

"You okay?" Julia asked, sensing something was on Katie's mind.

"I'm fine," Katie promised. "But, I do need to use your kitchen for a bit."

"Did you bring Betty with you?" Julia asked.

Katie laughed. "You are nuts, Riley."

"Probably. Did you?"

Katie shook her head. "I don't need Betty for this one," she said. "Now, let me go so I can get started, or you'll be having those cheesecake brownies you love so much for breakfast again and not for dessert."

"It's an acceptable breakfast food," Julia called after Katie as she walked away. Katie just waved her off.

"What are you yelling about breakfast foods for?" John asked.

"Katie's making brownies," Julia grinned. John scrunched his face in confusion. "I like them for breakfast," Julia explained.

John regarded her with pursed lips. "Does she make brownies for you in the morning often?" he asked.

"No, she makes them at night. I just eat them in the morning," Julia said.

John rolled his eyes. "You two are made for each other," he mumbled.

"What?"

"Oh, just admiring your little picture of domesticity," John fluttered his eyelashes.

"You're just jealous," Julia said.

"Of what? The princess's brownies? Honey, that is all your department," he said before turning and walking away.

"I like Katie's brownies," Julia muttered.

"There's some breaking news," John called back. "Better go tell her so she can inform the masses."

"Jealous. And, maybe I will do that."

అ అ అ

Julia had been sidelined by Michael and Bess on her way to check on Katie. They were both curious about the girl Jake seemed to be infatuated with. Julia smiled and assured them that Monica seemed polite, intelligent, and that she was attractive. Julia was reasonably sure that Jake and Monica had started seeing each other, but she had no intention of gossiping about her son's love life, even if it was with his father. Jake had matured over the last year. Julia respected his privacy and trusted his decisions. She was attempting to make her exit when a voice rang out through the house.

"Mom!" Jordan yelled.

Julia rolled her eyes and headed toward Jordan's voice when a crashing sound startled the entire room. Julia's slow saunter immediately turned to a frantic sprint.

ॐ ॐ ॐ

"Are you making brownies?" Jordan asked Katie.

"I am."

"Awesome," Jordan voiced her approval. "Can Ian stay here tonight?" Jordan asked.

Katie looked at Jordan curiously. "What are you two up to?" she asked.

"Nothing. Just want to watch some movies," Jordan told her.

"Uh-huh."

"Can he?" Jordan asked.

"That is up to your mom," Katie said, turning to retrieve the pan of brownies from the oven.

"Mom!" Jordan yelled.

Katie's cell phone rang just as she was pulling the pan out of the oven. She juggled to answer it and keep the pan from falling out of her gloved grasp.

"Hello? Oh, hey, Dad. What's wrong?" Katie's knees buckled as she listened to her father's voice through the phone. The pan flew out of her hands and across the counter onto the floor with a bang. "No."

ॐ ॐ ॐ

Julia was positive that she had stopped breathing. Katie was falling, and on a direct collision course with the kitchen floor.

"Katie!" Julia barely caught Katie before she hit the tile. She guided Katie gently to sit. "Katie," Julia called to her. Katie looked up at Julia with a vacant stare. Julia heard a voice through Katie's phone and took it out of her hand. "Hello?" Julia began.

"Julia?" Bob McAllister asked.

"Bob? What's going on?"

"It's Ruth," he said softly. "She's...She's gone, Julia. It was so fast. She just..."

Julia closed her eyes as a wave of grief and concern flooded her. She was completely unaware that anyone else had entered the room. Carrie silently directed Bess to steer the children clear of the kitchen. "I understand," Julia said sadly.

"Julia, Katie is she..."

"She's right here," Julia said. She lifted Katie's watery eyes to her own. "Katie, your dad wants to talk to you, okay?" Katie nodded. Julia kissed Katie's forehead, and sat beside her on the floor, rubbing Katie's back gently in support.

"Dad?"

"Katie, honey, I'm sorry."

"Are you okay, Dad?"

"Right now, I'm more worried about you, sweetheart," he said truthfully.

"I'm okay. I'll get there as soon as I can."

"Kate, don't you get in the car right now," he ordered.

"Daddy..."

"Katherine..."

Julia took the phone gently from Katie's hand. "Bob?"

"Julia, she shouldn't be driving."

"Don't worry about that," Julia assured Katie's father. "We'll be there as soon as we can. I'll have her call when we are leaving," she promised. She accepted Katie's father's thanks and then turned her attention to the woman beside her. Katie was in shock. "Katie?"

Katie looked at Julia helplessly. Julia folded Katie into her arms. "I know, sweetie. I know."

"I'm okay," Katie finally said.

"No, you're not, but you will be. I promise," Julia said. She helped Katie to her feet.

"I have to tell the kids. God, Julia…I…"

"I know. I think you should take a few minutes first, okay?"

Katie tried to calm herself. Her entire body was shaking. "I just talked to her last night."

"I know," Julia said.

"How am I going to tell the kids? They are supposed to see my parents next weekend when we…Oh, God, Julia…"

"Stop," Julia said gently as Katie finally began to cry. "I'm right here, whatever you need. Okay?" She felt Katie's warm tears roll down her neck as Katie collapsed into her. "I'm right here."

"Will you sit with me while I tell them?" Katie asked hopefully.

"Of course."

"Julia…I don't think I can handle this alone."

"You don't have to," Julia said. Katie nodded. "When you're ready, we'll go talk to them."

"I just need a minute," Katie said.

"Okay. I'll go check on…"

"No," Katie grabbed hold of Julia. "Just with you, just a minute."

Julia nodded and held Katie close. "Whatever you need, all you have to do is ask."

"I just need you," Katie whispered.

Julia gently tightened her hold on Katie. "Well, that's an easy one."

"I ruined your brownies," Katie chuckled through a sob.

Julia recognized the typical shift. She remembered the way her emotions turned on a dime when she had lost her parents. "They're fine," Julia said.

"They're on the floor," Katie replied with another teary giggle.

"My floors are clean."

Katie pulled back from Julia and looked into her eyes. "I love you, Julia," Katie told Julia.

"I know. I love you too."

Chapter Nineteen

Julia was worried about Katie. Telling Stephanie and Ian about their grandmother's death had proved more trying than Julia had expected. Ian had handled the news fairly well. Stephanie had erupted into a bout of inconsolable tears. Katie had sat and rocked her daughter for twenty minutes before Stephanie's sobs subsided. Carrie had pulled Julia aside and offered to take the kids for the weekend. It seemed a logical plan for everyone. Julia was stunned when Meghan came into the family room just as she was about to take Katie to her parents' house. Meghan politely asked if she could talk to her mother and Katie for a minute before they left. Julia and Katie looked at one another in surprise.

"What is it, Meg?" Julia asked.

Meghan looked at Katie wearily. "I'm sorry about your mom, Katie," she said sweetly. "She was a nice lady."

Katie smiled in earnest at Meghan. "Thank you, Meg. She was, and she liked you a great deal."

Meghan nodded and took a deep breath. "The thing is," she said, keeping her focus on Katie. "Steph and Ian kind of want to stay with us while you're gone."

Julia intervened. "Megs, Ma is going to take all of you back to her house," Julia explained.

Julia was confused by her daughter's statement. She had thought that they had made their plans clear. Carrie and Bess would take all of the kids back to their house until Katie and Julia returned. Then, Julia would take Katie, Stephanie, and Ian home. Julia's puzzled gaze lifted from Meghan as Carrie entered the doorway.

"No," Meghan said, turning her attention to her mother. "They want to stay at our house, and then you can both come home—here."

Katie looked at Meghan as a new truth descended upon her. She felt the trembling that started in her hands spread throughout her body. What Meghan was expressing—it was exactly the feeling that had prompted Katie's decision to move to Boston. Katie had needed to be with the people that she loved the most. That is exactly what her children needed now. They needed their family. Somewhere along the way, that is what this had become—a family. Katie looked at Julia, who was focused on Meghan. Katie watched as tears pooled in Julia's eyes. She wondered if Julia had suddenly realized the same thing.

Carrie decided to break the emotional tension. "It's fine with me," she said from the doorway. "We'll stay here until you two get home."

"Are you sure?" Julia asked Carrie. Carrie smiled. Julia turned to Katie. "What do you think?" Katie nodded her agreement. "Okay. I guess that's settled," Julia said.

"Thanks," Meghan said to the adults. She took a step forward and hugged Katie. "I really am sorry," she said.

Katie accepted Meghan's affection with grateful arms. "I know you are."

"Love you," Meghan told Katie.

Katie looked at Julia and then closed her eyes. The sincerity in Meghan's voice tugged at her heart. "I love you too, kiddo."

Meghan pulled away and moved to hug Julia. "Thanks, Mom."

"No, Meg, thank you," Julia said with a kiss to her daughter's head. She watched Meghan leave before turning to Katie. "You sure you are okay with this?"

"Yeah. Are you?"

Julia smiled and put out her hand. "Let's go," she said softly. "Maybe we can convince your dad to come back with us." Katie stopped in surprise. Julia just winked. "I have a big house," she reminded Katie.

"You need it to hold that big heart," Katie thought silently.

❧ ❧ ❧

All of the kids were asleep by the time Julia and Katie had returned home. Katie's father had declined their offer to come stay at Julia's. Katie had tried to nudge him a bit. Julia had pulled her aside when she was able to find a moment and suggested that maybe he just need to feel close to Katie's mother. He needed to be at his home to do that. Katie understood, but Julia could tell that Katie was concerned about leaving her father alone.

The day had taken a massive toll on Katie. She had spent the late afternoon making calls to family and friends, setting up an appointment with the funeral home, and checking in periodically with Carrie about the kids. Julia was feeling drained as well. She knew that Katie was emotionally and physically exhausted. She had hoped that Katie might be able to rest. Julia had suggested that Katie go and take a quick shower while Julia said goodbye to Carrie and Bess.

"How is she doing?" Carrie asked.

Julia shrugged. "You know how it is. She's in control right now. She's busy with details. When it gets quiet...."

"I remember," Carrie said to Julia.

"I know you do. It's a lot like Dad, Care. No one saw it coming. She just fell over."

"Do they know?"

"Yeah, brain aneurysm. She probably just felt dizzy. Didn't think anything until it was too late," Julia explained.

"Listen, if you need us…"

"We will. We have to meet with the funeral home tomorrow at one. We'll probably have to leave here by eleven."

"I'll be here before that," Carrie promised.

It hadn't escaped Carrie's notice that Julia referred to everything in the "we" and no longer in the "I". She doubted that Julia had a moment to ponder that reality. As much as Carrie had wished that Julia would wake up and realize the potential in her relationship with Katie, this was not the catalyst she had envisioned.

"Try and get some rest," Carrie said.

"It's not me that I'm worried about."

"I realize that," Carrie replied. "You can't take care of her if you are running on empty, Jules," Carrie reminded her. "Ask for help," Carrie said. Julia nodded. "I mean it."

"I will," Julia promised.

"I love you, Jules. She'll be okay," Carrie said.

"I hope so."

"She will. She has you," Carrie said with a smile.

Julia nodded. "Night, Care."

Julia closed the door softly and looked up the stairs. She remembered how the quiet had affected her when it finally settled in. Death was a strange experience for the living. There were so many tasks to complete and lists to check off during the day. At night, when silence finally fell, a feeling of emptiness tended to take over. There were moments that Julia recalled feeling hollow. Carrie had supported Julia though the loss of both of her parents. Julia took a deep breath as she approached the guest room. Katie was sitting on the edge of the bed looking at her phone.

"What are you doing?" Julia asked.

"Just checking to see if there are any messages I need to answer. Tommy was trying to book a flight home for Monday, and I still…" Katie's rant was cut short when Julia gently took the phone from her hands and placed it on the bedside table. "What are you doing? I need to…"

Julia smiled knowingly at Katie. "No. You need to rest."

"I don't want to rest, Julia," Katie snapped.

"I know."

"You know? You don't know! I can't close my eyes without seeing her. I keep hearing my father's voice…"

"I know," Julia said as she took a seat beside Katie on the bed.

"I don't know if I can do this," Katie confessed. Julia started to speak, and Katie stopped her. "If you say I know again, I swear I will…" Julia kissed Katie on the forehead tenderly. "I can't lose it now," Katie said with a sigh.

"Yes, you can," Julia said. Katie shook her head. "Yes, you can," Julia repeated. She pulled Katie to her just as Katie's emotional dam broke. Katie shook from the onslaught of raw pain and exhaustion. "Let it go," Julia whispered.

Julia remained silent. She lowered Katie onto the bed and held her. Katie held onto Julia as she sobbed until she thought for certain her tears had gone dry. Katie would catch her breath for a moment and another wave of sorrow would pull her under. She was angry. She was afraid. She was devastated.

"Why?" she asked Julia.

"I don't know, sweetheart. I wish I did," Julia said as Katie's tears gradually transformed into soft sniffles. "You're exhausted."

Katie held onto Julia firmly. "Don't leave," she implored Julia fearfully.

"I'm right here," Julia told her. "Go to sleep now."

"Don't let go," Katie whispered.

"I'm not going anywhere," Julia assured her. She listened as Katie's breathing deepened. "Not going anywhere, Katie." Julia pulled the blanket over them and closed her eyes. She stroked Katie's hair lovingly. "How am I going to tell you?" she wondered. "I can't lose you again," Julia whispered. "I love you too much."

❧ ❧ ❧

Funerals always unnerved Julia. She had thought that enduring her mother's and her father's funerals had been heart-wrenching. Watching Katie as she endeavored to control her emotions was agonizing for Julia. Outwardly, Katie was the picture of grace and collectedness. Julia could see the subtle hints of strain that Katie wore around her eyes. She was certain Katie's smile appeared genuine and heartfelt to each passerby. The sentiment behind Katie Brennan's photogenic smile was sincere, but its presentation was contrived. It was the product of the years of practice and hours of polish that Katie's career required.

Julia kept a close watch on Katie in the distance. Bob and Ruth McAllister's house was filled to capacity. There were family members, former co-workers, and friends everywhere to offer their support. Katie's younger brother Tommy had managed to get home for four days. Julia had enjoyed his company. She was thankful that his presence had brought Katie some solace. There was one wrinkle in the well-pressed plans Katie had orchestrated—Bill Brennan.

Bill Brennan had flown in on the morning of the wake. He arrived at the funeral home holding the hand of his quite visibly pregnant fiancée. Julia had jumped when he appeared, and she felt Katie reach for her hand and squeeze it in a death grip. Julia had only met Katie's ex-husband twice, and as far as Julia was concerned, that was enough for a lifetime. She stood in the corner of the living room, silently surveying the scene before her. Ian was standing in front of his father with a familiar expression on his face. His cheeks were growing redder by the second, almost to the tips of his ears. Julia tried not to laugh. It reminded her a bit of Jake when he was that age. Jake had provided an unexpected boost to Katie's spirits. He had flown home to surprise her. It hadn't been a request on anyone's part. Jake had insisted. It warmed Julia's heart. A deep affection had taken root between her son and Katie. Had it not been for Monica, Julia would have guessed Jake had a crush on the woman she loved.

"How are you doing?" Jake asked as he came up beside his mother.

"I'm fine, Jake. Just hoping Katie is all right."

"He's pissed," Jake gestured toward Ian.

"I'd say so," Julia chuckled. Before Jake could respond, Ian was standing in front of them.

"Do I have to go, Julia?" Ian asked.

Julia was perplexed. "Go where?" she asked.

"Do I have to go stay with my dad at the hotel?" he asked.

"What are you talking about, Ian?"

"He says that Steph and I need to go spend some time with him. I want to stay with Mom. So does Steph."

Jake looked at his mother and bit his lip. Julia seldom lost her temper. When it did happen, it reminded Jake of a tornado. Julia swooped in, sucked you right up, twirled you around, and then spit you back out. He had to admit, when his mother showed her anger, it tended to be justified, and she had just gone from simmering to steaming.

"Mom," Jake said softly.

"I'm going to ask Mom," Ian said.

Julia held Ian back gently. "No, Ian. You don't need to leave your mom. I'll talk to your father," Julia promised him. Ian nodded. "Nothing to your mom about this now, okay?"

"Okay," he agreed.

"Why don't you hang out here with Jake for a bit?" she suggested.

"What do you say?" Jake looked to Ian. "Your grandfather told me he set up the Ping-Pong table downstairs. You want to give it a go?" Jake asked. Ian nodded his approval. "Okay, I'll meet you there," Jake promised. "Mom…"

"Jake, don't worry. I can handle Bill Brennan."

Jake laughed. "It's not you I'm worried about." Julia snickered. Jake had grown up so much it was almost alarming. "I can't believe he's here," Jake commented.

"Well, he and Katie were together a long time," Julia said. "He has a right to be here. He doesn't have a right to make decisions about the kids without talking to her."

"What are you going to say?" Jake asked.

"That depends entirely on him," Julia answered. "Now, go entertain Ian for a bit."

"Good luck," Jake whispered. Julia just groaned.

≈≈ ≈≈ ≈≈

Katie stepped out onto the upstairs deck to catch her breath. It was unseasonably warm, which she considered a small blessing in a week full of upheaval. The sound of familiar voices drifted upward, and Katie smiled.

"Are you glad?" Stephanie asked.

"About Ma and Bess living together?" Meghan asked.

"Yeah. Do you think they'll get married?"

Megan laughed. "I don't know. Ma hasn't said anything about that. Probably. Feels like they already are," Meghan said.

"Do you like it there? I mean, living there?" Stephanie wondered.

"Yeah. I like Bess a lot, and I love Ma, so…"

"But?" Stephanie asked.

"Jordan's drumming gives me a headache. Plus, I miss my mom, and I miss you guys when I am there," Meghan admitted. "Don't you miss your dad?"

"Not really," Stephanie said. "Sometimes, but he wasn't home much anyway. It was always Mom, Ian, and me. I like it better here with all of you."

"You're with my mom more than I am," Meghan laughed.

"I love your mom," Stephanie said.

"Me too!" Meghan admitted. "She can be annoying, though."

Katie listened from above intently. She hated eavesdropping, but the conversation below her was so honest she couldn't help herself.

"What are you doing out here, Princess?" John called to Katie.

Katie shushed him with a finger and pointed below them. "Shhhh."

"My mom is annoying too," Stephanie said.

"Your mom is cool," Meghan disagreed.

"Yeah, because you don't live with her," Stephanie laughed.

"I wouldn't mind living with your mom," Meghan replied.

"Do you think that will happen?" Stephanie asked.

"I don't know," Meghan said with an exasperated sigh. "What do you think?"

"I don't know either. Do you really think your mom loves my mom?" Stephanie asked.

"Ummm… Yeah. Totally."

"Yeah, I think so too," Stephanie agreed. "So why doesn't she just tell my mom?"

"I don't know," Meghan said. "I asked Ma that."

"What did she say?" Stephanie asked.

"She said I should mind my own business," Meghan giggled. "But, I know she thinks they should be together. So does Jake."

"They said that?"

"Nah, I can just tell," Meghan explained.

"I don't get it. If they love each other, what's the problem?" Stephanie asked. "You know if they got married we would end up sisters."

"You're already like my sister," Meghan said.

"I know," Stephanie said. "But, it would still be cool."

"It would be easier."

"Yep," Stephanie agreed.

"But if they ever do, and we have to share a room, you cannot have pink and purple throw up in it," Meghan said seriously.

"Gross. I thought you liked my room."

"I do, with less pink and purple," Meghan said, sending them both into a fit of laughter.

"Come on, let's go see if Jake and Ian are still playing Ping-Pong," Stephanie suggested.

Katie covered her mouth with her hand and shook her head, listening as Meghan and Stephanie ran away giggling.

"Out of the mouths of babes," John said.

Katie sighed. "Why doesn't she tell me? If she does, I mean. I know she loves me," Katie looked at John. "That doesn't mean she's in love with me," she said.

"She's head over heels in the sand in love with you," John laughed.

"I don't know."

"Yeah, you do. Why haven't you told her?" John asked.

"I thought I would for Valentine's Day…. Then—this. We're cursed. We were supposed to be sitting at the symphony, not mourning at a wake."

"Hardly a curse, unless life is a curse…. Which, come to think of it, it might be!" John said. He watched Katie as she closed her eyes in pain. "You need to just take the bull by the horns. And by the bull, I mean Julia."

"Why does it have to be me?" Katie asked.

John took a deep breath. "Because, Kate, you walked away."

"I didn't…. I mean, we weren't even…"

"Exactly. You walked away when you were just beginning to have feelings for her. Don't you think she might be a wee bit reluctant to tell you that she's in love with you?"

Katie covered her face with her hands. "Shit. What if I lose her?"

"Kate," John said tenderly. Katie looked at her best friend. He always called her Kate when he was concerned. "Great rewards require great risk. If you love her as much as I think you do, what more is there? Look around you." Katie stood shell-shocked. "What? What did I say?" he asked.

"Nothing," Katie said softly. She let her tears fall as she recalled her mother's advice just a few weeks ago. *"If you want to have the big rewards, Kate, you have to take the big risks. Eventually, every-one leaves. That's part of life too. Take the ride while you can, sweetheart."*

"Katie? Are you okay?" John asked.

"Yeah. I think maybe I finally am."

༄ ༄ ༄

Julia made her way to Bill Brennan deliberately. "Oh, Julia! How are you?"

"I'm fine, Bill. I was wondering if I could steal you for a minute."

"Sure," he said.

Julia led Bill outside the front door near the driveway.

"Listen, thanks for everything. You've been a good friend to Katie. I'm glad she has someone to help out, especially now."

"You don't need to thank me," Julia said flatly. "Listen, Ian seems to be under the impression that he is staying with you tonight. He was kind of upset."

"Well, I'm sure Katie could use the break. You know how she is, I'm sure."

"No, I'm not sure I do. How is that?" Julia asked, keeping the emotion out of her voice.

"Well, her mother was her best friend. I'm sure she's emo-tional. When she's upset, she likes her space."

Julia nodded. She had come to understand a few things clearly about Katie through this ordeal. Katie did need space from time to time. Everyone did. The last week had given Julia some much-needed perspective on the distance that once crept between them. Katie had needed to settle her past before she could think about the future. Julia remained uncertain what the future held for them. She did understand Katie. Katie loved having her family close. When Katie was hurting, and Katie was torn apart right now, she wanted them closer than usual.

"See, the thing is Bill, I sort of wonder if you know Katie as well as you think you do," Julia said politely.

"I should. We were married for…"

"Well, I was married to my wife for almost fifteen years. I can read her pretty well most days, but she's not the woman I married all those years ago," Julia said. Bill seemed to be growing tense. "The thing is, Katie needs the kids around her right now. It's what's keeping her going."

"She has to be tired."

"She is. She's exhausted," Julia said.

"That's what I mean. She shouldn't have to handle this all alone. The least I can do is take the kids for a day."

"She's not alone," Julia replied. "I'm sure you mean well, but I'm also sure if you had asked Katie she would have told you that she wanted the kids to stay with her. And, if you listened to the kids, you'd know that's what they want too."

"I barely get to see them," he replied. "They need time with me too."

"Yeah. They do. Maybe not when they just lost their grand-mother, though."

"If Katie disagrees—fine. We'll just ask her."

Julia stopped Bill Brennan by putting her hand in the mid-dle of his chest. "I wish you would not do that," she said. "She's been through enough. Call her tomorrow afternoon and ask if you can take the kids for the night. Not tonight."

"I know you are close to Katie, but this is a family matter," he said.

Julia took a deep breath. "I agree. It is, and, Katie is part of mine."

Bill Brennan chuckled. "Are you two together?" he asked.

"That's none of your business," Julia said. "But, no. She's my best friend."

"Mm. Fine. I'll call her tomorrow."

"Thank you," Julia said.

"You know," Bill began. "I don't blame you. She is an extraordinary woman."

"Yes," Julia said with a smile. "She certainly is."

❧ ❧ ❧

Julia glanced over at Katie and received a smile that instantly stopped her heart. She instinctively returned the loving expression.

"Mom, you should see the old pictures of Katie," Jordan said.

Julia looked down at her daughter curiously. "Are they funnier than your baby pictures?"

"Mom!" Jordan whined.

"Okay," Julia laughed. "Lead the way. Maybe I can find some ammunition."

"What does that mean?" Jordan asked.

"Nothing," Julia sniggered as Jordan pulled her toward the family room.

Julia was enjoying looking through old photo albums with her daughter. Jordan's enthusiasm was short lived, made more so by an offer to come and join in the Ping-Pong tournament Jake was supervising in the basement. Julia just rolled her eyes and kept pouring over the pages of Katie's past.

"She was a hellion," Katie's father said. He sat down beside Julia and pointed to a picture of Katie in a snowsuit. "Into everything, that one," he said affectionately.

Julia chuckled. "I can believe that," she said. "How are you holding up?" she asked.

Bob McAllister offered the woman beside him a warm smile. "I'm all right." Julia just nodded. "It's good for me, having all these young people around," he told her. "Reminds me how much life there still is," Julia smiled softly at him. "I want to thank you, Julia. Katie and her mom, well…. They were always close. So much alike, those two," he said as he slipped into a memory. "When Kate was a teenager I thought they might kill each other a few times," he chuckled. "Somehow, they always made it to the other side. They just understood each other. Drove me nuts sometimes. Every time I look at Katherine, I can see a piece of Ruth."

Julia understood. Katie did look a great deal like her mother. Julia had always felt that way about Jake. The older Jake got, the more he resembled Julia's father. She often found herself studying Jake's expressions and finding her father there.

"I think I understand," Julia said.

"I'm sure you do. She is very lucky to have you," Bob said.

"Well, I am just thankful she fell into my life," Julia said honestly.

"That is how it happens, isn't it?" Bob asked. Julia's confusion made him chuckle. "Love," he clarified. He watched as Julia's posture slumped slightly, and he smiled. "I remember when I met Ruth," he said.

"Katie said you had been together since college."

"We met in college," Bob said. "Took us a while to get together." He shook his head. "Ruth was my roommate's girlfriend for two years," Bob said. He chuckled when Julia's eyes widened in surprise. "Katie left that out, I guess. Well, she was. David was my best friend. He was something. Handsome devil too."

"What happened?" Julia asked.

"David lived big. He was following in his father's footsteps. His parents were both educated. His father was a bigwig lawyer. They traveled a lot, skiing, snowmobiling, and yachting. That was David's life. He loved adventure. He had a bit of a reckless streak. Thought he was invincible. I think that's what drew Ruth to him. She was a wild child back then," he laughed. "And, she was beautiful," he said, taking a moment to picture his wife. Bob sighed and shook his head sadly. "He got a bit crazy one summer night with some of his high school friends. Drank a few too many of whatever they had, decided to dive off the side of a hill into a river near his parents' summer home. Snapped his neck on the landing. Killed him instantly."

Julia sucked in a breath and let it out slowly. "Jesus."

"Yeah," Bob agreed with her sentiment.

"Poor Ruth."

"It was terrible for everyone. Ruth was a wreck. But the truth is, we had sort of been watching each other for a while. Just friends, but we spent more time together than she ever did with David. I took what I could get for a long time."

"How did you...."

"Oh.... Well, it took a while. There were times I thought it would never happen," he laughed. "I was nothing like David, never had those aspirations—never relished recklessness as adventure. Ruth was brilliant, talented, and attractive. I guess I figured she wanted more. Part of me felt guilty," he admitted. "He was my best friend."

"But, you did end up together."

"We did. It took two years. We were sitting by a pond on campus one night, and she just turned to me and said that she loved me. I loved her. I told her that, but I said it would never work. I wanted to teach. I wanted a family. That was me. She needed more," he snickered softly. Julia gave Katie's father a puzzled look. "She was furious. Told me I was the most infuriating person she had ever met. How dare I tell her what she needed, and then she kissed me." Julia smiled at the story. Bob took a deep breath and looked at Julia knowingly. "I miss her."

"I can imagine," Julia said compassionately.

"She understood loss. She loved David. We both did, and we both lost him. Life is funny sometimes. It can get away from you if you let it. I'm glad we didn't waste more time," he said. Julia looked back at the photo album in her lap. "Well," Bob said as he placed a hand on Julia's knee. "I should go make the rounds one last time."

Bob watched Julia's hand unconsciously trace a picture in the album and smiled. He rose to make his way out of the room and passed Katie in the doorway. He kissed her on the cheek and winked.

"Trying to find my dirty laundry?" Katie asked as she plopped beside Julia.

"No," Julia laughed. "I already know where you keep that."

"I guess you do."

"Your dad is an interesting guy," Julia said.

"Yes, he is. What stories was he telling you?" Katie asked with some hesitancy.

Julia turned to Katie. "He told me how he ended up with your mom."

"Really?" Katie asked. Julia nodded. "He told you about David?"

"He did."

"Wow. Yeah, I've often wondered what would have happened if David had lived. Isn't that awful?" Katie asked.

"No," Julia said truthfully. "Things happen like they are supposed to," she said.

"You really believe that, don't you?" Katie asked. Julia nodded. "That's hard for me to believe right now."

"I know," Julia said. "I guess all we can do is the best we can with the time we've got."

Katie nodded and put her head on Julia's shoulder. "I hope we've got a lot left."

"Me too," Julia said. "Me too."

Chapter Twenty

Julia's Journal

Life is strange. I'm not certain that we are meant to understand it. I sometimes wonder in our quest to explain everything in our world, if we miss the entire point of living. Everything needs a box, and every box needs a label. That's how we are taught to navigate this experience that we call life. It needs to be understood, and it needs to be categorized. I spent most of my life searching for reasons. That search is what leads us all to need endless labeled boxes, on rows and rows of shelves. I gazed at the stars. I pondered the ocean. I mused over the changing seasons and puzzled over the passing of time. What does it all mean? What is it all telling me? Where is this journey taking me? All those long hours that I spent trying to understand my life did teach me a few things. I learned to listen as much as I spoke. I began to see more than just lights in the sky and fathom the existence of something much greater than myself. But, nothing, not one thing that I pondered, nothing I studied, or even considered brought me more reason or understanding than love—the love I have felt holding my children. The love I felt when my mother cradled me. The love I feel each day that I wake up beside the woman who shares my life.

I am tempted many days to ponder love itself. That is human nature, I think. There is a need to justify and explain everything.

The greatest discovery of my life happened once I allowed myself to close my eyes and free-fall into love. Love doesn't exist beyond life. It doesn't transcend time. It doesn't occupy space. Love is life. It is living. Love exists within, without, and through everything. Life is love, and love is meant to be felt, not boxed, labeled, or shelved. Love is the air of life. It took me a while to understand that. Every day I fall. Every day she catches me, even when I can't see her there. Life is a strange thing. Love makes it worth living.

MARCH 2016

"Jules, you look tired," Carrie said.

"I am tired," Julia snapped.

"And grumpy," Carrie joked.

"I'm sorry. It's been crazy all week. I feel like I just caught my breath after the funeral and boom! I had to hit the ground running again," Julia said.

"How is Katie?" Carrie asked.

"Good, I think. I mean, as good as you can be when you lose someone you love so much. To tell you the truth we haven't seen each other much these last two weeks. We sort of pass each other; you know? She was away for those three days in Los Angeles. I think I see her kids more than I do her sometimes," Julia laughed.

Carrie grinned. "Julia…"

"I know where this is headed, and the answer is no. I have not said anything to her."

"I thought for sure after everything that happened you would tell her."

"I told you, I haven't seen her much. That's the truth," Julia said.

"Well, you will see her tomorrow."

"Yes, I will," Julia agreed.

"And, Jake will be here to watch the kids. Here as in at *my* house," Carrie winked at Julia.

"Do you have *Matchmaker, Matchmaker* on repeat or something?"

"No. Come on, what is stopping you? You have to know by now that she loves you," Carrie said flatly.

Julia nodded. "Maybe, but Care...Katie's life...I mean Katie's career..."

"Katie's a big girl, Julia."

"Mm."

"Well, I'll tell you what, you had better make up your mind to let her go if you don't want to be with her," Carrie gave Julia her frank assessment of the situation. Julia shook her head. "You're so worried about losing her, and that's exactly where you'll end up if you're not careful," Carrie said.

Julia sighed. "I know. Every time I think I'm ready...."

"You chicken out."

"Pretty much," Julia admitted.

Carrie laughed as she walked Julia out her door. "Just do what I did with you," she said.

"What's that?" Julia asked curiously.

"Just kiss the girl," Carrie said. Julia grinned and kissed Carrie on the cheek, winked, and headed for her car.

"Doesn't count!" Carrie called out.

"What doesn't count, Ma?" Jordan asked Carrie.

"Your mother can be so difficult sometimes," Carrie chuckled.

"Yeah, that's what Katie said the other day after Mom dropped me and Meg off there. I heard her say she was gonna hit Mom over the head pretty soon."

Carrie laughed. "Maybe there's hope yet."

❧ ❧ ❧

"What's shaking, Princess?" John asked when Katie appeared in the door.

"Not me," Katie answered. "How are things here?" she asked John.

"Crazy."

"How is Julia?" Katie asked.

"Crazier."

"Other than the obvious," Katie chuckled.

"She's Julia. Herding the cattle and such, you know her," he said.

"Yes, I do."

"She's out at the site with some of our larger sponsors for tomorrow's groundbreaking ceremony. She'll be back soon, though," John told Katie.

"I didn't come to see Julia," Katie said.

"No? You're here for mwah? Oh, do tell. Is Cinderella finally ready to go to the ball?" he asked.

"Something like that," Katie answered with a smirk. "Interested?"

John beamed. "Does it involve shopping?"

"Maybe."

"Do I get lunch?"

"Probably."

"Will there be shoes?"

"If I need them."

"I didn't mean for you, Princess," John laughed.

"Of course not," Katie laughed. "So, can you get away?"

"I suppose so. You know how I feel about charity work."

"No wonder you two work so well together," Katie said. "You're both insane."

"Possibly, but that's why you love us," he replied. Katie laughed. "So, let's go. Oh, and as payment for my services, I expect details."

"I never kiss and tell," Katie said with a wink.

John grinned evilly. "So, there will be kissing?"

"One can only hope," Katie said.

❧ ❧ ❧

"Over there," Julia instructed some of the venue staff.

"How's it going?" Carrie asked.

"So far, no major catastrophes, so in my estimation—good," Julia said. "You look great, by the way," she complimented her ex-wife.

"Thanks. You look pretty amazing yourself Julia," Carrie said. "Where is Katie?"

"She had an interview to tape late this afternoon for Monday's show. I had to be here early. Believe it or not, Everett is picking her up," Julia laughed.

"He must be delirious with excitement."

"He's delirious all of the time," Julia joked. "But, yeah, I'm sure he is. Too bad Jake and Monica couldn't be here," she said. "I feel a bit badly that they are stuck with the kids."

"They seemed fine," Carrie said quietly.

"What's the matter? Don't you like Monica?" Julia asked.

"I like her just fine. She seems like a nice girl," Carrie said.

"She's twenty-one," Julia laughed. "She's not exactly a girl."

"Yes, I noticed."

"You're just upset you didn't get to play matchmaker with our son."

"You make it sound like he's headed to the altar," Carrie whispered.

"You never know."

Carrie smacked Julia. "Watch it. I have plenty I can share with Ms. Morning Coffee."

"You're too busy playing Yente to tell her where I hide the candy," Julia deadpanned.

"You're really okay with this? Jake and Monica, I mean?" Carrie asked.

Julia smiled. "He's got a good head on his shoulders, Care. So does she."

Carrie sighed. "I know. You know, he might beat *you* to the altar if you don't get the lead out," Carrie said.

"Me? What about you?" Julia poked her ex-wife gently. Carrie just smirked. "Holy shit. Are you and Bess getting married?"

"Not exactly how I planned on telling you."

"I think that's great, Care. I really do," Julia told Carrie sincerely.

"It's important to Bess."

Julia nodded. "Well, I'm glad."

"Honestly?" Carrie asked as Bess approached the pair.

"Yeah, now you will have something to occupy your time besides my love life."

Carrie leaned in and kissed Julia on the cheek. "If you would just get one, I wouldn't have to worry," she whispered before accepting her girlfriend's hand to be led away to the dance floor.

Julia stood silently shaking her head. "It never ceases to be strange," she muttered.

"What's strange?" Michael asked as he made his way to Julia.

"My ex-wife trying to find me a new wife," Julia explained.

"Sounds like a worthy endeavor," he said.

Julia smacked her ex-husband. "Don't start."

"I wouldn't dream of it," he said. "Not my specialty."

"Good," Julia said as her gaze shifted around the room.

Michael rolled his eyes. "Lose something?" he asked.

"What?"

"Oh, nothing," he brushed off the question. "So, tell me more about Monica."

ù ù ù

Julia was standing with Michael and Bess enjoying the soft music and the amusing conversation about Jake and his new girl-friend. It still felt surreal to her that her little boy was in college. Whenever Jake came home for a visit, Julia seemed to miss him twice as much when he headed back to school. Listening to Bess and Michael, she realized that she was not alone in that reality. Bess was prattling on about how Carrie had cleaned their house endlessly when Jake had announced he was bringing a girl home. Julia laughed as her eyes occasionally scanned the room for any sign of Katie. The week had been filled over capacity with meetings and preparation for the groundbreaking ceremony. That event had taken place earlier in the morning. Julia had only seen Katie twice all week, and both had been brief visits. Late night phone conversations were a pathetic substitute for the time Julia had come to cherish with Katie. The morning had been hurried, and Julia's attention was required by so many people that she had barely managed to share a personal hello and a smile with Katie. She glanced around the room again, hoping to catch sight of the popular morning show host.

Michael chuckled when he saw Julia's cheeks turn a deeper shade of pink and her eyes begin to gloss over. "See something interesting?" he chuckled knowingly.

Katie stopped briefly to acknowledge some familiar faces, but not before offering a smiling glance to the woman she desperately wanted to make her way to.

"Jesus," Julia whispered. "She is beautiful." Her words escaped unexpectedly and without apology.

Bess and Michael exchanged a smirk just as Katie managed to pull herself away from her small group of admirers. Julia couldn't take her eyes off the vision that approached her. She had made a concentrated effort to conceal the growing attraction she felt for Katie. As much as Julia wanted to believe that Katie might share her emotional feelings, she remained skeptical that those feelings would ever translate into a romantic relationship. Julia's eyes were riveted to Katie when Katie finally reached her.

Katie smiled at Michael and Bess and offered the usual pleasantries between friends. Julia found herself completely captivated. Katie was wearing a full-length, navy blue gown that hung off her shoulders. It seemed to deepen the blue eyes that Julia willingly lost herself in repeatedly. Julia could hear the conversation taking place around her, but she was not processing any of it. She stared dumbly at the woman she loved. Finally, after all the time they had spent apart, all the moments they had shared together, the emotions she had fought to justify, comprehend, even suppress, she spoke the words in her thoughts. "I am in love with her. Oh, my God," Julia thought silently. "I can't hide it anymore. I have to tell her. I am in love with her."

The music changed, and Katie offered a crooked smile to Julia. "You haven't danced at all, have you?" she inquired, already knowing the answer.

Julia narrowed her gaze playfully. "It's not my parent's base-ment. There are no 8-tracks here. I don't dance, remember? Two wrong feet," she offered.

Katie put out her hand. "Perhaps you just haven't found the right partner," she suggested.

Julia felt her body tremble at the deeper meaning she was certain Katie's innocent statement was meant to convey. "Are you asking me to dance?" Julia asked. Katie smiled. "Here?" Julia whis-pered in astonishment. "Katie, there are so many people here."

"Are you suggesting I can't lead, or that you are incapable of following?" Katie asked.

"I," Julia faltered. One of Julia's greatest reservations in crossing any lines with Katie were the implications she feared it might have, not just for their friendship, but for Katie's career. "Katie, there are a lot of people here. You know people will think that..."

Katie gently tugged Julia's hand and guided her to the dance floor. She stopped and looked at Julia seriously. "I don't care what anyone thinks."

Julia attempted to steady her breathing as Katie's arms slipped around her. Their dance started at a slight distance, two pairs of eyes searching for any evidence of hesitation. Julia followed Katie's lead—a lead Katie was taking in much more than their move-ment on the dance floor. This dance, they both knew, held something much greater within it. It was an admission without words. It was the final bridge that they had been reluctant to cross. Julia felt Katie pull her closer. Katie's cheek caressed hers, and Julia closed her eyes.

"See? You can dance," Katie whispered.

"Maybe I just found the right partner," Julia whispered emo-tionally.

Katie inhaled a deep breath. "Julia?"

Julia was lost in their movement and the emotional sea churning between them. "Hum?" Julia barely managed to respond.

Katie licked her lips and placed them against Julia's ear. "Take me home," she said simply.

Julia's heart skipped several beats before thundering at a pace she had never experienced. There was no mistaking the implication in Katie's request. "You just got here," Julia fumbled.

Katie pulled back slightly and smiled. She could feel Julia's unsteadiness. "Well, let's make the necessary rounds," she said. "Together. And, let's go. I missed you this week."

Julia managed a slight nod. Half of her wanted to make the excuse that she had to stay longer. She could say that she hadn't been present long enough and needed to circulate more, but in the dark, music-filled room, no one would miss her. Katie would see that argument for exactly what it was—Julia's fear. And, Julia was suddenly both terrified and elated. She knew the truth about her feelings was tonight's inevitability. She would have to face her truth for all its wonderment and all its vulnerability now. She would tell Katie Brennan that truth. Julia loved Katie more than she could comprehend. More than that, she wanted Katie in her life, every facet of it.

As they made their way through the large room, Katie could sense Julia's nervousness increasing. When they finally reached Julia's car, and Julia opened Katie's door, their long time roles reversed. Katie took Julia's hand tenderly. "It will all work out," Katie said with a smile that reflected more love than Julia could fathom.

Julia kissed Katie on the forehead and let her lips linger. "I know."

જી જી જી

Katie made her way into the living room carrying two glasses of wine. She stopped and watched as Julia stood gazing out of the large picture window. She closed her eyes and savored a deep breath. Julia's black dress fit her perfectly. Her curly hair spilled softly over her shoulders. Katie felt such an incredible surge of love pass through her that she was surprised it didn't knock her down. She wanted to hold Julia now, more than she had ever wanted anything in her life. Right now, she wanted to pull Julia to her, look into her eyes and say the words that had too long been left only a silent realization. She closed her eyes again and steadied herself. Katie looked at the glasses of wine in her hands and smirked. "No more distractions," she thought. She placed them on the small table that sat against the wall and made her way to Julia.

Julia sensed Katie's presence behind her. She studied the clear night sky outside the window, musing over the stars. Her Nana had always told her that whenever you saw a shooting star it meant that someone had just fallen in love. It was a romantic notion that Julia had carried with her throughout her life. She didn't need any shooting stars to convince her that she had fallen in love with the woman behind her. Julia felt Katie's hands tenderly fall onto her shoulders and coax her to turn. She finally managed to look at Katie. Katie's soft smile greeted her, and Julia's tears began to spill over.

Katie lifted her hands to Julia's face and brushed away the falling tears. "What is it?" Katie asked gently.

"I don't want to miss you again," Julia confessed.

Katie's smile never faded as she closed the distance between them, caressing Julia's cheek and bringing their lips together for the first time. The kiss was timid at first, but it deepened quickly. Julia's hands now held Katie's as each attempted to convey what neither had found the strength or perhaps adequate words to explain. Katie pulled back slowly and continued to tenderly stroke Julia's cheek.

"Don't you know by now?" Katie asked. Julia looked at Katie, knowing in her heart what Katie was about to say. "That I am in love with you," Katie told her.

Julia traced the creases at the corners of Katie's eyes. She loved the way Katie's eyes crinkled in amusement and affection. She had no conscious thought as her emotions finally found a voice. "I fell in love with you a long time ago," Julia confessed. "Katie…"

Katie was certain that Julia's mind had already begun its spinning rationalizations. That was Julia. That was the Julia she had fallen in love with. She loved everything about the woman standing before her—every quirk, every wall, and every hidden vulnerability.

"Stop," Katie said. "Don't put anything between us that doesn't need to be."

"Katie, what about your career?"

Katie shook her head as her smile grew wider. "There are plenty of lesbians on television," she reminded Julia with a chuckle.

Julia let out a sigh. She wasn't certain if she was more afraid of losing Katie now, or of never truly holding her.

"Julia," Katie said. "None of that means anything without you. I didn't come back here just to be closer to John, or even to my parents. I missed you every minute that we were apart. I still do now," Katie said as she closed her eyes.

"Katie?" Julia softly called.

Katie stroked Julia's cheek again and sighed. She needed Julia to understand. "I felt you holding me, so often, Julia. I thought I was crazy at first. That first night that we sat in your living room in front of the fire—I swear, I could feel you holding me. I didn't know what it meant, but when we were apart, I would close my eyes and travel back to that moment. I never really let you go," she choked on her tears. "I want to hold you," Katie said. "I need you to hold me for as long as you are willing."

Julia allowed her tears to fall without restraint. "Katie," her voice cracked. "I love you so much."

Katie kissed the tears on Julia's eyelids and cheeks. "I know," she said as her kiss moved back to Julia's lips. "Now, hold me and don't let me go. I don't want to miss another minute."

ત્જ ત્જ ત્જ

Julia felt Katie's hands as they steadily traveled along her back, finding the zipper that kept her confined. Her pulse had become so rapid that she momentarily wondered if its intensity would allow her to remain standing. She was grateful for the strength of Katie's embrace. It was the only thing steadying her. The desire Julia felt for Katie consumed any rational thought, and Julia felt no inclination to search her thoughts now. Her hands matched the motions in Katie's. Katie's dress fell away, and Julia stepped back to breathe in the sight before her.

"You are so beautiful," Julia remarked in awe as she marveled at the woman before her. She knew they were not her most eloquent words. They were simple and sincere.

"So are you," Katie complimented with a smile.

Katie lightly brushed her hand against the swell of Julia's breasts and she lingered there, enjoying the softness that fueled her need to feel Julia closer. She lost her breath instantly at the faint sensation of Julia's lips traveling down her neck to her shoulder. Julia was touching her with a reverence that simultaneously grounded and transported Katie outside of herself. She had never experienced such a sense of anticipation in her life. She wanted to give herself completely to Julia. As Julia led her to the bed, Katie realized that her nakedness went much deeper than the physical state in which she now found herself. Any barriers either woman had erected instantly demolished—completely and forever. Julia no longer surrounded her; she had become a part of Katie. No air, no thought, no space existed between them now. They moved as one. Katie ran her hands through Julia's hair as Julia looked down at her. There was no need for questions or commentary. Anything that Julia's eyes may have failed to reveal coursed through Katie in Julia's tender kiss, a delicate kiss that began at Katie's lips and deliberately sought every inch of skin on its journey downward. Katie's eyes fell shut with a passionate sigh as Julia's kiss caressed her breast, taking Katie to heights she had never imagined could exist.

Julia drank in all that was Katie. The softness of Katie's skin was intoxicating. The warmth that radiated from the body beneath her inflamed Julia's desire to make love to Katie—to make love to her. Julia was positive that she could spend the rest of her existence touching Katie. She loved the feel of Katie's hands on her. She longed for Katie's touch, but making love to Katie overwhelmed Julia's senses and her emotions unlike anything she could recall. If she could, Julia would lose herself here forever. Feeling Katie against her, Julia realized that she would never be able to get close enough to the woman she loved to satisfy the ache that had claimed permanent residence in her soul. That reality drove Julia to savor every sensation touching Katie produced.

Julia felt the slight quiver in Katie's body as her touch drifted lower. Slowly and tenderly, she allowed her hand to find Katie's need and meet it. Julia brought her lips to Katie's and darkened blue eyes opened to meet Julia's. Julia witnessed Katie's silent plea for her to end Katie's longing. She sensed Katie's frustration intensifying and smiled.

"Trust me," Julia whispered. "I want you to feel me, to know that you are a part of me," Julia told her lover.

The weight of Julia's words coupled with the sensation of Julia's breath on her neck brought Katie to a precipice she had never before reached. She pulled Julia closer, feeling a white hot energy surge through every nerve in her body. She felt as if she might drown in Julia's embrace.

Julia sensed the emotional and physical overload building in her lover when Katie shuddered. "Let go," Julia said. "I'll catch you. Let go," she promised.

Katie's grip tightened on Julia. She called out to Julia helplessly as Julia steadied her through a series of hills and valleys of pleasure and passion. Julia did not let Katie pull away. Each time she felt Katie begin to rise again, she simply held her closer until Katie fell into her arms. Katie drew Julia as close as possible. She nestled her face into Julia's neck, and Julia felt the warmth of Katie's tears bathe her cheek.

"I'm right here," Julia promised. "I love you, Katie, more than I have ever loved anyone."

Katie reached up and brushed Julia's hair aside. "I love you," she said softly.

Katie reversed their positions and Julia closed her eyes in a sweet surrender that no dream could ever hope to capture. For a moment, all Katie could do was gaze at the woman beneath her. So many feelings ran through her that she could not separate them. Julia was everything. She was the piece of Katie's life that gave it both balance and purpose. Katie reached out and traced the outline of Julia's face.

Julia took hold of Katie's hand and kissed it in reassurance. Katie lowered her kiss to Julia's forehead, her eyelids, her nose, her lips, her chin, and then traced a pathway delicately across Julia's breasts until she heard Julia reflexively moan in pleasure. The response Julia's sighs produced in Katie's body startled her slightly.

She found it impossible to believe that her need could resurface so quickly. If Katie had been able to think clearly, she would have made a journalistic inquiry of Julia about that reality. In this place, thought had no purpose. Katie indulged her hands in the warmth of Julia's body. Every touch sought to communicate the connection that Katie felt to the woman she loved. There was no destination on this journey, only a never-ending pathway of love and acceptance.

"Katie," Julia barely whispered as her hips rose to meet Katie's touch.

Katie was surprised momentarily by the feel of Julia's hand touching her again, but she could not mount a protest. Less than an instant had passed before Katie fell into Julia at the same time Julia's entire body rose to meet hers. It was sublime. It was completion.

Katie collapsed onto Julia with a sigh. "You had better never leave me, Riley," Katie whispered.

"Who?" Julia asked playfully.

Katie kissed Julia's neck. "Just don't ever do it, whatever you want to call yourself."

Julia kissed Katie's head. "You do realize what you are saying?" she asked.

Katie laughed. She did realize what she was saying. She had no illusions about what had just transpired, what this new dimension in their relationship meant. In Katie's mind, she had just promised Julia forever. Katie wanted nothing less than that with the woman who held her. She kissed the skin beneath her lips.

"Ummm…Five kids, two ex-husbands, one ex-wife, a Jawa challenged queen, and a whole lot of unexpected upheavals," Katie listed off her assessment of their future. "Oh, and one extremely charming, incredibly intelligent and witty, and occasionally frustrating woman."

"I don't think you are all that frustrating," Julia said flatly.

Katie lifted herself onto her elbow to look at her lover. "You in for that ride?"

Julia smiled. "Of course, I am. I waited in line a long time for this one," Julia said.

Katie chuckled. "I guess you did," she admitted. She leaned in for a tender kiss. "You know," she said as she snuggled into Julia's arms. "I saw a shooting star tonight."

"Really?" Julia asked as she ran her hand up and down Katie's back tenderly.

"Mm-hm. You know they say every time you see one that means someone fell in love."

Julia smiled. It was the same tale she had grown up believing. She hadn't needed any proof that Katie was the love of her life. Thinking back, she had known that for a long time. But, if anyone wanted to send her a sign, this one was perfect.

"Who is this *they* I keep hearing about?" Julia asked.

Katie laughed. "Do you believe it?"

Julia shifted her position to look at Katie and took Katie's face in her hands. "I don't need any shooting stars to know that I have fallen in love with you," she said. "But, yes, I do believe it."

Katie nodded. "You really are a sap at heart, Riley. You know that?"

Julia groaned slightly and pulled Katie back into her arms. "Yeah, well, don't you go telling anyone."

"Scouts honor," Katie promised with a yawn.

"Hey…. Were you ever even a Girl Scout?" Julia asked. "Katie?" Julia chuckled affectionately and kissed her sleeping lover. "That's what I thought," she whispered. "I love you, Katie."

Epilogue

THIRTY YEARS LATER

Julia sat on the front porch swing, rocking it gently and sipping a glass of wine. The sun was just beginning its slow retreat behind distant hills. A hint of lilac tickled her nose as it drifted on the breeze. Julia closed her eyes as images of this place and the woman she had shared so many memories with—sunsets and sunrises, children at play, and children moving away flooded her thoughts. An odd mixture of melancholy and gratefulness washed over her. She'd needed an escape from the chatter inside, just a few moments of solitude.

"Nana?" a voice barely whispered.

Julia turned her head to greet a pair of familiar eyes, a soft, gentle brown staring at her from under fair bangs. From behind the short, fair-haired girl, another set of eyes implored her. Familiar too, was this gaze. Colors that changed from the vibrant blue of a summer sky to the tinges of green that often painted ocean waves twinkled in the fading sunlight as Julia lifted her eyebrow to greet them.

"Well?" Julia asked. "Oh, come on. Pop a squat beside me." She set down her glass and welcomed the two girls on either side. "Bored with the all the old people?" she asked.

"No," the blue-eyed girl giggled.

"Riley, you are worse at lying than either your mother or your grandmother," Julia laughed.

"Nana?" the other girl began. Julia shifted her focus with a smile. "Are you sad?" Emma asked.

Julia took a deep breath and looked skyward for a moment. Riley and Emma were very much like their grandmothers. It often amused Julia. Emma looked so much like Carrie when Carrie was young and had such a similar temperament, that Julia often found herself having to stop and remember not to call her Care. Riley, on the other hand, did not look as much like Katie as she mirrored her grandmother's personality, unless, of course, you were looking into her eyes. Riley's eyes sparkled with mischief, curiosity, and intelligence just like Katie's.

Julia loved to spend time with Riley. She had never been one for favoritism, but if she were to be honest, even just with herself, Riley had captured her heart instantly. She and Katie had often mused about what kind of trouble Riley would lead Emma into. The two girls were the best of friends. Julia and Katie had hoped that Emma would ground Riley as much as Riley cajoled Emma into questionable adventures. Loss was not new in the family, but this loss—this loss was the greatest for any of them so far. Julia felt the place in her soul that had now been left vacant. It was a void that she was certain she would feel for the rest of her life.

"Oh," Julia began. "Sure, I am sad. I will miss your grandma. That's why I came out here. This place makes me feel closer to her," Julia said quietly. Emma looked at Riley and gave her an encouraging nod. Julia narrowed her gaze, first at Emma and then at Riley. "Okay, you two—out with it," Julia instructed them.

"Uncle John said Grandma was the best friend you could ask for," Emma told Julia.

Julia smiled. "Did he? Well, sometimes your Uncle John does make sense," she laughed. Her voice softened as she continued. "That's true," Julia agreed. Riley cleared her throat a little and moved closer to Julia. "Why do I think there is something more you wanted to ask me?" Julia asked with a playful lift of her eyebrow.

Riley and Emma were both about to turn thirteen, and they were insatiably curious about everything. Katie had joked to Julia that Julia had better prepare herself for some colorful questions soon. The pair seemed to gravitate to their grandmothers' home. Five children and seven grandchildren had given what Julia once called *The Riley Door Policy* an entirely new meaning. Of all of their children and grandchildren, it was the two that now sat on the swing that had exercised their rights to that policy the most frequently. Riley and Emma would find any excuse to spend time with Julia and Katie—any reason, any way possible. Julia looked at Emma, but Emma just looked down at her lap. She turned her gaze to Riley and received a customary sigh.

"Well…. Just…We were listening, you know?" Riley began to explain. Julia nodded for her to continue. "Well, to everyone talking. Uncle Jake said that the best thing in life is finding someone to love forever and that he was happy his moms both found that. So…I mean…We were wondering…. How do you know if you are in love?" Riley finally managed to ask her question.

Julia looked at Riley curiously and then turned to regard Emma. She was ready to make a crack about the pair hiding boyfriends when she realized that both their eyes had grown misty. Julia wondered what conversation they had overheard to compel this question. Riley let out another sigh.

"How did you know you were in love with Grandma?" Riley asked quietly. Julia felt the air in her lungs escape rapidly. "Nana?" Riley looked at Julia.

Julia cleared her throat slightly against a surge of emotion. She closed her eyes for a moment to gather her thoughts. A tender smile tugged at her lips as she pictured Katie. "You know, girls, I have thought about that for years. I'm not certain I can answer that the way you would like me to." Julia took a deep breath and her smile widened. "Katie," she whispered the name. "Every moment with your grandma was an adventure. There was never a minute that I didn't miss her, even when she was beside me. I guess that's how I knew I was in love with her. Every time I looked at her, she became more beautiful."

"Like she looked the same to you? I heard Uncle Michael say that once. You mean she was as beautiful as when you met her, even when you got old?" Emma asked innocently.

Julia suppressed a chuckle. "No," she said. "No, I mean that I noticed every subtle change," Julia explained. "Every added crease in the corner of her eyes, every tiny change in the color of her hair—everything. And, each and every tiny thing I noticed made me love her more, like I was seeing her for the first time."

"Did you ever fight?" Riley asked curiously.

Julia laughed. "Did we ever fight?" she repeated the question. "Oh, well, your grandma and I were never known to be reserved in our opinions," Julia said. "So, yes, we argued. Sometimes I think we argued just for the entertainment," she chuckled. "But, I loved her even then. Even when she tested my patience, or I tested hers." Julia felt tears filling her eyes. "There hasn't been a moment since I met your grandma that I didn't love her." It was a reality that Julia was not certain she had ever voiced to anyone, not even Katie. "I don't exactly know when I realized it," she said. "But now," Julia smiled. "Well, I can't remember a time when I didn't love her. I'm just grateful that I found her." Julia turned and kissed each of her granddaughters on the forehead. "One day, you will both find that person," she told them. "The person that sees you for all that you are, even the not so terrific parts," she winked. "And, still loves you."

"But, how do we know?" Riley asked.

"You'll know," Julia told her. "You'll know because you will never have to pretend to be anyone or feel anything that is not true, and that person will still love you. You'll know because every time that person walks into the room, you'll feel a bit like you are falling, but you won't want to stop it."

"Like a roller coaster?" Emma asked.

"Yes, Emma. It's a lot like a roller coaster. There are lots of twists and turns, and some of the hills are a bit scary, but you stay on the ride just to feel the thrill of that fall again," Julia said. "And, when you find that person, no matter where you are in life, don't you be afraid to take that ride," she instructed the girls. "Hold on up the hills, and let go during the falls, just like you do on the roller coaster."

Riley kissed her Nana's cheek. "I love you, Nana," she said.

"Me too," Emma said with a kiss.

Julia winked at them. "I love you too," she said as they scurried off together. Julia closed her eyes and breathed in the brisk night air. A sudden weight beside her rocked the swing gently. She smiled at the sensation of the head on her shoulder.

"You know, Riley, you really are a sap."

Julia chuckled. "You think so?" she asked.

"No, I know so," Katie answered. "I'll miss her too," she said, wiping a falling tear from Julia's cheek.

"I just can't believe she is really gone," Julia confessed. Julia placed her arm around the woman she loved and felt Katie grasp her hand gently.

"I can't imagine losing you," Katie's voice quivered slightly at the sentiment.

"Katie...."

"It's true. I don't even want to think about it. I don't think a hundred years would be long enough."

Julia nodded. She already missed Carrie more than she could express. She had found herself needing to hold Katie closer than ever over the last few days. Life was short. There would never be enough time with the woman beside her. All she could do was love Katie in every moment.

"Worth the roller coaster ride?" Katie asked Julia playfully.

"Every twist and every turn," Julia replied.

Julia felt Katie's head take up residence again on her shoulder and closed her eyes in contentment. The future, Julia had learned was only a moment. Perhaps more time stretched out behind them than lay ahead. The sound of children running through their home brought another smile to Julia's lips. She opened her eyes and looked up at the stars in the sky again. Silently, she offered a thought to the woman who had once shared her life and had long been her closest friend. "Some things are forever, Care," she said as tears bathed her cheeks.

"Still think everything happens for a reason?" Katie asked.

As if on cue, Riley's voice broke through. "Come on, Nana! Grandma, you're missing it!" she called out through the door. "You gonna stay out there all night?"

"Leave those old lovebirds alone!" John's voice followed closely behind. "They need their beauty rest."

Julia chuckled. "I think it leads us exactly where we need to go," she said. "And right now, I am thinking the girls should put on their hoodies. It's getting chilly."

"You are evil," Katie snickered.

"Devious," Julia corrected her wife. She cast her gaze skyward again. "Look," Julia pointed to the sky.

"A shooting star," Katie observed as she cuddled closer. "You know what that means?" Katie asked. "Someone just fell in love."

"Yes, they did," Julia said. She turned and took Katie's face in her hands. Katie placed her forehead against Julia's and accepted a tender kiss. "Falling in love with you is the best part of every moment," Julia said honestly. "Do you remember when I told you I never wanted to miss you again?"

"Yes, I do," Katie smiled.

Julia nodded. "I never want to miss you again, Katie," she said.

"You won't," Katie promised. "Just hold me while when we climb that last hill."

"It's the letting go that scares me," Julia whispered.

"No," Katie said, taking Julia's face in her hands. "We've never held on too tightly to each other. That's how we keep falling in love," she reminded Julia. "I'll always be there to catch you, Julia, even then."

Julia accepted Katie's kiss and closed her eyes. Somehow she knew that was true. "I love you, Katie."

"I know you do, Riley."

"Couldn't you, just once, call me Gallagher?"

"No."

Julia laughed at her wife's response. "No matter how much things change; they stay the same."

Katie stood up and pulled Julia along as the sound of laughter a few feet away lifted them both. "I would have fallen in love with you no matter what you called yourself," Katie winked.

"Oh, really?"

"Yes, now let's go see what your namesake is giggling about in there."

Julia stopped short and pulled Katie into her arms. "You know, if I could do it all over, any of it...I wouldn't change one thing."

"Nothing?" Katie asked.

"Well, maybe my hair," Julia confessed.

Katie smacked Julia gently. "You'll never change."

"Probably a safe bet," Julia agreed.

"Let's go get these heathens in line. I have plans for you later," Katie whispered. Julia watched as her wife headed through the door. She closed her eyes and tilted her head toward the sky above.

"What are you doing Nana?" Emma asked.

"Falling," Julia answered. "Right through shooting stars."

Katie stood inside the door and watched as Emma approached her Nana. Julia had always said everything that happened in life had a purpose. Life had not always led Katie where she had expected to go. It had led her where she needed to be. Julia was right, no matter how much things changed, one thing remained constant in their lives. Every day since they met, Julia and Katie fell helplessly, right into the safety of each other's arms. It was the unexpected path in their lives that proved there was always a purpose in everything that came to pass. Katie exchanged a knowing smile with the woman she loved in the distance.

"You okay?" John whispered in Katie's ear.

Katie nodded and kept her gaze on Julia. "Grateful I took your advice all those years ago and showed up to the ball," she told him. He smiled. "Just grateful."

Other Books by
NANCY ANN HEALY

THE ALEX AND CASSIDY SERIES
Intersection

Betrayal

Commitment

Conspiracy

The Collaborative – Coming Soon

Writing as J.A. Armstrong
OFF SCREEN SERIES
Off Screen

The Red Carpet

Dim All the Lights

Writer's Block

Casting Call

Intermission

Waiting in the Wings – August 2016

BY DESIGN SERIES
By Design

Under Construction

Solid Foundation

Rough Drafts

New Addition

Renovations

Building Blocks

Road Blocks – Fall 2016

CPSIA information can be obtained
at www.ICGtesting.com
Printed in the USA
LVHW031559060619
620404LV00036B/635